A Time for Change?

Nick Udall

PublishNation
www.publishnation.co.uk

For Dodo. Always my inspiration.

Chapter 1

It was a day that seemed very unusual. Not because 'Greenings' were interviewing for a new senior accountant, but due to the fact that the only candidate was a woman. It was a unique situation and one that had taken the company's staff by surprise. It was October 1963 and although many women worked as accounts clerks, few took the ACA exams to become qualified chartered accountants. The profession was a male preserve and most members believed it was the way things should stay.

Concepcion Maria Campbell, known as Connie to her friends, was different however. Left a legacy by her father, she had been able to stay at school and take her A-levels. Achieving excellent results, she was fortunate to be articled to the Manchester firm of John Francis and Co. Liberal minded, Francis believed in giving opportunities to clever young women. Once Connie had passed her exams, Francis had recognised that her talents were constrained by the limitations of his small business. When he heard that Greenings, a flourishing local company, had an opening, he used his friendship with the firm's founder, Joseph Greening, to convince him that Connie was worth an interview.

It was easy for Connie to get to Greenings from her home in Howard Avenue, Ardwick. The company was located on the corner of Oldham Street, so she could catch a bus into Piccadilly and then walk across the gardens to her destination. Their offices were located in Clayton House, an imposing six storey edifice, designed in the style of the Flemish Revival. With impressive decorations around its numerous large windows, the building was topped with an imposing central gable. It had been built at the turn of the century, when Manchester was a confident city and dominated the world's cotton trade. As such, the building was a statement of wealth, pride and solidity. A perfect location for a dynamic local company.

Reaching the entrance, Connie climbed the stairs to reception and introduced herself. She was then taken to a pleasant young woman wearing a blue shirtwaister dress, her long, black hair piled up into a fashionable 'beehive.' She smiled warmly at Connie.

"Hello. I'm Paula, Mr Greening's secretary. I assume that you're Miss Campbell, here for the interview."

"Yes, that's right. Connie Campbell."

Connie stretched out her hand and smiled. Paula was surprised. At work she had never shaken any one's hand. It seemed very masculine.

Yet, she took the hand on offer and shook it warmly. It may have been a simple act, but one that suggested to Paula that Connie was different. Although being considered for a senior position, she clearly regarded her as an equal.

"If you take a seat Miss Campbell, I'll let Mr Greening know that you're here."

Connie took off her coat and sat down. She looked to the side of Paula's desk, noting the presence of an oak panelled door with a shiny brass plate and the name Joseph Greening picked out in black letters upon it.

Lifting the receiver from the phone on her desk, Paula rang through to inform her boss that Connie had arrived. Having listened to his reply, Paula turned her attention back to Connie.

"Mr Greening shouldn't be very long."

Connie nodded, Paula noting that she seemed quite calm and relaxed.

Paula wasn't the only one favourably impressed by Connie's arrival. Observing her were two of the company's senior accountants, Ralph and Tom. Stood chatting at the entrance to an adjoining office, they were stunned by her appearance. They had both been intrigued by the actions of 'Old Joe' in calling a woman for interview. On first hearing the news they had thought it was a joke; someone was 'pulling their leg'. It didn't seem possible for a woman to be qualified for the position. Yet it turned out to be true and as time progressed, it was clear that 'Old Joe' was sticking to his decision and his senior accountants knew better than to question him on the matter. Still relatively young, they needed to act with due deference. For Ralph Greening however, it was less of a concern. Joe's nephew, Ralph seemed destined to take over the company, given that his uncle had no children of his own.

When Connie had first arrived, the two men had mistaken her for a client. Petite, she had light brown wavy hair, which framed a beautiful face. Her high, sculptured cheekbones gave her a classical appearance. Penetrating green eyes, a cute and perfectly proportioned nose, above soft, sensual lips. When she slowly removed her coat and reached up to hang it at the side of Paula's desk, they could see the pleasing outline of her shapely figure. Connie was dressed in a pretty, fashionable but functional black skirt suit. She was wearing a white blouse underneath her jacket and a skirt that reached to just below her knees. Unconsciously, the two men were drawn towards her beautifully defined calves, which tapered towards her slim, attractive ankles and a pair of black stiletto heels.

"Wow!" whispered Ralph. "I hope the 'old man' gives me her account."

"No," replied Tom, quietly. "I don't think she's a client. She's here about the job. I'm sure I heard Paula mention it to her."

"No Tom," said Ralph, shaking his head. "She can't be."

Ralph was stunned. He found it difficult to accept what Tom was telling him. Ralph had a natural suspicion of intelligent women. Mainly, although he would never admit it, because he felt slightly intimidated by them. Conditioned by the gender stereotypes of the time, Ralph didn't regard high intelligence as a particularly feminine characteristic. Consequently, he had assumed that the candidate would prove to be plain and uninspiring. Accountancy was perceived to be a dull affair and he couldn't imagine that any pretty and lively young woman would believe that they could shine in such an environment.

Tom was starting to feel a little embarrassed. After all, the young woman could become a colleague and therefore their actions and conversation were inappropriate. He could also empathise with her situation, recognising that as a woman, she must have achieved a lot to have got this far. Tom had also encountered social disadvantages. The son of industrious, working-class parents, he'd worked exceptionally hard at grammar school and been articled to Greenings, where his ability and maturity had seen him progress very quickly. At twenty-seven, Tom was three years younger than Ralph, but 'Old Joe' regarded him as an indispensable member of the firm, in comparison to his somewhat lazy and complacent nephew.

Suddenly, the door to Joe Greening's office opened and the company's senior partner strode out purposely towards Paula's desk. Halting, he looked across towards Ralph and Tom, both of whom were still loitering around the entrance to the nearby office. Shaking his head, he addressed them sharply, fully aware that they were taking the opportunity to admire his pretty interviewee.

"Haven't you two got anything better to do? The company doesn't pay you to stand there gawking and passing the time of day."

"We were just getting on to it," said Ralph. "No problem."

"There'd better not be!" replied Joe, fixing the pair of them with a steely stare.

Connie smiled, immediately warming to the old man. He was clearly keen on work and order and if she were to be given a job here, it would be solely because of her ability. Proud of her professional expertise, Connie didn't want men like Ralph and Tom falling all over her because they thought she was pretty. She wanted to gain their respect as a competent and hard-working colleague.

"This is Miss Campbell, Mr Greening. Here for the interview."

Paula gestured over towards Connie who, rising from her seat, approached Joe and held out her hand towards him.

"Hello my dear. I hope you had a good journey in. We're easy enough to find I think."

Taking her hand, he shook it gently.

"It's certainly a central location," replied Connie, confidently. "Very easy to get to. An address that's reassuring to your clients I would expect."

Connie's calm and assured manner impressed the old man. He'd been told that she was pretty, but he needed to know that she had substance. The early signs seemed promising. She wouldn't be overawed working in a growing company that dealt with large contracts and powerful and demanding clients.

"Well, if you'll come through into my office, I've got your application and references on my desk and we can talk about the job."

Joe pushed the office door open and standing to the side, held it as Connie thanked him and made her way in.

"Take a seat young lady."

Joe gestured towards the front of his desk and then moved behind it to ease himself into a rather comfortable leather chair.

Looking across at him, Connie saw an elderly man of seventy years of age, but one who still exuded ambition and determination. He had built the firm up in the testing days of the Depression and now Greening & Co were one of the largest firms of chartered accountants in the north-west of England, with its senior partner harbouring ambitions to become the biggest. Wearing a fashionable, grey three-piece suit and navy and white tie, Joe looked smart and business like. He still had a fine head of hair. Although grey, it gave him a distinguished look, reinforced by his neatly trimmed eyebrows, moustache and sideburns. A strong chin, yet gentle nose and lips and smiling blue eyes, completed his features, the latter giving Connie the impression that she was confronted by a favourite uncle. Leaning forward and placing his elbows on the desk, Joe clasped his hands together and Connie could see an impressive gold wristwatch, which would have taken her many weeks of working to afford. It was clear that he liked expensive clothes and possessions and although an accountant, wouldn't hesitate to spend money on such items.

"Well, I have to say that I'm impressed by your references and not just the written ones. It's clear that you're very highly thought of Miss Campbell. I always check out potential employees scrupulously and with my connections in the city, I've talked to a lot of John's clients. I couldn't find anyone who'd say a bad word about you. Hard-working, diligent, professional and very good at your job. Several doubted your ability to handle their accounts, but it's clear that you've won them over. You've overcome their initial doubts by making them focus on your expertise, not on the fact that you're a woman."

Joe paused. He was keen to see how Connie would react to his words, particularly his reference to her gender. Would she merely remain silent and be grateful for his compliments? He hoped not. He wanted to see if this young lady had fire in her belly.

Connie had known that the issue of her gender would arise in any interview. Qualified female accountants were something of a rarity and she was aware that if she were to be successful, she would have to impress a prospective employer far more than any male competitor. For Connie, it was a simple fact of life. Any notions of female equality had to be relegated to the theoretical discussions she had with her friends. Today she had to accept the practical realities of the business world and deal with them as effectively as possible. If she could convince Joe Greening that she would work harder and more effectively than anyone else, being a woman wouldn't be an issue. The fact that Greening had granted her an interview, made Connie optimistic that he would deal fairly with her. As such, her response was measured, but determined.

"Being a woman has nothing to do with it, Mr Greening," said Connie, firmly. "I want to be judged on my ability to do my job compared to other accountants, whether they be male or female. I just want to do the best I can and by doing so, hopefully earn an opportunity to further my career."

It was a response that pleased Greening. He nodded appreciatively at the earnest young lady in front of him.

"That's what I hoped you'd say, Connie." He paused, then continued. "Oh, do you mind me calling you Connie, Miss Campbell?"

"No, of course not," replied Connie, smiling.

"I may be old, but like John, who I've known for many years, I don't believe that obstacles should be put in front of anyone who has ability. You intrigue me, Connie. Your family is working-class and you still live in Ardwick. You're a woman in a man's world and yet you're building a successful career. To do that, tells me everything I need to know about you. You're a winner who overcomes difficulties. I have no doubt that you've had to deal with a lot of hostility and resentment over the last few years."

Greening paused giving Connie time to respond.

"Well, some, but I think that would probably be the case regardless. The workplace, wherever it is, can prove difficult. My experiences are no different to most other people."

Greening nodded appreciatively. The more the young lady talked, the more he was impressed with her modest and pragmatic nature. He felt certain that she would cope with the pressures and demands placed on her by working for his company.

"You can rest assured Connie that I want you to work for us because I believe that you're the best accountant we can get. Speaking to you now, only confirms my research and convinces me that it would be right to offer you the job, that is if you want it. I'm sure that you'll find the package we offer you very competitive and well in excess of what you're earning with John."

Connie was taken by surprise, uncertain of what she'd actually heard. Was he really offering her the job? It seemed so quick. She had expected a gruelling interview and then to be sent away before receiving a written response several days from now.

"I'm sorry Mr Greening," said Connie, hesitantly. "Did you just offer me the job?"

She felt nervous, worried that she'd appear foolish and his response to her question, although it must have come reasonably quickly, seemed an age in arriving.

"Yes," said Joe, smiling, "I certainly did and I'm hoping that you're going to accept. Subject to your satisfaction with the terms of the contract of course."

Connie seemed lost for words, almost confused. Events had unfolded so quickly.

Greening laughed. He could see the bemused look on Connie's face. He was well aware that the young lady hadn't expected to get a decision so quickly.

"It's as I told you Connie," he said, trying to reassure her. "I do my research and I was pretty certain that you would be good for the company. I just needed to meet you and see what you were like. I'm confident that I can rely on you. You seem a strong character."

Greening's brief, but logical explanation made sense. Looking at him, Connie realised that he was still awaiting an answer and at last she pulled herself together and gave him the response that he was looking for.

"I'd be delighted to take the position Mr Greening. I'm grateful that you're giving me the opportunity and I'm sure that the contract will be fine."

In reality, the latter wasn't of great concern, given that Connie fully expected that a senior position in a much larger company would naturally be better remunerated. What mattered was that if she carried out the job successfully, it would put her in a position where, regardless of her gender, she would have to be given the respect that her experience warranted. In time, this job could open up a whole range of possibilities for her.

"Well," said Greening, getting out of his chair and walking round to the front of his desk. "I suppose we should shake on the deal."

Joe held out his hand to Connie. She grasped it firmly and smiled.

"I'll leave you with Paula and she'll give you a copy of our standard contract. It has all the necessary details: pay; expenses; holidays. I believe you'll find that we're a very generous employer. Let me know if you have any concerns and if you can sign and return it, I'd like you to start next Monday. I've already spoken to John and he's got plans for a replacement should you join us. Initially, I want you working mainly in our audit department. In time, your main role will be to review our client's financial systems and provide them with risk analysis and business support. It's an area that's going to be important for the company's future. You'll be working closely with Ralph, my nephew and Tom, the two young chaps who were outside. Both know that you'll have my full backing and that you're here to work. I'm certain that you feel the same Connie."

Connie nodded.

"Yes, I'm sure that we'll get on just fine."

Joe smiled.

"Yes, I'm sure that you all will."

It was the only allusion he'd made to the fact that she was a pretty young woman. Yet it hadn't affected his judgement, which had been based solely on her character and ability. Yet Joe wasn't naïve and he knew that younger men like Ralph and Tom, would certainly find her attractive and that his nephew in particular, wouldn't hesitate to try and ingratiate himself with her. Yet Joe had no fears for Connie. John had made it clear that she refused to be pestered by the men she worked with. Connie may be friendly and possess a very generous nature, but she was always scrupulously professional.

Outside the office, Joe handed Connie over to Paula.

"Everything being satisfactory, we'll expect to see you next Monday morning at eight-thirty. Goodbye, Connie."

"Goodbye, Mr Greening."

"Well, it seems congratulations are in order," said Paula, after Joe had returned to his office.

"Yes, it seems so. I'm Connie by the way. I'm looking forward to working with you Paula."

Paula smiled. She was pleased with Connie's success, believing that her presence at Greenings may bring new, more feminine qualities, to the operations of the company.

Connie appreciated the warm welcome that Paula had given to her. It was a fact that most of the resentment Connie had to face, wasn't from men, but from other women. Many from her mother's generation believed that by not raising a family, she was failing in her womanly duties. Younger women, could be just as hostile. Many were envious that Connie had opened up opportunities that seemed well beyond themselves. It also didn't help that she was pretty and that men found her attractive. In such cases, the resentment was born out of a sense of personal inadequacy. It was only Connie's generous nature, a refusal to acknowledge the secret whispers and disparaging looks, that could, to some extent, overcome their jealousy. Connie recognised that Paula was different and hoped that the two of them could become good friends.

Having been given a copy of the proposed contract, Connie said goodbye to Paula, made her way out of the office, down the stairs and out into the bright morning light of Piccadilly. It was a mild day, pleasant and Connie felt a sense of relief as she walked over to the bus stop, ready for the journey back home. Sat waiting for the bus to depart, she considered the morning's events. She recognised how fortunate she had been to meet so unusual a man as Joseph Greening. Elderly and born in late Victorian England, he had an unusually liberal disposition. He had been prepared to give her a chance, when very few others would have even acknowledged her application or taken it seriously. She knew that she would be eternally grateful for the opportunity he had given her.

Back in his office, 'Old Joe' was also contemplating his decision. He felt pleased with himself, eager for his company to be breaking new ground in a world in which, unlike his business contemporaries, he believed change was inevitable. Connie would be providing a pathway that other clever and determined young women could follow. Joe had seen many changes during his lifetime. He'd started his company in the 'Twenties,' had got it through the Depression and seen it prosper as it took on work for the government during the Second World War. Having fought on the Western Front in the Great War, captured by the Germans during their assault on 'Manchester Hill' in April 1918, Joe believed that he'd made enough of a sacrifice for his country, to have no qualms about the fact that his company had emerged from the war against the Nazis, in a much stronger position than they had entered it.

Yet the war had also brought him personal tragedy. It had taken away the very essence of the meaning in his life. In the early hours of Christmas Eve 1940, his beloved wife Elizabeth had been killed in the second night of Luftwaffe raids on the city. Without any children of their own, Joe had just one nephew, the son of his only sibling, his younger brother Ben, who had died whilst Ralph was a baby. Necessarily, Joe had supported his sister-in-law in bringing up Ralph and providing him with a suitable education and position in the firm. Joe knew that it was his duty, but also that Elizabeth expected nothing less of him. His wife had been a determined woman. A crusader, she fought injustice and had been active in local politics. She had worked tirelessly in Manchester's most deprived communities. She never stood on convention and frequently upset the sensibilities of the staid and conservative men her husband did business with. And Joe loved her for it. And the reality was that the young woman who had come into his office that morning, reminded him so much of his darling Elizabeth. She was a breath of fresh air. Pretty, confident and able to overcome all the obstacles and prejudice that had been put in front of her. It was for the memory of his wife, just as much as for the impressive professional credentials she possessed, that led to Joe's conviction that in appointing Connie, he had done the right thing.

Chapter 2

It was mid-morning when Connie boarded the bus home to Ardwick. It contained few passengers and as it emerged from Piccadilly and set off down towards London Road, past the railway station and on to Downing Street, Connie was able to look beyond the oncoming traffic and towards the familiar scenery on the far side of the road.

A fact that continued to impress Connie was the growing number of cars parked along the route, far more than just a couple of years ago. There were also increasing numbers of young men riding motor scooters and as a result, every time she passed Russell Street and saw 'Regal Cars,' the Ford dealer, with their large showroom and nearby lot, she considered the possibility that she should learn to drive. After all, surely any liberated young woman would be thinking of doing so. Gender equality should be measured in the proportion of female drivers thought Connie. Why was driving yet another area that seemed reserved for men? Once, she had actually taken her pen and diary from her handbag and written down the telephone number emblazoned above the 'Regal Cars' sign: Ardwick 4581. She had contemplated phoning them to ask the price of the smart blue Ford Anglia she'd seen in the showroom window. Then, she'd realised just how good the public transport system was in Manchester, with its plentiful supply of buses and trains. Connie therefore decided that she had no real need to drive and practical as ever, decided that she wasn't going to buy a car just to make a political point.

The bus slowed down as it met a line of traffic. Glancing to her left, Connie saw the queue outside Ardwick Post Office and then, looking across to Grosvenor Street, she could see the premises of 'James C Broomes.' A prominent wooden hoarding on the edge of their slate tiled roof, boldly proclaimed that the company's business was 'Funerals.' It was a sign that reminded passers-by of their mortality and Connie had often noticed that passengers on the bus would invariably avert their eyes once they had seen it. Although the sign had never bothered her, Connie understood that if she was older, it may well have made her feel uncomfortable.

Opposite 'Broomes,' on the corner of Gaskin Street, with its large plate glass windows and displays of clothes and shoes, was the large Co-op store, well patronized by the residents of Ardwick and Chorlton-on-Medlock. It was a proud and substantial building boldly proclaiming its name in large letters across the top of its frontage. No one could fail to note that this was the 'Manchester and Salford Equitable Co-operative Society Limited.' The very name suggested a permanence about the business. It was an organisation founded for the benefit of the working classes, who had continued to remain its loyal customers and members. Yet Connie knew that the emergence of a post-war generation, with more disposable income and a younger age profile, meant that fashions were continually evolving, expectations were rising and new retail outlets were more responsive to those needs than the conservative Co-op. As an accountant, Connie was well aware that in the changing world of the 'Sixties,' businesses simply couldn't stand still. The Co-op may retain the loyalty of its older customers, but Connie seriously doubted whether the large store would still be there in the future.

Continuing on its journey, the bus headed up Downing Street to stop at the corner of Ardwick Green. So far, the scenery had been familiar, but Manchester was on the verge of change. Not just socially, but physically too. A glance across to Rusholme Road reinforced the fact. Just a year ago, Connie would have been looking at a local landmark; the striking mock Tudor pub, the 'Minshull Arms Hotel.' Now it was gone, as were most of the buildings going down Rusholme Road towards Brook Street. It was a sign that the wheels of development were beginning to turn. Demands to implement the Corporation's slum clearance programme, had become ever louder. Not just from inside the office of the planning department and among politicians obsessed with modernity, but also from local entrepreneurs eager for the chance to exploit new construction opportunities. Yet here, Connie saw only a wasteland. A few stray bricks, mortar and small piles of rubble, that somehow had failed to be cleared away by the demolition firms who'd razed the old terraces to the ground. It was quite eerie to see the pattern of remaining streets and roads bereft of their houses and people, with no inkling of what would be put in their place and how long it would take to happen.

Pressing on, the bus went past the park and across the roundabout to the ABC and on to Stockport Road. Getting out of her seat, Connie walked slowly down the aisle towards the platform at the back of the bus, ready to disembark at Devonshire Street. Stood waiting for her was the conductor. He was a young man and not unattractive. Connie smiled as she noticed him checking that his cap was securely on his head and that his hair lay tidily over his ears.

The conductor's actions indicated that he was impressed with the young woman walking towards him. It was a part of the job that he always appreciated. Thousands of passengers travelled on his bus every week and among them were some of Manchester's most beautiful women. The opportunity to have even a brief conversation with them, provided him with memorable highlights throughout the day. Yet he just wished that he didn't have to wear his standard issue uniform. It made him appear like an old man. Although he found it frustrating, it didn't stop him from attempting to catch his pretty passengers' attention. His driver, Bill, an older married man, would constantly shake his head at him. Only this morning he had been berating him during their tea break at the terminus café.

"Arthur, why do you get yourself so worked up about talking to these young birds? Nothing will ever come of it. They're off the bus and you'll never see them again."

"I know Bill, but that's not the point. To see a thing of beauty and not appreciate it, that's what's wrong. A few words with them, is an opportunity and who knows?"

"I know lad. The trouble is that you need a dose of reality. I tell you what, you won't be so keen on women when you're married. You sound like one of those poets; lovey this, lovey that. Just wait till they take your beer money off you and start demanding that you fix things in the house after you've been working all day. There won't be much romance then. Birds change once they've got a ring on their finger!"

"Oh, come off it, Bill. You love your Peggy. I know you do. You can't fool me."

"Well," replied Bill, chuckling. "I do. I don't know what I'd do without her. It's a fact. We'd all be buggered if it wasn't for our wives. Everything would go to pot."

With that Bill had turned back to his mug, unceremoniously closing the conversation by slurping on his tea.

Now, as Connie reached the back of the bus, Arthur was ready to savour his few, fleeting moments with her.

"Next stop love?"

"Yes please," replied Connie.

Arthur smiled at her. He found her particularly attractive in her fetching black two-piece suit, white blouse and heels. She had a beautiful face and lovely figure and provided a pleasant and enticing sight before him. He looked at her left hand. He couldn't help doing it with beautiful women. By doing so he could perhaps entertain the fantasy, even if ever so briefly, that she could perhaps be his. Surprisingly, he could see no wedding or engagement ring on her finger. For a woman as pretty as her to be unattached, seemed rather unusual. Perhaps, she was one of the new, liberated women that he'd heard so much about. More sophisticated than most of the girls in his neighbourhood, they were the type of women who excited a young, working-class lad like himself. Women who were fast-moving, clever and who were in charge; women you wouldn't mind taking control. And the thought once entertained, made the young man involuntarily shudder with pleasure.

"Had a nice morning love?"

"Yes, I have as a matter of fact," replied Connie, smiling at his eagerness to engage her in conversation.

"Good," replied Arthur.

But his time was up. The button had been pressed and the bell had rung. Devonshire Street was approaching and Bill was bringing the bus to a halt.

"Take care," said Arthur, as Connie stepped down from the platform and on to the pavement.

"Thank you, I will."

Arthur's moment of pleasure was at an end. With a sigh he pressed the button twice, the two rings signalling to Bill that it was safe to move on. He gazed back down Stockport Road and watched Connie walking along the pavement, her figure diminishing by the second. Never mind he thought, how privileged he was to be able to talk to such a beautiful woman and it wouldn't be long before he could focus on the next stunning young lady who stepped on to his bus.

Yes, thought Arthur, Bill had got one thing right. It was great to be single!

Chapter 3

Alighting from the bus, Connie began to walk back down Stockport Road. On her right was the 'Devonshire,' a large white public house with its own car park. It wasn't quite as grand as it once had been, yet still had the classic moulded colonnades attached to the exterior of the building and the splendid arches over the large sash windows on its upstairs floor. Downstairs, the Devonshire appeared plain and functional. Long gone were the days in which it had been a hotel and had hosted grand dances and celebrations. In a sense, the building reflected how the whole area had become tired. Expecting demolition, landlords and local businessmen were reluctant to invest in improving the existing properties.

It was just past opening time when Connie reached the 'Devonshire,' but there were only a couple of vehicles in the car park. Few drivers pulled in off Stockport Road to sample its attractions and there wouldn't be many locals inside, given that it was Monday. The best the pub could hope for was the custom of a few old, retired men and the odd couple of workmen nipping in for a 'swift one' during their dinner break. Moving on, Connie continued towards Syndall Street, turned at the corner and then proceeded past the 'Rutland,' the signs above its doors proclaiming that the establishment was a proud purveyor of 'Chesters ales and stouts.' Walking on, Connie soon reached Howard Avenue. Crossing over to the far side, she made her way down the row of terraced houses to where she lived at number fifteen.

Effectively, the Avenue was a cul-de-sac, its far end blocked off by the properties of Exeter Street, which backed on to it. This made for an even greater sense of community. The street was no thoroughfare, so when they weren't at school, the kids would be out on the pavements and in the road playing hopscotch, jacks, skipping rope or playing football or cricket. Many young lads had made their way to United, City or Lancashire, after honing their skills on the cobbled streets of Ardwick. The fact that so few residents possessed cars, meant that modernity had yet to impact on the traditional world of 'playing out'. The gangs of happy kids who greeted Connie when she walked down Howard Avenue, both in the evening and at weekends, never ceased to provide her with a sense of satisfaction.

There was no doubt however, that the street looked weary. The houses, two-up, two-down terraces, were almost exclusively rented. Yet they all had small front gardens which had originally been enclosed by picket fences and gates a couple of feet high. Some landlords had planted privet hedges. It emphasised that their properties were a notch above the terraced houses whose front doors opened straight on to the pavement. Unlike her neighbours, Connie usually entered her home through the front door, not accessing the property via the alley off Syndall Street, which led to the backyard with its outside toilet and the door to the kitchen. Defying convention, Connie didn't consider her front room as sacrosanct. She used it every day, not limiting it to entertaining guests on special occasions. In most homes, the kitchen functioned as the eating, living and bathroom. If the family had a television, there it would be. Families lived closely in this one room, young and old having to get along together, with the woman of the house ensuring that they did.

Opening the door, Connie entered her front room. It was well decorated and furnished, a sign of a household that had money. Connie had paid for everything 'on the nail.' It wasn't that she was against the increasing popularity of hire purchase, which had helped to fuel the recent consumer boom, it was because as a woman, she wasn't considered a suitable risk. Yet Connie also knew that many of Manchester's retailers would turn down men who applied for credit, once they had given their Ardwick address. Being working-class and from an area of the city perceived to be poor, was enough to label anyone as unsuitable, regardless of their job or gender.

Connie had been eager to acquire furniture of contemporary Scandinavian design. She had therefore decided to buy items from the 'G Plan' range, where her pieces could be selected individually. At first, she had bought a Teak, two-seater settee with a small, matching coffee table. To complement them, Connie then acquired two chairs which she placed in the recesses on either side of the fire breast wall. Finally, Connie purchased a Teak radiogram from 'Lewis's', to go under the front window and the item she took most pride in, a small, rosewood sideboard produced by 'Faarup' and based on the designs of Ib Kofod Larsen. Yet the traditional had not been forgotten. Like all the other houses in Howard Avenue, Connie had put up net curtains at her front window. They afforded a sense of propriety and just like her neighbours, Connie took great pride in her 'nets' being sparkling white.

It did nevertheless, seem somewhat bizarre that the front room of a terraced house in Ardwick, contained such valuable and exquisite items. They certainly seemed incongruous in their surroundings, far more suited it could be argued, to properties in Gatley or Northenden. Yet Connie was a young woman who defied convention and there was something else that marked her out as different to her neighbours. That was because

Connie was in the process of buying number fifteen. A year ago, her landlord, Jim Stevens, believed that if Labour won the next general election, it was likely that Manchester's slum clearance programme would go ahead. Consequently, he had taken the unusual step of offering Connie the opportunity to buy the house from him. As she'd lived there all of her life, Jim had known her for many years. He'd seen her work hard at school and then qualify as an accountant. He was surprised that she had remained in Howard Avenue. Young, pretty and fashionable, she would surely have wanted to move away. He wondered if it was because as a single woman, she was finding it hard to rent elsewhere. He had therefore offered to help. After all, he knew most of the letting agents in Manchester and beyond. Yet Connie had insisted that Howard Avenue was home. It was where she felt comfortable and she had no intention of moving.

Connie's response had resulted in Jim's offer. It was an unusual agreement that was drawn up between them, whereby Stevens continued to receive Connie's rent payments as interest, whilst she paid off the purchase price through additional weekly amounts. It was a deal that suited both parties. Connie had been given the property at a reasonable price. One which would be covered by compensation if redevelopment was quick to go ahead. Her landlord had given Connie the opportunity to get on the property ladder, something which the banks and building societies, regardless of her substantial savings, would never have done.

Pleased as she was to have her investment, Connie couldn't help but consider how the morning's events may force her to re-evaluate her situation. Although Joseph Greening had no qualms about giving a senior position to someone from Ardwick, Connie knew that as she dealt with increasingly wealthy and influential clients, their attitudes may well be different. Others, less enlightened in their thinking, with snobbish and elitist attitudes, would be less appreciative of her social background. Connie therefore wondered how long it would be before she would have to choose between her attachment to her roots and the need to move away for the benefit of her career. Compromises may well have to be made if Connie desired the latter. The word compromise however, wasn't one that this strong-minded young woman was normally prepared to countenance.

Chapter 4

Later that evening, Connie was sat quietly on the settee in the kitchen, reading the 'Manchester Evening News' with the radio quietly playing music in the background. Connie had a television, but unlike the enthusiasm that most of the country showed towards the powerful and engrossing new media, Connie chose her programmes selectively. Dramas and documentaries were her favourites, but she still preferred to get her news via the radio and the local and national press. Tonight's 'Evening News' held a particular interest for her, containing as it did an article on the Labour Party, whose aspirations Connie generally supported. The writer was considering how, if there was a Labour victory at the next general election, it would impact upon the region. It was a topic of great concern to Connie, given that Manchester and the North-West were going through difficult economic times. Manufacturing jobs had been steadily declining since the end of the War. Furthermore, the city's redevelopment was seemingly at a standstill, with public funds unavailable to sustain it, private finance seemingly reluctant to do so and too little thought given to the wishes of the communities that any changes would impact upon. The article certainly wasn't complimentary to the Party and Connie found it hard to disagree with their judgement. There was still so much that needed to be achieved.

There had been great optimism following Labour's landslide victory in 1945. Connie acknowledged that the National Health Service was a laudable achievement and there had been the nationalisation of key industries too. Yet almost twenty years later in Ardwick, Connie still saw distress and poverty. Disadvantaged children who had little chance of sharing in the greater affluence that was emerging in the early 1960s. There had been lots of fine words and good intentions from local party heavyweights. Men like Ardwick's own MP, Leslie Lever, a man utterly committed to his constituents. Yet they hadn't managed to get all Mancunians on their side and in successive general elections, there had been a significant return of Tory MPs among the city's constituencies. Nationally, Labour had also failed to take the people of the country with them. The Tories had come storming back in 1951 and they had held power ever since. Perhaps too many members of Labour's national leadership were 'champagne socialists.' They weren't radical enough to be prepared to alleviate the ongoing distress of the working classes, at the risk of undermining the national coalition of interests that they believed was needed to return them to power.

Connie prided herself on the fact that she had never denied her working-class heritage, when it would have been so easy for her to have done so. It was a badge of honour for her that she still lived in Ardwick, in the same house that she had shared with her mother until the latter's departure when Connie was eighteen. Connie was a child who had been born out of love and passion. Her mother Doris had met Wilfred, her father, during his studies in engineering at the University. The Campbells were a wealthy family and having experienced a sheltered upbringing, Wilf was shocked by the poverty he saw in the streets of Chorlton-on-Medlock, so close to where he studied. It was 1934 and the Great Depression seemed hardly to have released the iron grip of its fingers on the working classes of Northern England. Wilf's conscience had jolted him into action and he threw himself into local protests and charitable work. Without realising it, he gradually took on the socialist aspirations that made him see the world in a different way. To Wilf, life had become a struggle between good and evil. It was a conflict that went beyond the shores of his own country, as he watched the rising tide of fascism sweep over the continent.

And then he had met Doris, a beautiful, working-class girl from Ardwick, at a protest against Mosley's fascists in Salford in 1935. Wilf couldn't help but be enchanted by the fiery, proud young woman, so confident in herself and eager to tell him of her part in stopping Mosley's speech at Belle Vue during the previous year. She too was taken by the handsome young man who, like herself, so earnestly desired to change the World. Although their backgrounds were so far apart, they were united by their idealism and even though Doris would tease him for being a 'toff,' she never doubted the sincerity in his heart. And it was a heart that he'd made clear was devoted to her. When Wilf completed his studies the following year, inheriting a significant legacy from his grandfather, the two were married at All Saints Register Office. It was a union disapproved of by Wilf's family, unable to accept a daughter-in-law who they considered well beneath their social standing. Their attitude had meant that Doris required much persuasion from Wilf to marry him, but eventually she had agreed and the couple had moved into the house on Howard Avenue.

Within a short time, Doris was expecting, but Wilf wasn't destined to be present for the birth of their child. With the attack by Franco's forces on the Republican Government in Spain, the couple saw a watershed moment; a time to decisively halt the fascist menace. It was Doris who insisted. There could be no question. Wilf had to go and play his part in the struggle and she would remain behind. Otherwise, they were hypocrites, putting their own selfish interests before their principles. Doris's parents had passed on and she had no immediate family. Wilfred had therefore written to his parents asking them to help care for his child should he fail to return. The letter came back unopened. The young couple were on their own. Regardless, Wilf joined the British Battalion of the International Brigade. In early 1937 he arrived in Spain. Letters to and from home were inevitably delayed, but Wilf finally received the news that he had become father to a baby girl. To mark his fight for the Republican cause, Doris had given her the Spanish names of Concepcion and Maria, determined that their daughter would never forget the principles and courage of a father who would see action at Jarama and Brunete, before being wounded at Aragon.

Wilf was back in Manchester by early 1938. Finally, he was able to meet his daughter and settle down to a blissful period of happy family life, following the vicious fighting and atrocities he'd experienced in Spain. Although, like his comrades, he'd been regarded with suspicion by the authorities when he'd left, concerns about his leftist sympathies had mostly disappeared on his return. Hitler was now on the march and perceived as a clear threat to the country and having risked his life to resist the fascist onslaught in Spain, Wilf was now regarded as a hero and a patriot. Yet it had taken several months to fully recover from his injuries and it wasn't long after he'd found employment as a civil engineer, that Germany invaded Poland and Wilf found himself called up to serve in the army. Given his sacrifice in Spain and his desire to continue to confront the fascist menace, once he was fit, Wilf had joined the 'Territorials' and so had been first in line to be called up. His combat experience and social background had led to officer training and a commission in the Territorials and by the end of 1939, Wilf was out in Belgium.

Having got her husband back safely from Spain, Doris's attitude towards the political struggle had changed. Their separation hadn't been easy. Doris now realised that she couldn't live without him. And once he returned, she was convinced that Wilf had more than played his part. She therefore opposed his decision to join the Territorials, insisting that his past injuries should excuse him from ever having to fight again. Yet Wilf ignored her and when he was called up, Doris felt a growing sense of unease. As the weeks and months passed, she became convinced that she wouldn't see Wilf again and it therefore came as no surprise when she received a telegram informing her, that her husband had been killed on the beaches of Dunkirk. A letter from his battalion commander commended Wilf's bravery in bringing his isolated troops through the German lines to safety. The letter however, provided little in the way of consolation for Doris, although it would remain a source of great pride to her daughter.

Doris was fortunate that Wilf had left a regular income for his daughter. Connie was a bright and inquisitive little girl. She had inherited the determination of both her parents and was exceptionally clever at school. With no financial pressure, like most families around them, Doris could allow Connie to stay on at school. Yet as the years passed, Doris found it increasingly difficult to cope with her loss and from her early grammar school years, Connie had effectively looked after herself, as her mam went through bouts of depression. Doris began to blame herself for her husband's death. She believed that by supporting his decision to go to Spain, it had later convinced him that he'd lose her respect if he didn't face up to the Nazis. She was wrong, but had never believed Wilf when he had told her so. Full of remorse, time had brought the slow disintegration of a once proud woman. Under the influence of drink, she had sought solace in the arms of men she had picked up in town centre pubs. Thankfully, she retained enough pride to keep her activities away from Ardwick, the neighbours and her daughter.

In her periods of relative stability, Doris marvelled at how Connie continued to thrive. Her daughter was so grown up and capable of coping on her own. Nothing seemed to hold her back. When Connie was eighteen and had obtained a job with John Francis, Doris arranged for Wilf's legacy to be paid directly to her daughter who, with her salary, could comfortably support herself. Doris had found a new man, Frank Rhodes, moving in to his house in Harpurhey. Connie hadn't been impressed with Frank. When her mam visited, she often looked battered and bruised, but would always insist that it was the result of an accident. Eventually, the two women had argued. Doris wouldn't accept any criticism of Frank and there was a parting of the ways. Doris moved and Connie was unable to find her. Still only eighteen, Connie had the security of a home in Howard Avenue and as long as the rent was paid, the landlord wasn't concerned that he never saw Doris when he came to collect it. When Connie was twenty-one, she was able to reveal her mother's absence and take on the tenancy in her own name.

To many, it would have seemed a difficult upbringing, but Connie never saw it like that. In reality she had never felt vulnerable. She was part of a wider community that gave her a sense of belonging and a feeling of security. Regardless of how poor most of the people of Ardwick were, they looked after one another. Howard Avenue was her home and growing up in a tough environment, had given her the political and social aspirations that her parents had shared in the 1930s. Regardless of being part of the upwardly mobile post-war generation, Connie had no intention of leaving her roots behind.

Chapter 5

Thirty years old, Ralph Greening was exactly where he liked to be. It was Monday morning, just before nine and Ralph was holding court in the presence of the typists and secretaries of Greenings main office. The younger women adored him. He was the boss's nephew and for those who were still unmarried, Ralph offered up the fantasy that they could be the one who would capture this eligible bachelor's heart. There had been many that had tried, but all had failed. Nevertheless, the stories of Ralph's ruthlessness in discarding those he'd gone out with, didn't seem to dampen the ambition of others who were convinced that they could reform him. The dark side of his character was rarely on show however. This morning, as usual, he was cheerful and his jocular behaviour made him seem kind and appealing. He had a winning smile and the looks to go with it. Ralph was handsome and he knew it. He had striking blonde hair, blue eyes and finely chiselled features. To his female admirers, he was no less than a modern Adonis. Moreover, he was supremely confident and together with his good looks and impending fortune, Ralph simply swept women off their feet. He boasted to his colleague Tom, that if he so desired, he could make love to any woman he wanted and for Ralph, his claim was entirely serious.

This morning however, Ralph's discourse was interrupted by the arrival of his uncle and with him was the young lady that was joining the audit department as its new senior accountant.

"Time we were getting down to work," said 'Old Joe.' "Clients don't pay us to sit around doing nothing."

There was no hint of menace to be detected in Joe's voice. He was regarded as a kind employer by all who worked for him. Nevertheless, his words carried weight and whether they did it because they liked and respected him, or recognised the truth of his comment, the result was the same. Quickly, everyone got back to their desks.

"This is my nephew, Ralph," said Joe, introducing him to Connie.

"Hello," said Connie, looking straight at Ralph and holding out her hand towards him. "I'm Connie. I'm pleased to meet you."

Taking Connie's hand, Ralph gently shook it. He felt pleasure at the soft touch of her palm and her delicate fingers. Momentarily, he took in the vision of loveliness that was stood before him. She seemed even more desirable than before. Once again, she exhibited a sense of style that though simple, exuded beauty and class. Her hair was immaculate and there was only the faintest hint of make-up around her adorable green eyes. Her outfit could be considered plain, yet it was perfect for the office. She was wearing a white, crisp blouse, black pencil skirt, black stockings and high heels. Yet the clothes accentuated her gorgeous figure and her blouse, unbuttoned at the top, gave Ralph an almost uncontrollable desire to lean forward and delicately kiss the soft, perfect skin of her neck.

"It's nice to finally meet you Connie," said Ralph, at last. "My uncle told me a lot about you and I'm sure we'll work well together."

"Yes, I'm sure we will," replied Connie.

"Well, I'll leave you two to get on," said Joe. "I'm sure you'll soon settle in Connie. Any problems, let me know right away."

Joe glanced at his nephew, a suggestion that his final comment was aimed more at him than Connie.

"I'm sure everything will be fine Mr Greening. I'm looking forward to getting started."

With 'Old Joe' gone, Connie was left together with Ralph.

"We're located on the next floor Connie. Everything concerning the audit work is concentrated there. I'll take you up, show you your office and then introduce you to Tom, he's the other senior accountant, as well as the other members of staff."

The two of them set off, continuing their conversation.

"Uncle Joe, as you know, is very forward-looking. He's all for this American idea of an 'open door' policy. He says that senior staff should, unless they're dealing confidentially with clients, or discussing sensitive matters with staff, work with their office doors open. It means that we can be approached at any time. I just thought I'd warn you, in case it's different to what you're used to."

"It sounds like a good idea Ralph. Where I've come from is only a small firm. There was really only John Francis, our boss, who spent much time alone in his office. The rest of us tended to work together."

"Oh, right," said Ralph.

Reaching the audit department, Connie found herself in a large office, similar to the one that she had been in downstairs. Around her were desks at which a number of secretaries and typists were working. At the far end she could see a corridor and Ralph guided her towards it. Their pace was checked however, by the fact that the younger women in the office, noting Ralph's presence, were eager to acknowledge him. Ralph smiled and pleasantly responded to their greetings. Connie noted that he clearly enjoyed the attention, but she didn't regard him as 'big headed' or arrogant. Connie understood that for Ralph, adulation came naturally. It was a fact that was unsurprising, as she had already recognised that he was extremely handsome.

Finally reaching the corridor, Ralph turned towards her.

"Our offices are along here Connie. Yours is down on the right, mine further along on the left."

Ralph then pointed to an open door.

"We'll pop in here to see Tom first. He's the other senior chap in auditing. He's a good lad, I'm sure you'll get on with him. Everyone does."

Moving towards the entrance, Ralph tapped on the open door and walked into the office, followed closely by Connie. At a large desk sat a young man staring down at a series of documents. It was clear that he was so engrossed in his work that he had failed to hear the knock on the door, or the footsteps of Ralph and Connie as they had entered the room. The two visitors stopped before the desk and looked down at him. There was still no reaction. Ralph smiled and Connie sensed that he was about to take drastic action. Bending down towards Tom, Ralph suddenly bellowed.

"Fire! Fire! Quick, evacuate the building!"

Tom leapt out of his seat, banging his knees on the desk in the process and throwing his pen up in the air. Stood up, he let out a sigh, grimacing as he rubbed his knees.

"What the…"

Connie knew that Tom was annoyed, but having seen her, he'd suppressed the curse that had been coming following Ralph's antics.

"Come on. Wakey, wakey Tom," said Ralph, in between fits of laughter. "You need to be alert to what's going on around you. Too devoted to the job by far. It won't get you anywhere you know."

Tom's face was a picture. A mixture of shock and irritation. Try as she might, Connie couldn't help but laugh, as still looking stunned, Tom seemed rooted to the spot.

"I'm sorry, I didn't mean to laugh, but I just couldn't help it," said Connie, chuckling once more as Tom, blushing like a beetroot, stared blankly at her.

For all the humour of the situation, Connie couldn't help but feel sorry for him. She recognised that he felt embarrassed and so asked him if he was all right in order to help him break his awkward silence.

"Are your knees okay Tom?" she asked, sympathetically. "They took a bit of a knock there, didn't they?"

"Yes, they did," he replied, "but I'm sure I'll be fine. It was more the shock of it I think."

Connie nodded her agreement.

"I'm Connie by the way," she continued. "I expect you know that."

"Yes. I saw you briefly outside Mr Greening's office when you came for your interview. I'm pleased to meet you, Connie. I'm sure that you're all ready to get started."

"Yes. I must say that I am," replied Connie, smiling.

"We're going out to analyse the financial management systems at Brown Engineering in Bolton later this week and I've been going through some preparatory documents. It's a big task and all three of us, Ralph, you and I, will be going out there."

There was a clear and immediate difference to the impression that Tom made on Connie, when compared to her interactions with Ralph. Whereas Ralph was outwardly charming and sociable, this young man was serious and focused on his job. Conscientious, Tom always wanted to do his best and unlike Ralph, wasn't easily diverted from his work.

Tom Clarke had taken his articles with Greenings. Twenty-seven years old, he had been a qualified accountant for over five years and had quickly become indispensable to the firm. Yet he was a quiet and considered young man. Given that they had worked closely together for many years, he was the obvious foil for the extrovert Ralph. All the women in the office liked Tom, but in a different way to Ralph. Tom was kind and considerate. There was no suggestion of impropriety about him and he felt uncomfortable when on occasions, Ralph's behaviour towards young women could be considered to be inappropriate, regardless of the fact that his colleague would dismiss it as 'just a bit of fun.'

"Well, I'm sure you'll want Ralph to show you your office," continued Tom. "Once you've settled in, the three of us can start planning the work at 'Browns'."

"Oh, not me," said Ralph. "The 'old man' is expecting me to accompany him to a meeting later on this morning. I'm not supposed to say, but we've a chance of getting into McVitie's."

"Oh," said Tom, surprised.

"Yes," continued Ralph. "The 'old man' wants it kept under wraps. Doesn't want any of the competition to find out."

Connie could see that Tom was disappointed not to have known of Joe Greening's plans. Yet it seemed logical that his nephew was more likely to be taken into Joe's confidence. It was a family firm and that would always prove a disadvantage to those who, regardless of their ability, weren't related to the owners. As a woman, Connie knew that in business she would be disadvantaged because of her gender, but she was aware that young men without social connections, could also face prejudicial treatment.

"Well," said Connie, "I'm sure that the two of us will be able to work through it."

"Yes, that'll be great Connie," said Tom, smiling.

Departing with Ralph, Connie was taken to her office. She was delighted. It contained a large desk, bookcase, some attractive plants on the window sill and chairs at the side of the room for clients or staff.

"Feel free to bring in any pictures, if you want to make it more homely," suggested Ralph.

"Yes. I'm sure I will. Thanks Ralph."

"Well, I'd best get off back to my uncle. I'll see you again tomorrow, Connie. You know where Tom's office is. He'll show you the ropes."

"Yes. Thanks again," replied Connie.

With Ralph's departure, Connie felt pleased at how she was slowly easing herself into the job. No animosity had been shown towards her by either of the men who would be her closest colleagues. It was refreshing that neither of them seemed to have an issue with the fact that they would be working on equal terms with a woman. In reality, that didn't surprise her with Tom, but given Ralph's character and the adulation he received from the young women at Greenings, she found his positive attitude particularly notable.

Chapter 6

Connie spent the rest of the morning working with Tom in his office. He was impressed. She was just like a breath of fresh air. Ralph was often frustrating. He easily became distracted and could be accused of lacking direction. Connie, on the other hand, was serious and focused. She was a pleasure to work with. Glancing at his watch, Tom found that the time had flown by and suggested that it was an opportune moment for them to take a break.

"I'm sorry Connie. I'm forgetting. It's almost one o'clock and you've had nothing to eat. Would you like to come for some dinner? There's a nice café just around the corner."

Connie looked up at him.

"Oh. That is if you want to of course," continued Tom.

Connie noted that he was determined not to appear presumptuous.

"Yes, I'd like to. That would be nice. It's good to hear you call it dinner. We working classes have to stick together. No lunches for us," she continued, with a broad smile across her face.

Tom smiled back. It was the first time that he'd betrayed any real emotion.

"Yes. Guilty as charged. A young, working-class lad, here among the bastions of capitalism!"

The two of them laughed. Connie's comment had broken the ice. Rather than just being colleagues, there was now an opportunity for them to find out more about each other and possibly become friends.

The café was one that Connie had been to before. It was just around the corner, down Oldham Street at the junction with Hilton Street. It was a Lyons Café with its series of large plate glass windows. Inside were a number of tables and chairs and the counters behind which were an array of delectable pastries, tarts, buns and cream cakes. It was a perfect choice.

"What would you like Connie?" asked Tom, after they had sat down.

"It's all right Tom, I can get it."

"Well, if I pay this time, then you can get it next."

"Okay," replied Connie. "I'll have a cheese barm, a cup of tea and a vanilla."

Soon the waitress had served them and the two were happily eating and deep in conversation, finding out a wealth of details about one another. Importantly, the two recognised that they had much in common. Both of them were from working-class backgrounds, they supported the Labour

Party, were eager for further social and political change and the two of them loved music.

"Who's your favourite artist Connie?"

"Well, I've always loved Cliff and Billy Fury and I do like the Beatles now too."

"But don't you like any of the new Manchester groups? Billy Fury and the Beatles are 'Scousers.'"

Connie laughed. Referring to them as 'Scousers' certainly betrayed Tom's Mancunian heritage. It always had to be competitive between the two cities. It had been ever since the building of the ship canal. Yet his comments also showed that Tom felt at ease in her company; he wasn't having to soften his language for his middle-class colleagues or clients.

"The 'Hollies', the 'Dakotas', the 'Mindbenders' are all breaking through now Connie," he continued. "And there are a lot more, good up-and-coming Manchester groups too."

"It's so long since I've been out with my old friends Tom. We used to go to the coffee bars in town. We were the lucky ones with enough money to do it. But one by one, my friends got married, had kids and stayed at home. As I've remained single, it's meant that our lives have diverged. Without them, I've not made an effort to go out as much. I've always kept a love for music, but going out to see groups or artists, has just slipped away. So, unlike you, I've lost touch with what's going on. Until these groups get into the charts and get played on the radio, I'm in the dark about them."

"Well then Connie, you should come down to the 'Oasis.' They all play there."

"The 'Oasis.' I've heard a lot about it, but I've never been. It's a club, isn't it?"

"Yes," continued Tom. "They have lots of different artists and music. Not just the big acts, but they also give new groups a chance to play. You should come and show your support. You'd enjoy it."

"Well, I might just think about it," replied Connie, impressed by Tom's obvious enthusiasm.

It was a tantalising answer. For the first time during their conversation, Tom felt a sense of embarrassment and his face reddened slightly.

"Oh, I didn't mean that I was asking you to ..."

He hesitated. He was now starting to feel silly.

"But I'd be more than happy for you to come with me if you wanted to see what the club and the music's like," he added, hurriedly.

Connie smiled and there, at that moment, Tom knew that without even trying, she had him completely in the palm of her hand. He certainly hadn't meant to ask her out, but his reference to her going with him to the 'Oasis,' had made it sound like he had. And now he'd become flustered because he couldn't overcome how beautiful she was. When he'd found out that she was coming to Greenings, he was determined that he would treat her the same as anyone else. Yet the plan had failed. He'd fallen under Connie's spell and would now find it very difficult to regard her in other than a romantic light.

To Tom's relief, Connie came to his rescue. She was determined that there would be no awkwardness between them.

"If I do want to go, then I'd be grateful for you showing me around Tom. You seem to be a bit of an expert in musical matters. You'd be a good guide."

"Well, I'm hardly an expert," replied Tom.

Self-effacing, without any hint of arrogance, Connie discerned a real sense of decency about him.

"Come on Tom," said Connie, taking the initiative. "Time we were getting back."

Standing up, the two of them placed their chairs back under the table and made their way out into Oldham Street and back to the office.

Sitting on the bus on her way home from work, Connie reflected on her first day at Greenings. So far, it had gone well. The positive relationships she had quickly struck up with the men she would be working with, boded well for the future. Yet how different Ralph and Tom were. The former so confident and assured, with a calm, easy manner that made women feel very comfortable. Tom, on the other hand, was far less confident once he was outside the working environment and he had shown Connie that he was self-conscious when he thought that there was even a hint of intimacy between them. Yet Connie liked Tom. He had been so friendly to her and their conversation in Lyons Café had revealed that they had many interests in common. The pair considered themselves socialists and were eager to improve the lot of the working classes, to whose ranks they still felt they belonged. Given their background, both were having to prove themselves in order to make their way in their chosen profession. They had eagerly discussed their tastes in music, films and literature and they had enjoyed each other's company. Yet Connie found no romantic feelings emerging within her towards Tom. It wasn't that he was unattractive. Tom was tall, six foot, he had black, curly hair and a pleasant smile that revealed his even, white teeth. He had kind, soft brown eyes and although his nose could be considered to be slightly too big and his chin a little pronounced, she loved the cute dimple that she could see there. Yet for all that, Connie was a woman of deep passions and unfortunately for Tom, he simply didn't arouse them.

Chapter 7

Tom and Connie's relationship had quickly developed during their first week of working together. During their dinner breaks, they eagerly discussed the state of their city and the problems it was facing. These were intensified, they believed, by the failure to tackle the declining state of the city's housing stock, the increasing economic stagnation, which was threatening the supply of traditional working-class jobs and the seeming indifference of the current Tory government to the plight of not only Manchester, but other industrial areas too. Noting Connie's enthusiasm for the socialist cause Tom, an active Labour worker in Connie's own Ardwick constituency, expressed his surprise that he had never seen her at any of the local party meetings.

"You should take the plunge and join the Party Connie. We need enthusiastic and intelligent members. Instead of feeling angry about the inequalities you see around you, you should join us and make a difference."

"I suppose I've had my focus firmly on work," replied Connie. "It's not easy being a woman in our profession Tom. You can't afford to let anything slip. There are too many disgruntled men out there, just waiting for you to make a mistake. I've had to set very high expectations for myself and so I've been hesitant to take on any other major commitments."

"But you're fine here at work, Connie. You can see that everyone accepts you. Why, we don't even regard you as a woman."

Connie raised her eyebrows and stared at him with a feigned look of displeasure.

"Oh really! You don't even recognise me as a woman now!"

Connie watched as Tom's face went its characteristic shade of scarlet. She was teasing him, but knew that he was unable to recognise the fact.

"Oh, no. That wasn't what I meant. I…"

Tom paused, clearly frustrated. Yet if he hoped that Connie would alter the course of the conversation and come to his rescue, he was to be disappointed. Connie was amused by his response and hadn't finished with him yet.

"So, you're telling me that you don't see me as a woman. I'm just 'one of the boys.' Is that it?"

Connie tried hard to maintain her stern expression as Tom stumbled along trying to find a satisfactory answer for her.

"No. You've got it all wrong Connie. Of course, you're a woman."

"Well, that's reassuring to know!"

"Yes. No one could mistake you for anything else."

Tom paused. He was about to tell Connie that no one could fail to regard her as feminine, given how pretty she was. Yet he was afraid that she may see his words as a juvenile attempt at a chat-up line. So, as a result, he remained silent, unable to think of anything else he could say, to safely extricate himself from his predicament.

"It's okay Tom," said Connie, laughing gently. "I know what you meant."

Seeing her lovely, warm smile and playful sparkling eyes, Tom was relieved. He was pleased to know that she wasn't angry with him and not annoyed that she had been teasing him all along. It gave him a nice, warm feeling to know that he hadn't upset her. Able to express his ideas once more, Tom returned to the question of Connie joining the Party.

"Why don't you come along to a meeting and see what you think? There's going to be one tomorrow night on education policy for Manchester's schools. There's a big push for comprehensives, especially after the reports by Newsom and Robbins."

"I'm not convinced that comprehensives are going to be the answer that their supporters are claiming," replied Connie. "It all seems a rather simplistic solution to overcoming the disadvantages of poor kids."

"Well, that's why you should come Connie. As a party, we're supposed to be a broad church. It's good to hear different opinions."

Tom smiled at her. Once more, he was talking confidently, willing her to accompany him to the meeting. She found his enthusiasm for the cause genuine and infectious.

"Okay. Why not? I'll come. You've persuaded me."

Tom couldn't hide his pleasure at her decision.

"That's great Connie. If you like, we can go and get something to eat together after we finish work tomorrow and then go on from there."

"Yes, okay Tom. I doubt that I'd have time to get back home anyway. It seems a good idea."

Perhaps it was time that Connie considered turning her political interests into action. After all, it was no good being critical of social inequalities, if she wasn't prepared to do something about them. And Tom was right. She was secure at Greenings. Connie had sacrificed so much in pursuing her career. Now, there seemed to be no reason why she couldn't turn her attention to other purposes and ambitions.

Chapter 8

The two of them arrived slightly late. The meeting was already underway as they entered the hall. Walking across the outer lobby and through the double doors into the main room, Connie was struck by the dull glare of the electric lights, the smoke from numerous cigarettes casting a shimmering haze over the proceedings. There wasn't a particularly large audience, so Tom led Connie down the central aisle towards a couple of seats on the end of a row near the front. Glancing around her, Connie was pleased to see that the audience was mixed. There were working men with their obligatory caps in their hands, a few women and a smattering of what appeared to be students from the University. All of them were listening intently to the words of a serious looking man, who was stood behind a long table placed on a small stage at the front. He spoke with passion, seriousness and intensity, as he outlined the Party's desire to implement a new programme of comprehensive education in Manchester's schools.

"Who's that?" whispered Connie to Tom.

"It's Harry. Harry Thomas."

"Oh yes. I thought I knew him. He's one of the councillors in Ardwick, isn't he?"

"Yes," replied Tom. "He's highly respected and very committed, but a good man to work with. I'll introduce you to him later."

Connie looked more closely at Harry. Thirty-one years of age, his dark, brown hair was starting to recede and there were even flecks of grey visible in his sideburns and moustache. With his glasses, measured and thoughtful words and authoritative presence, Harry projected the aura of a political intellectual.

"What does he do? What's his job?" asked Connie, turning to Tom as the applause broke out to signify the end of Harry's speech.

He's the deputy head of a boys' secondary school in Hyde. It's reckoned that he'll soon be a headmaster. He's relatively young for it, but he's well thought of by the education committee. He's not married and since he lost his mother, who'd been ill for some time, he's devoted all his energies to work and the Party."

Connie nodded. Harry's persuasive and assured tones had made a positive impression on her and she found his mature and distinguished appearance pleasing to the eye.

As the applause ended, Harry sat back down. To the left of him a balding, older man, wearing small round-framed glasses and with a moustache and beard reminiscent of Lenin, stood up and motioned to the room to be quiet.

"That's Bill Perkins," said Tom, quietly to Connie. "He's a councillor for Levenshulme and on the left of the party. He used to be a Stalinist in the 'Thirties' and didn't join Labour until after the war."

"I suppose he realised then, that everything wasn't all sweetness and light in the Soviet Union," replied Connie.

"Well," said Tom, chuckling. "When you hear him, you might want to reconsider that idea."

"Why?" asked Connie.

"Just wait. You'll see."

Connie was intrigued by Tom's words and when Perkins started speaking, she listened intently.

"Comrades. It's clear to us all, the words of Newsom and Robbins in their recent reports for this pathetic Tory excuse for a government, confirm everything Comrade Thomas has noted in his magnificent speech. It's time to rip up these grammar schools. Time to crush privilege. A school system whose only purpose is to pander to the bourgeoisie and seduce working-class children who've managed to pass the eleven-plus, into continued subservience to the controlling, capitalist class! It's no good and we have to change. And by hell, we will!"

Connie turned to Tom as most of the audience cheered in agreement. She shook her head in acknowledgement of his previous words.

"I see what you mean Tom."

If Connie thought that Perkins was just making an opening impression, grabbing his listeners' attention by the use of powerful, aggressive and emotive phrases, she was wrong. His entire speech, delivered like a presidential address, continued in similar vein. He gave the impression of a man furious with everything; a man intolerant of opposition and unwilling to countenance compromise. His vision was clear. Labour would come to power and the local council, unhindered and controlled by socialists, would impose change from above. It wasn't just education that was his target, housing too was part of his agenda and just like with schools, changes would be imposed without any recourse to the opinions of those who would be affected by them. It was a classical Stalinist position. The state's interests were paramount and its bureaucrats would simply impose their policies. It was also a commitment to modernisation for its own sake; a desire for a new socialist utopia which would, without hesitation, sweep away the traditional and old as fundamentally worthless.

Yet it seemed that the small audience were captivated by the man, in agreement with all that he had said. It would be a brave person who would want to challenge him in the potential hostility of such an environment. Yet Connie had felt the anger rise up inside her as she had listened to him speak and when the chairman asked the meeting if anyone had any questions Connie, without hesitation, sprang to her feet.

"Yes, I have Mr Chairman."

The chairman looked down at the young woman just a few rows from the front. His gaze was followed by that of Harry Thomas and Bill Perkins to either side of him. He didn't recognise her. She hadn't been present at any meetings he'd ever been at, but he was pleased to see that the Party was attracting potential new recruits, especially one so pretty. Smiling at her, the chairman asked her to go ahead.

"It's a question for Councillor Perkins," said Connie.

"Yes, Comrade?" said Perkins, leaning forward towards the young woman and smiling.

Looking at Connie, Perkins underestimated the potential challenge that she could pose towards him. Surely her question wouldn't prove to be uncomfortable. Although a socialist with a supposedly modern outlook, Perkins was no different to so many men Connie had encountered. Whatever their social class or political persuasion, their views about the inherent intelligence and capabilities of women, were far from complimentary.

"Councillor Perkins, you made reference to the Newsom and Robbins Reports, didn't you?"

"Yes, young lady. That's right," replied Perkins, once again smiling at Connie.

"Well, I'm sorry to have to say it, but you've totally misrepresented the views in both of those documents. Your conclusions about grammar schools, stating that their removal will bring the end of social injustice and inequality, are wrong. Neither report states that."

Connie paused. She saw the startled look on Perkins face. She could sense that he was angry and uncomfortable about the fact that he was being challenged in front of an audience of acolytes. The hall was silent, momentarily shocked by the challenge thrown out to a man who to many of them, was their darling and hero. Nevertheless, Connie was determined to push on.

"The Newsom Report in particular, is clear about it. Schools themselves are just one element of the problem that results in children from so-called slum areas, underachieving. There are a host of issues involved: poor housing; one parent families; girls aspiring to get married at the earliest opportunity and so having no academic aspirations; poverty meaning that kids are leaving school at fifteen to earn money before they can take any qualifications and, most importantly, a lack of government funding to tackle these problems and give schools money to retain staff and introduce more technical and practical subjects to suit the less academic. Nowhere in the Newsom Report does it blame the existence of grammar schools for the failure of children in the secondary moderns. It doesn't support your argument."

"So, you're a supporter of grammar schools young lady and the inequality they breed, are you?" asked Perkins, fiercely.

"Not inequality," replied Connie, "but meritocracy. It's the same principle that operates in education in the Soviet Union and Red China. It's what gives bright kids from poor backgrounds in this country, a chance to compete with the children of the rich, who take their places at the independent schools. Why shouldn't pupils of all abilities, be able to thrive in a school that is best suited to their needs; either grammar, technical or secondary modern?"

As Connie paused, members of the audience started to boo her. Her arguments were clearly falling on deaf ears. A couple of shouts of "traitor!" came from behind and then a booming voice asking "who the bloody hell does she think she is?" Tom sensed the tension in the room. He hadn't expected that by bringing Connie along to the meeting, he may be placing her in physical danger. Yet before he could act, a new protector had thrust himself into the spotlight. Harry Thomas jumped to his feet, quickly got from behind the desk and moved to the front of the stage. Raising both arms, he then moved his hands up and down, motioning to the audience to be quiet. He spoke loudly, clearly and calmly. It was the voice of authority.

"Comrades. That's enough. That's the Tory way. We give everyone a chance here. We listen to one another. We might not like what we hear, but we consider it carefully, rationally, practically. It's what the working classes are all about. It's what our party is about. Calm discussion, leading to practical solutions for the benefit of us all. That's what I believe in and we should all defend the right of this young woman to contribute to our debate. Give her a chance, listen to what she has to say and if you disagree, tell her why."

As he spoke, the room quickly came over to his side. Harry was a man admired well beyond the confines of his own ward in Ardwick and had even come to the attention of members of Labour's National Executive. He was genuine, he cared and had helped so many individuals with their difficulties and thrown his weight behind so many causes. He was a natural, confident speaker. He could quickly sense the mood of an audience and knew the exact words to engage their attention. There was talk that once a safe parliamentary constituency became available around Manchester, Harry would be the preferred candidate. Still relatively young, Harry seemed to have a promising political future.

Bill Perkins had felt real animosity towards the young woman who'd had the temerity to challenge him so vigorously. Nevertheless, he had enough political nous to recognise that Harry's appeal had won over the room and that he couldn't simply intimidate or overpower her, as was his wont. Perkins was a shrewd politician, a man of experience who enjoyed his stature within the local party. He was, underneath his tough and abrasive exterior, clever enough to adopt a different, more rational and less emotional approach towards his opponent. Quickly, he stood up and took the initiative from Harry.

"Yes, comrades. Harry's right. We need to give the young lady her due. We've listened to her views and I for one, am happy to reply to her criticisms about what I've said on the subject of grammar schools. It will give me enormous pleasure to do so."

Smiling, he turned to Harry.

"It's all right Comrade. I'll take it from here."

The audience, now settled, looked forward to what Perkins was about to say. They felt confident that he was about to put this upstart in her place.

"Young lady," began Perkins, his condescending tone creating the impression that she couldn't possibly challenge the knowledge and experience of a party stalwart like himself.

"I'm afraid that if you'd read the Robbins report correctly, you'd know that the education system as it currently stands, with grammar schools at its centre, completely fails the sons and daughters of the poor. Only 2% of students from families of a skilled, working-class background, get to university and just 1% of those from semi-skilled or unskilled backgrounds do. That's one in a hundred! Well young lady, that proves to me that your beloved grammar schools are failing."

Shouts of "that's right Bill!" and "you told her!" rang out, as the audience expressed their appreciation of his words with loud applause.

"Comrades. Calm down," continued Perkins. "We must give the young lady the right to reply."

He stood confidently. He was sure that his telling statistics would bring no effective response. It would be as he'd expected; the young woman would prove to be an ineffective opponent. He'd come across her type before. Educated, middle-class he thought. A typical 'do-gooder' who'd had it easy and was coming along to a Labour meeting because she believed that she was sympathetic to the working classes. There were so many of them joining the party and he despised them. They'd never done a real job of work in their lives; hard graft with their hands for poor wages from cruel bosses. They hadn't a clue about what it was like to be exploited. They didn't understand that there was a class war going on and all this nonsense about compromising ideals, would never see the Workers triumphant. Perkins had come up through the union and he'd fought the bosses in bitter strikes and felt the crack of the police truncheons on his skull whilst he was manning the picket lines. How dare any of these comfortable, bourgeois intellectuals, try to dictate to him what socialism meant. To Perkins, grammar schools reflected privilege. They were a Tory creation, the work of Rab Butler in 1944. Their purpose was to uphold the existing class structure and the establishment, at a point in time when working-class soldiers from Britain and the Soviet Union, were gaining ascendancy over the Nazis. Grammar schools were just one part of an attempt to stop the socialist victory and deny the Workers their rights. Comprehensives would sweep it all away. Education would be on equal terms for all and become a key component of the new socialist society.

Yet Perkins had misjudged his opponent. He'd stereotyped her background and character, blindly compartmentalising her into the category of his typical party opponents. Connie would not be quiet. She didn't care if the room was against her. She wasn't about to back down when she believed that she was right. Once more, the vigour and passion that had seen her father fight for the Spanish Republican cause and had prompted her mam to name her Concepcion Maria, seemed to course through her veins.

"Before the Butler Act, the children of the working classes had no chance of gaining educational qualifications and through them, the chance to go to university or pursue more varied forms of employment. Grammar schools have changed that. Karl Marx himself said: 'From each according to his ability; to each according to his needs.' That's true of education. The 1944 act reflects that by creating grammar, technical and secondary modern schools to meet the abilities of all types of children. It is by getting the best out of every child, that we can challenge the dominance of the upper and middle classes over the socio-economic system. Grammar schools are all about meritocracy; a recognition of ability, regardless of class. That has to be the way forward if we are to improve society for everyone."

Connie paused for a few seconds to enable her message to sink in. Walking out into the aisle and to the front of the rows of chairs, she turned to the audience and continued.

"The problem is that you can't create the school structure in isolation and that, as I've said, is what both Newsom and Robbins have pointed out. Neither Tory or Labour governments have created the infrastructure, socially or economically, to provide the environment that poor children need in order to succeed in the education system. But grammar schools have been successful in getting many young, working-class men and women into our universities. Regardless of the statistics that Comrade Perkins has given, increasing numbers of them are achieving degrees and universities can no longer be considered institutions that are reserved for the upper and middle classes. And why do I feel so passionately about this? I'm from Ardwick and a grammar school education has helped provide me with a career that someone from my background, would never have achieved without it."

Connie's final statement provided a sting in the tail. It didn't just take Perkins by surprise, but the audience too. They'd assumed that this young woman, who they'd never seen before, was anything but working-class. Her clothes and the words she'd used, suggested to them otherwise. Few of them would reflect on the fact of their own innate prejudices, but once they knew that she was one of their own, their attitude softened towards her, even if they weren't prepared to be swayed by her arguments. With the pause in proceedings created by Connie's revelation, the chairman of the meeting took the opportunity to announce a recess.

"Well Comrades. We've certainly had some thought provoking and interesting ideas. I think that now would be a good time for a break. There's tea and biscuits available as usual from the servery. We'll reconvene in twenty minutes."

With the scraping of chair legs and the muffled sound of conversation, people began to make their way towards the servery and the welcoming sustenance of tea, custard creams and digestives.

Tom turned towards Connie. She still had that defiant and determined look in her eyes. His admiration for her was unbounded. He doubted whether he would have had the courage to face such a hostile audience and a pugnacious opponent like Bill Perkins. Yet it hadn't bothered her and even now there were no signs that the experience had upset her sense of equilibrium.

"Come on Connie. Let's go and get a drink. I'll introduce you to Harry as I promised."

"Yes. I'd like to meet him," said Connie. "He stood up for me, didn't he?"

"Yes, he did. It's what he would do. Harry's a decent chap."

"And open-minded too. Not a characteristic necessarily shared by the comrades," she replied, laughing.

Tom laughed too. He'd often had reason to question his party colleagues. So many were too dogmatic, too accepting of the 'articles of faith' handed down to them without question. Hopefully, Connie may have made them think again, but he doubted it.

The pair made their way to the servery. Purchasing two cups of tea and some biscuits, the money used to boost local party funds, Tom walked Connie over to Harry Thomas, who was stood at the rear of the room. Harry immediately acknowledged them.

"Hello Tom. Good to see you and who's your friend?" he asked, smiling at Connie.

"Connie, this is Harry. Harry Thomas."

"Hello," said Connie, extending her hand towards Harry.

Taking her hand, Harry shook it gently, but felt Connie grip his hand firmly in return. Her brave and passionate words had impressed him and now able to see her at close quarters, she seemed even prettier than when he'd observed her from the stage.

"So, where have you been hiding Connie?" he asked. "I've not seen you at any of our meetings or functions before."

"Well, I'm working with Tom now and he's the one responsible for bringing me. I'd say I was a Labour sympathiser and I believe a socialist, although I'm not sure that Comrade Perkins would agree. I've never felt though, that I could devote the necessary time to commit myself fully to the Party."

"I shouldn't worry too much about Bill," said Harry, laughing. "It was good to hear you put up such a convincing challenge against him. Interesting though. You certainly wouldn't be following the general party consensus in your defence of grammar schools. Then again, none of us agree with all the policies and I concur with you, that everything should be up for reconsideration and debate."

"So, you agree with me then? "

"No. Sorry to disappoint you Connie, but I don't. But unlike Bill and his supporters, I believe that I can agree to differ."

His response pleased Connie. He was honest, making no attempt to be charming or worse still, condescending. He'd defended her right to speak because it was the correct thing to do. As such, Connie couldn't fail to be impressed by his calm intelligence and generous qualities.

"Your commitment can be as much, or as little as you like Connie," continued Harry. "We all lead busy lives and few of us can put in the hours that we'd like. Why don't you accompany Tom and I on one of our ward rounds? You're from Ardwick. It wouldn't require too much time or trouble. You'd get a good insight into the difficulties we help people with. There are problems with landlords, the Council, employers, so many different things. And if it interests you, then you could help us. You know Ardwick and its people as well as I do. Decent, hard-working and a belief in standards. Yet they don't have the advantages that we have. When they try to deal with the authorities, they lack knowledge and confidence. That's where we can step in and help to defend their interests."

There was a gleam in his eyes as he spoke and Connie found his words persuasive. There was an emotion in his voice born of conviction. The conviction that it was his duty to help those less fortunate than himself. And that was what Connie understood to be the true meaning of any worthwhile political cause. Without hesitation, she responded affirmatively.

"Yes, I'd like to be involved in that."

Both Harry and Tom smiled at her.

"We'll be going out again next Thursday Connie," said Harry. "Tom will give you the details. I'm afraid that I'll have to get back to the hall before they notice that I'm missing!"

Connie looked around and realised that the three of them were the only ones still left in the room.

I look forward to seeing you again Connie," said Harry.

After watching him depart, Connie turned back to Tom.

"I think I'd like to go home now Tom. I've taken a big enough part in proceedings for one night."

"Okay. Do you want me to come with you?" asked Tom.

"No. It's all right, I'm a big girl now. I'm sure I can find my way home," replied Connie, laughing.

"But I can, if you want."

"Honestly Tom, you should stay. They may need you. I'll be fine."

"Okay Connie. Good night."

"Good night, Tom."

Tom made his way back to the hall whilst Connie set off home. The night's events had been an interesting experience and one that she had enjoyed. Even her joust with Bill Perkins had proved to be stimulating. She had met Harry too and he was a man who intrigued her. She was looking forward to seeing him again and in a situation where she could use her skills and knowledge for the benefit of the local community.

Chapter 9

Connie and Paula were sat in Lyons Café. It was dinner time and the two women were enjoying a break. Paula had made a pleasant impression on Connie when she had first met her and after she had started at Greenings, the two of them had formed a close friendship. As Connie spent most of her working day with Tom and Ralph, she appreciated the opportunity to get together with Paula and discuss matters from a woman's perspective. Almost inevitably, the conversation drifted on to matters at work.

"How are you getting on with Tom then Connie?"

"Fine. He's been so welcoming since the day I started. He's so easy to work with and now he's got me involved with the Ardwick Labour Party."

"How did that happen?" asked Paula.

"Well, I suppose I've developed more than a passing interest in politics from my parents. Both of them were involved in the struggle against fascism before the War. My mam got arrested for protesting against Mosley and his Blackshirts in Salford. My dad fought for the International Brigade against Franco in Spain. Then, living in Ardwick, I see so much poverty and distress and I feel that I really should try to do something about it. Tom's already a member of the Labour Party and he offered to take me along to a meeting. The local councillor asked me if I could spare some time to help those in difficulty and I thought that I would give it a try."

"That's pretty generous of you Connie, given all the work that you have to do for Greenings."

"Well, I think that I should be giving something back Paula. Any issues I might have in terms of time, are nothing compared to the problems faced by many of my neighbours."

"I've been meaning to ask you about that Connie. Why do you still live in Ardwick?"

"Because I'm buying a house there."

"But why not buy a house somewhere else?"

Connie laughed.

"We women aren't allowed to buy houses on our own Paula. They only give mortgages to men. I'd need the cash in the bank to buy one outright. Luckily, I have an arrangement with my landlord. He's selling me the house because he wants it off his hands before the Corporation issues a compulsory purchase order."

The explanation didn't satisfy Paula, who looked at her friend confused. After all, there was no way that if she earned Connie's salary, she would be remaining in a house that had no bathroom and an outside toilet. Paula lived in Burnage where this wasn't the case. After all, it was 1963 and there were modern houses available in what to her, were better areas. Connie's reasoning just didn't make sense.

"You could rent somewhere nicer. Surely?" continued Paula.

"I don't want to. Honestly, I feel at home in Ardwick and I might as well stay where I am until they either knock it all down or, and it would be a miracle if they did, improve the houses with bathrooms and inside toilets."

Paula breathed out audibly.

"Well Connie. I don't know if I should admire or pity you. Either way, I'd rather you than me!"

Connie laughed, amused by her friend's reaction. The facilities at Howard Avenue didn't bother her. She and a majority of Mancunians, had lived with them since birth. She was prepared to tolerate them for a bit longer. Changing the subject, Connie referred back to Tom.

"I was talking about music with Tom the other day and a couple of his friends are in a group that are performing at the 'Oasis' on Saturday night, so we're going to watch them. Hopefully, I'll enjoy it. I haven't been out to a club in ages."

"Who are they?" asked Paula, who, like Tom, was keenly interested in the local music scene.

"I don't know," replied Connie. "He didn't tell me and I didn't think to ask. I just thought that it would make a nice change to go somewhere and relax for once."

"And Tom?" asked Paula.

"Yes?" replied Connie.

"Are you going because you want to go out with him, or is it just to listen to the music?"

"What made you say that?" asked Connie, surprised by Paula's question.

Paula realised from Connie's reaction, that her enquiry was now redundant. Going on a date with Tom was clearly the furthest thing from her mind. Yet there was something that her friend hadn't realised and Paula felt that she had a responsibility to tell her. But she would make sure that she did it carefully and replying to Connie's question, she initially gave a cautious response.

"It's just the fact that you both get on so well together and seem to enjoy each other's company. I suppose I'm just being romantic."

"No, there's nothing like that Paula. I like Tom but he's just a friend. Nothing more. I'm not looking for romance."

"Not at all?"

"Well, not with Tom."

"Oh dear."

Connie looked closely at her friend.

"What is it, Paula?" she asked, quietly.

"Haven't you noticed the way he looks at you Connie?"

"Who?"

"Tom, of course!"

Paula found it difficult to comprehend how someone as intelligent as Connie, couldn't fail to recognise that Tom was falling in love with her.

"He hangs on your every word Connie. He watches your every move. It's clear that he idolises you. Surely, you must have noticed?"

"No," said Connie. "I haven't. Are you sure?"

"Yes, you need to be careful. He's going to be disappointed when he realises that there'll never be any romance between you. He's very kind and I suspect, sensitive too Connie. Try to let him down gently."

"Well, I'm sure that I've done nothing to encourage him, Paula. He's just a friend. I go out with him just the same as I would go out with you or anyone else. Surely, he can see that?"

"Men are different Connie. They aren't like us. When a woman agrees to go somewhere with them, they want to think that it's because they're attracted to them. Tom's feelings for you are clear and if you spend time with him outside work, it's more than likely that he'll assume that you share his feelings."

"But I don't Paula. He's a lovely guy, yet I just don't think of him in any other way than as a friend. I'm sure he realises that."

"Well, hopefully he will Connie. But don't say that I didn't warn you."

Noticing that it was time to return to work, the two women brought their conversation to an end. Later that evening, in the quiet of Howard Avenue, Connie reflected on what Paula had said. She was sure that she had done nothing to encourage any feelings other than those of friendship from Tom. She assured herself that she would continue to do that in the future. Nevertheless, she had appreciated the warning from Paula but was confident that if she continued to spend time with Tom outside work, it wouldn't lead to any difficult or compromising situations.

Chapter 10

They had arranged to meet in Albert Square on Saturday night at six thirty. The 'Oasis' was the successor of the '2Js Club', a jazz venue located in an old warehouse conversion on the corner of Lloyd Street and Albert Square. When she arrived, Connie found that Tom was already waiting for her by the Albert Memorial. He looked as if he had been there for some time. Seeing her, Tom's eyes lit up and a broad smile crossed his face.

"Have you been waiting very long Tom?" asked Connie.

"Not too long. I wanted to make sure that I was here in case you arrived early."

Connie laughed.

"I can look after myself you know. I've lived in Manchester as long as you have."

"I know," he replied. "I didn't want you thinking that I wasn't going to turn up."

"And why would I think that?"

Tom stood silent for a few moments. It was clear that he didn't know what to say. He blushed and Connie realised that what Paula had told her was true. Tom did have strong feelings towards her. She realised that she would have to stop teasing him so much. It was that, in particular, that seemed to cause him embarrassment and indicated the strong emotions that she aroused within him.

Ignoring her question, Tom changed the subject.

"It should be a good night, Connie. The Big Three are the main group; my friends are supporting them. There's normally a queue to get in if you turn up at seven thirty, but we can go round to the back and go in with my pals."

"Oh," said Connie. "Who are The Big Three?"

"Haven't you heard of them?" asked Tom, in disbelief.

His expression of surprise caused Connie to laugh.

"I've told you Tom, I'm out of touch these days. If they aren't in the charts or on the radio, I don't know them. We can't all be music aficionados like you. I'm sure you're the only person who's heard of most of the groups you talk to me about!"

Connie stopped herself before going any further, realising that once again she was teasing him and risking his embarrassment.

"Come on Tom, let's get moving."

The two of them walked across the Square towards Lloyd Street. They crossed the road and made their way to the rear of the club. Tom's friends hadn't arrived yet.

"Don't worry, they'll be here soon," said Tom. "They need time to unload and set up their equipment."

Stood waiting, Connie was keen to find out more about the group who were tonight's main attraction.

"You still haven't told me anything about The Big Three Tom."

"They're a Liverpool group."

"I thought you said that groups from Liverpool weren't as good as those from Manchester."

"Well, generally they're not."

"Even the Beatles?"

"Connie, anyone who's heard The Big Three agrees that they're much better than the Beatles. I can guarantee you that the club's going to be packed tonight."

"So, why aren't they having hits like the Beatles then?"

"Who knows? I suppose it's the nature of the record business. It's not always the best artists that make it."

"But surely Tom, you must like 'Love Me Do' and 'Please Please Me'"

"Yes, they're okay I suppose. The Beatles played here at the 'Oasis' back in February. Kids were queueing all around the block and loads couldn't get in. I can't deny it, the Beatles are certainly doing well."

As he was speaking, an old, blue Bedford CA van, with its distinctive pug nose, turned into view, pulling up beside them. The door of the passenger side slid open and out clambered a couple of young guys in T-shirts and jeans, sporting 'mop top' haircuts.

"Hi Tom," called out one. "We're running late. The van wouldn't start. Can you give us a hand with the gear?"

"Yes, sure Mitch," replied Tom.

Looking at the state of the van, Connie was surprised that it had got there at all. Steam was hissing out from under the bonnet and as they walked round to the back, she noticed that the bodywork was rusting badly. Connie stood there in disbelief. Surely, they hadn't risked their lives driving across Manchester in such a vehicle as this? Having got out of the van to join them, the driver, seeing the astonishment on Connie's face, nonchalantly offered some words of reassurance.

"Oh, she's all right love. Just a bit tired. A little problem with the radiator. Once it's cooled down, I'll soon be able to sort it out."

Moving to the rear of the vehicle, Connie stood back as Mitch went to open a pair of badly dented doors. They had been bashed about by the goods and equipment that had been hauled through them over the last decade. As he pulled each one of them towards him, they clanked and groaned in protest, demanding a superhuman effort from Mitch, before they finally opened wide enough to permit access to the van's interior.

Connie was startled as suddenly, a fourth man leapt out of the van to confront her.

"Thank the Lord for that. I couldn't have stayed in there much longer. I thought I was going to get crushed by the equipment when you were screeching around those corners Tony."

"Go on. It's luxury back there," replied Tony. "Far better than walking."

"Huh. I don't think so. It's someone else's turn to go in the back next time."

"Come on lads, we need to get on. There's not much time to get set up," said Mitch.

Energised, the four group members, with Tom helping, began to bring out a succession of amplifiers and speakers, instruments, drums and cymbals. The club had opened the back door for them and it wasn't long before it was all inside. Connie, offering to help, was designated the task of bringing in the microphones and the band's stage wear. Smart, black matching suits, white shirts and ties that had been carefully covered in a plastic sheet on one side of the van. The lads were clearly on their best behaviour. Although there had been trapped fingers, bumped heads and stubbed toes, as they had wrestled their equipment out of the van and into the club, she had heard no curses or swearing. Connie could only assume that for her, they were acting like gentlemen. She couldn't imagine that this was how they normally behaved. Four young, single men from a beat group, living their rock 'n' roll dream. It seemed highly unlikely.

Whilst the group went off to get changed, Tom took his and Connie's coats to the cloakroom for safe keeping. Connie looked at the group's equipment which had been set out on the smaller of the two stages in the venue. The bass drum proudly proclaimed the name of the group: *The Wayves*. The Big Three had already arrived and were set up on the main stage and in comparison, The Wayves appeared to be an equally professional outfit. Connie hoped that their performance wouldn't disappoint her. Looking around the large room, she saw lots of tables. The club offered food, but not of the greatest quality and common for venues in the city, there was no license to sell alcohol. Then again, many members of the club were under eighteen and those older, were there to listen to the music. After all, the latter were part of a Fifties generation that had been brought up alongside the new coffee bar culture and if anyone did want an alcoholic drink, they could get the back of their hand stamped and go to a local pub, before being readmitted. To the side of her, Connie noticed a large mural depicting an imaginary 'Oasis,' an attempt to create a kind of exotic ambience for the club. Connie doubted whether the young clientele would be concerned about such things. Good music and dancing, among like-minded individuals, would create a positive ambience in itself.

It wasn't long before Tom returned and shortly after The Wayves were there too. They were now ready for a quick sound check; a couple of minutes to get the balance right between instruments and vocals.

"It's only a rough guide," shouted Tom, through the music. "Once there are more bodies in here, they'll have to adjust it again."

Connie was impressed by the short burst of song that she heard. The group sounded tight and both singers had strong voices. Stopping, the lads put down their instruments and walked off the small stage towards Connie.

"Isn't it time that you introduced us to your friend Tom?" asked Mitch.

"Yes, sorry. This is Connie."

Connie smiled as Tom then went on to introduce the members of the group to her.

"This is Mitch, who plays bass."

"And sings," added Mitch.

"Yes. And sings. Then there's Alan, guitar and vocals; Johnny, who plays lead and Tony on the drums."

"Hi Connie!" shouted the four lads together, bowing down towards her.

Connie laughed. They were appealing characters; real comedians. In their turn, the boys were finding Connie a sight pleasing to their eyes. Wearing a pink sleeveless dress, fitted at the top to highlight her figure, it flared out at the bottom, so accentuating her femininity. With a pretty white collar below her beautiful face and neck, she looked stunning. Pleasant and friendly, she was fun to be with. Almost as one, the lads looked enquiringly at Tom. He sensed what they were thinking and responded to them quickly.

"Connie and I are friends. We work together."

"Oh," said Tony.

"Yes, I've been telling her all about the group and so she wanted to come and see you for herself. So, here we are."

"Well Connie," said Mitch. "I hope we don't disappoint you."

"I'm sure you won't," replied Connie.

"We'd best get back to the dressing room," said Johnny. "We've got to go on in ten minutes."

The room had begun to fill up quickly after the doors had been opened at seven thirty. Tom had been right. A huge queue had formed outside. The Big Three had a growing reputation and had gained lots of fans in Manchester, following their various performances in the city.

"It's a good break for the guys," said Tom. "There's a packed audience tonight and hopefully, a lot of them are going to be impressed by The Wayves. It's all about building a following Connie and acts from Manchester have got a real opportunity now. The Dakotas, The Hollies, The Dreamers, all of them have made it. Record companies will be looking for other Manchester groups. Perhaps the boys will get a chance."

The Wayves set was a combination of their own numbers, rock 'n' roll standards and a couple of contemporary hits. Connie was impressed and so were the audience, up and dancing at the steady beat, the insistent and measured rhythms and the tight harmonies between Mitch and Alan. The latter was quite an extrovert and had real stage presence, making him an excellent front man for the group and one whose good looks made him popular with the teenage girls in the audience. The Wayves ended with a storming rendition of Chuck Berry's 'Johnny B Goode' and after briefly acknowledging the cheers of the audience, they made their way off stage towards the dressing room.

"Well, what do you think?" asked Tom, as the cheering and applause died down.

"They were good," replied Connie.

"I told you they were," said Tom. He already knew that she'd enjoyed their performance. She'd been dancing away to the music and her face was glowing, her eyes shining.

"I've not enjoyed myself like this for ages Tom. I'm pleased that I came with you tonight."

Tom smiled, delighted that Connie was having such a good time. With the club DJ now slipping into action, the music began again, making it more difficult for the two of them to continue their conversation. Before Tom had time to suggest that he and Connie sit down, they saw Mitch making his way towards them. His progress was anything but straightforward however, as members of the audience stopped to congratulate him on the group's performance. Connie noticed that several girls had flung their arms around him, clearly wanting a kiss, but that Mitch carefully eased himself away from them. Nevertheless, the contented look on his face, indicated that he was flattered by their attention. Confident and an extrovert, Mitch had the ideal character and temperament to deal with any adulation that came his way. Having caught their eye, Mitch beckoned Tom and Connie over. Once they'd reached him, Mitch asked them to follow him through the back door and out into the cool, October night.

"That's better," said Connie. "Some fresh air. I needed it after dancing to The Wayves."

"So, you liked us then?" asked Mitch.

"Yes."

"Good," declared Mitch, clearly satisfied with her answer.

"I'm curious Mitch," continued Connie. "The girls who went to kiss you. There were some very pretty ones. Why did you turn them away?"

"Well, Connie. I've got to be honest and say that I didn't want to. You've got to be careful though. You don't know if they're with their boyfriends or not. Even if they aren't, some places you play, the lads don't like it if all the local talent is eyeing up the group. They get jealous." Mitch looked at Tom. "You remember what happened to Alan don't you Tom? Tell Connie."

"Yes, I do. All too well. It was when the three of us were in The Striders."

"The Striders!" interrupted Connie. "What kind of a name is that!"

Mitch and Tom couldn't help laughing.

"Well, you know," said Mitch, eventually. "It's not easy to think of a name. Anyway, let Tom finish the story."

"Sorry," said Connie.

"Well, we were playing at this club in Bolton and we were going down a storm. They really liked us. We had to play two sets and after the first, Alan went to the toilet and these lads followed him in. One of their girlfriends had been chatting and had said that she fancied Alan. Her boyfriend and his mates got to hear about it. Alan hadn't done anything. He hadn't even spoken to her, but they still cornered him and told him that they were going to sort him out. Luckily, we had a guy called Dave with us back then. He used to drive the van and help us with the gear. He'd been in Strangeways for ABH and he went in just as they started laying into Alan. He beat the hell out of them, but Alan got a black eye and a bloody nose before he pulled them off. We had to cancel the second part of the show and get out of there as quick as we could."

"Yeah. We've never been back since," added Mitch.

"Oh," said Connie, who was clearly shocked. "I didn't realise that things like that happened."

"Yes. It's not all glamour and plain sailing being a musician, Connie. You learn with experience though and at any venue you know that you have to be careful when girls or women approach you."

"Obviously. I see now," replied Connie.

Mitch nodded and turned to Tom.

"Did that have anything to do with you packing it in? You've never said."

"No," said Tom. "It wasn't pleasant, but it hadn't happened before. I just didn't think I was good enough to make it. I was doing well at work and I knew that it wouldn't be long before I would be earning really good money. I thought that I needed to put more time into the job and so the playing had to stop."

"But Tom, an accountant?" Mitch could hardly hide his disappointment. "It's just not rock 'n' roll. Is it?"

Connie burst out laughing.

"Hey, less of that. I'm one too!"

"No offence Connie. It's just that Tom, whatever he might say, is good enough."

Is he now?"

"What, you didn't know? asked Mitch, noting her surprise. "He's not told you?"

"No. He's forever talking about music, but he's said nothing about being in a group himself. I just thought that you were all his friends."

"No, far more than that Connie. Tom and I played together in different groups for about five years. And we made some good money. Enough to go professional. I did, but Tom never would. Then again, he did well at school and got into a profession. I keep telling him that it's not too late. That he might regret it, but he's not listening to me Connie."

"Well, you have surprised me."

Connie had kept glancing at Tom whilst Mitch had been talking. She'd noticed how he seemed uncomfortable. It wasn't only because he was naturally self-effacing, but that he felt ill at ease with himself because he didn't want to take the risk of plunging into the unknown; to join Mitch on the uncertain road to musical success. Whereas his friend was trying to shoot for the stars, with no way of knowing whether he would be successful or not, Tom had chosen a life of conformity with safe rewards. Although it would provide him with little in the way of creative fulfilment, it would give him financial security. Connie knew that as lovely a man as he was, Tom would never be a risk taker. For Connie he was too safe, too predictable and although she had very quickly grown fond of him as a friend, she could never envisage him as a lover. Connie wanted someone who would surprise and challenge her and Tom would never be that man.

"Time for us to get back inside if we want to see The Big Three," said Tom.

Connie involuntarily shivered. She realised that she'd been standing outside, without a coat, for some time and she was now feeling cold.

"Yes. I need to warm up a bit."

"You'll like The Big Three Connie," said Mitch. "They're great lads and a top group."

"Yes. Tom's told me."

As the three of them made their way back inside, they reached the front of the main stage just as the group came on. There was loud and sustained cheering. It seemed really packed and Connie could see lots of the audience were standing on the chairs and tables further back to get a better view. With no introduction, the group launched straight into 'Some other guy.' It was loud, louder than any group she'd ever heard. Connie was struck by their power; a driving beat that had the audience dancing deliriously around her. They were good, on top of their game and Connie realised that if these lads weren't household names and had yet to break out successfully from the North-West, then The Wayves, regardless of Mitch's optimism, had a hard road ahead of them. The Big Three moved effortlessly through a performance that included some of their own compositions, as well as blues, soul and rock 'n' roll standards. They ended the show with 'What'd I say', the frenzied voices of the audience joining in a call and response, before the song was over and the performance at an end.

Although the music, courtesy of the resident DJ, continued on into the early hours of the morning, younger teenagers, needing to catch the last bus home, made their way to the cloakroom and then to the exit. Connie had enjoyed her night out. She'd been surprised by the quality of The Big Three and The Wayves too. She and Tom said farewell to Mitch and the lads, collected their coats and made their way to the bus station in Piccadilly. Tom insisted on waiting with her until her bus arrived, regardless of the fact that it would probably mean that he would miss his own. Connie, like earlier in the evening, pointed out that she was quite capable of looking after herself, but not wanting to risk upsetting Tom's evening by pressing the point, acquiesced in his wishes.

As her bus arrived, Connie sensed that Tom was slightly uncomfortable. As she said farewell to him before getting on board, he was hesitant. He seemed uncertain of what to say. Once again, Connie was slow to pick up on the signs that others, such as Paula, could see all too readily. There was a yearning look in Tom's eyes. She had enchanted him all evening and he was desperate to express his feelings for her, to ask Connie if she would be his girlfriend. He wanted to put his arms around her and gently kiss her on the cheek, but he knew that he couldn't do such a thing. She'd given him no indication that she would encourage his advances and he wasn't someone who would take that chance, fearing her rejection as much as he did.

Pulling himself together, Tom smiled at her.

"Good night, Connie. I'm glad you enjoyed it."

"Yes Tom. It was great. I'll see you on Monday morning."

Connie stepped on to the bus and took a seat near the front where Tom could still see her from the pavement. As the bus pulled away, they waved to one another but then she was gone. Tom had missed his bus, but he didn't care. He could have got a taxi but he needed time to reflect and a long walk home didn't concern him. He could think of nothing but Connie and by the time he'd reached home, had resolved that he would ask her out on a date and determined that it would be when they were alone together on Monday.

Chapter 11

It was ten to nine on a cold Monday morning in November and Connie was stood opposite Duncan and Foster's head office on York Street. The building was stylish and pristine. It had a symmetrical design; two stories of three double windows on either side, decoratively picked out with stonework features. Classically styled, the building had a central portico with an impressive looking pediment that projected forward from the sloped, tiled roof. To the rear of the building, Connie could see a large delivery bay and attached to that was a huge three-storey bakery. Connie was here to conduct an audit of the company's financial management systems and she would be working together with Tom, whose presence she was awaiting. Duncan and Foster Ltd were a successful firm of Manchester bakers, selling their produce through a chain of their own shops and cafés in the city and beyond. As they proudly proclaimed, Duncan and Foster were also 'purveyors to hotels, cafés, clubs and institutions.' Looking at their impressive offices, Connie couldn't deny that the company projected an image of confidence and stability.

The company were located just behind All Saints, York Street running parallel with Oxford Road towards the city centre. This area of Chorlton-on-Medlock was a mixture of terraced houses, factories and workshops. To cater for the local community, opposite Duncan and Fosters and close to where Connie waited, were two public houses on either corner of the junction of Berwick Street. The All Saints Tavern was a pub that sold Cornbrook ales, whilst the Wellington Inn was tied to Threlfall's Brewery. Unlike the gleaming offices opposite, both pubs' external decor left much to be desired. This was especially the case with the All Saints Tavern, where the exterior white paint was peeling off the walls. It was a reflection of the difficulties that both hostelries were beginning to experience, due to the planned redevelopment of the area. This had been hastened by the approval of Parliament to construct an elevated dual carriageway across Central Manchester and so speed up east-west traffic along the A57. Known in its design phase as link road 17/7, later called the Mancunian Way, the scheme's construction depended on the compulsory purchase and demolition, of a wide band of properties that stretched for well over a mile.

York Street was right in the middle of the development and looking down the road towards town, Connie could see evidence of the handiwork of the demolition teams who were beginning to take down the houses and factories that lined the street. Bizarrely, it hadn't affected those who worked in the shops and offices of Oxford Road and who still chose to park their cars on the street. With stray bricks and rubble littering the pavements and carriageway, their decision seemed ill considered. It certainly was a bleak and distressing landscape and the houses at the end of York Street, clearly reflected the disintegration of the area around them.

Looking past the All Saints Tavern and down Hill Street, Connie could see obvious signs of neglect. Until recently, wives and mothers had kept their doorsteps brown stoned and the pavements swept. Now the debris was building up. Residents knew that their communities were breaking up and that they had no control over the process. Many now saw little point in following convention. The older generation however, still stuck to their principles and Connie could see an old woman on bended knees, brown stoning her front step as she always did. It must be so upsetting for her, thought Connie. She had probably spent all her married life in that house and now had to watch the community that had provided her with friendship and security, slowly dying around her.

Connie glanced at her watch. It was almost nine o'clock, the time that they were expected to arrive for their appointment. Just then, she saw a taxi coming down the road towards her. It pulled up outside Duncan and Foster and Tom got out. Quickly, she crossed over to meet him.

"I was starting to get worried Tom. It isn't like you to be late. I thought that there might be a problem."

"I'm sorry Connie. 'Old Joe' kept me back at the office. He said we had to make sure that we did a good job. He's hoping for more work from Duncan and Foster. So, there's no pressure on us!"

He smiled, his eyes lighting up as Connie smiled in return.

"Well, I'm sure we won't disappoint him," said Connie.

Noticing that Tom's tie was slightly askew, Connie instinctively reached over and adjusted it. It was an unexpected move and one that gave Tom a thrill of satisfaction, as he felt Connie's soft fingers delicately touch his neck.

"Come on Tom. You're done. Smart enough to face the most demanding of taskmasters. Let's get weaving!"

Tom followed behind as she strode through the entrance of Duncan and Foster. Approaching the reception, Connie confidently announced their presence.

"Hello, I'm Connie Campbell and this is Tom Clarke. We're with Greening and Co and are expected at nine."

"Ah, yes," said the young lady at the desk. "You're down on the list. I'll just phone through and someone will be out to take care of you."

It wasn't long before the accounts manager came out to see them and they were soon upstairs working through a mountain of paperwork. Quickly, they realised that there were important adjustments that could be made to the recording and verification of returns from the company's various outlets. These changes would prove valuable and more than justify the hiring of their services. As dinner time approached, the two of them were told that if they walked around the corner to Oxford Road, they would find a Duncan and Foster café. Connie was handed a form to cover the cost of anything that they wished to order. It was a perk given to anyone who came to work for the company.

Tom now had the opportunity to act on the resolution he'd made after taking Connie to the 'Oasis.' They were out of the office, had no junior staff with them and when they went for their break, he would have the privacy he needed to talk openly about his feelings towards her.

The café looked fairly plain from the outside. Its sign was rather unexciting; standard white letters against a black background. However, through its large glass windows it looked clean and inviting. It wasn't as large as the Lyons Café, which made it seem a little more intimate. There were enough people at the tables though, to show that the food on offer was good. The buzz of conversation also gave Tom the confidence to open his heart to Connie, safe in the knowledge that other customers were too busily discussing their own affairs, to hear anything of his. Tom and Connie were seated at a table towards the back of the room and their order soon arrived. Following some general conversation, Tom felt that the time had come to tell Connie of his feelings for her.

"Connie?" he asked, quietly.

"Yes?"

"You enjoyed being at the 'Oasis,' didn't you?"

"I did Tom. I thought both of the groups were great."

Connie, assuming that Tom was going to ask if she wanted to go again, was in for a surprise.

"I did too Connie."

Tom paused briefly before continuing, digging deep to find the resolution to ask the question that could change his life.

"I loved spending the evening with you Connie and I wondered if we could be more than friends. Connie, will you go out with me?"

Connie was silent. Momentarily stunned. She hadn't expected this. It had come without any warning. Tom had been the same as usual that morning. There was nothing in his disposition to alert her to the likelihood of hearing the question that he'd put to her.

Fearing that he may face an instant refusal, Tom took Connie's silence as an encouragement to continue. His words became almost philosophical.

"Do you know how very unlikely it is to find that one person Connie? There are millions of people on this planet, but for each of us there is only one, perfect partner. The person who will fulfil every one of our physical, emotional and spiritual needs. I believe that you're that woman Connie and I'd like you to give me the chance to prove that I'm the man for you."

The words had come so naturally. There was a sincerity behind them. Connie couldn't fail to be impressed by the intensity of his emotion but as she listened, she was already feeling desperately sorry for him, knowing that she couldn't possibly agree to his request. Tom looked expectantly at her. Connie's mind raced, considering a host of potential replies that she hoped wouldn't upset him. It was a virtually impossible task. Nevertheless, she gave Tom her reply.

"Tom, how can you say that I'm that special person? We've not known one another long enough. It's too soon. In time you'll see my faults and I can assure you that I've got lots of them!"

She smiled, hoping that her words would ease the tension. Looking at Tom however, it was clear that his ardour had lost none of its intensity.

"No, Connie. Time isn't important. Romantics talk about love at first sight, but I'd agree that you can't love someone just on the basis of physical attraction. Yet I do believe that within a short space of time, after talking to, working with and being with someone, you just instinctively know that they're the one."

He looked intently into her beautiful, green eyes, willing her to say yes. Connie could feel the weight of his expectations. She felt her heart sink, her chest was heavy and she breathed deeply. It felt unpleasant. She wished that she had taken far more notice of Paula. If she had, she could have prepared for this eventuality, or have given subtle, but clear indications to Tom, that she had no desire for romance with him. Her real problem was that she liked Tom and he was a friend that she wished to keep. To do that, Connie realised that she had to treat him with kindness and sympathy.

"Tom, you've been so good to me since I started at Greenings. I do like you and I really want us to be friends, but I can't commit to anything else. We work so well together and I don't want to jeopardise that."

Connie's words were measured and thoughtful, but she'd still left room for Tom to probe further.

"So, perhaps in the future, when you've had more time to get to know me, you may feel differently?"

"That's not fair Tom. You shouldn't try to put expectations on me."

Connie's firm response, though necessary from her perspective, resulted in a severe blow to Tom's confidence. His head dropped and unconsciously he picked up a spoon and began to stir his tea. Placing it back on the table he was quiet and Connie had no doubt that deep inside, he was hurting. Against her better judgement she moved her hand across the table and lay it gently on his. She wanted to reassure him that everything was fine; he'd asked her a question and she'd declined. It was no reason for their current relationship to change. Yet in doing so, her show of sympathy had given Tom hope. This time she had said no but perhaps, he thought, sometime in the future, she would change her mind. She still wanted to be close friends with him and they could still spend time working for the Party. They wouldn't be a couple, but they would be together. Looking up at her, Tom smiled.

"I understand Connie. I'm sorry you felt that I put pressure on you. I didn't mean to."

"It's okay Tom. Let's forget about it."

"Yes Connie. We'd best be getting back. They're not paying us to sit around chatting!"

Connie smiled.

"Too true Tom. You sound just like 'Old Joe.'"

The pair of them laughed and as they left the café and walked back down Oxford Road, it seemed to Connie that everything would continue as normal. Her relationship with Tom was back on its previous footing. In that she was right, except for one thing. Tom still loved her and just how deeply, Connie could never have imagined. He idolised her; was in love with everything about her. And regardless of their conversation, he would always remain convinced that Connie was the one for him. No other woman would ever capture his heart in the way that she had.

Chapter 12

Connie had been eager to take up the offer from Harry Thomas of accompanying him on a ward round in Ardwick. Tom arranged for her to meet him outside the ABC on Stockport Road, at seven on the second Thursday in November.

"Harry's rounds always take place on the second and fourth Thursdays of every month," said Tom. "It's when he goes to see people who find it difficult to get into the office. It'll give you a good idea of the variety of problems that we try to help with."

"Will you be coming too Tom?"

"I'll be meeting Harry with you, but we've got so many people needing advice, that we'll be splitting up for the night. Harry's far better at explaining the ins and outs of our work than I am. He lives and breathes it."

"Yes, I got that impression from talking to him," said Connie.

On the appointed day, the two of them had left work early and Connie had taken Tom home with her. On the way, they decided that they would have 'chippy' for their tea and so they headed to 'Chiappe's,' where Connie bought a meat and potato pie, chips and peas for herself and cod, chips and peas for Tom. Eager to keep their wrapped meals hot, they walked quickly down Syndall Street and then nipped down the alley at the back of Howard Avenue, into Connie's backyard and then through the back door and into the kitchen.

"I'd leave your coat on for a while Tom. It's too cold. I'll light the gas fire. Take a seat at the table."

Tom watched as Connie put the package of food down on a tray beside the sink and then went to the cupboard to take out a box of matches with which to light the gas fire.

"Careful," said Tom, as he watched her bending down near the fire.

"Don't worry," said Connie. "I can keep the gas fairly low whilst I light it."

Nevertheless, there was a characteristic *'whooosh'* as the gas ignited, but Connie was well clear of any potential danger.

"The damn ignition buttons never work, do they?" asked Tom.

"No, I'm afraid not. I always have to use a match. But as long as you're careful, you shouldn't have a problem."

"Well, I've been singed a few times," replied Tom.

Connie looked at him and laughed.

"Why doesn't that surprise me?" she asked.

Tom blushed, his usual reaction when Connie teased him. He looked down in order to cover his embarrassment, causing Connie to laugh even more.

Taking a pretty green and white patterned tablecloth, Connie laid it over the table. She then distributed a number of mats upon which she placed their two plates and the salt and vinegar. Adding knives and forks, the two of them were ready to eat.

"Did you want any bread-and-butter Tom?" asked Connie. "I can soon make some."

"Oh, that'd be great Connie. Thanks."

Connie had already placed the butter dish on the hearth below the gas fire, softening it so that she could easily spread it on to a couple of slices of bread for Tom.

"It's best butter Tom. What my mam always said we should use. Actually, 'Lurpak.' But it amounts to the same thing."

Connie smiled, recalling one of the pleasant memories of her youth.

"Yes, my Gran always insisted on 'Adam's best butter,'" said Tom.

Connie fetched the wrapped meals and placed them on the plates.

"I'd leave them in the paper Tom. The plates aren't very warm."

Tom nodded and the two of them were soon tucking contentedly into their food. They were hungry and they both believed that 'chippy' was one of the best meals that anyone could have. Whilst eating, Tom looked around the kitchen, which also served as Connie's living room. It was brightly decorated and inviting. A comfortable settee to the side and a television and radio for entertainment. The window was covered by a white net curtain, along with some expensive, lined beige curtains to the sides. The whole room was gleaming, not a speck of dust in sight. Besides being a successful accountant, Connie very much fitted the mould of an intensely house-proud, working-class woman. He was impressed. Knowing how much work she brought home with her, it must have required a supreme effort to keep her house so spick and span. What other woman in her position would have done it? The middle classes employed their domestics; cleaners who would do the household chores for them. Give them a beautiful home which they could take the credit for, without having to do any of the associated hard work. Connie could have taken that route quite easily herself, but she hadn't. Tom couldn't think of anything other than how wonderful she was.

"Your home's lovely," said Tom.

"You've only seen the kitchen," replied Connie. "When we've finished eating, I'll show you the front room."

Tom nodded appreciatively and after they'd finished, washed and wiped the pots and Connie had cleared the table, she took him to see her inner sanctum, proudly describing her prized pieces of furniture to him.

"It's so modern," remarked Tom.

"Yes, everyone says that," replied Connie. "I suppose it seems such a contrast to the old exterior of the house and the Avenue. But it's my only extravagance and it's a good, solid investment. Furniture that will last and a couple of pieces that may be worth something in the future."

"Ah, the voice of an accountant," said Tom.

"Well, I don't suppose we can ever lose that, can we?" asked Connie.

"No, I suppose we can't."

Connie ushered Tom out of the front room and switched off the light. It was time for them to be getting off to the ABC to meet up with Harry.

Chapter 13

Outside the ABC at seven, Tom and Connie didn't have long to wait for Harry's arrival.

"Here he comes," said Tom.

"Where?" replied Connie, scanning the pavement to both sides of her.

"Here."

Tom pointed as a car slowed to a halt just past where they were standing. The lights of the cinema illuminated a green, two-door Austin A40. It looked in good condition, but it was by no means new. It had gleaming, chrome hubcaps, mirrors and headlamp mounts and a fancy strip down its side. Nevertheless, it was a People's car. It was cheap and cheerful, reliable and effective in getting its occupants safely from A to B. There were lots of them on the road and for a socialist like Harry, its functionality was all that mattered. Ostentatious vehicles were not in his remit.

Tom and Connie walked over to the car. The passenger door opened out towards them and bending down, Connie could see Harry leaning back into his seat as he released his hand on the internal door handle.

"Hello Connie. Nice to see you."

"Hi," replied Connie.

"We've got quite a few people to visit this evening," continued Harry. "We should be able to see them a bit quicker with the car."

Bending down towards the car door, Tom joined the conversation.

"Connie's eager to get started Harry. Have you got the details about the people I'm seeing?"

"Yes, Tom."

Harry picked up a folder resting on the front passenger seat and handed it to Tom.

"I've given you the appointments behind Ardwick Green Tom. There aren't too many and we can catch up on what needs doing tomorrow night. Is that okay?"

"Yes, fine Harry. I'll give you a ring tomorrow morning at school."

Tom said his farewells and started walking towards Hyde Road, so as to cross over to Ardwick Green.

"Get in then Connie," said Harry. "Mind the paperwork."

Connie picked up another folder that remained on the seat and eased herself into position. Closing the door, she indicated to Harry that she was ready. Carefully, he pulled away from the kerb and they were on their way to their first appointment.

"I'm pleased that you've come Connie, you're going to experience lots of the familiar problems that confront people in Ardwick. I suppose though, given that Tom told me that you still live here..."

"Yes, in Howard Avenue," said Connie, interrupting.

"... that they won't come as much of a surprise."

"Well, perhaps not," replied Connie. "I'm most interested though, in finding out what you're able to do to help people."

"Not enough I'm afraid," replied Harry. "People here are forgotten, even by many in our own party. There's a sense that things are improving. That technology is on the march and so soon, everything will be fine in a new, modern Britain. I wish it was that simple. I liked it at the meeting when you questioned that. It was good that you were thinking the issues through. I respected that."

Connie couldn't help but experience a sense of satisfaction at hearing his complimentary words. Harry had very quickly made an impression upon her. It was a meeting of minds. He was studious, clever and considerate. In fact, he was the first man who had truly treated her as a colleague, unaffected by her femininity. Connie wasn't naïve. She knew that men found her attractive and regardless of whether they intended it or not, their feelings, or more correctly, their desires, inevitably affected the way they reacted to her. That wasn't the case with Harry and the time she spent with him provided a refreshing change.

The familiar problems that Harry had referred to, were anything but ordinary. Houses with leaking roofs, water pipes or toilets. Rising damp and unhealthy living conditions that, regardless of the efforts of the tenants, could only be remedied by the resources available to their landlords. There were illegal attempts to raise the rent and subsequent threats of eviction if the tenant complained. Others who contacted Harry wanted help with problems at work or with their child's school. Whatever the issue, Connie was impressed by Harry's expansive knowledge of the law and the rights that people were entitled to. Most importantly, he was never flustered, always calm and caring and invariably left people in a far happier frame of mind than when he'd arrived.

Back in the car, Harry told Connie of someone that he wanted her to see.

"It's an old lady called Kath. She's in her seventies and as sharp as they come. She's had an amazing life. She's an inspiration to us all. She only lives off Apsley Grove, not far from you."

It wasn't long before the car pulled up on Apsley Grove and Connie and Harry got out. Connie immediately recognised where they were. She walked past here almost every day, to and from the bus stop on Stockport Road. Harry parked the car outside 'Mastersons,' a large wholesale food distribution company. It was located on the corner of Pleasant View, a small, closed off street which on its opposite side had a row of eight terraced houses; two-up two-down and straight on to the pavement. Crossing over, Harry led her past the end house to the entrance to the ginnel that gave access to the backyards of the properties. Opening the gate, he held it for Connie to follow him through, then he approached the back step, weakly illuminated by the light penetrating through the curtains at the kitchen window and knocked.

"It's okay," he shouted. "It's only me, Harry."

After a short pause, Connie saw the back door slowly open and there, in the glare of the electric light, stood Kath.

"Come in. I thought that you might be dropping in," said Kath, smiling.

"I've brought a young lady with me. She's thinking of helping the Party."

"That's good," said Kath.

Connie moved slowly up the steps, following behind Harry.

"Hello, I'm Connie."

"Make yourself comfortable love."

Instinctively, Kath moved towards the sink and was soon filling the kettle and placing it on the gas cooker.

"I'll make us a brew. I'm sure you could both do with one."

Lighting the gas, Kath turned to Connie, who was still stood near the door.

"Sit down love."

Connie sat at the table under the window. It was where every table in every kitchen in Ardwick seemed to be located. It was a familiar scene and together with the warm welcome extended by Kath, Connie quickly felt at ease. Harry joined her at the table, taking the opportunity to relax after working through the night's problems. Kath looked at him and then turned to Connie.

"He works too hard love. Never stops. That's his trouble."

Harry seemed lost in thought, oblivious to what Kath was saying.

"He doesn't even know that we're talking about him, does he?" asked Kath.

Connie smiled.

"No, he doesn't Kath."

"I'll bet you've had nothing to eat tonight, have you Harry?" asked Kath.

"Hey? What?" said Harry.

"You, having nothing to eat. You haven't, have you?" asked Kath, once more.

"Well, no. But I'm not hungry."

Kath turned back to Connie.

"He stays at that school, then rushes out doing his ward rounds without any thought for himself. They won't thank him for it you know. He'll never learn."

Kath walked over to the recessed cupboard next to the chimney breast wall. She took out some bread and the butter dish and placed them on the table. She then went over to open the door to the cellar steps behind which, on the small landing in the relative cold, she stored her milk, meat and cheese. Picking up a couple of items, she returned, placing them on top of some large plates that she'd collected from the draining board by the sink. Cutting the bread into thick slices, she buttered it and then spread potted meat, with its layer of dripping on top, together with piccalilli, over the bread. Putting the sandwiches in the centre of the table, she gave a small plate each to Harry and Connie and told them to help themselves.

"I've got biscuits, digestives and custard creams, if you prefer Connie."

"Yes please," said Connie. "Unlike Harry, I did manage to have my tea before I came out."

Meanwhile, Harry was enjoying his sandwiches. Kath looked at him and tutted, her eyes raised playfully.

"I thought you weren't hungry," said Kath.

Enjoying his sandwich, Harry was oblivious to her words and chewed on regardless. Kath looked at Connie and the two of them burst out laughing. Harry looked at them blankly, unaware that his actions were responsible for their merriment.

"He's in a little world all of his own," said Kath.

"Yes, it does seem so," replied Connie.

Having made them all a cup of tea, Kath sat down with Harry and Connie at the kitchen table. Looking at her, Connie saw a neat and tidy old lady with grey hair which had been carefully placed in a bun on top of her head. Her blue eyes were expressive and unlike many women her age, her skin was relatively free of wrinkles. She was wearing, given the season, a thick cardigan, under which she wore a neat, pressed blouse and a long, black woollen skirt. Connie felt comfortable with her. Regardless of the age difference between them, the two women had hit it off immediately, laughing and joking together at the expense of Harry. Connie could see why Harry liked to visit, but he'd indicated to her that there was a little more to Kath's character than just her friendly and pleasant disposition and Connie looked forward to finding out what it was.

It went without saying, that Kath was extremely house proud. The kitchen was spotless, not a thing out of place. Catching Connie's eye in particular, was a beautiful green vase on the mantelpiece over the fireplace.

"That's a nice vase Kath."

"Yes," replied Kath, looking towards it.

Getting up, she walked over to the mantelpiece, picked up the vase and returned to her seat, placing the ornament on the table in front of Connie.

"My husband, Stan, got it for me just after we were married. I remember telling him off for getting it. We'd been in Lewis's and I'd seen it and had remarked on how nice it was. A couple of weeks later he gave it to me. I don't how much it was. He told me that he'd won some money on the horses. I'm not sure that he did, but he couldn't take it back."

Connie looked admiringly at the vase.

"It's all right, you can pick it up love," said Kath.

Carefully, Connie examined it. It was a drip vase with lines of red, white, green and brown running and blending under the glaze. Underneath, she could see that it was an English vase made by 'Bretby' with the code '02B' imprinted upon it.

"It's beautiful. What a lovely present."

"Yes. It means a lot to me. Every time I look at it, I think of Stan and I smile when I remember how I told him off for buying it when we had so little money. Secretly though, I was pleased that he did. But I wasn't going to tell him that. Men need keeping in their place."

Connie laughed.

"They do love," insisted Kath.

She spoke with an air of certainty, of wisdom and experience. It hadn't escaped Connie's notice that Harry, who normally appeared so confident and assured, was relegated in Kath's presence, to the role of a wayward child needing direction and guidance. Without thinking or objecting, he had dutifully eaten his sandwiches, drunk his tea and listened to a 'telling off' by Kath, as if it was the most natural thing to do.

Connie handed the vase back to Kath, who replaced it carefully on the mantelpiece. Harry, having finished eating, looked at the clock on the wall opposite. It was quarter to ten.

"It's getting on Kath. We'd best be going," said Harry.

"Oh! Is that the time?" replied Kath, looking at the clock herself and sounding surprised. "It goes so quickly, doesn't it?"

She turned to Connie.

"It's been nice meeting you love."

"Yes," replied Connie. "Thanks for the tea and biscuits."

"I should have brought Connie around earlier," said Harry. "I wanted her to learn about the struggles that you've been through. Let her know that young women can play a big role in the Party."

"I think lots of women have done far more than me."

"I don't think so. You're too modest."

"And you don't need to flatter me to get my vote young man."

Connie laughed. She noted how there was a sharply focused humour in many of Kath's responses. Undeterred, Harry continued.

"Connie only lives on Howard Avenue. Just off Syndall Street."

"Yes, I know it. Well love," she said, turning to Connie. "You're welcome any time. Just drop in."

"I'd like that," said Connie.

"Well, that's settled then," said Kath. "Don't be a stranger."

Saying their farewells, Harry and Connie returned to the car.

"Do you want me to drop you off Connie?"

"No, I'm just around the corner Harry. You get off home."

"Okay."

Harry opened the car door and got in. He wound down his window so he could speak to her.

"I've enjoyed tonight, Harry. I definitely want to get involved in helping with the problems I've seen. I can arrange that with Tom, can't I?"

"Yes."

"Kath's lovely Harry. I'm pleased you took me to see her."

"Yes. She's fascinating. As you'll find out when you get to know her better."

"Well, thanks again Harry. I'll see you again soon."

"Yes. Goodbye Connie."

Harry wound up the window and Connie moved around the car and on to the kerb. As he pulled away, she waved to him. He was so different to Tom. Not once had he given her any hint that he found her attractive, or that there was even a glimmer of any romantic intentions towards her. Their relationship was friendly, but business like. He treated her as a colleague. Connie though, felt fine. She respected Harry and shared his concerns for social justice. What's more, he had introduced her to Kath and true to the conventions of hospitality in Ardwick, Kath had made it clear that there was an open invitation to visit her at any time she wished. By expressing her intention to do so, Connie was now effectively obligated to return. It was however, a commitment that she welcomed. Connie resolved that she would return to see Kath on the following Thursday night, looking forward to what she would learn about her life.

Chapter 14

The following day, Connie received a surprise. Joe Greening had been impressed with her progress during her first weeks with the company. Consequently, he called Connie into his office and told her that she'd be working with Ralph on the acquisition of a new client's account. The client was Joyce and Hitchcock Engineering Ltd, who were based on Crossley Road on the border between Burnage and Stockport. Its managing director was Mike Joyce, a local businessman that Joe had known for several years. The company were expanding and wanted advice on their financial restructuring and business development.

"Moving forward, this could be a very valuable account for us Connie. Mike Joyce is well connected. If he's pleased with our ideas, we get the contract and are successful, he'll spread the word about us."

"I see," said Connie.

She was wondering why he had chosen her, rather than Tom, to support Ralph, but wasn't about to ask him in case it made her appear uncertain of her own abilities. Joe had however, already anticipated her desire for an explanation.

"I've chosen you for this Connie due to the excellent reports I've received from Duncan and Foster. They were delighted with your recommendations and impressed by your ability to present them with clarity. That's the approach I need here Connie. Mike Joyce is no 'mug' and between you and me, he'll soon see through any 'bull' that Ralph might give him. He'll need solid suggestions as to exactly how we can help them. I'm afraid that if I send Tom, he may hold back and let Ralph do all the talking. I know you won't do that and you'll keep my nephew in check. And before you ask, I've already told Ralph that you'll be presenting all the technical details and that he's there as a family representative of the firm."

"I understand Mr Greening," replied Connie.

"You and Ralph are going to need to get together. You'll both meet Mike next Tuesday afternoon at Joyce and Hitchcock's offices. It only gives you a couple of days to study the details of the company and their plans and to put together a presentation."

"Thank you, Mr Greening. I'll go over to Ralph's office right away."

Excited, Connie was quickly on her way to see Ralph. As was company policy, the door to his office was open and she could see him talking to a young, pretty typist called Veronica, who had some files in her arms. Seeing Connie approaching, Ralph called out to her.

"Come in Connie. We're all ready to get started. Veronica has brought us all the necessary information on Joyce and Hitchcock. Haven't you Veronica?"

He smiled at the young woman and took the files off her.

Veronica nodded and Connie noticed that she was blushing, affected by her close proximity to Ralph and his genial disposition. She was very pretty. Seventeen, she had long blonde hair, blue eyes and her young age gave her an aura of vulnerability that made her more appealing to older men. She was dressed in a pale blue blouse, unbuttoned at the neck and a grey, pleated skirt which had been taken up to just above the knee, unusually short for more conservative office attire. A pair of brown stilettos accentuated her long and shapely legs. Had she been older, it would have been considered that she dressed in order to attract attention. However, Connie saw her attire as a natural inclination to be fashionable. Connie recognised a refreshing naivety about Veronica, that failed to appreciate the predatory instincts of many of the men around her. Nevertheless, it seemed clear to Connie that the young lady had fallen for the charms of her handsome boss, although Connie had seen no evidence to suggest that Ralph was encouraging her. He was just being his pleasant and approachable self.

After Veronica had left, Connie and Ralph quickly got down to their assignment. Not having worked with Ralph before, Connie was impressed. He was more focused than she'd expected and the pair of them had soon mapped out the key aspects of their submission. Ralph also made it clear that he understood that Connie would lead the presentation and that he would support her when necessary. It was reassuring to her that she detected no resentment from Ralph about his uncle's arrangement. As they reached the end of the day, Connie suggested that she would work further on the task over the weekend and the pair of them could refine the final details on Monday morning.

"That's a splendid idea," said Ralph. "You must have known that I was planning a weekend away."

"Oh. Are you going anywhere nice?"

"I'm just meeting up with a few of the chaps from university."

"A weekend for the boys," said Connie, smiling. "Behave yourself Ralph. I don't want to be going on my own on Tuesday!"

"Of course, I will Connie. I'm a model of impeccable behaviour."

The two of them laughed.

She couldn't help it. Connie liked Ralph. He was utterly charming and he seemed genuine. He was naturally friendly and hadn't once made an inappropriate comment or looked at her in a suggestive way. And why would he? With his natural good looks, Ralph had no need to chase after women.

By Tuesday, Connie had put the finishing touches to the presentation. As dinner time approached, she was feeling nervous. She had taken special care over her appearance that morning and she was wearing a conservative, black two-piece suit, with a white blouse and black heels. She wanted to reinforce the impression of herself as a serious and competent businesswoman. When she walked into Ralph's office however, he saw her appearance as far more striking. A beautiful young woman, elegant and sophisticated. Ralph had no doubts that Connie would hold the rapt attention of the staff at Joyce and Hitchcock.

Ralph noticed that she seemed a little ill at ease, constantly looking at the clock on the wall behind his desk.

"Don't worry Connie. You'll be fine. Just relax. We've come up with some great ideas. You'll impress them with no problems at all."

He smiled at her and Connie felt a modicum of relief.

"Yes, thanks Ralph. I suppose it's the first really important task that your uncle has given me, so I'm bound to be a little nervous."

"No, Connie. The work for Duncan and Foster was equally important and you made a great impression there."

Connie appreciated Ralph's support. Again, there wasn't a hint of jealousy about Connie being in charge. He wanted her to succeed. His concern was for Connie and the firm, not for himself.

"Well, come on Connie. It's time we got moving. I'm taking us in the car. You'll get to experience my driving."

"Oh no!" said Connie, pretending to be shocked. "Now, I'm really nervous!"

Ralph laughed and Connie quickly joined in.

Leaving the office, the two of them collected their coats and made their way out into Piccadilly and the weak sunshine of a November day. Walking down to Portland Street, Ralph led Connie to a large car park, a blighted open space created by the destruction wrought by the Luftwaffe in the Manchester Blitz. It was an area that had yet to attract the attention of the developers. Ralph made his way through the rows of stationary vehicles and then stopped by the side of a red sports car.

"Here we are Connie," he said, appreciatively. "My pride and joy."

Connie stood looking down at the sleek vehicle before her.

"It's a 1962 Daimler SP 250 Dart Convertible," explained Ralph, precisely. "It's got a 2.5 Litre V8 engine producing 140 horse power. She'll do well over a hundred without any difficulty."

Connie looked at him uneasily. She wasn't sure that she fancied getting in. Noticing her apprehension, Ralph was quick to reassure her.

"Of course, I haven't driven her at that speed and we won't be going much above thirty today. It's busy traffic all the way."

Connie relaxed. It certainly was a beautiful looking car. Close to the ground, it had a distinctive chrome grille above which was a smooth, aerodynamic fibreglass body, two circular headlamps projecting from round housings fused into the front wings. Stylish too were the distinctive wire wheels and the rear fins, which contained the brake lights and the indicators. The car was finished off with two chrome bumpers with their distinctive 'whiskers.' Given the cold weather, Ralph made no attempt to bring down the convertible roof. He had bought the vehicle with the intention of driving it open-topped in the sunshine on a hot summer's day. It was a car for a bachelor and a motor enthusiast. One that was meant to be impressive to beautiful women with its dazzling looks and power.

As befitted the purpose of the sports car, the interior was small and functional. Just two seats separated by a central column housing the gear stick. Once Connie got into the car, she found that she had plenty of legroom and the leather seat soon felt comfortable when she had settled into it. Ralph was aware that Connie was warming to the Dart. He turned the key in the ignition and the car immediately came to life. Pressing his foot on the accelerator, he elicited a growl from the V8 engine and turned to smile at Connie. Releasing the clutch, the car moved slowly forward, Ralph carefully navigating his way out of the car park.

"They were built for the American market Connie. The Yanks love them and so do I."

For Ralph and many of his female passengers, the car's stateside connection made it seem more glamorous. Connie however, showed no signs of being impressed. She did like the Dart but her thoughts were directed towards the car she'd been in with Harry, the ubiquitous Austin A40. The two vehicles were a reflection of the contrasting characters of their owners. Harry was content with functionality and simply getting to his destination, whilst Ralph believed that a journey should be carried out in style and his car had to be a thing of beauty. To Ralph, simply getting there wasn't enough and what Harry regarded as unnecessary and ostentatious, Ralph saw as a necessity. Had Harry been asked to give his opinion on the Dart, Connie felt sure that he would dismiss its purchase as extravagant.

Yet Connie couldn't be critical of Ralph. After all, she also loved beautiful things. She had purchased elegant furniture for her front room. And she was finding Ralph increasingly appealing. There was so much that should have made this impossible. He was unashamedly a member of the upper-middle classes. He was clearly no socialist. And he'd been born with all the advantages. His position in the company had been handed to him by his uncle. He hadn't needed to work for it like Tom and Connie and normally, she would have steered well clear of a man with a reputation as a womaniser. But she'd been open-minded and had seen no evidence of the latter. She had to admit that he was exceptionally handsome, but that in itself wouldn't count for too much. What she did find in Ralph, was a pleasant colleague who seemed helpful, caring and to a degree, sensitive. Undeniably, he was fun too. With wit and charm, it was very hard not to like him and she couldn't think of one instance where he had acted towards her with even a hint of impropriety.

Proceeding down London Road, then on to Downing Street and past Ardwick Green, they negotiated the roundabout at the start of Hyde Road, went past the ABC and on to Stockport Road. As he promised, Ralph was driving carefully but Connie, once again getting nervous about the meeting, wasn't feeling too relaxed.

"You live around here, don't you Connie?"

"Yes, at the back there. Off Syndall Street, just here."

Connie pointed to the left as they moved past the junction with the latter.

"Oh," said Ralph, with more than a hint of disappointment.

"It doesn't meet with your approval then, Ardwick?"

"Well. No disrespect intended Connie. But, Ardwick!"

"What's wrong with Ardwick?"

"What's right with it?"

Ralph smiled and continued.

"Surely you can afford to live somewhere better? Come on Connie."

"I've always lived here. I like it."

"Oh no. We've got ourselves a social crusader here, haven't we?"

Ralph smiled. There was a glint in his eye. Amused, he waited eagerly for her to respond. Connie wanted to shout at him, but she couldn't. She simply shook her head.

"It's all right for you to live in a decent area Connie. You're not letting your comrades down if you do. I don't know, you and Tom. Accept it. You've done well. It's time for you to move on."

"It won't work," said Connie.

"What won't work?"

"I'm not falling for the bait."

"I'm making an observation Connie."

As they proceeded down through Longsight and into Levenshulme, their conversation on the merits of living in Ardwick continued. Connie, whether she liked it or not, felt obligated to defend her community.

Before she had realised, they had reached the turning for Crossley Road and were soon parking next to Joyce and Hitchcock's offices.

"Here we are Connie. All ready to go. It did work, didn't it?"

"What did?" asked Connie, confused.

"All those points defending Ardwick. You've driven away the stress now, haven't you?"

"Yes, but I still know that you disagree with me for staying there."

"I do. But it's your choice, misguided as it may be. The important thing is that we need you confident and at your best for the meeting and now you're fine."

Connie shook her head, but the smile on her face made it clear to Ralph that any disapproval of him, wasn't genuine. The fact was that she'd understood what he'd done and now, she was more than ready to deliver her presentation.

"You'll find that Mike's a decent chap. He'll give you a fair hearing Connie."

Once inside, Connie and Ralph were shown to a small conference room where Mike Joyce, his company accountant and works manager were sat waiting at a large table. In his late forties, Mike was a 'hands-on' boss, which could be seen from his appearance. He wore no jacket or tie, just an open-necked shirt under a plain pullover. He had just been on the factory floor helping a couple of his apprentices who were training on a refrigeration unit. He was still sweating and Connie found herself looking at a balding, red-faced man with a thick grey moustache and a prominent nose. Mike had started the company, together with Pete Hitchcock, twenty years ago. He'd subsequently bought out his partner and had moved the business towards the servicing and development of machinery for food processing and packaging, as well as refrigeration. Correctly, he'd judged it to be an area of market growth and subsequently, his company had been acquiring an increasing number of prestigious local customers. As the operation expanded, Mike was well aware that there needed to be a restructuring of management, the introduction of new financial systems and an evaluation of options for the injection of capital, which would arise if the company continued to grow. It was Greenings remit to provide potential solutions for these issues.

As Connie approached the table, Mike stood up and walked towards her. Extending his hand, Connie took it. Mike felt her firm grip and noticed how she looked him directly in the eye. His first impression of her was positive. She was a confident young lady who was likely to justify the faith Joe Greening was placing in her.

"Hello Mr Joyce. I'm Connie Campbell and I believe that you've met Ralph."

"Yes, I have. Please, call me Mike. There's no need to be so formal."

Ralph, sat at the table and distributed copies of the presentation to Mike and his team. Connie remained standing, going through the details of their proposals. Connie's presentation was clear and precise. They had put together a number of models to clarify their ideas and Connie gave Ralph the opportunity to provide further explanations when necessary. In fact, the two of them proved to be a very effective team and when the presentation was over, Mike seemed genuine in his appreciation of their efforts. Escorting them out of the building, his parting remarks offered them real hope of success.

"You've given us lots of good ideas to think about. We'll study them further and I'm sure that I'll be back in touch."

Driving back to the office, Connie enjoyed a feeling of satisfaction.

"You did really well Connie," said Ralph. "I have a feeling that we're going to be working closely with Joyce and Hitchcock. What do you think?"

"Well, let's not count our chickens yet Ralph. We mustn't be too optimistic when we see your uncle."

"Oh, nonsense Connie. You had Mike in the palm of your hand."

"I don't think so!"

Connie knew that she had far more riding on the outcome of the meeting than Ralph. Success would further strengthen her position at Greenings. This was something that Ralph, secure as the boss's nephew, had never had to contemplate. Not that she envied Ralph. It was just the way things were. Nevertheless, she did feel that when making the presentation, she had done her best. Ultimately, that was all she could do and although she didn't say so to Ralph, she too felt optimistic that the two of them would secure a deal.

Chapter 15

On Thursday morning, Connie received a summons to Joe Greening's office. Approaching Paula's desk, she was greeted warmly by her friend.

"Well Connie, how does it feel to be the boss's favourite girl?"

Connie looked surprised. She'd no idea why 'Old Joe' had wanted to see her, as it seemed too soon for Mike Joyce to have come to a decision.

"About ten minutes ago," said Paula, "I took a phone call and put it through to the 'old man'. After a few minutes he was out here, with a huge smile on his face, asking me to send for you. He had Ralph in his office and as he went back in, I heard him mention how pleased he was that we now have Joyce and Hitchcock as clients. Congratulations Connie. You did it!"

Paula threw her arms around Connie and gave her a hug, delighted with her friend's success.

"It's best that you don't let on that you already know Connie. Make sure that you look surprised when they tell you. I don't want to get into trouble."

"Thanks Paula. It's a relief. I wasn't sure why he wanted to see me."

"That's why I had to tell you."

Connie waited, taking time to ensure that she would appear calm and collected. She felt relieved. She had known how important the acquisition of Joyce and Hitchcock's account was to Greenings. She had begun to worry that failure could well halt the progress of a career that she had worked so very hard to establish. Ready, Connie asked Paula to call through to say that she'd arrived. Almost immediately, the office door opened and Ralph appeared in the doorway.

"Come in Connie. My uncle's waiting for you."

Connie nodded and walked through the door, held open for her by Ralph. He was smiling and winked at her as she moved past him, in his own way reassuring her that everything was all right. 'Old Joe' was sat behind his desk and he had a broad smile on his face.

"There you are young lady. Take a seat."

He indicated to the chairs in front of him. Ralph moved to the side of the desk, standing against one of the bookshelves. Connie sat down, giving no indication that she knew why she was there.

"I've had a call this morning from Mike Joyce," said Joe. "He's considered the proposals that you and Ralph made to him and he's eager to start working with us. He's asked specifically for you to lead our team.

You've really impressed him young lady. I'm delighted at what you've done for us. Thank you."

Connie was touched by his compliment. Yet, generous as ever, she didn't feel justified in taking so much of the credit for herself.

"Ralph was just as instrumental in putting together our proposals," replied Connie. "He's supported me throughout. He's just as responsible for securing Joyce and Hitchcock's business as I am."

"No," said Ralph. "You did far more in putting together the presentation. You're the one who reassured Mike and his team and persuaded them to work with us. You shouldn't be so modest Connie."

"Yes, Ralph's right," confirmed Joe. "I've had nothing but good reports about you. Mike Joyce, Duncan and Foster; you've won them over. And I hope you don't mind me saying this Connie, but you've overcome any nonsense about you being a woman. I knew that Mike Joyce would give you a fair hearing, but others are harder to convince. You'll be leading our team at Joyce and Hitchcock and I've every confidence that this contract will help us to get others."

Connie felt embarrassed. She wasn't used to such unstinting praise. She found it difficult to give any kind of response and continued to sit quietly in her chair. Sensing her discomfort, Ralph came to the rescue.

"I think that we've rather overwhelmed you with our excitement at the news. Perhaps you'd like to go back to your office and have the chance to take it all in Connie."

"Yes. I think so," replied Connie.

Getting slowly out of her chair, Connie turned back to her boss.

"Thank you, Mr Greening. You've been very kind. I'm looking forward to getting on with the work at Joyce and Hitchcock."

"You'll be spending quite a bit of time there now Connie," replied Joe. "I'm sending Tom with you. We need a couple of senior accountants there, not just you and some of our juniors. We must assure Mike that his account is our number one priority. I'd send Ralph, but I want him to keep an eye on things here."

Following Connie's departure, Ralph took a seat in front of his uncle's desk. Lounging back in the chair, he questioned Joe over his decision to send Tom.

"Wouldn't it have been better for me to have gone with Connie? After all, Tom hasn't worked as much on the account as I have."

Joe looked at his nephew closely. He paused, carefully considering the words of advice he was about to utter. Satisfied, he addressed Ralph in a quiet, calm voice.

"You like Connie, don't you?"

The question took Ralph by surprise. It seemed to have little to do with providing an explanation for his uncle's decision.

"Yes, of course. Why?"

"She's very pretty Ralph. A charming personality. I've no doubt that they're the first things our clients notice. Then they realise that she's such a clever young lady and really knows what she's talking about. She's a real asset for this firm and that's the way I want it to stay."

Joe stared intently at his nephew. Ralph appeared perplexed, unsure of the point, if any, that his uncle was making.

"And?" asked Ralph, inviting Joe to elaborate further.

"I think you know Ralph."

It was as if he was hesitant to reveal the true meaning behind his words, wanting Ralph to acknowledge it without the necessity of spelling it out. Unfortunately, Ralph was showing no inclination towards indicating that he'd understood. Consequently, Joe had no alternative but to lay his cards clearly on the table.

"I sent you with Connie to see Mike, because besides me, you're the face of Greenings. As my nephew, you represent the company at the highest level. Your presence offers reassurance to our clients. It tells them of our keen, personal attention to their needs. That's not necessary at Joyce and Hitchcock now. Mike's happy for Connie to lead the team. The fact is Ralph, that at the moment I don't want you working with Connie too often. I know you all too well. You won't be able to see her as just another colleague. It's your weakness for pretty women. You can't help yourself and Connie is far too important to us. I don't want her leaving, like other good women we've had. Excellent staff who, through your stupidity, have been lost to us."

Joe paused, giving Ralph time to digest his words. His nephew was well aware of the difficulties he'd caused his uncle. More than once, Joe had been forced to smooth over the problems caused by his cavalier treatment of women. Joe had provided 'golden handshakes' for some and found new positions for others. His uncle had made clear to him that, but for his family connection, he would have been moved on long ago. Nevertheless, Ralph still felt that his uncle was being unfair and he was prepared to tell him so.

"I've been stupid in the past, I agree. Yet I've worked closely with Connie and not once have I acted inappropriately. And I never will. You're right. She's not just pretty, she's clever, witty and such a joy to be with. And if I tried it on with her, she'd knock me down straightaway and I'd never have another chance. You've no reason to fear me working with her."

"I'm pleased to see that Connie's made a positive impression on you Ralph, but I'm sticking with my decision. There's plenty of time to work with Connie after she's finished at Joyce and Hitchcock. If what you tell me is true, then I won't have to worry about things, will I?"

"No, certainly not," replied Ralph, firmly.

"Remember, you'll be taking over from me some day and you have to learn that the good of the firm takes priority over your own personal interests. Nothing would give me greater pleasure than to see you settle down. You're thirty, for goodness sake! You should be married and have responsibilities to take care of. It would give you stability and security and I'd feel far more comfortable about your prospects of taking the company forward."

"Yes, I know uncle Joe, but I just haven't found the right woman and I do like the life of a bachelor."

Getting up, Ralph walked towards the door.

"Think on what I've said. I do want the best for you Ralph."

"I know."

The two of them ended their conversation on relatively good terms and as Ralph returned to his office, for a moment he considered that his uncle was right. At thirty, he was hardly a young man anymore. Then turning into the corridor, the sight of Veronica walking towards him, her hips swaying, a welcoming smile on her face, quickly banished such thoughts from his mind.

"Are you okay Veronica?" he asked, stopping.

"Yes, I am. Thank you Mr Greening," said Veronica, pleased at his interest in her.

Veronica was trying hard not to blush. She didn't want to make it obvious that she was attracted to him. Yet averting her eyes, she gave herself away.

"Well, I mustn't stop you from getting on Veronica. You'll be getting me into trouble."

Veronica smiled. More confident, she lifted her eyes and made contact with Ralph's. Her long lashes fluttered enticingly and Ralph, gazing at the top of her open blouse, found it hard to suppress his desire.

"Yes, Mr Greening," she said, her voice suddenly sounding soft and husky.

"Call me Ralph, Veronica. Don't be so formal. We're all one happy family here at Greenings."

Returning to his office, Ralph stared out of the window. He'd not lied to his uncle. He'd not shown any disrespect to Connie. She was special, someone he could consider himself settling down with. Yet if he were to go out with her, it would require from him a sincerity that he'd been unable to show to any other woman. He sensed that she liked him but that it would be a difficult challenge to win her over. Nevertheless, he was determined to try. The problem was whether he could do it whilst losing his desire for other women. For Ralph was well aware that if Connie did agree to go out with him, she would never be prepared to share him with anyone else.

Chapter 16

Connie left work on the stroke of five. She was eager to get home. It was the night that she had decided to visit Kath and she was keen to learn more about the old lady's life. Having finished her tea and cleared away the pots, she then made her way out of the back door and out through the yard and down the alley to Syndall Street. She turned right towards the Richmond pub and saw two young men walking towards her. Recognising Connie, they quickened their pace and stopped to talk to her.

Connie had known Johnny and Bob for many years. The two friends had grown up together on Howard Avenue. Now eighteen, they were eight years younger than Connie and she had often earned extra pocket money by babysitting them when she was a teenager. The lads idolised her. Johnny's mam had recently told Connie that her son was in love with her, or at least he thought he was, she had added, laughing. Connie didn't see the revelation as amusing, but as rather touching. Given his relative youth, the knowledge of his feelings didn't cause her any embarrassment when she spoke to him. Johnny however, was always shy and reserved around her. Tonight, both lads were looking very dapper. They were wearing fashionable beatle suits, shirts and ties and smart, black winkle picker shoes. Johnny, with his shock of red hair and freckled face, smiled nervously, whilst Bob, his black hair styled into a quiff, winked and grinned.

"You're both looking very smart," said Connie.

"Do you think so?" asked Johnny, quietly.

"Of course. She wouldn't have said it otherwise," remarked Bob. "Would you Connie?"

Bob, far more confident around beautiful women, smiled at her.

"No. You know me boys. I'd only ever tell you the truth."

"There you are," said Bob, nudging Johnny with his elbow.

Johnny looked down. Bob gently shook his head. He recognised that his friend was embarrassed. He was so close to the woman of his dreams, but afraid to attempt to engage her in conversation.

"You've made his night for him now Connie," continued Bob, mischievously. "Those other girls won't stand a chance!"

To ease Johnny's embarrassment, Connie ignored the meaning of Bob's remark, pretending to have misunderstood him.

"Yes Bob," she replied. "Johnny's going to be a big hit with the girls tonight. I've no doubt that the pair of you will soon be courting."

"No, love 'em and leave 'em, Connie. That's the way," replied Bob, smiling.

"Speak for yourself," said Johnny, looking quite animated for once.

"Our Johnny's a real romantic Connie. Aren't you?" he asked, turning to his friend.

Bob was playfully 'pulling his leg,' but Johnny, with his strong feelings for Connie, didn't see the funny side of the situation. It was time for Connie to step in and calm things down.

"I'm sure that you'll both find a nice girl to settle down with. A good pair of hard-working and decent lads like you. There won't be any shortage of takers."

She turned to Johnny who, basking in the radiance of her smile, found his animosity towards his friend, vanishing as quickly as it had appeared.

"Anyway boys," continued Connie, "I'd best be getting on, I've got someone expecting me."

"Bye Connie," said Johnny, quietly.

"Yes, see you soon," said Bob.

The two lads walked on. As they made their way down towards Stockport Road, Connie could hear them chattering away. She was pleased that Johnny's irritation with Bob had been fleeting and that she had quickly smoothed things over. Crossing Syndall Street, Connie turned the corner into Apsley Grove and in double quick time, she was outside Kath's back door. Knocking, she announced her presence and from behind the door, she heard Kath telling her to come in. The kitchen was warm and bright and Kath, by the sink, had the kettle in her hand.

"I'm just making a brew love. I'm sure you could do with one."

"Yes. That would be lovely. Thanks Kath."

"You can get the biscuits and mugs out of the cupboard for me love, if you will. I've got different ones in the tin. Custard creams, bourbons, coconut rings and some chocolate digestives. I topped up at the weekend thinking you'd be coming to see me."

Connie went to the cupboard, collected the tin and brought it over to the kitchen table.

"Take your coat off love, you can hang it up over there."

Kath pointed over to some coat hooks near the door to the bottom of the stairs. Walking towards them, Connie took off her coat, hung it up and returned to sit at the table.

"It's nice and warm Kath."

"Yes, it soon heats up with the gas fire on. The doors and windows don't let in too many drafts."

"Not like a lot of the houses around here," said Connie.

"That's right love, but my landlord's a good 'un. I can't complain."

"It's a shame that there aren't more like that," replied Connie.

"Yes," said Kath. "Do you know Connie, I've lived here since before the Great War and the houses back then, were in a far better condition than they are today. It's so sad to see it. There's progress for you."

Connie nodded in agreement.

With the kettle whistling on the stove, Kath turned her attention to making the tea. She filled the pot, stirring the tea leaves around in the hot water, before replacing the lid and covering it with a colourful, striped cosy. She brought it over to the table and placed it on a thick mat located in the centre of a bright, yellow tablecloth.

"I'll just leave it to brew for a while," said Kath.

Pouring milk into the mugs, she then picked up the teapot and filled them before returning the pot to the centre of the table.

"Sugar?" she asked.

"Yes, one please," replied Connie.

"Good," said Kath smiling. "It's nice to see that you're not obsessed about your weight, like so many young women these days. Then again, with a lovely figure like yours, sugar in your tea obviously isn't making a difference."

"Oh," said Connie, feeling slightly embarrassed by Kath's compliment.

"Well, it's true love. You're very pretty and there's no getting away from it."

Connie didn't reply, busying herself by taking a chocolate digestive from the tin. Kath, watching her, smiled.

"You're a modest lass Connie. I like that about you. Harry told me about your job and to think that you still choose to live in Ardwick. There's not many that would. That's why I knew that I'd be seeing you again and bought in the biscuits. When you said you'd come to see me, I knew you were genuine and not just being polite."

"Well, I would hope so," said Connie.

"Yes, but not everyone's like you and Harry. There's a lot in the Party who don't really like the working classes, even though they profess to all and sundry that they want to help them. I've met a lot of them in my time."

Kath paused to take a sip of her tea. She seemed to be recollecting the individuals that she'd referred to. Connie, wanting to know more, asked Kath a question.

"When did you first join the Party?"

"It all goes back to the Great War love. My Stan was a 'territorial,' a member of the Manchester Regiment, long before 1914. He joined to earn some extra money with a few of his friends from work. Their boss encouraged them, by giving them paid time off for exercises and training.

The regiment formed a battalion in Ardwick and they trained regularly. When war was declared, they were asked if they would volunteer to go and fight overseas and nearly all of them, including Stan, did. They left in May 1915 for Alexandria and from there they were packed off to Gallipoli. Stan fought at Krithia. They lost a lot of men and after everyone was pulled out, they went to Egypt where they kept on fighting the Turks. I've got Stan's medals for it."

Kath paused. She took another drink of tea and then continued.

"With Stan fighting abroad, I wanted to do my bit too. Yet I didn't want to just make uniforms. I wanted to do something more and the chance came to work in the new shell factory that they'd set up in the tram depot on Hyde Road. The same building that they use for the buses today. It was 1916 and we were making 4½ inch shells for the Western Front. Stan's battalion got sent there at the start of 1917. It was tough work. Long hours and extra shifts, but we did it because we knew we were standing side by side with our husbands and sweethearts."

Connie nodded. She understood Kath's emotions. Her own mother had felt the same way in her father's fight against fascism in Spain.

"I was a 'Turner,' working on a lathe, turning the shells to get them to the right size and depth for the guns."

"You weren't one of the 'Canaries' then Kath?" asked Connie.

"No, love. We sent the casings to be filled at other factories. I'm thankful I didn't end up doing that. But of course, none of us really knew how dangerous that job was until the explosion at Hooley Hill in Ashton. The blast killed kids, as well as those in the factory. It was terrible."

"Did you see the Labour Party as a way to stop war and the misery it caused to everyone?" asked Connie.

"Back then, no Connie. Labour was behind the war effort, we all were. We knew our men were in danger and we wanted to help them win. There weren't many people thinking about pacifism until the fighting ended."

"So, what did make you get involved?"

"At first, 'dilution.' The Labour Party was against its use to exploit workers and I signed up to join the fight too. You see, they were trying to destroy our husbands' jobs; use the War to take away their skills, bargaining power and wages for when they returned home. They broke down complex, skilled jobs into separate tasks, which semi-skilled or unskilled workers could do. They said that as we were women, it wouldn't be possible for us to learn every part of the job and 'dilution' would speed up production. It meant that they could also pay workers less in the future too; not just women, as they were already doing. We didn't want our men risking their lives at the Front to come home to diluted jobs that wouldn't pay a decent wage. One thing we also did, was that we agreed that when our men came home, the women doing their jobs, would give them up."

"But wasn't that unfair on the women who wanted to keep doing them?"

"We didn't think like that. Union leaders were angry at first that we were being used in the factories. They thought that we'd let the bosses exploit us and destroy men's livelihoods. But they found out different. We fought for equal conditions and wages for women, but we also fought to get employers and the government to recognise that when the war ended and the soldiers returned, they would have their old jobs back. We threatened to go on strike to get our own wages up and to get promises for our husbands. The unions and Labour learned that we women can fight for working-class rights, just as well as any man."

Connie smiled at hearing the pride in Kath's voice. She and the women working with her, were formidable indeed.

"It must have felt good for women to have such unity and influence Kath."

"Well, the unity wasn't always there Connie. I told you that not all our party members are genuinely concerned for the poor. I served on the factory committee and was in the 'Women's Labour League.' It always struck me how so many of our 'leaders' were upper or middle-class women. It was the same in the factory. They were always the 'forewomen' or the 'welfare supervisors.' Many were condescending and spoke down to us and the bosses expected that we'd do everything they told us, as they were supposed to be our social superiors. So many of these women professed to be socialists, but they never mixed with us and if they weren't from around here and needed accommodation, they were always given better lodgings than the ordinary girls."

"I see," said Connie. "I didn't know."

"People don't love. If you're a woman and working-class, the history books don't want to know."

"Yes," said Connie. "I suppose women's history is just Florence Nightingale, Elizabeth I and Queen Victoria."

"But you must have experienced it yourself love."

"Experienced what?" asked Connie.

"You're living in Ardwick and working as an accountant. How do the wives of the men you work with react when you meet them?"

"I've not met any of them yet."

"Well, you just wait and see. Quite a few of them will think that being from Ardwick is the same as being from the gutter. And what will make them worse, is that you're clever and pretty. They'll have nothing but their snobbery to fall back on."

It was an incisive comment, but said without any hint of bitterness. It was a statement of fact, from a woman with decades of experiencing social injustice and who hoped that perhaps one day, things would be different.

"But you'll be all right Connie. Stay as you are. Be proud of your heritage. You've got real qualities of warmth and humanity and that's the only chance we have of ever making this world better."

She reached over the top of the table and placed her hand on Connie's.

"I'm sorry love. I've been rambling on a bit, haven't I? I've not let you get a word in edgeways."

Connie looked into her eyes and smiled.

"You've told me so much more about what I thought I knew. Real history is nothing like the textbooks, is it?"

"It isn't love."

"I often think that we haven't really moved on Kath. Look around us. The same families in the same houses, with the same problems and Macmillan telling us that we've never had it so good!"

Connie shook her head.

"It's not as bad as when I was young, Connie. There were no doctors, social services or proper pensions. Look at you. A good education, qualifications and an important job. Even upper-class women didn't have that when I was a girl. So, it can get better and we need people like you to fight for the cause."

"Well, I certainly want to help Harry to give support to people who need it."

"He's a good lad Harry," said Kath. "He genuinely respects a woman's opinion. You'll find that for all they claim to be modern and broad-minded, most Labour men are traditionalists. They like their tea on the table when they get home and their wives to dutifully clean the house, care for the kids and not speak their minds."

Kath paused, considering her words before continuing.

"Stick to your guns Connie. Don't let any man try to force any of that on you."

"Don't worry," replied Connie, laughing. "There's no chance of that."

"Find a kind, decent man like my Stan. And if you do, hold on to him. For if you don't ever truly love someone, your time in this world will have been for nothing."

The two women were silent as they contemplated Kath's words. Their relationship had grown closer as their conversation had unfolded. Finally, looking up towards the clock, Kath noticed that it was getting late. They had been getting along so well, that they hadn't realised how long they'd been talking.

"I'm sorry Connie. I forgot that you have to go to work tomorrow morning."

"That's okay. I've enjoyed it."

"And the chocolate biscuits?" asked Kath, smiling.

"Yes, especially them."

"You're welcome to come anytime Connie. It's been lovely having you here."

"Thanks. I will."

Walking home, Connie reflected on her visit. Kath had so much experience, a wealth of knowledge gained throughout a long and challenging life. It was becoming all too common for society to ignore the accumulated wisdom of the older generation, condemning it as old-fashioned and out of touch with the modern world. It was a view that Connie didn't share. Kath and Joe Greening made a nonsense of it. Two people who Connie would always be prepared to listen to and take advice from. They were older citizens prepared to accept that the world was changing, but who still believed that society could benefit from more traditional values and ideas. And in that, Connie concurred. She had no doubt that she would be visiting Kath again soon. Despite the fact that they were from different generations, she already felt that Kath would prove to be a close and true friend.

Chapter 17

Although Connie had disappointed Tom's hopes of romance, their relationship remained strong. Tom hadn't given up on the hope that in the future, Connie may change her mind. He was more than prepared to wait, content with the fact that he spent so much time with her at Joyce and Hitchcock. Tom had assumed that Ralph would be the one to work closely with Connie on the project. Therefore, when 'Old Joe' informed him that he had been chosen to carry out the role, it seemed as if he was receiving his Christmas present early. Tom also found that Connie's increasing involvement with the Party, meant that they were also sharing time together outside work too. With an important meeting on Manchester's slum clearance programme coming up, Connie and Tom decided that they would go together.

The subject was one that was close to Connie's heart. She hated the use of the word 'slums.' She knew that in a way it was well meant. Its purpose was to draw attention to inadequate housing. It was an emotive word. It would gain the sympathy and support necessary to release the purse strings of central government and deliver better homes. But to the proud families who occupied such properties, they were anything but 'slums.' Doorsteps were brown stoned, pavements swept clean, windows were gleaming and brilliant white net curtains were hung on the inside. Proud wives and mothers kept their homes 'spick and span', so many adhering to the old adage of cleanliness being next to godliness. These homes were loved and the communities they spawned felt a sense of belonging, that could never be found in more affluent and privileged areas. She feared that this was misunderstood or ignored. Politicians were intent on imposing solutions from above. They were failing to recognise the deep, emotional attachment of people to homes which they had no desire to leave.

The meeting was different in that it was organised on a Saturday and wasn't just a local event. It would be bringing in delegates from all over the city. Nevertheless, the event was only being held in a small hall. Tom explained that as 'United' were playing at home, the organisers knew that numbers would be down, as members showed their preference for football over politics. On entering, the two of them took seats on the front row close to the stage. The audience was different to that Connie had seen in Ardwick. Here, many of the delegates were middle-class. There were members of the professions: teachers, lecturers, doctors, solicitors, engineers, interspersed with working-class, union men. Once again, she found that members of her own gender were very much in the minority. Just before the conference began, she and Tom were joined by Harry. Unusually, he wasn't going to be on the stage, even though he had a serious interest in the issue being considered.

Connie listened to an introduction by the presiding officer, who introduced the speakers for the day. They included Bill Perkins, Connie's recent adversary. The day's programme ended with a questions-and-answers session. This would allow those attending to raise any issues of concern.

As the speeches got underway, Connie listened carefully. There was concern that the Corporation were being denied funds by national government to provide for a meaningful programme of works to address the housing situation. Nevertheless, there was optimism that when, not if, Labour won the next general election, the new government would address the problem. There were also references to Harold Wilson's 'white heat of technology' speech, delivered just a couple of months ago. In essence, he'd argued that the progress of science, technology and engineering, would address long-standing social problems. This would create a strong Britain and provide a brave, new world where inequalities between classes would be eradicated. Wilson was suggesting a new direction for the Party, one that would be popular with middle-class supporters. It suggested that there was no longer any need to pursue 'Clause IV' of Labour's constitution; the "common ownership of the means of production, distribution and exchange."

Wilson's words however, hadn't gone down well with many of the unions. Lots of their members supported the Bevanite wing of the party. They stuck to a firm belief in the necessity for nationalisation, so references by speakers to the Labour leader, necessarily elicited groans from some sections of the audience. When it was Bill Perkins turn to speak, he unequivocally advocated the imposition of housing change from above. With a bureaucratic attention to detail, he made clear that there could be no deviation from the plan. Houses would be demolished and people rehoused on brand new estates, many of them miles beyond the city. If the new socialist community was to be established, argued Perkins, then nothing could be allowed to stand in its way. It was foolhardy to have fond memories of the old neighbourhoods. It was now time to forge new communities and argued Perkins, even Wilson would agree to that; using new industrial building processes to create new housing units. It would bring with it a new residential landscape and a true socialist city.

The solution seemed brutal and when the opportunity came for members of the audience to express their concerns, Connie raised her hand. It seemed however, that she was destined to be ignored. That is until Harry, sat beside her, raised his own hand. Immediately recognised, Harry was granted the floor. Standing up, he turned to the side and pointed down at Connie.

"I'd like this young lady to speak on my behalf. She's been trying to catch your eye for quite some time now."

He beckoned to Connie to stand up. Harry's calm assurance, allied to his stature in the Party, encouraged the presiding officer to accede to his demand. Confidently Connie began.

"The 'white heat of technology' is all well and good. The scientists, the engineers, the planners who will bring us our new, model communities in a precise and clinical fashion. But there's a real danger here. It seems to me, listening to the proposals of the proponents of this plan, that it is all so cold and sterile. Where is the heart, the soul, the appreciation of the human beings at the centre of it all? Who has asked the people of Hulme, of Greenheys, of Chorlton-on-Medlock, of Ardwick, of Gorton and all the other areas of so-called slum housing in our city, what they want? Because it's their lives and their communities. The people who live around me, in Ardwick, don't want to move. Old people who have lived there all their lives, with their families and friends around them. It's familiar to them and it's home. Planners can talk all they want about new houses, flats and estates. You need more than the fabric of a building to create a real home. Homes are an intangible thing. They're not the bricks and mortar from which they are built, but are created by the presence and emotions of the people who dwell within."

Conscious of the hushed and attentive atmosphere within the room, so different to the heckling that she'd received at the previous meeting, Connie dared to pause a few seconds in order to allow her words to have more impact. She glanced down to the side of her. Harry, who'd been listening with intent, nodded his head in encouragement.

"I want to say to everyone here today," she continued, "that there is an alternative to the wholesale destruction of our neighbourhoods. It is that we refurbish the old terraced houses. Modernise them with inside bathrooms and toilets, repair the leaky roofs and windows and tackle the damp. It can be done. The Corporation have done it before and if the works are costed properly, it will require no more resources and in fact, it will definitely be much cheaper than the demolition of houses, removal of tenants and construction of homes on newly purchased land. Most important of all, there will be no human costs associated with such a scheme. No distress for residents desperate to stay in the communities so familiar to them. Any new building should be confined to providing housing for the homeless, the elderly and disabled, who need specialised accommodation, or for newly-wed couples looking to start a home of their own. When I hear speakers here today, obsessed about driving through these huge schemes, without a thought for the people who will be affected by them, I'm afraid to say that it is reminiscent of the worst kind of soviet state planning in the Stalinist era. We cannot have people being forced into compliance by heartless ideologues, insistent on the unquestioned wisdom and supremacy of the state. I would hope that we in Manchester will think very carefully about how we take our housing programme forward."

Connie sat down. Rising applause went around the hall and when it had stopped, the presiding officer thanked Connie for her contribution. He glanced towards Bill Perkins, most clearly the individual who'd been the focus of Connie's words, to see if he wished to reply. Perkins had recognised Connie the moment she had stood up and felt it prudent to avoid jousting with her again, especially as today she seemed to have the sympathy of many in the room. After all, Perkins knew that the real decisions wouldn't be made here, but with the Corporation's Planning Committee. Voices such as Connie's, would carry very little weight there. Powerful words they may have been but ultimately, he knew that they would be ineffective.

With the meeting ended, Connie, Harry and Tom drifted slowly outside. The two men had been astounded by the power and emotion of Connie's speech and neither of them could hide their admiration for her.

"That was a wonderful speech Connie," remarked Harry. "Truly powerful and I have to say, it certainly won me over."

Connie smiled.

"And a lot of others too," added Tom.

"Yes, perhaps," said Connie. "Then again, men like Bill Perkins will make the final decisions and I'm afraid I don't see any evidence that they'll try to consult with members of the local communities. They'll insist that they know best and it's very hard to see how they can be stopped and made to properly consider the alternatives."

"Nevertheless," said Harry, "you've put an alternative view forward. And very convincingly. So, you never know."

"I'm afraid politics is about compromise Connie," said Tom. "It's the irony of it. We all have such strongly felt beliefs and we join political parties to help promote our ideas. Yet most of the time we never get what we want, or have to be satisfied with a compromise that dilutes our objectives so much, that it's as if they had never been achieved."

"It's inevitable Connie," continued Harry. "You mentioned Stalin and I know you're having a go at Bill Perkins there…"

"That's right," interrupted Connie. "He shares that mentality of driving through change regardless. A belief in the infallibility of the leadership, over the mass of the party members."

"Yet, think on Connie," replied Harry. "There are those in the party who favour Bill's approach. They look to the failed promises of the new Labour dawn under Attlee's post-war government. Compromise from the start. Caving in to the doctors over the NHS; employers over the Industrial Injuries Act; low benefits for National Assistance and poor pensions. There was no real attempt to threaten the interests of the rich and powerful and that was because Attlee's Cabinet didn't want to threaten the status quo. That's why the working classes have never got the housing improvements we're talking about today. The 'old boys club' that Wilson referred to, are still pulling the strings behind the scenes, whilst Wilson shifts the party ever more towards the centre."

"You sound like a true radical Harry," said Connie.

"Actually, I'm not. I learned a long time ago that you have to be a realist. This country has never been ripe for revolution. The Somme and Passchendaele couldn't bring it about and the opportunity provided by the General Strike, came and went. The British working classes have shown that they want a fairer society, but most of them won't abandon parliamentary democracy to get it. So that's the path that all of us must continue to tread, but we should also understand the views of those such as Bill Perkins, whose ultimate ambitions may be different."

"Well, I think you've already worked out that I'm no slavish follower of party policy," continued Connie. "My views on education and housing, don't correspond with the official line I've heard in the last two meetings. And I suppose, working as an accountant, I can't profess to have any sympathy with the full implementation of 'Clause IV.'"

"Like many, Connie," remarked Tom. "You're certainly in the majority there."

Tom was worried that Connie was on the verge of renouncing her interest in Labour politics. He had encouraged her to come to the meetings, but she had dipped her toe in the water and hadn't found the temperature to her liking. Perhaps, she would now turn away.

"We're in the Labour Party Connie," continued Tom, "because all of us, including you, know that it's the only true party for the working-class. The Tories will always give preferential treatment to the privileged few, anything they throw to the working-class, is just crumbs off the table. Like you, I work in and for a capitalist world, but it doesn't stop me fighting for social justice and to gain political power, so that we can redistribute the resources of the state to those most needy. You, Harry and I were born into the working-class. We have joined the privileged, but we must never betray our roots and do all we can for those less fortunate. The Party needs you, Connie. Don't get disillusioned. Rome wasn't built in a day."

"Or the new Jerusalem!" added Harry, smiling.

Connie laughed gently. She'd been touched by Tom's impassioned appeal. His cheeks were reddening. He was slightly embarrassed, feeling he'd perhaps been a bit too melodramatic.

"No, Tom. You're right and I feel the same way, but I'll always take every issue on its merits. I'll never toe the party line when I don't agree with it. I want to help people with their everyday problems and through Harry and the Party's connection with them, I can do that."

Connie's words summed up her attitude perfectly. She wanted to do good and that would be achieved on the ground with real people and real problems that she could help to address. Connie didn't believe that she would be attending many more meetings. She would leave that to those with greater political ambitions, who were intent on furthering their position within the Party. Too much energy was being spent on talking and meeting, with very little to show for it other than rancour and division between factions striving for dominance within the Party. Bevanites and Gaitskellites. Were their different standpoints anything other than to justify their opposition to one another? And at the end of the day, did it not just come down to egotism and personal ambition? In reality, it was a clash of personalities and not policies. Connie wanted no part of that and although she had a growing respect for Harry, she had no ambition to follow him into any political office.

Chapter 18

It was the evening of Thursday, December 12th and Christmas 1963 was rapidly approaching. Having been out on their ward visits, Connie took Tom to see Kath.

"Take a seat love," said Kath, looking at Tom who was standing quietly behind Connie.

"Thank you," said Tom.

"There's some biscuits on the table, or I could make you a nice sandwich if you like."

"No, it's fine. I've already eaten," replied Tom, rather hesitantly.

"Go on. You know you want one," said Connie.

"No, honestly I don't."

Tom's words sounded unconvincing.

"Just make him one Kath. He thinks he's being polite," said Connie.

"We don't need any 'airs and graces' around here love," said Kath, smiling at Tom. "Just take me as you find me. After all that traipsing around, you must be famished."

"Yes, I suppose I am," said Tom, smiling.

"Will Cheshire Cheese be all right?"

"That'll be great. Thank you," said Tom.

"Do you want a bit of beetroot on it as well?"

"Oh, yes please! Thank you."

Tom's eyes lit up. Cheese and beetroot had been his favourite since being a kid.

Satisfied, Kath got on with making Tom's sandwich.

"I'll finish the tea," said Connie.

"All right love. Make sure you warm the pot though."

Connie always did, but had no intention of saying so. Carefully, she put hot water from the kettle into the empty pot, before returning the former to the cooker. Swilling the water around the sides, she felt the exterior of the pot becoming warm. As the kettle started to whistle, Connie emptied the teapot in the sink. She then added the tea, one spoon for each of them and another for the pot, before filling it with boiling water. In the meantime, Kath had given Tom his sandwich and had joined him at the kitchen table. Sat quietly, she watched him as he ate contentedly, his eyes following Connie's every move. It would have been pointless for Kath to try and engage him in conversation. Tom's mind was clearly elsewhere.

Having finished making the tea, Connie brought the mugs over to the table and put them down on the mats in front of Tom and Kath, before returning to get her own drink. Sitting down, Connie noticed that there was a sandwich for her too.

"I knew you'd be hungry Connie. You have to eat properly, given all the hours you spend working and helping Harry."

"Thanks Kath," said Connie, reaching across the table and gently squeezing her friend's hand.

"It's all right love," replied Kath, touched by Connie's show of affection.

Looking across at her other visitor, Kath continued.

"I think that I've met you before, haven't I Tom?"

"Yes, you have. I came once with Harry, but it was quite a long time ago. Last January, when the snow and ice was so bad. I remember that Harry was concerned about you, but you told him off, saying that there were others that he should worry about far more than you. You said that you may look old, but you could give him a run for his money any day and didn't need mollycoddling."

Connie burst out laughing. She could just imagine Harry and Tom's faces when Kath had said it. She was proud and independent. She wouldn't have anyone thinking that she couldn't take care of herself, regardless of her advanced years or the severity of the weather.

"It was a very bad winter though," said Kath. "It was just before Christmas when it started with the freezing snow and ice and it just seemed to carry on forever. A lot of my friends are worried that we might get the same again this year."

"I think we'll be all right," said Tom. "It's not expected again this winter."

"Weather forecasters! I don't put much faith in them. They never seem to get it right," replied Kath.

Connie nodded in agreement and as Tom didn't feel inclined to challenge their criticism of the weather service, the conversation moved rapidly on.

"How did the meeting go at the weekend Connie? Do we know what's going to be happening here in Ardwick?"

"Well, apparently there isn't the money to do very much unless Labour wins the next election. But if they do, I'm afraid the Corporation will just bulldoze everything down and we'll all end up who knows where."

"Don't they understand that we don't want that?"

"No one seems to listen."

The room was silent. It struck Tom how true Connie's words at the meeting had been. The planners, the Party, had no inkling of the impact on local residents of the uncertainty created by the fear of losing their communities.

"It's no different to the 'Twenties' and 'Thirties,'" said Kath. "I was a union organiser then. I represented the girls and fought for equality, just like in the Great War and the union leaders ignored us. They didn't want women negotiating with the bosses. They wanted to reserve that for themselves. It was all very cosy. Boys together."

"It's felt like that at the meetings I've been to Kath. No disrespect to you or Harry," she added, looking at Tom, "but the Party is run by men, for men. There might be a few token women at the top table, but in reality, the leadership is just another 'old boys club.' Harold needs to take a look in the mirror!"

"It wasn't just being ignored that bothered me," continued Kath, "but that I suspected that those at the head of the union, were on familiar and even friendly terms with the bosses. You never knew if we were being encouraged to moderate our demands, or draw back from going on strike, because some of our officials were getting a 'backhander.' Greed is a terrible thing and it can cause people to forget their loyalties and values."

"I agree," said Tom. "Top union officials can easily lose touch with the workers they represent. They're no longer on the factory floor and so don't experience the daily struggles and inequalities of working life. Like Lenin argued, they have comfortable lives, a salary greater than the men they represent and spend more time with the bosses than they do with their fellow workers. In fact, their mentality becomes just the same as the bosses."

"So, why should we keep faith with the movement then?" asked Connie.

Tom, becoming animated by the conversation, stared into her eyes.

"It's because there are some good people working in the movement and I believe that now is a time of real change. A new, exciting period where education and scientific progress will eventually overcome inequality and society will provide equal opportunities for everyone."

"You're sounding just like Wilson," said Connie.

"Yes, because I believe that much of what he says is right. Technology has provided an opportunity to revolutionise all aspects of society. But I also agree with some of your concerns Connie."

His voice softened and Kath noticed how Tom seemed oblivious to everything around him, except for Connie. His eyes blazed brightly.

"We must never lose our heart and soul. Never forget about the needs of real people. And that's why the Party needs you Connie and others like you. You can ensure that the Party has that beating heart at its centre."

Kath watched him sit back in his chair. Not once had he taken his eyes off Connie, not only during his impassioned words to her, but throughout the time he'd been at the house. It was clear to Kath that the young man had fallen deeply in love with Connie. He couldn't hide the fact. Nevertheless, she wasn't sure whether Connie had truly grasped the reality of the situation.

Changing the subject, Kath asked Connie a question.

"Are you going to be on your own at Christmas Connie?"

"Yes, I usually am."

"Well, you're welcome to share it with me if you like. I always get a small turkey and make a Christmas pudding and you never know, there may even be a little Advocaat afterwards," she said, smiling.

"I'd like that. Thanks Kath."

"Well love, I'd best not keep you any longer. You and Tom have to get to work tomorrow."

Kath stood up, followed by Tom and Connie. The two women embraced warmly.

"I'll see you soon," said Connie.

"It was nice to meet you again Tom," said Kath. "You can drop in any time if you're down this way."

"Thanks," replied Tom.

As the two of them walked out into Apsley Grove, Tom remarked on how impressed he'd been with the warmth of Kath's welcome and her feisty personality.

"She's nice, isn't she?" asked Tom.

"I think so," replied Connie.

"So open-minded. She's not bitter or resentful at the opportunities we have, that she never did."

"Yes, Tom. If she were born today, there wouldn't be anything that she couldn't achieve. That is, if she wanted to."

"And that's why we have to make sure that all children get that opportunity," observed Tom.

It was a view that Connie wholeheartedly agreed with.

Chapter 19

The following morning was Connie's last at Joyce and Hitchcock. She and Tom had their final meeting with Mike and went through the new financial management systems they'd introduced. It had been decided that Tom would be returning on a regular basis to ensure that the new procedures were bedding in effectively. It seemed, said Mike, that 'Old Joe' had other plans for Connie, but he hoped that he would work with her again in the future. Returning to Greenings, Connie was met by Ralph who had some interesting news for her.

"It's good to see you back. My uncle's delighted. You're quite a star when it comes to impressing the clients. Mike can't speak highly enough of you."

"I'm sure you're exaggerating Ralph," replied Connie.

"No, I'm not. Why would I do that?" asked Ralph.

Connie couldn't help but smile.

"I'm being serious Connie. It's the truth and because we've got another important client lined up, the 'old man' wants you to go with me to the 'Midland' tonight to meet them."

"Oh," said Connie surprised. "And who would that be?" she asked.

"Keep it under your hat," warned Ralph, "but you remember I told you that we were in contact with McVitie's. Well, we've got a good chance of getting their audit work."

"I don't know if you've noticed Ralph," replied Connie, "but I haven't got a hat!"

"You know what I mean," said Ralph.

The two of them laughed.

"The 'Midland.' That's very posh. Are you sure you're allowed to take me?" asked Connie. "After all, I'm only an Ardwick lass!"

Ralph shook his head and smiled.

"Point taken. I suppose you're never going to forget about me casting aspersions on your blessed Ardwick, are you Connie?"

"That's right Ralph," replied Connie, with a twinkle in her eye.

"And what do you mean by 'posh?' I've been to the 'Midland' dozens of times. It's a perfect place to do business."

"I've no doubt that you have. You 'toffs' like your luxury, don't you?"

Connie smiled mischievously and Ralph laughed. He enjoyed it when she made fun of him. The more time they spent together, the more comfortable he felt in her company. It was Connie's personality; her warmth, her heart. He knew that he desired her, but with other women, that desire was all-consuming. In reality, it amounted to little more than lust. Connie, was someone he respected. She was immune to his charms and he knew that unless he was sincere, she would utterly reject him.

"We're meeting them at seven," continued Ralph. "If you'd like to, we can go a little earlier, so that we can relax before we see them."

"Yes, that seems a good idea. I'll need to go through everything you've had from them, if you can let me see it?"

"Of course," said Ralph. "I'll go along to my office now and send the papers over to you."

"No need to rush Ralph. I've arranged to go with Paula to have some dinner. I'll be back after one."

Connie hadn't seen Paula for a while and the two women had lots to catch up on. As they sat in Lyons Café, the conversation ebbed and flowed. It seemed almost inevitable that Ralph's name would come up and it did when Connie referred to the meeting at the 'Midland.'

"How do you feel about Ralph?" asked Paula.

"How do you mean?" replied Connie.

"He's got a reputation for being a bad 'un. Just be a bit wary of him."

"Why?" asked Connie.

"Well, there's been incidents with women in the office, especially some of the young trainees we've had."

"He's certainly very handsome Paula. I can see why women are attracted to him. Perhaps that's the root of the problem. Young women feeling that he doesn't give them enough attention."

"Yes, maybe so," said Paula, rather unconvincingly, although her less than ringing endorsement of Connie's suggestion, wasn't noticed by the latter.

"He's always acted like a gentleman towards me Paula. He'll laugh and joke, but he's never attempted to try it on and I can't say that I've seen any evidence of him doing it with anyone else. Perhaps he's grown up now."

"Yes. Perhaps so," said Paula.

"What about Tom? How was it working with him?" she continued.

"It's been fine. We're really good friends and I enjoyed being with him."

"He's still in love with you. You do know that, don't you?" asked Paula.

"No, I think he's accepted it now. He's fine about it."

"I hope so Connie. He's a lovely man."

Paula said no more. She'd wanted to warn Connie about Ralph's past and she had done so. Yet she was worried that Connie's defence of Ralph may suggest that she was starting to fall for him, just like so many others before her. It was such a shame, thought Paula, that Connie had spurned Tom's advances. She was positive that he would never have been unfaithful to Connie, or have hurt her. However, Paula realised that no one can fight against the dictates of their heart and for Connie, much as she liked Tom, he would never secure that special place in her affections that would convince her to go out with him.

Chapter 20

Ralph and Connie arrived outside the Midland Hotel at just after six thirty. Connie had passed it many times and never failed to be impressed by its appearance. It was now sixty years old and had been designed in the Gothic style by Charles Trubshaw, the architect of the Midland Railway Company. It was a huge building, covering two acres and towering upwards. Its lower floors were composed of pink granite, contrasting with its upper storeys of brick and brown glazed terracotta. Its hundreds of windows were highlighted by a profusion of ornamental details. It was a building of real substance and one of Manchester's finest. Its entrance consisted of two arches either side of a central column, a gentle flight of steps leading up towards the hotel doors and access to the lobby. As Connie walked through into the interior, she wasn't disappointed. It was finely decorated and furnished. She understood why the 'Midland' was the destination for all wealthy and important visitors to the city. No other hotel could compete with its opulence.

Whilst Connie sat down, Ralph went to the reception. Indicating where they were sitting, he asked to be informed when his guests arrived. Returning to Connie, the two of them went over the details that they would be covering that evening. This time Ralph would take the lead in the discussions and Connie would support him when necessary. The two of them were feeling confident, yet as the time ticked by, there was no sign of the representatives from McVitie's.

"Strange," said Ralph. "It's seven fifteen, they should have been here by now."

"Perhaps they've been delayed," said Connie. "After all, it is Friday night. They'll have to contend with all the extra traffic."

"Well, that may be so," replied Ralph, "but we took the precaution of setting off earlier to get here on time."

"Never mind," replied Connie. "Remember that the client is always right. That's the first thing I learned from John Francis, my old boss. He always pointed out that we were the ones that needed their business. They could choose to go to any firm of accountants. We just have to bite our tongue, smile and get on with it."

"Do you know Connie. Every time we talk, you sound more like my uncle. I think that when it's time for him to move aside, you'll be the one he gets to follow him."

"Don't be daft Ralph."

"No. I'm serious."

Ralph laughed and Connie smiled. She noticed that she rarely felt tense or concerned when she was with him. Here they were on the verge of a very important meeting and she was totally relaxed. Just then, a young lady approached them.

"I'm sorry sir," she said, addressing Ralph. "We've just had a message from Mr Connors at McVitie's. He says that unfortunately, they've had a problem at work and they won't be able to arrive for another hour at least. He suggested that the best thing is for you to contact him on Monday to rearrange the meeting. He says he's awfully sorry."

Ralph smiled at the young lady and thanked her. With the receptionist gone, Ralph looked at Connie and let out a huge sigh.

"Ah, ah!" said Connie. "Remember that the client is always right."

She could see the frustration etched into Ralph's face. He'd been keen for the meeting to go ahead. Getting McVitie's business would have been a real feather in his cap where his uncle was concerned.

"But we've been waiting all this time and…"

He had no chance of going any further. Connie suddenly burst out laughing.

"I'm sorry Ralph," she said, falteringly. "I can't help it. Your face. It was just so funny."

Confronted with her fits of laughter, Ralph couldn't help but smile. She was so beautiful when she laughed. Her eyes sparkled, her soft lips parted over her beautiful white teeth and her broad smile lit up the room. She was so special and at that moment, Ralph decided that he wouldn't let the evening pass without spending the rest of it in Connie's company.

"Connie," he said, as she gradually settled down. "I don't know about you, but we would have been spending the evening here if Connors and his chaps had arrived, so why don't we just go ahead and take advantage of the table booked for us all at 'The French?' You and I can have a nice meal and forget all about this disaster."

"That sounds lovely Ralph. But won't your uncle be unhappy at paying for an expensive meal without any obvious benefit for the company?"

"We've not had anything to eat Connie and besides, the firm owes you a lot for getting the Joyce and Hitchcock contract. The 'old man' never stops talking about it."

"Well, I'll agree on one condition."

"What's that?" asked Ralph.

"If your uncle is even a little bit unhappy, the two of us will pay for the meal ourselves."

"Oh, Connie. You can't expect a chap to allow a lady to do that."

"Well, it's either that, or we'll have to forget it."

Ralph shook his head. He recognised that she was determined that he wouldn't play the role of the chivalrous gentleman.

"I think these notions of equality are going a little too far when a chap has to agree to a lady paying for a night out," he continued, with more than a hint of disapproval in his voice.

"Well, I don't," said Connie, firmly.

She looked straight into his eyes, defiant and determined and he knew that unless he agreed, the night was over. Yet that defiance, the confidence that swept away his protestations, was thrilling. It actually made him tingle with excitement. It was all so new for him. A beautiful woman who was impervious to his charm and good looks. She was a real challenge. Connie had put herself in charge. Ralph was facing the unfamiliar and that made her even more desirable to him.

"Okay, I agree."

"That?"

"If my uncle isn't happy, then the two of us will share the cost of the meal."

"Good," said Connie, smiling. "Come on then, let's go and see this fancy restaurant."

Ralph led her to 'The French.' It was the Midland Hotel's much lauded restaurant. It was famous in the region for its excellent cuisine and was a place for gourmets. It was also very expensive. When Connie saw the menu, she was shocked by how much she would have to pay if Joe Greening didn't honour the bill. Yet, she had no second thoughts. She had acted on principle and to Connie, that meant far more than pounds, shillings and pence.

Connie watched as Ralph went through the menu and the wine list. He had been born to this. He was privileged and he settled easily into his role of directing the waiters, choosing the wine and explaining to her the selections of food on offer. To Connie, whose favourite meal was steak and kidney pudding, chips and mushy peas from 'Chiappe's,' the intricacies of the menu at the French were mystifying. She couldn't understand why there was such an obsession with something as basic as food. Simple food was good enough for her, but she had no wish to deny the pleasure that Ralph was getting from helping her to make her selections and his belief that he was introducing her to the finer things in life.

"If the firm can acquire even more important clients, we'll be doing a lot of entertaining at places like this. The bigger the business, the more they'll expect it."

"Well, not always," replied Connie. "I can't see someone like Mike Joyce being impressed by being wined and dined."

"Yes, but most of them aren't like Mike and ironically Connie, it's the self-made men who normally want to come to places like this. It makes them feel that socially, they've arrived."

"Well, more fool them," said Connie.

Ralph smiled. She was so independent. He could never see her forgetting her roots. Yet neither would he. Fortunately, the two of them could happily agree to differ on notions of status and class.

When they had finished eating, Connie began to collect the used plates and cutlery and started stacking them in the centre of the table. Ralph, watched her in fascination. He was astounded by her behaviour.

"What on earth are you doing Connie?"

"What do you mean Ralph? I think it's quite obvious."

"No, Connie," he replied. "I don't have a clue what you're doing."

"I'm clearing the table. What do you think I'm doing?" asked Connie, equally surprised by Ralph's reaction.

"But they have people for that kind of thing Connie. Stop it, you'll embarrass yourself," he continued, clearly concerned that the other diners would be disapproving of her actions.

Connie laughed, but continued to tidy up the table.

"Well, I can see that you've never had to clean up after yourself, have you Ralph? I never go out to eat anywhere without tidying the table. It's slovenly not to do so. Consider yourself told off!"

At that moment, the waiter came over to the table. He was shocked to see the neat piles of pots and cutlery at its centre. Just as he went to take away the plates, Connie asked him to hold on. She took a spoon and carefully scooped up some potatoes that had fallen on the table next to where Ralph had been eating.

"Sorry," said Connie to the waiter. "I nearly missed that."

"Thank you, madam," replied the waiter, politely.

"Oh Lord," said Ralph, as the waiter retreated. "Would you stop it? I'll never live this down."

Connie chuckled.

"No, I won't Ralph."

"You'll be going into the kitchen next and asking them if you can help with the washing up!"

"Don't be silly," replied Connie. "I only feel that I should tidy up the table where we've been sitting."

Ralph shook his head several times and took in a deep breath.

"That's just like the working classes, Connie. I knew a chap that was on the management over at 'The Grand.' He said that they always knew when they had couples who weren't particularly well off staying there, because they always left the room tidy. The staff never thought any better of them for doing it, especially the maids and cleaners."

"Well, that's not the point, as you well know Ralph."

She smiled at him, her pretty, radiant face, eliciting a warm smile from Ralph in return.

"Oh, what are we going to do with you Connie?" continued Ralph, shaking his head.

"Well, we could have a final drink in the bar and then you can get me a taxi home, if you will please."

Riding back in the taxi to Howard Avenue, Connie went over the night's events. She felt happy and contented. She had enjoyed her time with Ralph. What was supposed to be a tricky and challenging evening, satisfying the concerns of prospective new clients, had turned into an intimate occasion. The two of them had been able to relax and get to know one another outside the confines of work. And yes, the two of them came from backgrounds that were so far apart and they had such different perspectives on life. Yet their disagreements were without any hint of rancour. They were content to accept each other's opinions. And regardless of the differences between them, Connie understood that increasingly she was attracted to Ralph. She had given no indication to him of the fact, but it was clear by his own actions, that Ralph certainly felt affection towards her. Yet contrary to Paula's warnings, his actions had been those of a true gentleman and she began to feel that should romance develop between them, Ralph would prove to be a steadfast and reliable lover.

Chapter 21

Connie was finding it a challenge to juggle her commitments to helping Harry and the local community, with the increasing responsibilities she was assuming at Greenings. The job was going far better than she could ever have imagined. Together with Ralph and Tom, she was part of a successful team and Joe Greening was delighted with her progress. He was happy to authorise the payment of Ralph and Connie's meal at 'The French.' It was, he told his nephew, a suitable reward for her intelligence and hard work. Connie had recognised early in her career that she had to focus on making herself indispensable. If she was excellent at her job, kept improving her abilities and widening her experience, then finally the issue of her gender would be a matter of no consequence. At that point she would be judged solely on her capabilities. At present however, Connie knew that she couldn't afford to take anything for granted. She had to stay focused and keep on impressing her boss.

Connie's Thursday night rounds in Ardwick had deeply affected her. She was coming into contact with an increasing number of people who were vulnerable and afraid. Yet, through kindness and conversation, she provided plans to deal with their issues and a promise to support them through to their resolution. The look of relief and gratitude that she subsequently saw on people's faces, gave her an enormous sense of satisfaction. Consequently, regardless of the extra demands it placed upon her, Connie was determined that she would maintain her support for those of her neighbours who needed her.

In work on Tuesday morning, Connie's concentration was distracted by the putting up of the Christmas decorations. It was December 17th and the countdown to Christmas was on. Starting to think about the festive period, Connie recognised that the season of goodwill usually had little impact on her, given that she lived alone. Kath's recent invitation to dinner however, meant that for the first time in years, Connie would have someone to spend Christmas Day with and given her growing affection for Kath, it was something that she was looking forward to.

Deep in thought, Connie didn't notice as Tom made his way into her office. Stood waiting for her attention, Connie finally acknowledged his presence.

"Oh, hi Tom. I'm sorry. I was miles away."

"I hope it was somewhere nice," replied Tom, smiling.

Connie laughed. Her lips parting invitingly, sending a warm tingle down Tom's spine. He marvelled at how she could do that to him. Just a simple movement, like pushing back a stray lock of hair from her face, or reaching up to fetch a folder from a shelf and he would feel his pulse race with excitement.

"Are you free tomorrow evening Connie?" asked Tom.

"I can be. Why?"

"Harry's going over to Hulme. There's a meeting with a group of West Indian residents and business owners. The Party's trying to make more contact with them. There's too much prejudice, even among our own members. We need the whole community together, black and white, fighting for the common cause."

"I protested against Hesketh, Mosley and his Union Movement Party two years ago Tom. You don't have to tell me about prejudice."

"Yes, the Moss Side By-election. I protested too," replied Tom.

"It was the first time politically, that I felt close to my dad," continued Connie. "He and my mam demonstrated against Mosley in the 'Thirties.' When I protested, I felt I was fighting fascism just like them. Of course, my dad did far more, putting his life on the line in Spain."

"Wow Connie," said Tom, impressed. "He was in the International Brigade?"

"Yes."

"You must be proud."

"I am," replied Connie.

"That election leaflet they put out in Moss Side was a disgrace," continued Tom. "Blaming immigration for poor homes and threatening jobs."

"Yes, I remember," said Connie. "They claimed that immigrants were bringing TB, VD and leprosy into the country. How could any decent person do that?"

"Well," said Tom, "they aren't decent, are they? But it didn't do them any good. They only managed to get around a thousand votes. Once again, Mosley was sent packing from Manchester with his tail between his legs."

"The Tories played the anti-immigration issue too though, didn't they?" continued Connie. "They were calling for limits on immigration during the election and Frank Taylor still held on to the seat for them. We can't simply assume that because Mosley's been seen off, that there aren't many racist views remaining in Manchester, or the country as a whole. The Tories recognised that there are, by passing the Commonwealth Immigrants Act last year."

"Are you going to come along then Connie?" asked Tom. "It starts at seven."

"Yes. We can finish up around five-thirty, have something to eat and get a taxi over."

When they arrived, the meeting was well attended. There were just a few empty seats. It was clear that the local West Indian community felt that their grievances were being ignored. There were many white faces to be seen too and Connie was pleased that they had come to express their solidarity with their black neighbours. Harry, together with a group of community leaders, was already on the stage. It was explained that he had come to outline Labour's policies towards improving neighbourhoods like Hulme, Moss Side and Greenheys, where it was reckoned 10,000 of Manchester's black residents lived. Harry didn't expect to receive an unqualified and enthusiastic response and he was proved right as he faced some residents who were keen to voice their frustration and anger. They complained of their inability to rent decent properties and their exclusion from a range of jobs at the labour exchange, because employers refused to take on black workers. They had come to Britain hoping for a new life of opportunity and their lives were as unpromising as the cold and damp weather they experienced. Connie noted that on the whole, speakers expressed their desire to live peacefully within their local communities. It was noted that the Irish too, were victims of prejudice and discrimination. After all, it was commonly noted that many boarding houses carried notices that they wouldn't accept any 'blacks, Irish or pets.' Yet some of the younger men took a more assertive and potentially aggressive tone. They made clear that anyone coming to tell them that they should 'go back home,' would find themselves 'getting chased off.' Harry made it clear that this was the last thing he wanted to see happen and the community leaders on stage endorsed his view, pointing out that any violence would merely be ammunition for the racists to use against them.

The meeting had raised more questions than answers, yet Harry tried hard to persuade his audience that positive changes would come eventually.

"You've seen," he said, "that by Labour's support for the Bristol bus boycott, you can trust our party to bring about change when we win power. Bristol's Labour MP, Tony Benn, fought hard to remove the colour bar from Bristol's buses and Harold Wilson has steadfastly shown his support. And change did come. Our leadership have taken note of the discrimination that immigrants face, not only those from the Caribbean, but the Indian subcontinent too. These matters will be addressed by the passing of new laws when Labour are in government. Meanwhile, we local party councillors promise to help you to our utmost if you're facing injustice."

It was a reassuring final address to the room and most of the audience applauded Harry warmly. It was another example, if one was needed, of Harry the accomplished politician. He was always prepared to take on a difficult topic or audience, even at the risk of damaging his own popularity or reputation. When Connie listened to him speak, she didn't regard him as a political chancer. He was genuine and his words were spoken with sincerity.

When the meeting ended, the majority of the audience remained behind. Young men had started piling up the chairs, removing some to a storeroom, whilst relocating others to the sides of the hall. On the front of the stage were placed a record player and two huge, home-made speakers, whilst boxes of records were put down on a nearby table. In the meantime, Tom and Connie had been joined by Harry, who was talking to Abel, a small, smartly dressed Jamaican. He was balding and had a small moustache. He was wearing a suit underneath which was a colourful waistcoat, shirt and tie. Introduced by Harry, he smiled generously at Connie.

"Abel is a local business owner Connie. He helped to set up tonight's meeting."

Connie held out her hand to Abel. He took it carefully and shook it warmly. Whilst Tom and Harry moved off to talk to other local leaders, Connie remained talking to Abel.

"What kind of business do you have Abel?" asked Connie.

"I've got a shop on Princess Road. I sell everything and try and get food from Jamaica you know. And records."

"Records?"

"Yes. Ska darling."

"What's that?" asked Connie, never having heard of the genre before.

"Real, good dance music you can let yourself go to. Forget your troubles. The cold, the rain. Be back in the sunshine in Kingston."

Abel smiled. Connie looked confused.

"Stay around Connie, then you can hear some."

"Oh?"

"Yes."

Abel pointed towards the stage where the sound system had been set up.

"We arranged a dance to get some young people in. There aren't too many places that young men can go. Pubs and working men's clubs don't make us welcome. We have to entertain ourselves."

"Yes, I've heard of the shebeens."

"Yes, darling. People's houses. The sound men set up and play music all night long."

Connie had heard of these house parties. Many young, white Mancunians went to them too. Like Connie, they could understand that new arrivals from the Caribbean had brought a new culture to the city and they were willing to experience it, whether it be food, clothing, art or music. Connie hoped that through cultural exchange, prejudice could eventually be defeated. Common enjoyment, could bring mutual respect.

At that moment, Harry and Tom returned.

"I've got to leave now Abel. I have to get to another meeting. We'll keep in touch," said Harry.

"Yes, sure," replied Abel.

Saying farewell to Tom and Connie, Harry departed. Tom looked at Connie, wondering what she wanted to do.

"Abel has invited us to stay for the music and dancing. I'm keen, are you Tom?"

"Yes, Connie. I'm not a very good dancer though."

"That's no matter," said Abel.

Tom hoped it wasn't. He didn't want to make a fool of himself in front of Connie, but if she wanted to stay and dance, he didn't want to deny her the pleasure.

"We've got food and drink at the back of the hall if you want it," said Abel.

"No, I just want to dance," said Connie.

The sound man in place, the first record hit the turntable and the music erupted through the speakers. So, this was Ska. A thumping bass and drums, an offbeat rhythm that just forced you to dance and what seemed like a clipped guitar, accompanied by upbeat vocals. Without realising, Connie was moving to the music. She'd always loved dancing, her supple limbs, swaying hips and innate sense of timing and rhythm, had made her the envy of many of her friends. Watching her, Abel began to dance himself.

"Come on Connie," he said, invitingly. "Let's get on the dance floor."

The two of them moved out to the centre of the hall to join the scores of dancers already there. Surprised by Abel and Connie's quick departure, Tom stood back. He was out of his comfort zone and somewhat appreciative that Abel had stepped in and saved him from potential embarrassment. Watching the two of them move, he could see that Abel was an accomplished dancer. Any woman would enjoy a turn on the dance floor with him. Tom's main focus though was on Connie. She had danced at the 'Oasis' but there the crowd had been packed and there had been little chance for Connie to express herself as freely as she could here. Now, he was absolutely mesmerised by her. The way her body swayed, the accentuation of her figure, her movements seamless. He'd never experienced a scene so sexually charged. There was something earthy, primordial about her, that stimulated an almost irresistible desire to make love to her.

Connie was certainly enjoying herself. Once on the dance floor, she had become captivated by the music. Dancing through a succession of records, Abel finally found himself unable to keep up with her and suggested that they take a break. Connie nodded her agreement and the two of them made their way back over to Tom.

"Phew Connie!" said Abel. "You can't half dance girl."

"You're pretty good yourself," replied Connie.

I need a drink Connie. Do you want one? asked Abel.

"Yes, please."

"A Coke all right?"

"That's great."

"What about you Tom?" asked Abel.

"It's okay, I'm fine."

Abel went off to get the Cokes. As this wasn't a house party, no alcohol was available. Connie looked at Tom.

"Why didn't you come and dance Tom?"

"Oh, it's all right. I enjoyed watching you two."

"You don't have to be brilliant. No one's judging you."

"I know."

"Just give it a go," said Connie, reassuringly.

"You never mentioned that you were so keen on dancing Connie."

"Well, I don't go very often now. I went with my friends all the time when I was younger. We used to enter the jiving competitions at the Ritz."

"Did you win?"

"Yes, sometimes."

Returning, Abel gave Connie her drink.

"Well, how do you like Ska Connie?"

"It's great Abel. Perfect to dance to."

"Yes, lots of rhythm."

Abel turned to Tom.

"You need to get out there yourself. Enjoy the music, dance."

"Yes Tom," said Connie, in agreement.

"I've already told him Abel, that no one cares how good he is. Everyone's here to enjoy themselves."

"That's right Connie," replied Abel.

Although he was still reluctant, once Abel and Connie had finished their drinks, Tom knew that he'd have to go out on to the dance floor.

"You two go," said Abel. "You can teach Tom a few moves Connie."

As the two of them moved slowly towards the centre of the room, Connie could see the look of trepidation on her partner's face. She smiled and tried to lighten Tom's mood.

"I'm not leading you to your execution Tom!"

Her playful words relaxed Tom slightly, but as the next song started and Connie began to move, he was finding it hard to concentrate. At the side of the room, he had been able to savour her performance from afar, unchecked by any fear of embarrassment that she would be aware of how intensely her dancing was affecting him. Now, she was right in front of him and he was having to work hard to rein in his emotions. That intensity of focus meant that Tom could hardly move at all.

"Come on Tom. Try," said Connie, encouragingly.

Fearing that he was spoiling her enjoyment, Tom forced himself to begin dancing. But he was stiff and mechanical. His movements didn't flow, they stuttered along like a misfiring engine. The harder he tried, the more exaggerated and ridiculous his movements appeared. Watching Connie dance with Abel had been a pleasure; trying to dance with her himself, was pure torture.

Connie sensed Tom's despair. She knew that he wanted her to enjoy the dance and was concerned that his ineptitude was ruining her experience. She stopped dancing and put her hand softly on his arm, the music slowly fading at the end of the song.

"It's okay Tom. You're doing fine. Come on, try and follow me."

When the music once more burst into life, Connie moved slower, her arms, legs and body more restrained. Tom tried hard to follow her example, encouraged by her smile, a nod of the head and mouthed words of encouragement under the noise of the throbbing music. Connie despaired of Tom ever becoming a competent dancer, but she never gave him even a hint of criticism. And Tom loved her all the more for it. She understood that he was out of his depth, but her kindness towards him was there as ever. Tonight, he had seen yet another side of Connie and it had excited him. He knew that it would be very hard for him to focus on anything but the picture of her dancing, so deeply etched into his mind, for many days to come. He was hopelessly and desperately in love with her.

Chapter 22

Returning home from work the following day, Connie had settled down to look through some paperwork that Tom had given her, regarding his work for Joyce and Hitchcock. Carefully, she had read each document in turn, underlining key passages and making notes in the margins. On a separate piece of paper, she was noting down comments for Tom. Connie was eager to continue her input, feeling somewhat responsible for their new client, bearing in mind she had been instrumental in securing their business. Glancing up at the clock, she noticed that it was almost eight fifteen. Presently, a knock came to the back door. It took Connie by surprise. If it was one of the neighbours, they would have shouted through to her, but there was silence. Connie knew it must be someone else. But who could be visiting her at this time? Getting out of her chair, Connie moved towards the back door. Opening it, she was speechless, unable to move as she stared at the figure in front of her.

"You look like you've seen a ghost," said the visitor.

Connie couldn't reply. She simply stared back, her face displaying shock and disbelief.

"Well, aren't you going to let your mother in?"

Connie blinked. It really was her mother and after all this time.

"Mam, of course. Come in."

Connie stood to the side, allowing Doris to enter the kitchen before closing the door behind her. Then she turned to her mam and smiled, before throwing her arms around her and hugging her tightly, as if she was determined not to let go. The two women stood, tears in their eyes, their embrace making them aware of the long years of separation. Finally, Doris eased herself from her daughter's arms. She stood back and looked closely at Connie.

"Why, look at you. What a beautiful young woman you are," said Doris, her voice full of admiration.

Connie found herself falling back on her responsibilities as a host. It was perhaps a way of getting her emotions in check.

"Are you warm enough Mam? It's cold out there tonight. I can turn the gas fire up if you like."

"No, I'm fine Connie."

"Well, you must want a brew."

"Yes, that'd be lovely."

"I've got some biscuits. Chocolate digestives."

Connie went over to the cupboard and brought out the biscuit tin. She moved over to the table and realised it was covered with her work.

"Can you take these please Mam?"

Connie handed the biscuit tin to Doris and busily set about stacking up the paper work at the far end of the table.

"Well, you look busy love," observed Doris.

"Yes. It's some work that I've brought home."

"Oh. Are you still with John Francis?"

"No, Mam. I've got a new job now. I'll tell you all about it once I've got the kettle on."

Connie got out a tablecloth and covered the top of the table. She put a large place mat in the centre for the biscuits and two smaller ones by their seats for the mugs.

"Sit down, Mam and get yourself a biscuit."

Doris sat down.

Connie went over to the sink to fill the kettle and put it on the stove. Getting the teapot and mugs ready, she put them on a tray on top of the draining board.

"You said you've got a new job Connie."

"Yes, Mam. It's at a firm called Greenings in Piccadilly. They're much larger than John Francis and I'm one of their senior accountants."

Doris couldn't hide her satisfaction. A huge smile spread across her face.

"I knew you'd do it Connie. Nothing could ever hold you back."

"But it's a lot more work, Mam."

"But you enjoy it, don't you?"

"Oh, yes. I'm getting the chance to work at a level that I feared I never would."

"Your dad would be so proud of you Connie. I wish he was here to see it."

"Yes, Mam. I know."

The kettle whistled. Connie filled the pot, added the tea and brought it over on the tray with the mugs, milk and sugar, to the table. After a suitable amount of time, to ensure a decent brew, the tea was poured out.

So far, the conversation between mother and daughter had been measured and polite. Necessarily, this was the way that the two women had to progress, given the length of time since they had last spoken. In particular, Connie had concerns about her mam's welfare but was determined not to raise them until later, not wanting to spark a similar disagreement to that which had caused the parting of the ways eight years ago. Necessarily therefore, Connie talked about her job, the people she worked with and her work with the local Labour Party.

"Your dad would be pleased to know that you're a good socialist Connie."

"Well, I think it's more that I want to try and help people, rather than seeing myself as a true socialist. I've had a few disagreements with some of the local Labour leaders already."

Doris smiled. Her daughter's words reflected the fiercely independent and strong-willed girl that she'd known in the past.

"There's nothing wrong with that Connie. There were always big arguments in the Party when me and your dad were involved in the 'Thirties.'"

"Yes, I suppose so," replied Connie.

Looking around the kitchen, Doris was impressed.

"You've got it nice Connie. I like it."

"Do you want to have a look at the rest of the house?"

"That'd be nice," replied Doris.

"We'll go upstairs first," said Connie, eager for her mam to see how the house had changed in her absence.

Connie led Doris to the door to the stairwell and the two of them went through and climbed the steep stairs. Having looked at the bedrooms, Connie led her mam back downstairs and then opened the door to the front room. She had saved her favourite room, with its beautiful furniture, until last. Doris followed her in and looked around, impressed by the changes that Connie had made.

"Oh! It's beautiful Connie. And the furniture!"

Connie glowed with pride. Her mam's approval pleasing her more than she could ever have imagined.

"You must be doing very well Connie, to have all these wonderful things. Haven't you wanted to move and rent somewhere else? I was surprised when I asked around and found out that you were still living here."

"I'm buying the house, Mam."

"Buying it?"

Doris was clearly surprised, but after Connie had explained her agreement with the landlord, she nodded her approval.

"Yes, Connie. You've used your head, love."

Returning to the kitchen, they sat down. Connie offered to make another tea and busied herself at the kitchen sink, washing and drying the mugs. Stood there, she took a close look at her mam. Doris looked older than she remembered. But that was to be expected. Her brown hair was showing signs of grey and around her eyes there was evidence of wrinkles, but she seemed in good health. She was also in good spirits and she had come to the house without any evidence that she had been drinking.

Connie realised that so far, she had told her mam almost everything about her own life and work. Doris however, had told her nothing about her own situation and whether she was still living with Frank. Connie was also wondering why her mam had suddenly turned up, when she hadn't been in touch for so long. Connie decided that she needed to find an opportunity to try and get some answers. It came when Doris asked her if there were any special men in her life.

"I wasn't sure if I would find you living with someone. Married. Maybe with a family Connie."

"No. Not yet."

"A pretty young woman like you. I'm sure you've got lots of men running after you."

Connie smiled, but said nothing.

"I won't think that you're being big-headed if you tell me that you have," continued Doris, trying to elicit a response.

"Well, there's a couple of men at work I get on with, but whether it will ever come to anything, I don't know."

"Who are they?"

"Well, there's Tom, but I can't ever see me going out with him, whereas with Ralph," she paused, thinking carefully about what to say. "Ralph, who I find quite attractive. Nice looking, but kind too."

"Oh!" replied Doris, clearly intrigued. "Tell me more."

"Well, he's the boss's nephew, but that's of no concern to me. He's witty and good company. I've been told that I need to watch out for him, that he's a bit of a Casanova. I can't say that I've seen any evidence of it. He's never tried it on with me."

"Hmm. You have to watch out for the bosses. They think they can take liberties with the girls in the office."

Connie smiled.

"You're not really the best person to give me advice on my love life, are you Mam?"

Connie's question was posed without any hint of acrimony and Doris took it with good humour.

"No, you're not far wrong there Connie," she replied, then added more seriously, "but I don't want you to make the same mistakes that I have."

The two women paused to consider Doris's words. Connie realised it was now time to find out about her situation.

"Are you living with anyone Mam?"

"Yes," replied Doris. "I'm still with Frank."

Connie's heart sank. A look of disappointment crossed her face which didn't go unnoticed by Doris, who immediately sprang to her boyfriend's defence.

"He's changed Connie. We get on like Darby and Joan. You'd never know him now if you met him."

Her words were delivered in a voice that lacked conviction. It was almost as if she was pleading with Connie to believe her.

"Oh," said Connie, quietly.

"Yes, the reason I've come here tonight, is that we've moved into a house on Polygon Avenue. I'm not far away now. Near enough to come and see you."

"Is Frank okay with you being here?"

"Of course, love."

"So, he knows that you've come to see me?"

"Yes."

"Oh," said Connie. She wasn't convinced that Doris was telling the truth, but tried hard to disguise her misgivings.

"You'll come again, won't you Mam?"

"Yes, of course Connie. It's been lovely to see you. I'm so proud of you."

Doris's top lip began to quiver and her eyes moistened. Connie hoped that it was caused by the emotion of seeing her only child after so many years, rather than the darker thought that Frank didn't know or approve of her visit and it may be that the two women wouldn't see each other again. Connie remained strong, holding her emotions in check. Turning to more simple matters, she made her mam an offer.

"I'm having Christmas dinner with a friend. You're very welcome to join us, Mam."

"I'd love to Connie, but I've already arranged it for me and Frank."

"Oh, never mind."

Suddenly, Connie felt relieved. Perhaps Doris had thought that she was inviting Frank too, which she certainly wasn't. A potential fallout had therefore been avoided.

"I'd best be going," said Doris. "I want to be home for when Frank gets back."

"Yes, of course," said Connie.

The two of them kissed and embraced before Connie opened the back door.

"You're welcome any time Mam. I'm in most nights except Thursdays. I've a lot of work that I have to do at home."

"Well, it's only just around the corner Connie. There's no harm done if I turn up and you're not in."

As Doris disappeared through the back gate, Connie closed the door and sat down at the table. Her mam's visit had come out of the blue. With the passage of time, Connie had accepted that there was little possibility that Doris would come back into her life. Now, her mam had returned. Yet Connie was experienced enough to understand that life doesn't always have a happy ending. She really wanted a close relationship with her mam, but knew that the odds of that happening with Frank on the scene, weren't good. Connie accepted that she would have to prepare herself for disappointment. For the moment however, she would appreciate the fact that she was back in contact with Doris again.

Chapter 23

Connie didn't have long to wait before she became aware of the nature of Doris and Frank's relationship. It was the Friday before Christmas and Connie had gone to bed early, following a succession of late nights. She slept in the front bedroom, which overlooked her small front garden and the road and pavement beyond. Suddenly, she woke up with a start, a cacophony of sound disturbing her slumber. Not fully awake, Connie sat up in bed, blinking her eyes in an attempt to see through the gloom, only a faint chink of light from a nearby street lamp penetrating through a tiny gap in the curtains. The noise continued. She realised that someone was pounding on her front door. Connie was shocked rather than afraid. She wondered what it could be and then she heard a woman's voice shrieking out in a cry for help.

"Connie! Connie! Please! Let me in!"

Connie threw back the sheets and dived out of bed. She quickly put on her dressing gown and moved across to the window. Drawing the curtains, she peered down into the front garden and saw a dimly lit figure waving her arms at her. From the upturned face, she realised that it was her mam. Without a second thought, Connie raced out of the room and down the steep stairs, almost falling in her haste to get to Doris. Through into the front room, she opened the door.

"Thank God. Thank God. Oh Connie, help me!"

Emotionally and physically spent, Doris fell, a limp and listless figure, into her daughter's arms.

"Come in Mam. Let's get inside and shut the door."

Doris was hyperventilating. There was no point in Connie trying to ask her any questions, as she was incapable of answering them. Connie had to calm her down and keep her warm. After all, it was December and the front room was cold.

"Come on Mam, sit down," said Connie, calmly.

Connie knew how important it was that she held her own feelings in check and didn't allow herself to get upset over her mam's condition. Doris needed reassurance and her daughter had to be strong. Leading her mam over to the settee, Connie sat her down. She fetched an outdoor coat and placed it around her mam's shoulders. Then she lit the gas fire.

"It'll soon be nice and warm Mam."

Calmer, Doris's breathing was starting to settle down. Connie sat on the settee beside her and took hold of her hand, stroking it gently. Finally, she felt her mam's fingers tighten around her own. It was the first response that Connie had received from her. It was getting warmer now. That heavy type of heat, unique to a gas fire, that made one feel content and drowsy.

"I'll go and make us a nice cup of tea," said Connie, getting up.

"No, don't leave me," said Doris, weakly. "I'll come with you."

Doris stood up uncertainly, Connie holding on to her to make sure that she didn't fall. It was clear that she had been through a traumatic experience and she was just beginning to understand its true horror.

"I'm okay love," said Doris. "I can make it. Don't worry."

The two women walked through to the kitchen. Doris sat on the settee opposite the fireplace, whilst Connie lit the gas fire. Connie now remembered hearing that keeping someone warm would help stop them from going into shock. Setting about making the tea, Connie remained quiet. Her mam needed time. She would have to wait longer to find out what had been going on, but looking at her closely, there were certainly clues as to what it could be. On the right side of Doris's face was a huge red mark and there were signs of bruising beginning to appear. It seemed likely that she had either fallen down or had been struck a blow. Although Doris smelt faintly of alcohol, there were no signs that she was under the influence. Naturally, Connie began to think that it was Frank who was responsible.

Having finished making the drinks, Connie brought them over to the settee. The two women sat side by side, Doris staring down into her mug, trying to make sense of what had happened to her.

"We were in the 'Shakespeare'," said Doris, eventually.

"Yes," replied Connie, inviting her to continue.

"There was this man. He was sat with his friends across the room from us. He looked over a couple of times. Then, when I went to the toilet, I passed his table and he said hello and smiled at me. That was it."

Doris paused. She was thinking deeply. Wondering whether anything else had happened. Whether she'd given him any encouragement at all. She felt sure that she hadn't. Slowly, she continued.

"I passed him again on the way back and purposely avoided looking at him. That was it. Nothing else."

"And?" asked Connie, quietly.

"Nothing at first. It was early on. Everything seemed fine. We had some more drinks and were talking to our friends and then I noticed Frank staring."

"Go on," said Connie.

"He suddenly jumped up. Knocked all the drinks over. Glasses on the floor. He swore at me. Hit me. Called me a prostitute. Threw me on the floor and then charged across the room to get the man who'd spoken to me. Everyone scattered. The two of them were at it. Eventually the landlord and some of the regulars dived in and pulled them apart. They had to jump on Frank and pin him down and he started screaming and shouting that he was going to get me. The landlord told me to go, get away from him. I got out and started walking up to the corner of Syndall Street. Then I heard him shouting after me. He'd got away from them. I ran and ran. I just thought that if I could get to you. If I could just keep away from him…"

Doris had related the events in a voice devoid of any emotion. It was as if she was purposely trying to disconnect herself from the events that had happened.

"You can stay here Mam. You don't have to go back. There's always room for you, whenever you want."

Connie's caring words finally penetrated her mam's defences. They were in stark contrast to the brutish violence and selfish behaviour of her partner. Slowly, the tears trickled down Doris's cheeks and she sobbed quietly. Connie put her arm around her shoulders and gave her a gentle hug.

"You're so kind Connie. I'm so sorry I've brought my troubles to your door."

"Don't be daft Mam."

"No. It's not fair. I shouldn't have. I just didn't know where else I could go. It all happened so fast."

"I know," replied Connie, softly.

With Doris seemingly over the worst of her experience, Connie was considering just how she was going to help her. She had never understood how her mam could possibly put up with Frank. Her loyalty to him made no sense. Just then, came a huge crash from the front room and the sound of breaking glass.

"Oh God, please no. It's Frank, he's found me!" exclaimed Doris.

Leaping to her feet, Connie told her mam to stay put whilst she moved quickly into the front room. Turning on the light, she could see her 'nets' peeping out between the heavy curtains she had covering her front windows. She went over to the radiogram, reaching behind it. She pulled the curtains slightly apart and looked behind them. She could see a piece of broken paving stone, together with shards of broken glass. Restrained by the heavy fabric of the curtains, the furniture had escaped damage.

Connie couldn't hear anything, which suggested that the perpetrator had gone. She knew that she would have to go out and take a look. She went back to the kitchen to get her shoes and to fetch her broom from the top of the cellar steps. If there was someone out there, she needed a weapon and it was the first thing that came to mind. Going back to the front room, she now heard a man's voice coming from outside. It was loud, but faltering and it was obvious that the speaker was drunk.

"Get her out… Go on, get her out… She's a liar… a cheat and a liar…"

The sound of the voice had carried through to the kitchen. Doris, recognising it, rushed straight into the front room.

"Go away Frank. Go away!"

"No Mam!" said Connie, firmly. "Get back in the kitchen!"

"But you don't know what he's like Connie. Leave him to me."

"Do you think I'm scared of the likes of him!"

Connie spoke with real venom. She was furious. How dare he come to her home and think that he could intimidate her. She knew no fear, just anger and she was determined that she would go out and drive him away. Approaching the front door, she grabbed hold of the catch. Doris, who'd remained in the front room, grabbed hold of her arm.

"No, Connie. Please. Stay here," pleaded Doris.

"No. There's only one way to deal with a bully."

Removing Doris's hand from her arm, Connie opened the door and strode out into the garden, her broom at the ready. But Frank wasn't there. She moved through the gate and looking across the road, she saw him lying on the floor. Standing above him were Johnny and Bob, with other neighbours stood to the side. It was clear that her two young admirers had taken matters into their own hands and if they hadn't, there were plenty of others waiting to do so. In fact, as Connie looked up and down Howard Avenue, she could see that most of the houses had their front bedroom or front room lights on. If people weren't out on the pavement, then they were stood staring out of their bedroom windows. The commotion caused by Frank had woken the whole street and Connie's friends and neighbours were quick to come to her aid. Although ready to confront Frank herself, she hadn't needed to. Looking back across the road, she saw Frank get back to his feet and then swing his arm wildly at Bob, who responded by punching him squarely on the jaw and knocking him straight back down.

Connie quickly ran across the road. She stared at Frank on the ground. She could see the familiar scar on the side of his face, the legacy of a fight in his youth. He seemed far older than when she had seen him last. His hair was almost gone and his face was drawn. She could see that his nose was broken, his lip split and there was blood all over him.

"No more. He's had enough Bob. Don't hit him again. I don't want you getting into any trouble."

"He deserves it Connie," said Johnny. "Don't feel sorry for him."

"I don't. I just don't want the police arresting you. They'll be here any minute. You need to get off."

"Yes, that's right lads," said a voice from behind.

Connie turned around to see the figure of Eddie Taylor.

"The police are on their way," continued Eddie. "Clear off. Make yourselves scarce."

Johnny and Bob didn't move. They still seemed disinclined to take the advice.

"Please lads," said Connie. "I'm really grateful for your help, but I'd never forgive myself if you got into trouble because of me."

"Oh, it'd be worth it Connie," said Bob, cheekily. "Wouldn't it, Johnny?"

Embarrassed, Johnny pretended not to hear his comment.

"Come on Bob. Connie's right," said Johnny. "Let's go."

"Okay then," replied Bob. "It's been a good night. Some lovely girls at the 'Three Coins' and a bit of boxing to round off the evening!"

Connie shook her head. Was anything in life serious for Bob? She didn't think so, but she was certainly grateful for the help that he, Johnny and all her neighbours had given her that evening.

With the lads departing, a couple of men moved in to stand guard over Frank. He was a spent force now and lay curled up on the floor, hands clasped to his head, occasionally letting out a groan. But he received no sympathy. Drunk or not, throwing a paving slab through a young woman's window had put him beyond the pale. Eddie's wife, Edna, joined Connie and her husband.

"Connie love. You get inside. You can't see the broken window behind your hedge. The police won't notice it. We'll just tell them that this idiot was shouting and bawling and started on a couple of other men he was with. He's ended up getting battered and the others have cleared off. You don't want the coppers coming to you."

"But he did it because my mam's with me. He's her boyfriend. He'll say that."

"He's drunk love. I don't think he's got any idea now where he is, or why he's here. Anyway, the coppers will just think he's rambling on."

"Oh, I don't know," said Connie, uncertainly.

"Connie love, you can't afford it. How do you think it'll go down at your office, if they hear about this? You've worked hard for what you've got. Don't risk it all now."

Eddie, Edna and all the neighbours respected Connie. They were amazed at what she'd achieved and loved the fact that she stayed around, proud to be part of their community. They regarded Connie's success as if it were their own. As such, Edna was determined to protect her neighbour's reputation.

"Okay," said Connie, accepting the logic of Edna's advice. "But if the police start to get awkward, you must tell them to come and see me."

"Of course," said Edna, knowing full well that she had no intention of doing so.

Returning home, Connie saw Doris peering out from behind the front door. Connie was pleased that she hadn't ventured outside. She had been worried that if her mam had seen the state of Frank, then she would have felt sorry for him. She wouldn't have stayed the night to get the respite that she so clearly needed. Purposely, Connie withheld her knowledge of Frank's injuries. Coming into the house, she closed the door behind her.

"Nothing to worry about, Mam. Frank's gone."

"What about the window Connie?" asked Doris.

"It'll be all right. I'll get a glazier tomorrow. No one would risk trying to get through that. It's too dangerous. The curtains are thick, they'll keep the drafts out. Anyway, it's time you were getting to bed. You need some rest. You can come in the front bedroom with me. The bed in the back hasn't been aired. It'll be too cold and probably feel damp."

"Thanks love," said Doris. "Aren't I lucky to have you for a daughter?"

"Come on," said Connie. "Let's go up."

Outside, the police arrived, ready to pick up Frank. Seeing his injuries, they immediately called for an ambulance. True to their word, Eddie, Edna and those neighbours who'd remained to keep an eye on Frank, successfully feigned ignorance over what had transpired that evening. For the police, it was a scene that was all too familiar after the pubs closed on Friday and Saturday nights. Fights and injuries were an annoying drain on their time and resources. It simply wasn't worth the effort to delve too deeply into what had happened. Frank was clearly drunk and although injured, his wounds were certainly not life-threatening. There were other calls to attend and as far as the police were concerned, the incident was over.

Chapter 24

Next morning, Connie woke up early as she always did. She glanced at the bedside cabinet and towards the clock which was indicating that it was six twenty. Realising that her mam was asleep beside her, Connie slipped carefully out from under the covers. Putting on her slippers and dressing gown, she collected her clothes ready to get washed and dressed downstairs. Just as she was about to open the bedroom door, Connie remembered to check that she hadn't set her alarm clock. Now, she felt confident that her mam would continue to rest undisturbed, something that would benefit her after the trauma of the previous evening.

Down in the kitchen, Connie switched the transistor radio on. She enjoyed the background music but made sure that the volume was low. She then set about filling a large plastic bowl with hot water from the Ascot boiler over the sink. Placing the bowl on a mat to cover the floor underneath her, she proceeded to have a stripped wash. Had there been no uncertainty over the future of the houses on Howard Avenue, Connie would have gone ahead and had an inside bathroom and toilet fitted into the attic. She knew of houses in Ardwick where this conversion had been carried out. It certainly wasn't a difficult job, but she had no intention of spending money that may not be refunded to her, if the Corporation went ahead with their plans for compulsory purchase. However, given that she'd lived all her life without the luxury of a bathroom, she felt sure that she could continue doing so for a little bit longer.

Making herself a brew, Connie sat at the kitchen table and started to read yesterday's 'Evening News.' Given her heavy commitments at work, she felt that she was getting a little out of touch with local developments and so appreciated the opportunity to catch up. When she'd almost completed working her way through the paper, she heard the heavy and uncertain tread of her mam coming down the stairs. Connie glanced at the clock. It was almost nine. Getting up from the table, Connie went straight over to the cooker, picked up the kettle, filled it with water and put it on to boil. She looked around to see Doris emerge through the door from the stairwell.

"Hello sleepyhead," said Connie, smiling.

Doris moved over towards Connie. She put her arms around her, squeezing and kissing her. Stepping back, Connie noticed that the bruising had now come out around her mam's right eye and cheekbone. It was dark purple.

"Oh Mam! Your face. You need to get it looked at."

Doris had already felt the soreness underneath her eye and her face had felt tender when she had touched it. Consequently, she had examined it in the large swivel mirror on the top of the dressing table in the front bedroom. She couldn't hide from the fact that the damage had been inflicted upon her by Frank. Yet in front of her daughter, she was determined to treat her injury with an air of nonchalance. Moving towards the mirror on the fire breast wall, she studied herself as if for the first time.

"Oh, yes. It does look bad, doesn't it?"

"You need to go to Casualty, Mam. We can have some tea and toast, then you can get washed and we'll get off to the MRI."

"No, Connie. I'm all right. There's no need for that."

"But you might have a broken cheek bone or eye socket. A doctor needs to have a look at it."

Doris was adamant. She wouldn't go.

"I hate going to Casualty Connie. It's a waste of time. You're there for ages and you end up being fine in any case."

Connie shook her head. She knew that she couldn't compel Doris to go. Her mam made her own decisions and for the last eight years, the significant one for Connie, was that she hadn't kept in contact with her or let her know where she was. Connie knew that Doris was hardly likely to do what she wanted now.

"Okay, Mam," said Connie, with a sigh. "But promise me that you'll go if it doesn't get better. If it keeps hurting, then there could be something wrong."

"Yes, of course I will love," replied Doris, pleased that her daughter wasn't going to pursue the matter any further.

Connie suspected that the real reason her mam didn't want to go to Casualty, was because she would have to face some difficult questions about how she had sustained her injuries. She was probably worried too, that if Connie went with her, she would tell them about Frank and perhaps the police would be called. And that thought led Connie to the realisation that even though Doris wouldn't want her to broach the subject, she needed to get clarification of her mam's future plans and how much Frank would be a part of them. Connie understood that she couldn't accept her mother's abusive relationship; stand idly by whilst able to see what Frank was doing to her. Connie's pleas to her mam to leave him, had led to the latter's disappearance eight years ago. Much as Connie wanted Doris back in her life, with Frank still around, it was too big a price to pay.

"Mam, we have to talk. Sit down and I'll finish the tea."

Doris was feeling uncomfortable, but she did as her daughter asked. Connie finished making the toast. She buttered it and handed it on a plate to her mam, then placed some jam and marmalade on the table.

"I'm not really hungry," said Doris, weakly.

"You need something Mam."

"Okay, love."

Reluctantly, Doris opened the marmalade, inserted a knife into the jar and extracted enough of the contents to spread it on a slice of toast. It was obvious that she was only doing it for Connie's benefit. Placing the knife by the side of her plate, she tentatively took the piece of toast, then winced as she tried to chew it.

"Hmm," said Connie. "It's troubling you, isn't it? Moving your mouth."

"No," replied Doris. "I don't normally eat breakfast. The toast just got stuck."

Connie said no more. Doris was determined to make out that her face wasn't causing her any pain.

"Mam?"

"Yes, love."

"What Frank did last night. You know it was wrong. He hasn't changed, has he? It's still the same as it was when you first met him."

"No. No love, it isn't," replied Doris. "It wasn't his fault."

"Wasn't his fault!"

Connie could feel herself becoming angry. She hated Frank and just couldn't understand how her mam could possibly defend him. But she fought hard to keep her emotions in check. If she didn't, there was no chance of them having a calm and constructive conversation. Without that, she had little chance of getting Doris to reconsider her loyalty to Frank.

"Last night, you told me that Frank 'lost it' because he thought that you were encouraging another man in the pub. That didn't give him the right to hit you Mam," continued Connie.

"I've been thinking Connie. I shouldn't have spoken to the man. I know how upset Frank gets. I should have thought about that."

Connie took a deep breath. She felt the urge to yell at her mam, but looking at her bruised and battered face, she immediately felt guilty. She also knew that Doris would retreat into silence if she didn't choose her words carefully. As calmly as possible, Connie replied.

"You said Mam, that the guy simply said hello when you passed his table; that you didn't have a conversation."

"Well, yes. But he was looking at me too. He made Frank jealous."

"Okay Mam," said Connie. "But that wasn't your fault. Men look at women all the time. It's nice to know that men find you attractive. Looking doesn't mean that they're trying to get you into bed. And even if a man is thinking that, you're giving them no encouragement. And if you did, Frank still has no right to lift a finger against you, or use violence against any man who wants to speak to you. Frank is jealous and dangerous. You aren't safe with him."

"No, Connie. He's changed. I've told you. He's nothing like he was. He's just been through a bad time. He was laid off and it's hurt his pride. He just had too much to drink. It was me. I shouldn't have looked at the man."

"You could hardly avoid it when you had to pass his table."

"No, Connie. I shouldn't have."

"Mam, if you're saying that it's just the drink, you know that Frank's not going to stop going to the pub. In that case, the beatings are only going to continue."

"No. Frank is getting better. It was a 'one-off.' He'll be distraught now, wondering what he's done to me. He won't do it again."

Connie could see that she was getting nowhere. For whatever reason, her mam was determined that she would stay loyal to Frank. Understanding that her considered approach towards Doris had no chance of success, she decided to say exactly what was on her mind.

"I want you to come back here Mam. You can live with me. You'll be safe. It's your home as much as it's mine. You don't owe Frank anything."

"No, I don't want to Connie."

"But why Frank? Do you think that you can't get anyone else? Of course, you can find another man. One who's kind and gentle. You're still attractive. Leave Frank. Come here and if you meet the right man, then you can get married and live together."

"I don't want to be on my own Connie."

"But you won't be on your own Mam. You'll be here with me."

"I need a man, Connie."

"But you don't need him!"

"I love him."

"I don't believe that. How can you? He's nothing like my father was."

"How do you know Connie? You were far too young."

"Because you told me Mam and so did the neighbours."

Doris was silent. She had no option but to accept Connie's words. She knew that her daughter was right. Wilf was the only true love of her life but he was a fading memory and Frank was the man she'd chosen to be with now.

"Do you think that the jealousy and aggression he shows towards other men, means that he's in love with you? You're wrong Mam. Frank's pure evil."

"No. He's not. I've told you. He has changed. He isn't like he was," insisted Doris.

The conversation had reached its natural conclusion. Any further words that Connie could have said, would be simply redundant. She knew it and she suspected that she was about to lose her mother again too. It hurt, but just as when she was eighteen, Connie couldn't accept Doris's abusive relationship with Frank. She suspected that it wouldn't be long before her mam was on the move once more and doubted whether she would keep in touch. Connie wanted so much to have her mam in her life, but given Doris's insistence that Connie accept her relationship with Frank, she knew that it couldn't happen. Such an acceptance would make her complicit in the abuse that Frank gave to her mother. Connie would never place herself in such a situation.

Just before noon, Doris bade Connie farewell, explaining that she would have to get back to see Frank.

"Remember Mam," said Connie, as the two women embraced at the back door. "You can move in with me anytime you want. And you know that I work at Greenings and if you ever need my help, you mustn't hesitate to contact me there."

As the two women separated, both were finding it hard to keep their tears in check. Doris reached out for her daughter's hand and gripped it firmly.

"I'm so proud of you Connie. For what you've achieved and how kind you are to me. I know I've not been a great mother, but please don't be angry with me for going back to Frank."

"I could never be angry with you, Mam. Frustrated, because I love you, but never angry."

Under the circumstances, it was the kindest parting of the ways that mother and daughter could have had. Yet as Doris disappeared out of the backyard and into the alley, Connie believed that it would be a very long time before she would see her mam again.

Chapter 25

Christmas morning had arrived. Connie had bought some Advocaat, as Kath had requested, some fruit, nuts, chocolate and crackers to take round to her friend. She had also bought a couple of cardigans, useful gifts for this time of year. Fortunately, the weather was mild and when she carried her bags, full of 'goodies,' up Syndall Street and down Apsley Grove, there wasn't a hint of snow or ice on the ground. Kath had told her to turn up around ten, insisting that she would take care of all the preparations for the meal.

"I don't invite you for Christmas dinner and then expect you to help me with it. No love. It just isn't done."

Connie had nodded, accepting her friend's words as final. Kath had planned to make the day a full one. She was aware of Doris's visit and was worried that Connie may be feeling isolated, on the one day of the year that was traditionally so family orientated. The two of them would be having a good time. Kath would make sure of it.

It was an enjoyable walk for Connie. Saying 'merry Christmas' to neighbours who were supervising their young children, or grandchildren, as they took their first faltering steps on their new roller skates, or balanced precariously on the bicycles they had been brought by Santa. Connie looked at the bright, smiling faces and listened to the excited squeals of laughter. She was taken back to a time when she too was so much younger and innocent of the trials and tribulations that came as an adult.

Entering the alley behind Pleasant View, Connie walked the short distance to Kath's backyard. Opening the gate, she advanced to the back step and knocked on the door.

"It's only me Kath," she said, loudly.

"Come in love," came the reply.

Opening the door, she entered the kitchen. The smell of the turkey roasting in the oven filled the air. It was comforting and inviting. Connie could see a number of pans on top of the draining board. They contained vegetables that had been peeled and were ready to be boiled for their dinner. On the cooker she could see the Christmas pudding, wrapped in tinfoil, gently simmering in a pan. It was one that Kath had made herself and Connie was looking forward to trying it, together with the brandy custard that would accompany it.

Kath, stood by the sink, turned towards Connie. She noticed the two full bags by her side.

"What on earth have you got their love? I told you. You only needed to bring yourself and a bottle of Advocaat."

"It's nothing much. Some fruit, nuts and chocolate. Oh, and I didn't know if you had any Christmas crackers."

"Of course, I have. It wouldn't be the same without pulling a few crackers now, would it?"

"No."

"Never mind. We'll just have twice the amount," said Kath, smiling.

Connie began to empty her bags, placing the objects in the middle of the kitchen table.

"And, I've got you a present Kath. Well, two presents I suppose."

Kath watched her as she took the two cardigans, individually wrapped in green and red Christmas paper, out of the bags and placed them on the table.

"I hope you like them."

"Oh, Connie. You shouldn't have."

"Of course, I should."

It was clear from Kath's face that she was delighted to receive Connie's gifts, but she still insisted on telling her friend off.

"You shouldn't be spending money on presents for me young lady. Christmas is for kids, not adults!"

"Well, I did! So there!" replied Connie, playfully.

The two of them burst out laughing.

"Go on then, open them," said Connie, impatiently.

It was obvious to Kath, by the feel of the packages, that she had been bought items of clothing, but it didn't stop her expressing genuine pleasure when she saw the two beautiful Shetland wool cardigans that Connie had bought her; one an attractive light blue, the other a subtle, pale yellow. Trying them on, they both fitted her perfectly.

"They're very stylish Connie."

"Yes, I thought so when I saw them. I got them from 'Marks.'"

"Yes, you can't beat them for quality Connie. But still, you shouldn't have bought them," continued Kath, smiling. "Come here love. Give me a hug."

Connie threw her arms around Kath. The two embraced and then Kath stood back.

"And I've got something for you too Connie."

She walked over to the cupboard, opened it and brought out a small package.

"Here you are."

Connie took it and shook her head.

"I don't know Kath. You've just had a go at me for buying you a present!"

"Yes, I did. But then I'm older than you and we old people get to say what we want. It's a privilege that comes with age."

She smiled broadly, causing Connie to burst out laughing.

"Come on then. Open it."

Just like Connie, Kath was impatient to see her friend's reaction to her gift.

The package was tightly wrapped and with it being small, Connie found it hard to make an impression on the wrapping paper. Finally, she managed to lift a little of the Sellotape, which allowed her to rip the paper. Having removed it, she saw that it had been covering a small jewellery box. Opening the box, she saw a beautiful, gold cable chain necklace with a distinctive charm; two lovers sitting on a crescent moon.

"Oh, it's lovely Kath. It's so unusual," said Connie, stunned by the beauty of her gift.

"I thought you'd like it."

Connie nodded and smiled. Once more she threw her arms around Kath and hugged her warmly. It was one of the nicest presents that she'd ever received. It was touching that Kath had put so much thought into it.

"Hopefully, that will be you and a kind, handsome young man," said Kath, referring to the charm on the necklace.

"Yes. Perhaps so," replied Connie.

"Well, sit yourself down whilst I take a look at the turkey. I think I'll need to get the vegetables on soon. Did you want a brew?"

"No, I'm all right at the moment."

Connie sat down at the kitchen table and watched Kath open the oven door, take out the metal tray and place it by the sink. She then removed the tinfoil and put a fork into the turkey.

"It'll be another couple of hours yet, but the 'roasties' can go in now."

Picking up a basin, to the side of her, Kath drained off the water and then carefully placed the cut potatoes inside it, into the tray around the turkey. Replacing the foil, she put the tray back into the oven, closed the door, declared herself satisfied and sat down with Connie.

"Did you want a drink of Advocaat?" asked Connie.

"Yes. But only one. I want to be able to finish the dinner!"

Connie smiled. She fetched a glass from the cupboard and poured her friend a drink.

"Aren't you having one?" asked Kath.

"I'll have one later, after my dinner."

"I've got some sweet sherry if you'd rather," continued Kath.

"No, I'll be fine."

"But it doesn't feel very polite, drinking on my own."

Connie understood.

"Okay, I'll have a sherry, but just a small one. I'll get it, don't get up. Where is it?" she asked.

"On the shelf above the glasses."

"Oh. I must be blind," said Connie. "I've just been over there."

Fetching the bottle of 'Harveys Bristol Cream', Connie opened it and poured herself a small amount. The taste was rich, thick and heavy, although sweet and Connie was able to take a small sip, enough to persuade Kath that she wasn't drinking alone.

"Drinking sherry in the morning, it makes it really seem like Christmas. Doesn't it, Kath?"

"That's right love. We wouldn't do it any other time, would we?"

"No."

Having to wait for the turkey, Kath could relax after her exertions preparing the dinner. It meant that the two friends could talk and one of their favourite topics, women's rights, was soon on the agenda. Connie continued to be fascinated by the fact that Kath had led such a rich and varied life and had been at the forefront of the struggle for women's equality, going all the way back to the Great War. She wondered how many women of her own generation would ever equal her achievements, or appreciate just how much Kath and her contemporaries had struggled to make conditions better for themselves. Most of all, Connie was impressed by Kath's wisdom and her warnings that, regardless of increasing education and life slowly being improved by technology, women in the 1960s were just as susceptible to exploitation as much as they had ever been.

"The necklace is important Connie. The charm shows true love. Dedication and commitment. A mutual respect. There can be no other type of relationship for us women."

Connie nodded her agreement and Kath continued.

"The necklace is you, Connie. You're a sensible young woman. You judge men carefully and you don't get carried away. You know that whoever you choose, he has to be the right one."

"Well, yes. I suppose I do feel that," replied Connie.

"I worry Connie," continued Kath. "This contraceptive pill. Many women say that it brings them freedom. Well, yes. I see that if they're married, then it can. It means that they don't have to be tied down by a large family; struggling to provide for kids that they can't really afford. But what about if they're single?"

She paused. Connie looked intently at her, inviting her to continue.

"What freedom is there for a young, unmarried woman, who makes herself available to men, because she no longer fears getting pregnant? She's allowing them to use her. No, all the benefits, all the freedoms, are for men, not women. They get their way without fearing the consequences of responsibility, should they get a woman pregnant. Young women need to be aware of that."

"I think that most of them are Kath. Most young women fear the consequences of gaining a reputation for being easy and available. And with that knowledge they're showing an awareness of the fact that today, there certainly isn't real equality between the sexes. We all know that men can do as they please, but let a woman make just one error of judgement and they're marked for life."

"Yes, Connie. But there are still too many young women who don't realise it."

"And then unfortunately, there are a lot of them who don't care," said Connie. "Perhaps contraception at least stops them from getting pregnant. Then they don't have to get stuck in a loveless marriage with a bullying husband. What's really important, is that these young women are educated to access the pill, so that they don't end up like that."

"Yes Connie, I can see that. Practical as ever young lady. But I'm still convinced that 'the pill' was introduced for the benefit of men, not women."

Connie nodded. They both took a sip of their drinks and Kath smiled.

"Well, we are being very solemn, aren't we?" she observed. "We'd better lighten up a bit. It is Christmas after all."

Connie laughed.

Going back to the cooker, Kath took another look at the turkey. Removing the foil, she basted and turned the potatoes and put the tray back into the oven. She then turned on the gas under the pans of vegetables, so that they would be ready with the turkey. Kath and Connie then prepared the table, putting out a series of mats, cutlery and condiments. Kath had provided cranberry jelly, horseradish sauce and mustard. Importantly, they laid out half a dozen crackers on the table. They pulled two of them immediately, so that they could put on the paper hats they contained in order to promote the Christmas spirit.

By one o'clock, the turkey was in the centre of the table, the vegetables and stuffing were on the plates.

"Would you like to do the honours Connie?" asked Kath, offering her a large knife with which to carve the turkey.

Connie took the knife.

"Did you want a leg?" she asked.

"No, just some breast please."

Carefully, Connie used a fork to hold the turkey steady with one hand, whilst carving the meat, using the knife, with the other. She picked up the slices with the fork and placed them carefully on Kath's plate. Preferring a leg herself, she delicately removed it and put it down on her own plate. The two of them sat down, ready to eat.

"Ah! The gravy. Silly me," said Kath.

She jumped up and moved quickly to the cooker. She emptied the gravy from a pan into a jug and returned to the table.

"I used the giblets and put a bit of Marmite in it," said Kath. "The vegetables would be a bit dry without it."

"You must have known. I love Marmite gravy. You really are spoiling me," replied Connie, appreciatively.

The two women realised how hungry they were. Neither of them had eaten anything in anticipation of the big dinner that they'd be having. The turkey had been cooked to perfection. It was moist and full of flavour. Connie quickly expressed her satisfaction.

"The dinner's lovely Kath and the turkey's beautiful."

"You can't beat Dewhurst's. I've always gone there," Kath replied. "He always picks me out a nice one."

Kath's attention to detail, her organisation and planning, had produced a gastronomic triumph. Connie thought about how she would have eaten very simply if she'd been at home. She was so grateful to Kath for allowing her to share this wonderful meal. Clearing her plate, Connie was surprised. It was something that she very rarely did.

"Well, it looks like you've enjoyed your food," said Kath, approvingly.

"I certainly have Kath. Thanks."

"I hope that you've still got some room for your Christmas 'pud.'"

Connie had been enjoying her turkey dinner so much, that she'd forgotten that there was going to be 'afters.' A concerned look flitted across her face, the result of a fear that she may find it difficult to eat any of Kath's home-made pudding. Observant as ever, her host quickly put her mind at rest.

"I tell you what Connie. I've eaten quite a bit. Do you mind if I give it half an hour or so, before I serve the pudding?"

"No," said Connie, relieved. "I think that I'm going to need time to make room for it too."

"Let's go and sit on the settee," said Kath. "We can let our dinner settle and see what's on the 'telly.'"

"That sounds good to me," replied Connie.

Having eaten more than usual, Connie felt a little tired. So too did Kath, who'd been working hard since early that morning. Switching on the television, she sat back into the comfort of her settee, joined by Connie. Opening the 'Evening News,' with its Christmas TV Guide, she offered her guest a choice of programmes.

"Well love. It's either 'Christmas Swing Time' on ITV or 'Walt Disney' on the BBC. They're both on until three. I'm not bothered what we watch. It's up to you."

Kath handed the newspaper to Connie who could see that Cliff and the Shadows were part of 'Christmas Swing Time,' yet she didn't much care for the other acts who'd been lined up to perform.

"I think I prefer 'Walt Disney.' They may show some clips from 'Snow White,' 'Dumbo' or 'Sleeping Beauty.' It seems more Christmassy," suggested Connie.

"Well, let's hope that the TV comes on before the programme's finished!" said Kath, in frustration.

Connie looked at the screen. The white dot was still in the centre, the picture yet to burst into life. The valves took so long to warm up. If you wanted to watch something, you always had to remember to turn the set on a good five minutes in advance.

"It'll get there. Don't worry," said Connie.

"Well, I put the sixpence in the slot. It's certainly paid for."

The two of them began to laugh. Kath had drunk a couple of large 'snowballs' and Connie had sipped her way through a couple of sherries. The two of them were now feeling relaxed and a little 'merry.' Finally, the picture emerged, grainy at first but then clearing up as it filled out the screen. Contentedly, the two friends sat through the various clips. As the programme ended, Connie had a thought.

"You didn't want to watch the Queen's message did you Kath? It's on the other side."

"Huh, no love. I'm not for the Royals. I had enough of 'King and Country' when my Stan was in the trenches."

Connie smiled.

"You're pretty much the same as me then."

So, it was on to 'Billy Smart's Circus' and inevitably the two of them nodded off. Woken by the zany antics of Abbott and Costello, who were meeting Captain Kidd in the movie that followed, Connie went over to the sink and started to wash the pots. She had almost finished wiping them, when Kath also woke up from her slumbers. Pulling herself together, Kath got on to putting out the Christmas pudding, once she had made her special brandy custard. The pudding was rich, fruity and luxurious. Kath had used only the finest of ingredients. It was a pudding fit for a banquet and was followed by a frantic pulling of crackers and a reading out of the terrible jokes contained within them. So bad were they that, influenced by the effects of Advocaat and sherry, the two women couldn't stop themselves from breaking out into fits of giggling, just like they were mischievous little girls.

Returning to the settee, the pair were well supplied with their drinks and the fruit, nuts and chocolate that Connie had brought with her. Exhausted, they sat back contentedly, able to do little other than stare at the television. There was one programme however, that Kath hadn't wanted to miss. Like eighteen million other British viewers, Kath was hooked on 'Coronation Street,' now into its fourth year of production. A special Christmas edition was based on the idea of the Street's residents creating a 'This is your Life' presentation for the 'Rovers Return' landlady, Annie Walker. Connie couldn't fail to be amused by the shocked look on Kath's face, when Dennis Tanner's presentation of Annie's life, revealed the latter's appearance as Lady Godiva some thirty years earlier.

"Well, I never!" said Kath. "Who'd have thought that of Annie Walker? So prim and proper!"

Connie had to laugh. Kath was like all the fans of the programme that she knew. It was almost as if they were convinced that the events and characters portrayed were real. Paula was the same. She always watched 'the Street' and had looked at Connie in astonishment when her friend suggested 'it was only a TV show.' No, Paula had replied, it was far more than that! Yet Connie couldn't deny that the programme had certainly caught the public's imagination.

With the episode over Kath, the perfect host, asked if Connie fancied a turkey sandwich.

"Oh, I couldn't eat another thing," replied Connie.

"Well, I'll cut you some turkey and wrap it in foil. You'll be able to take it with you. There's far too much left for me."

"No, keep it Kath. I'll come again tomorrow and we can have some turkey sandwiches. Have you got enough bread? I can bring some. I got worried with the shops being shut and I bought a couple of extra loaves."

"That's great. Thanks Connie. It's always the problem over Christmas. You can easily run out of everything. At least the shops will be open again on Friday."

"And I'll be back in work unfortunately," said Connie. "Anyway, let me get the pudding pots washed and then I think I'll have to be getting off."

"You wipe and I'll wash" said Kath, getting to the sink first.

When the pots were finished, it was getting on for nine o'clock and time for Connie to go home. She took her coat and scarf from the bottom of the stairs and bundled herself up ready to face the cold night air.

"It's been a lovely day. Thank you so much for inviting me round."
"Nonsense love. It's been great spending the day with you."
The two women hugged one another.
"Go carefully down the alley love. Don't trip over. The lamp at the end has been on the blink lately."
"I will."
Opening the back gate, Connie turned and shouted farewell to Kath, then was off down the alley to Apsley Grove. It had been a wonderful day, the first proper Christmas that Connie had experienced in years. Her relationship with Kath had developed so quickly, to a point where both of them felt a genuine warmth and affection for one another. Connie, who had been estranged from her real mother for so long, had now developed a closeness to Kath that made her feel as if she was 'family.'

Chapter 26

The New Year had come and gone and Greenings was full of activity and optimism. The company was expanding its client base and its expectations. 'Old Joe' was delighted and couldn't hide the fact from his nephew, who he believed was starting to develop the maturity that his years in the business warranted. Joe knew that much of this was down to the presence of Connie. She had brought out a real sense of responsibility in his nephew, who had finally met his match in a pretty young woman who refused to be overwhelmed by his good looks and charming personality. Although pleased to see the changes, Joe reserved his judgement. Ralph still had some way to go before his uncle would be convinced that the corner had finally been turned.

Joe was right about Connie's impact. Ralph had been unable to get her out of his mind. He was determined to woo and win her, yet she was proving to be something of a challenge. Although the two of them got on well together, there wasn't even the slightest hint of intimacy between them. And as he spent more time with Connie, Ralph began to understand that he found her wit, intelligence and kind heart, as attractive as her physical beauty. For the first time in his life, he realised that he was falling in love. Yet how could he win her affection? She wasn't interested in his money, or his prospects of taking over at Greenings. Being wined and dined at 'The French' hadn't affected her either. She had enjoyed the evening, but that would have been the case wherever they had been. Everything that impressed his previous conquests, meant absolutely nothing to her.

Ralph therefore decided that in order to win Connie's heart, it would take perseverance and time. Importantly, he would have to change his habits. This included distancing himself from other women in the office. It didn't mean that he would stop being affable, but any hint of impropriety must be eliminated. This did have an unfortunate consequence however, in that Sandra, a typist Ralph had gone out with, became upset with his attitude towards her. Paula had found her crying and she'd been insistent that it was because Ralph was being cruel. He'd done her a terrible wrong and now wouldn't speak to her. Sat with Connie in Lyons Café, Paula relayed the details to her friend.

"Are you sure that she's not exaggerating Paula?"

"She seemed far too upset Connie. She was one of Ralph's conquests. She was charmed by him, as they usually are. It wouldn't be surprising if he'd had his way with her and then moved on to someone else."

"Do you know that for definite though Paula?"

"Well, she wouldn't be the first Connie."

"I don't know," said Connie, expressing her doubts. "It may be that she's just become infatuated with him."

Looking at Paula, Connie could see that her friend was unconvinced.

"It's just that I've not seen it in him Paula," continued Connie. "Whatever he may have done in the past, it doesn't mean that he's necessarily guilty now."

"Well, yes. I can see what you're saying Connie. Perhaps she is being too hard on him."

It was a comment that enabled Paula to draw a line under the subject, before the two of them set off back to work.

Later that evening, Paula thought about her conversation with Connie. It reminded her of the one that they'd had before her friend had gone to the 'Midland' with Ralph. Perhaps, what she had sensed then, that Connie was becoming fond of Ralph, was the reason for her dismissal of Sandra's claims. Paula recognised that she would have to tread warily. Continuing to warn her friend against Ralph, could well push her into his arms. Ralph would become her cause and she would resolutely defend him. Paula knew that there was no alternative other than to wait, hoping that Connie would recognise for herself, the potential dangers of embarking on a relationship with Ralph.

Chapter 27

It was early February, 1964 and Connie was in the party office, helping Harry with his preparations for his upcoming election campaign. The two of them had developed a close association based on mutual respect. Connie had been particularly pleased by Harry's support for many of the ideas she had put forward in her opposition to the views of Bill Perkins. Unlike some members of the local and national party leadership, Harry was no misogynist. He clearly respected women and defended their right to air their opinions. Harry was struck by the intelligence and originality of his new political friend. He admired her fearlessness and her determination to support her ideas against fierce opposition, when she believed them to be right. The Party desperately needed more young women like Connie and he hoped that she would keep working for the movement for many years to come. Engrossed in their work, the pair were interrupted by the arrival of a young woman with a baby in a pushchair. She had been shown into the room having turned up at the office looking for advice from Harry. It was clear that she had been crying, her eyes red and swollen and in such circumstances, it was felt appropriate that she should see Harry immediately.

"Come in young lady," said Harry. "Who have we got here then?"

Harry walked over to the pushchair and smiled at the baby, who was wrapped up snugly in a warm coat and mittens and covered by blankets.

"His name is Andrew," said the young woman.

"He's a 'smasher' isn't he?" remarked Harry.

"Yes, he is," said his mam. Harry's soothing tones and calm, friendly nature having given her a sense of reassurance.

Connie fetched a chair from the side of the room for the young woman to sit on.

"Hello. I'm Connie."

"Gillian. Gillian Matthews."

"Hello, Gillian."

Connie smiled. Gillian now seemed calm. Like Connie, she was petite. She had short, black curly hair and what was potentially an attractive face, but one blighted by the signs of the stresses and strains of a testing existence. She was wearing slacks, a jumper and an anorak. Her shoes looked worn, in sharp contrast to the almost pristine condition of Andrew's clothes and blankets. Connie could recognise that she was a mother who cared deeply for her child, sacrificing any concerns about her own welfare, to ensure that he was properly provided for. She couldn't have been more than eighteen or nineteen at the most. Connie believed that she didn't deserve to have these responsibilities heaped upon her at such a young age. But unfortunately, that's the way it was for so many teenage mothers.

Connie and Harry moved their chairs from around the desk so that they could sit closer to their visitor.

"How can I help?" asked Harry.

"I didn't want to come, but I've nowhere else to go. I haven't had the money to pay the rent for the last two weeks and I'm sure the landlord will throw us out."

Harry noticed the wedding ring on Gillian's finger.

"What about Andrew's dad?" he asked.

"He's been out of work. He got sacked for being late and he's only just found a new job. That's why I owe money on the rent."

"Didn't you claim unemployment benefit?" asked Connie.

"I can't. Steve, my husband, has to. I tried at the labour exchange, but they told me that he was the one who had to go in and talk to them."

"So, why didn't he?" asked Connie.

"He said he wasn't going to show himself up. That we'd manage until he found something else."

"Couldn't social services give you anything? asked Harry. "They can make emergency payments if you're desperate."

"No. I'm not contacting them. They'll take Andrew away from me."

"I'm sure they wouldn't," replied Harry.

"I'm sorry Mr Thomas, but I'm not taking the risk."

"How much is the rent?" asked Connie.

"One pound, eight shillings a week."

"Where do you live?"

"Smith Street, off Higher Ardwick."

Connie and Harry looked at one another. Harry shook his head and sighed.

"One pound eight shillings. That's a lot. It's a two-up, two-down, isn't it?"

"Yes."

"That's too much Gillian."

"I know, but me and Steve are teenagers. We were lucky to get anywhere. Other landlords wouldn't have considered us."

It was the harsh reality that Harry had come across since the Tory Rent Act of 1957. It had effectively removed controls on landlords and allowed them to raise rents significantly when taking on new tenants. The fact that Gillian and Steve were such a young couple, made them even more ripe for exploitation.

"I'm not complaining about the rent," continued Gillian. "I just don't want us to get thrown out. I need to pay the landlord something. Steve's just got another job. He's promised me he'll get up and get there on time. If I can just pay something to the landlord, I'm sure that I can hold him off for a bit."

Given his long experience as a councillor, Harry had quickly identified the key issue that lay at the heart of Gillian's problem. It was Steve. He was too young to be married. Just a boy who'd never understood the consequences of making his girlfriend pregnant. It was obvious that he couldn't get himself out of bed in the morning and Gillian had no way of making him. His past employers, quite naturally, weren't standing for it. Harry felt that it would probably be best for Gillian to make a clean break with him, but then he knew that she wouldn't. He wondered if she had parents who were able to help her. He had to assume that she didn't, otherwise she and Andrew would have been with them and not come to him.

"Have you no relatives you can stay with?" asked Harry.

"No. My mam won't help me as long as I stay with Steve. She says she's being cruel to be kind. That he's no good for me. Steve doesn't know where his parents are and his Gran's too old to help us."

Fearing that Harry couldn't provide a solution to her problems, Gillian's bottom lip began to quiver and tears welled up in her eyes. Harry had been her final hope and now it seemed that all was lost.

"When's the rent next due?" asked Connie.

"Tomorrow night. The rent man comes around seven."

"What number on Smith Street do you live at?"

"Sixteen. Why?" asked Gillian.

"I'll come to the house tomorrow night and talk to him on your behalf," explained Connie. "We'll sort something out and keep you in your home until Steve's wages start coming in again."

"Oh, thank you! Thank you! You're so kind."

Gillian reached forward, picked up Connie's hand and kissed it, before pulling it towards her face. Connie could feel the tears on her cheek. She was taken by surprise. It was a reaction that she hadn't expected, but she now realised just how grateful Gillian was for her offer of help.

"No, no Gillian. It's fine. We're here to help you."

"But you don't have to," said Gillian.

Taking control of a situation that was becoming a little too emotional for his liking, Harry stood up and indicated to Gillian that it was time for her to leave.

"Well, Gillian. You'd best be getting little Andrew back home. Give our best to Steve and tell him that we're all counting on him holding down his next job. Connie will be along to see you tomorrow."

"Right. Thank you, Mr Thomas. Thank you, Connie."

Back on her feet, Gillian took hold of Andrew's pushchair and wheeled him out of the room. Harry followed and closed the door behind her.

"You do realise what you've done Connie, don't you?"

Connie looked at him confused.

"You've not just given Gillian hope, you've all but guaranteed it to her. You have to be very careful. We don't always have all the answers and in Gillian's case, the answers are beyond our control."

"Why?" asked Connie.

"Because you and I know that we can't possibly solve Gillian's problem."

"And why's that?"

"Because Steve is the problem and how do we cure him?"

"You heard what she said Harry, he's got another job. That means that they can get back on their feet again."

"Oh, Connie," said Harry, shaking his head sympathetically. "Intelligent as you are, you do sometimes let your heart rule your head. Do you think that there's a realistic chance that Steve's going to change?"

Connie looked at him. She could have felt, if she didn't know him better, that Harry was being condescending.

"I know it's tough," continued Harry. "It was for me, when I first became a councillor. You want to put the whole world to rights but sometimes you just can't. People can be their own worst enemies and you simply can't get them to see that. Do you think for one moment that Gillian will accept that her husband is the reason that she had to come here; that he's got no sense of responsibility and he never will have?"

"But how can you be so sure that Steve won't change?"

"Because it was the same for my mother."

There was a pause. Connie was surprised by his revelation. It was the first time that he'd ever told her anything about his personal life. Their relationship, though friendly, had always been so professional.

"My father left us when I was five," continued Harry. "I don't remember very much about him. It's hard to recollect seeing him. I know, from what my grandparents told me, that he let my mother down from the day she married him. He spent all his wages on himself, was out drinking and probably, womanising. My mum had three cleaning jobs and my grandparents helped and somehow, we got by. My dad just disappeared. We never heard from him again."

Harry hesitated. Connie felt the urge to offer her understanding and support.

"It must have proved very difficult for you, Harry. I never knew my father too, as he was killed at Dunkirk, but he did leave my mam and I provided for. I still found it tough though, but I always knew that dad had loved us and that always helped. I suppose it gave me a sense of hope. That life could move on and improve. Although even I have to admit, that things can look bleak at times."

Encouraged by her words, Harry continued.

"What my dad did, has turned me into someone who regards life so seriously. And that's continued because I still see so much anguish in the world."

Connie nodded. She understood that Harry was a product of his environment. It was why she wanted to create a better world for those like Gillian and little Andrew. She wanted to provide them with prosperity and stability, so that they could take advantage of a brighter future. Perhaps, as Harry had suggested, she was too optimistic, but to go down the road of negativity could never, she believed, provide any substantial improvement in the human condition.

"When you go to see Gillian, don't be tempted to give her any money Connie," said Harry, changing the subject.

"Why would I do that?" she asked, trying to convince him that she'd not thought of such a thing.

"Because I suspect that you will," continued Harry. "The rent man will be there and you'll think that you can settle their arrears and keep their home for them."

"But if there's a chance of that and I can afford to help them out, shouldn't I?"

"No."

"Why not?"

"Because it won't help. All you're doing is postponing the inevitable and you'll never see your money again. The best thing for Gillian, as I've said, would be to leave Steve and move in with her mother, but she doesn't want to do that. If you help her out with money, then you're not allowing her to see the reality of her situation. Then there's no chance of her doing something about it."

"But she loves him, Harry."

"But does he love her? I don't think so."

"How can you say that, Harry?" asked Connie, frustrated and a little angry at his response. "If you could help someone who'd fallen on hard times, someone truly deserving, wouldn't you? You must see such cases all the time, when misfortune isn't down to the personal inadequacies of someone like Steve. Don't you ever feel like giving financial help to someone when you can afford to do so? You know yourself what it's like to struggle. How can you say that you wouldn't ever give anyone money?"

"Because there's absolutely no chance that I could ever give money to every deserving case that I come across. I won't play God, stepping in to help one family, whilst others are simply left by the wayside. I wouldn't ever feel comfortable making that decision. We live in an imperfect world, but I'll move heaven and earth to try and get every form of public assistance for those I represent. I can fight for the laws we need to create a society where we can eventually eliminate poverty and distress."

Connie had to acknowledge that Harry's heart was in the right place. He'd shown real emotional awareness when relating the events of his childhood. However, he had soon buried those feelings beneath his usually calm and logical exterior.

"You know Connie," said Harry. "It would be wonderful if you were able to devote all your time to political work. It's what I want to do. I want to be adopted as a parliamentary candidate. Go to Westminster and try to make a real difference. Not just in Manchester, but in the country as a whole. If ever I do get the chance, I'd love you to help me Connie."

It was the closest that Harry had come to suggesting that he had more than a professional interest in her. But it was an ambiguous statement and one which he didn't seem inclined to elaborate on. Harry's difficult early life had encouraged him to shield his emotions. Yet, where Connie was concerned, he had been prepared to lower his defences and it had pleased her. But for the present, her thoughts towards him were based on respect for the hard work he carried out for those he represented. Harry's attitude towards Connie however, was changing. Working closely with her, he had come to recognise what an accomplished young woman she was. It wouldn't be long before Harry would be dreaming of a future at Westminster, in which Connie, as his beautiful wife, would be by his side.

Chapter 28

Connie arrived at Smith Street at six thirty. She got off the bus at the ABC and walked back across Hyde Road. She then followed Higher Ardwick up and around to the right and to the entrance to Smith Street, with its rows of small, two-up two-down terraced houses. Reaching the door to number sixteen, she saw that the front room light was on and she could hear music coming from within. Knocking loudly on the front door, she stood and waited. After a brief delay, she heard the sound of someone behind the door and then watched as it slowly began to open, the light penetrating out into the dimly lit street. Open wide, Connie was confronted by the sight of a young man whose striking blonde hair had been styled into the almost obligatory 'Beatle cut.' Wearing a white shirt and black tie, suit trousers and gleaming black, winkle picker shoes, the young man hesitated and then, when he saw Connie, his face broke out into a broad smile.

"Yes, love?"

"I've come to see Gillian. She's expecting me. My name's Connie. Are you Steve?" she asked.

"Yes, that's me."

Steve smiled at her again.

"You'd better come in Connie. I'll take you through to Gillian in the kitchen."

Connie entered and stood to the side as Steve closed the front door.

"I'll just turn this off," said Steve, walking over to a transistor radio on the top of the sideboard. The task completed, he led Connie through the door to the bottom of the stairwell.

"You've got a visitor," Steve announced, as they continued into the kitchen.

Connie lifted her hand in acknowledgement to Gillian, who was feeding Andrew in his high chair next to the kitchen table.

"Hi Gillian. I hope I'm not too early."

"No, Connie. Thanks ever so much for coming."

Gillian appeared relieved. It was clear that she'd been concerned that Connie might not turn up.

"This is the lady I was telling you about Steve. The one I met with Councillor Thomas last night."

"Oh," said Steve. "I didn't expect you to be as young as you are Connie. I thought anyone on the Council would be old. They always seem to be."

"No, councillors are often quite young. But I'm not one Steve. I just help Harry."

"If politicians were all like you, then people would be more interested in listening to them."

Steve winked at Connie and smiled. He didn't seem to care that Gillian was there and in fact his wife took it all in good humour.

"Get off with you Steve. Don't be daft," said Gillian.

"Is the rent man usually on time?" asked Connie, changing the subject.

"Yes," replied Gillian. " If he isn't, he's never more than a few minutes late."

"Well, you said that you owed him two weeks rent and I'm assuming it will be three with the rent due again today. Is that right?"

"Yes Connie. Steve's had to work a week in hand, so we won't be able to pay the rent until next week, but then we can pay it weekly and pay some off the arrears as well. Isn't that right Steve?"

Steve wasn't listening. His eyes had been fixed on Connie the whole time, not realising that she had noticed how he was weighing her up, from head to toe.

"Steve!" repeated Gillian, loudly.

"Oh yes, sorry?"

"Men!" Gillian shook her head. "Just a waste of time!"

"Sorry love," said Steve smiling. "I didn't catch what you were saying."

"That you'll have your wages for the rent next week."

"Oh, yes."

"Good," said Connie. "We can let the rent man know what we intend to do about the arrears."

"You can take care of that, can't you Gillian? I need to be making a move if I'm going to meet up with the lads in town."

Steve smiled at his wife in the knowledge that she had no option but to agree.

The two women stared at him. Gillian with a look of resignation, Connie with surprise. Surely, she thought, it wasn't too much to expect him to remain a little longer and show support for his wife? But it was clear that he wouldn't. No, it was far more important to Steve that he went out 'on the pull' with his mates. Like them, he was eager to find some accommodating young woman who was looking for a good time. Fetching his suit jacket, he put it on. He looked at himself in the mirror, declared himself satisfied, gave Gillian a quick kiss and was gone.

"He means well," said Gillian. "He's not very good at dealing with people. I do all that."

Connie knew that Gillian was making excuses for her husband, but she had no intention of being judgemental. The situation was how it was and something they simply had to work with.

"I don't know," said Gillian, turning to Andrew, "just what are we going to do with your daddy?"

Taking Andrew out of his high chair, she held him with one arm whilst trying to move the chair with the other.

"Do you want me to take him?" asked Connie.

"Oh, would you?" replied Gillian, smiling.

"Of course."

Taking careful hold of Andrew, Connie couldn't help but give him a cuddle.

"You are a lovely little boy, aren't you?"

Connie's voice was soft and soothing and Andrew showed no signs of missing his mother. Walking around the kitchen, Connie gently rocked Andrew in her arms. He was quiet and contented. Connie looked around the room. The furniture was old and tattered. No doubt the house had been let as furnished to allow the landlord to charge more rent. The items were left over from previous tenancies, having been replaced, when necessary, by pieces from the local junk shops. The rooms were smaller than in Howard Avenue and the rent, at one pound eight shillings a week, was too high. Gillian and Steve were definitely being overcharged. Noticing that Gillian had finished cleaning the chair and was ready to take Andrew once more, she prepared to hand him back.

"Oh Connie, it looks like you've sent him off to sleep. He's dead to the world."

Connie looked down and noticed that Andrew had shut his eyes.

"Hang on," said Gillian. "We'll put him down on the settee."

Gillian unfolded some small blankets that were on the settee. She took one to cover the seats and asked Connie to lay Andrew down, with his head on a pillow that she had placed at one end. Connie did so gently, ensuring that she didn't disturb him. Comfortable, Andrew was covered with a couple of blankets, the two women then retiring to sit at the kitchen table.

"I'm sorry Connie, I've not offered you a brew."

"I can wait Gillian. The rent man should be here soon, let's deal with him first."

Almost as soon as she had spoken, a knock came to the door. Not waiting for a reply, the handle was turned and the door pushed open. Into the room emerged a small man who was wearing a trilby, a long, black overcoat and a beige scarf around his neck. By his side, he was carrying a large satchel. Looking closely at him, Connie could see that he was quite elderly. His face was drawn and he had grey eyebrows and a small, grey moustache. Seeing the two women, he smiled warmly and certainly didn't give Connie the impression of someone who was tough and intimidating. Yet, he had walked into the house without waiting for an invitation, an action that made it clear that although Gillian rented the property, she didn't have any right to deny him access.

"Hello love," said the man, looking towards Gillian. "It's perishing out there tonight."

He walked over to the gas fire and bent down towards it, rubbing his hands in front of the flames.

"That's better. It's nice and warm in here."

"Yes, Mr Yates. I've got to keep it warm for Andrew. I have to keep money back for the gas meter," said Gillian.

"Of course you do love," replied Yates. "No one could expect you to do anything different."

The man looked at her reassuringly. He'd worked as a rent collector since before the War and he knew how tough it was for many of the families who lived in these houses. 'Make do and mend,' the great wartime slogan, was still a way of life for these people. And he knew that Gillian was worried that being behind with the rent, he may criticise her for spending money on the gas fire that could be used to pay off her arrears. Nevertheless, although he wanted to show understanding towards her, there had to be a limit. His boss, Josiah Mulgrew, who owned hundreds of houses all over Manchester, expected that his tenants paid up and if they didn't, eviction would swiftly follow. Mulgrew had to be told when any of his tenants missed their rent and no matter how much sympathy Yates may have for vulnerable families like Gillian's, he would never dare to try and cover up the problems that they were having. If arrears mounted and Mulgrew wasn't told, it would be Yates's own head on the block and he wasn't prepared to risk that. No one crossed Josiah Mulgrew.

While standing by the gas fire, Yates looked closely at the young lady who was sat with Gillian at the table. He'd never seen her before and had immediately noted that she was out of place here. She was wearing a very smart, light blue, two-piece suit, with a brilliant white blouse and fashionable blue heels on her feet. Her stylish clothes indicated that she had money and in addition, he couldn't help but notice how very pretty she was; so pleasing to an old man's eye. Her presence intrigued him.

"And who's your friend then Gillian? Aren't you going to introduce me?"

There was more than a hint of formality in his words, a recognition, whether Connie liked it or not, that he regarded her as having a higher social status than the people he usually mixed with.

"Oh, sorry Mr Yates. This is Connie."

"Hello Connie."

"Hello Mr Yates."

"Oh please, call me Bill."

Yates smiled but was then surprised as Connie stood up and thrust out her hand towards him. Hesitant at first, Yates saw that the hand wasn't going to be withdrawn and so took it. He couldn't ever remember shaking hands with a woman and certainly not any of the women who lived in these houses and who he collected rents from. He understood that he was presented with a young lady who wasn't only pretty and well off, but who was educated, confident and knowledgeable too. He immediately suspected that she was here to support Gillian over the matter of the rent, a fact that was soon confirmed by the tenant herself.

"Mr Yates, I've asked Connie to come and help me over the rent arrears, if that's all right?"

Yates stood silently for a few moments and then nodded his head.

"Okay. What did you have in mind?" he asked, turning to Connie.

"I believe that with the rent due today, Gillian and Steve owe you three weeks in payments. Is that correct?"

"Yes, that's about the size of it," replied Yates.

"Well Bill, I'm prepared to pay you two weeks rent now and as Steve has started a new job and will get his first wages next week, I'm proposing that you allow them to miss this week's rent, which they can catch up over the following four weeks. They will, of course, be paying the full weekly rent again from next week."

"I see," said Yates. "So, just to get it straight, from next week they'll pay one pound and eight shillings, plus an extra seven shillings over four weeks to pay off the arrears."

"Yes," said Connie.

"And you can manage that can you Gillian?" asked Yates.

"Yes," replied Gillian. "Of course, we can."

"And you're sure that husband of yours will keep his job."

"Yes. Yes. He knows that he's got to," replied Gillian.

"Well, the only problem I can see is that four weeks seems too long to pay off the arrears. Can't you pay them off in two or three weeks?"

"Well, yes. I suppose that we could," replied Gillian, worried that Yates was about to turn them down.

"No, you couldn't!" insisted Connie.

Gillian looked down, afraid that Connie had overstepped the mark. Raising her eyes slowly, she looked subserviently at Yates.

"Well, I'm sure that we could manage it, if that's what Mr Yates wanted," she said meekly, almost apologetically.

"No, you can't manage it," said Connie. "Our offer is very reasonable. I'm giving Bill two thirds of what you owe today and the landlord will have it all, five weeks from now. If the landlord wanted to evict you, he wouldn't get anything and then the house would be empty until he got another tenant. How much additional money would he lose then? And there's another fact that Bill hasn't considered."

She paused and looked straight into his eyes. Connie was in a determined mood and Yates found himself pushed firmly back on the defensive.

"Oh, and what's that?" asked Yates, quietly.

"The rent. It's far too high. One pound and eight shillings a week for this? I can't believe that you'd get that off anyone else."

"No, no Connie!" exclaimed Gillian. "The rent's fine! We've got no complaints! We're happy with it, Mr Yates."

Gillian was in a panic. She was terrified, not expecting that Connie would criticise Yates so fiercely. In fact, she hadn't considered that Connie would do so at all. Downtrodden for so long, feeling that she and her family were at rock bottom, Gillian could never contemplate answering back to those she perceived as being above her. By virtue of his job, Yates automatically obtained her respect, whether he deserved it or not. All Gillian had wanted that night, was for Yates to accept Connie's request to give them more time. She had been shocked by Connie's generosity in offering to pay two weeks arrears of rent on her behalf, but she didn't want anything more. Gillian's whole life was one rooted in fear. Unlike Connie, she didn't have the education or experience to challenge the injustices that beset her. It seemed that she was always just one step away from disaster and she felt that in order to survive, you had to remain quiet and keep your head down.

Connie understood Gillian's fears, but she had the confidence to know that her words made financial sense. The landlord would lose far more by rejecting her offer. Yates understood it too. Moreover, he felt guilty when he observed the fearful state of his young tenant and looked at the little boy asleep on the settee. It was at times like this that he felt as much a victim of his job, as the tenants he pursued. Usually, he felt justified in his work. Bad tenants deserved no sympathy, but Gillian and her little boy, that was different. Yet, he too had a home to pay for and a wife to support and most importantly, a hard and uncompromising boss, who expected him to get results.

"Okay Connie," said Yates. "I can assure you though that the rent is very reasonable and anyway, that doesn't matter. Gillian and Steve took it on. They didn't have to. We didn't force them. I think that the landlord will accept the deal, so if you give me the two pounds and sixteen shillings, I'll write it up in the rent book and then put in the expected amount of one pound and fifteen shillings for the next four weeks, in order to get everything straight."

Yates moved over to the table and sat down. He picked up the rent book that Gillian had placed there and proceeded to fill in the details. Having completed his task, he passed the rent book to Connie for her approval.

"Are you happy Connie?" he asked.

"Yes, that's fine," she said, returning it.

Going to her handbag, Connie opened it and took out her purse. She counted out the money for the next two weeks rent and gave it to Yates, who put it safely away in his satchel and then signed the amount off in the rent book. Looking up, Yates gave a word of warning to Gillian.

"You're very lucky that Connie has helped you. Without the two weeks rent, Mr Mulgrew would've wanted you out. He doesn't let his tenants get away with owing arrears. You must make sure that you stick to the agreement. If you don't, I can't give you any more chances. You do understand that, don't you?"

"Oh yes. Yes, Mr Yates. Thank you."

Yates stood up from the table.

"Well, I've got to be going. It was nice to meet you, Connie."

He smiled and Connie politely, smiled back.

"Don't forget your satchel," said Connie.

"Oh yes, thanks. I wouldn't get far without that."

Yates picked it up from beside the leg of the kitchen table where he'd left it.

"Isn't it a bit risky walking around with all that money Bill?" asked Connie.

"No. Not at all. All the thieves around here know who I work for. No one would dare take anything from Josiah Mulgrew. He'd move heaven and earth to find out who'd done it and when he did, it wouldn't end up being a pretty sight."

Yates grinned as if his words were of no real consequence, but for Connie, their meaning was quite chilling. With his departure, the two women were left to consider the night's events.

"Well Gillian, I think we've done as much as we can. You've got a good chance to get straight now. You need to make sure that you keep on at Steve. He's got to hold on to his job, you and Andrew depend on it."

"I wouldn't have a problem, if I were like you Connie. Would I?"

"Don't be daft Gillian, what you're doing here is brilliant. Looking after Andrew, keeping your family together, doing everything you can to keep your home. I don't have to cope with any of the worries that you do."

"But it's how you can deal with men. Mr Yates has never told me to call him Bill. I watched him. He was scared of you. What you said, how sure of yourself you were. Nothing he said bothered you at all."

"I just made him see sense Gillian. It was more costly to Mulgrew to throw you out. I just pointed that out to him. Money always makes them see things differently."

"You'd think that with all his money, Mulgrew would be more reasonable," said Gillian.

"I wish it was so," replied Connie. "But you usually find that the more money people have, the more they want. That's why we need more council houses Gillian. Then we'll have a landlord who's there to help tenants, not bully and exploit them."

"The money, Connie. I didn't expect you to pay that for us. I won't be able to give it you back until after we've straightened the rent arrears out."

"That's okay Gillian. I can wait."

"I'm sorry though."

"The main thing, is to worry about paying Mulgrew, not me."

"I know Connie."

"I'll have to be getting off home now Gillian. I'll come back next Friday, around the same time, to see how you're getting on. If that's okay?"

"Of course, Connie. You can come any time you want."

Walking the short distance home, Connie recalled Harry's warning to her not to give Gillian any money. She accepted that it was unlikely she would ever get it back, but Connie knew that it was the only deal she could have made, in order to keep Gillian and Andrew in the house. But, for how long? She'd met Steve and Harry's concerns were justified. He hadn't got any sense of responsibility and was carrying on as if he was single and fancy free. It was a problem of education and background. Steve was just another young, working-class lad, who'd been brought up to believe that hearth and home were a woman's domain. Steve may have fathered a child, but that was where his obligations ended. Connie knew that it would be extremely difficult for Gillian to keep pushing her husband. He would never stop wanting to go out or buy fashionable clothes that they couldn't afford.

Harry had the answer. Gillian should leave Steve and move back to live with her mother. It was the only solution that would give Gillian the chance to build a new life and claim back her self-respect. Yet that would only be possible in an ideal world and Connie knew that life in Ardwick was far from ideal. Connie now accepted, as Harry had suggested, that she herself was too emotional. Too often, she did let her heart rule her head. There were so many young mothers like Gillian and she couldn't possibly dip into her purse and help them all. It meant that if she continued to work with Harry, then she would have to become tougher. She must accept the limits of what was possible, however frustrating that may be. As an accountant, dealing logically with facts and figures, she should have had the qualities to do that. Yet, when confronted with the sight of little Andrew, sleeping on the settee, oblivious to the danger of his home being taken away from him, it simply wasn't that easy. When she had left Gillian, she had given her the address and phone number of Greenings. She had told Gillian to contact her if she needed help. Connie knew that if Gillian did, she wouldn't hesitate to give it.

Chapter 29

The following Friday, having finished work, Connie was as good as her word. Getting off the bus at the ABC, she made her way to Higher Ardwick and along to Smith Street. Approaching the front door to number sixteen, she suddenly stopped. The house was boarded up and in the glare of the nearby street light, she could see that the walls were blackened. It was obvious that there had been a fire, one so serious that the house was now uninhabitable. Usually so calm, Connie felt a sickening sense of foreboding. What had happened to Gillian and Andrew? Were they all right? Connie noticed that there was a light on in the front room at number fourteen. Maybe the resident would be able to provide her with some answers. Connie walked up to the front door and knocked. Waiting, she noticed the curtains twitch to the side and a face peer out through the window. Connie stood further back so that she could be clearly seen, a young woman who wouldn't pose them any threat. The sight of her must have been reassuring, as she soon heard the sound of a catch being released and the door swung open to reveal an elderly lady.

"Hello love," said the lady, smiling.

"Hello. I'm sorry to bother you, but my name's Connie and I'm a friend of Gillian's at number sixteen. I'd arranged to see her tonight and now I'm really worried. I've heard nothing from her and I can see that they've had a fire. I wondered if you happen to know if all of them are all right."

"Yes love. As far as I know. Gillian and the baby weren't here when it set on fire. Just that excuse for a husband and one of his women."

"Were they alright?" asked Connie.

"Oh, yes love, they both got out. The firemen put a ladder up to the front bedroom. They smashed the window and they both climbed out. With a bit of luck, it'll shock the lad into not being such a swine in future."

"Do you know how it started?" asked Connie.

"We're not sure. He was probably drunk. Perhaps a lit cig. It was a good job the Fire Brigade were here quickly. Me and my hubby had to get out of the house. We thought it might go up too."

"When did it happen?"

"On Monday night. That burnt, sooty smell is only just starting to wear off. They've gone, but we've still got to live with it!" continued the old lady, clearly unimpressed with the situation.

"Thank you," said Connie. "I suppose Gillian's got more important things to worry about then contacting me. Hopefully she'll get in touch again soon."

"Yes, love. That Steve. It's terrible how he messes her about. She's so good with the little 'un. I do feel sorry for her."

She tutted and shook her head in sympathy. Connie nodded in agreement.

"Well, I'd best be getting off. Thanks again," continued Connie.

"That's alright love. When you do see Gillian, you tell her that we're all thinking about her."

"Yes, I will," replied Connie.

Connie felt a sense of relief but still had concerns about Gillian and Andrew's welfare. She'd become involved in their problems and had made an emotional investment in trying to secure a solution. She didn't just want to walk away, but unless Gillian contacted her, it seemed as though that would have to be the case. That was until the following Tuesday when, just before dinner, Connie received a message from Paula asking her to come to see her. When she arrived, she was surprised to see Gillian sat waiting for her.

"There's a young lady here for you Connie," said Paula, sat at her desk.

"Thanks Paula," replied Connie.

She walked straight over to Gillian who stood up. Connie smiled, she threw out her arms and gave her a hug, the warmth of which took Gillian by surprise.

"I'm so relieved to see you," said Connie. "Is Andrew okay?"

"Yes, he's fine," said Gillian. "My mam is looking after him while I'm here."

"That's good," replied Connie. "Shall we go and get a drink and something to eat? It's almost time for my break."

Gillian nodded. Connie felt that they could talk more openly away from the office. She was confident that Gillian would be more inclined to let her know the true state of affairs, if they were sat in a more convivial environment.

"Yes, that would be nice Connie. Thank you."

Letting Paula know that she was leaving the office, Connie then took Gillian to Lyons Café, buying them both a ham and tomato barm, a vanilla and a cup of tea. As she ate, Gillian slowly began to unburden herself to Connie.

"I didn't know who else I could tell Connie. I have to tell someone, but not my mam or my sister. They can never know."

Gillian was hesitant and nervous. She was torn between confiding in Connie and the fear of the latter's disapproval of her when she did. Connie sensed how uneasy Gillian felt. It was becoming clear that she was about to be privy to some very serious information. She realised that she must encourage Gillian to continue, but braced herself to be shocked by what she was about to hear.

"Go on Gillian," said Connie, quietly.

"Please don't think badly of me Connie. I didn't realise what I was doing," continued Gillian. "It was me who started the fire."

She paused, half expecting Connie to angrily denounce her actions. Instinctively, she bent her head down towards the table, averting her eyes from her benefactor. But Connie was calm. Moving her hand across the table, she softly patted Gillian's shoulder.

"It's all right Gillian. Just tell me what happened," she said, reassuringly.

"I'd arranged to take Andrew to my mam's and stay the night," continued Gillian, quietly and slowly. "Steve had come home early at dinner. He was surprised that I hadn't already left. He said that his boss had sent them all home early, as they'd been let down on the materials for a job. It didn't seem right to me and I know that I haven't told you Connie, but I've had to keep my eye on him since Andrew was born."

"Oh?" asked Connie, pretending to be surprised.

"Yes. My friends have told me that they've heard he's been with other women. But you know how you are, you just ignore it. You don't want to believe it. But something told me that he was planning to bring another woman into the house when I wasn't there."

"A woman's intuition?" suggested Connie.

"Yes, I suppose so," said Gillian.

"It was then," she continued, "that I decided to go back to the house at night. I made an excuse to my mam. I wouldn't have told her what I was doing. She hates Steve and I couldn't bear her going on and saying 'I told you so', like she always does. I got there around eight and I had my key and I could see that the front bedroom light was on. I went quietly in through the front door, crept over to the bottom of the stairs and listened. I could hear him at it with someone in my bed, in my bedroom! I felt like murdering the swine and then it came to me. I'd set the house on fire, burn the place down. I never wanted to set foot in that house again."

"So, what did you do?" asked Connie, calmly.

"I went into the kitchen, got some damp washing and put it on the 'clothes horse' and then turned the gas fire on and put the clothes right up against it. I knew they'd soon set on fire. I let myself out of the back door and checked that there was no one in the ginnel and I crept back down to the end of the street and waited. I was so angry, but then I started to worry and I went back, intending to go in the kitchen and turn off the fire. But it was too late. I saw the flames coming from the yard and I ran to the phone box and rang 999. It was me. I called the fire engine. I was worried sick for Steve. I didn't care about her! I watched from the end of the street and saw them rescued through the front bedroom window."

"Did anyone see you?" asked Connie.

"No one, except Steve."

"Steve!" Connie was shocked.

"Yes. He looked down the street and recognised me on the corner."

"How do you know?"

"He came to my mam's house early the next morning."

"Oh, no! Gillian, no!"

There was real anguish in Connie's voice. She now feared that she would be unable to help.

"I suppose he's threatening to tell the police?" she added, expecting to hear the worst.

"No."

"No?" asked Connie, confused.

"He told me that he hadn't realised just how much I loved him."

"You almost killed him!" said Connie, in astonishment.

"I know I did. But he said it showed how deeply I felt about him. That I loved him so much that I couldn't bear to see him with anyone else."

Connie was utterly amazed. She could hardly believe what she was hearing.

"And he was right Connie. Then he said that he really loved me, more than anyone else ever. That other women meant nothing to him and he begged me to forgive him."

"And did you?" asked Connie, calmly.

"Yes, I did."

Connie nodded. She had no intention of appearing judgemental. In any case, it was clear that Gillian had already made her decision. What was important now, was how Gillian, Steve and Andrew were going to move forward.

"Gillian. You must never tell another soul what you've just told me. You have to think of Andrew. He needs his mam. You could go to prison if anyone finds out."

"I know Connie. Steve's been to the police station. They asked him what happened and he said that he must have forgotten to turn off the gas fire, after he'd left the washing to dry. They said that the fire officer looked in the house and told them the same thing. We don't have insurance. They know that Steve didn't start it on purpose in order to claim some money. They're not interested in seeing him again. So, it should be okay."

"Where are you staying now Gillian? At your mam's?"

"No. She won't allow Steve to stay, but we're with my sister Carol in Harpurhey at the moment."

"What's that like?"

"Well, Carol's told us that we can't stay for too long. She's had to put all her kids in one bedroom to make room for us. Her hubby, Pete, isn't too happy."

"You really need to get somewhere of your own, don't you?" asked Connie

"Yes, but we've got the money that we were going to pay to Mr Yates and we can save a little more by living with Carol. That should give us enough to rent somewhere else."

Connie was worried. She knew that Gillian was being naïve. It wasn't Yates that they owed the money to, but Josiah Mulgrew. They had been his tenants and his house had been burned to a shell. Moreover, they'd disappeared without a word of explanation. Connie had made enquiries about Mulgrew and what she'd heard, worried her. She was sure that he wouldn't rest until he'd tracked them down.

"Gillian. How are you going to be able to rent somewhere else? Mr Mulgrew, your landlord, knows everyone in the letting business. He'll find you. He'll want money and explanations.

"Steve has thought of that. We'll just change our names."

"But then how is Steve going to work? What about his national insurance cards? What happens if you want to stay on the council housing list? It's not that easy Gillian."

For the first time, Gillian looked concerned. Connie could see that her eyes were beginning to fill with tears.

"I knew it Connie. I told Steve that it couldn't be that simple. But everything seems so easy to him. That's why I came to talk to you. I could trust you to be honest with me and if you can Connie, help us, please."

"Don't cry. It'll be all right" said Connie, taking hold of Gillian's hand.

"I'll have to figure out how to approach Mulgrew. If you're going to stay in Manchester, we have to make things right with him."

"Maybe, we should just leave," said Gillian. "Really disappear. But I don't know where we could go. What Steve could do. We've never been anywhere but Manchester."

"No. There has to be a way, Gillian. I can arrange to go and see Mulgrew. I'm working for the local councillor. He can't do anything to me and so you needn't do anything silly. Stay with Carol, telephone me at work on Friday morning and hopefully, I'll have some better news for you."

Having said goodbye, Connie walked back down Oldham Street towards Clayton House. She thought over her final words to Gillian. She realised that she had made her a huge promise. She thought of Harry and knew that he wouldn't agree with the course of action she was taking, especially as Gillian was guilty of a criminal offence. Furthermore, Mulgrew's reputation was such, that Connie would be ill advised to approach him over any matter that he considered detrimental to his interests. Once again, Connie was being governed by her emotions. She wasn't someone who could readily subscribe to the view of discretion being the better part of valour, especially when she considered the safety of little Andrew. Meeting Mulgrew would be difficult, but she knew that she had to do it. A young family's future depended on it.

Chapter 30

Arriving back at work, Connie headed straight for Tom's office. She was eager to talk about the action she intended to take in relation to Gillian's family and their predicament with Mulgrew. Connie was careful not to tell him that it was Gillian who had started the fire, feeling sure that he wouldn't offer her his support if he was aware of it. Tom suggested that as Harry would be working in the party office that evening, they could meet with him to see what he thought about the matter. Connie agreed and so Tom phoned Harry's school and left a message to say that they would see him that evening at seven.

Together at the appointed time, Connie was able to apprise Harry of the details of her conversation with Gillian. She made it clear that a meeting with Josiah Mulgrew was unavoidable. It was the only way to ensure that he didn't hold the family responsible for the damage to his property.

"I've heard all kinds of stories about Mulgrew," she said. "How he pursues his tenants for the last penny of arrears and employs thugs to evict defenceless families. I'm worried that he'll be after Gillian and Steve and they simply aren't in a position to pay him anything. They need to get another house quickly, or I can see Gillian's sister throwing them out on the street."

"Steady on Connie," said Harry. "You don't know for certain that Mulgrew is that bad. He's never been investigated by the police and the Corporation regularly use his building and development company for local contracts. They seem to be happy enough with him."

"Well, Harry. I've got to say that I've heard stories similar to Connie," said Tom, coming to her defence. "The reason there are no complaints against him is obvious. No one in their right mind would dare complain about him to the police."

"Tom's right Harry," continued Connie. "When I went to Smith Street to see Gillian, the rent man, Bill Yates, made it quite clear that no one crosses Mulgrew. Even the local criminals know better than to try and grab his rent money. The man rules by fear and if he decides to go after Gillian and Steve, they've had it. I'm sure that if I hadn't paid a couple of weeks rent for them, Mulgrew would have thrown them out the very next day."

"I thought I advised you not to give them any money Connie. It doesn't help. It would have been better if they had left the house before it burned down."

"I had to do it Harry. I couldn't stand by when I knew I could make a difference and it's the same now. I know what Gillian's situation is and I can't pretend otherwise. I just can't walk away and have it on my conscience. So, I am going to go and see Mulgrew."

Harry sighed, shook his head and raised his eyes to the ceiling.

"Oh, Connie. You do worry me. I'm beginning to think that I shouldn't have ever asked you to get involved with any of my council work. This is all my fault."

"No," replied Connie. "Don't be daft Harry. I do the work because I want to, irrespective of whether you asked me to do it or not."

"Still," said Harry. "This is a mess and although I'm not going along with what you and Tom are suggesting about Mulgrew, I'm concerned enough to ask you to think again. The problem here has been caused by Steve. If he worked hard and consistently, didn't keep getting himself sacked and woke up to his responsibilities, then they would never have been in arrears in the first place. This problem isn't your responsibility, Connie."

"But that's how things are Harry. Should we simply condemn Steve, which then means that we abandon Gillian and Andrew? No. That's not what we're supposed to believe in. If young fathers like Steve act in the way they do, it's because society has failed to support and educate them. Their failure is our failure too. Until those issues get addressed, we're duty bound to help those who are weak and vulnerable."

"I can see that I'm not going to get anywhere with you Connie, am I?" replied Harry, with an air of resignation. "But one thing you must do, if you meet with Mulgrew, is to be diplomatic. His views are unlikely to be anywhere near the same as yours."

Tom had remained quiet. He could see that both of his friends' arguments had merits, yet instinctively his sympathies lay on the side of Gillian and her family. He believed that Connie would need his support and now he offered it to her.

"I'll come with you Connie. With the two of us together, it may give us a little more leverage."

"No Tom," said Connie. "It's something best done on my own. If Mulgrew is as ruthless as people say, just dealing with a woman may restrain him a little."

Tom understood her logic, yet he wasn't prepared to abandon her completely.

"Well, there's no reason I shouldn't come along with you. I don't have to be in the meeting, but at least I can give you moral support on the way."

"All right Tom, but I insist that you wait for me outside his office. I don't want him to feel that we're trying to pressure him. That would be a disaster."

Tom nodded in agreement.

"You don't even know that he's going to see you," said Harry.

"I'll make sure that he does," said Connie. "He's an astute businessman. I'm sure he'll want to deal with this without too much fuss."

Connie had stuck to her decision to see Mulgrew, yet without a ringing endorsement from Harry. Next morning, Connie phoned the offices of 'Mulgrew & Co Ltd' to arrange an appointment. Speaking to his personal secretary, Connie explained that she desired to see her boss in order to discuss his former tenants, Steve and Gillian Matthews. She was put on hold whilst the secretary spoke to Mulgrew. Asked to confirm her name, the secretary then informed her that Mr Mulgrew would be delighted to see her tomorrow, Thursday, at two o'clock. The meeting was set up. Connie now had to hope that she would make a favourable impression on him.

Chapter 31

The offices of Mulgrew & Company were located in St Andrews House at 53 Portland Street. They were located only a very short distance from Greenings. Coming out of Clayton House, Tom and Connie walked down to the start of Portland Street and then moved briskly along to their destination.

As they looked ahead of them, they could see the changing landscape around Piccadilly Gardens and the new building that was beginning to transform the city centre. By the late 1950s post-war austerity was coming to an end, the economy was growing and property developers were gaining the confidence to invest in new construction projects. Manchester, the key regional centre in the North of England, was a city of administrative and commercial importance. National companies looked to expand their interests in the city and developers were keen to invest in new properties before land values became excessive. Opposite Clayton House, across Piccadilly Gardens, a huge construction project was underway to create Piccadilly Plaza. The development would eventually consist of a nine-storey hotel, resting on a huge concrete cradle, an office block of twenty-four storeys and an additional seven-storey building. These uniform, concrete structures, with their imposing height, seemed cold and anonymous to Connie. As they walked opposite the Plaza development and over Minshull Street, Connie was struck by the contrast of the beautiful Victorian architecture, proudly displayed by the Watts Warehouse building, on their side of Portland Street.

Watts Warehouse was a famous Manchester landmark, it's five storeys displaying different architectural styles: Elizabethan, Italian and French Renaissance. The building was topped with a deep frieze. Its windows and walls were covered by ornate strapwork and tracery, its rose windows reminiscent of French Gothic cathedrals. To Connie, the building had heart and soul and it reflected a more caring city; a proud city. The new architecture gave her no such feelings. Functional capitalism at its worst. As they crossed Chorlton Street, her opinion was reinforced, as she looked up at the recently completed St Andrews House and Telephone House beyond. The latter was typical of the new high-rise buildings constructed over the last few years. It had a ground floor podium which filled the site boundary, yet a high tower block rising within it, to allow light to the nearby buildings. These structures, with their many storeys, provided for a higher floor space. It meant that rents could be maximised to a point where even expensive land values didn't deter the developers. St Andrews House, with its twenty storeys, was an extremely lucrative property once it had been filled with tenants. Mulgrew, even though his interests were mainly in the realm of residential developments, would no doubt have approved of the economics of scale.

Entering St Andrews House, Connie and Tom made their way to the reception desk. Stating that she was here for a two o'clock appointment with Mr Mulgrew, Connie was directed to the lift and told to get out on the twelfth floor.

"Tom. You need to wait down here. I don't anticipate that I'll be too long. I'm going to be fine."

Tom nodded and took a seat whilst Connie moved smartly into the lift. When it arrived at the twelfth floor and its doors opened, Connie stepped out into a large reception area. There was a desk in front of her, behind which two women were seated. Walking over to them, she could see passages branching off to the left and right, leading to a number of rooms and offices. Reaching the desk, Connie addressed one of the receptionists, who'd stood up to greet her.

"Hello. I'm Connie Campbell, I'm here to see Mr Mulgrew at two."

"Yes, Miss Campbell. We've been expecting you. I'll let Mr Mulgrew know that you're here."

Picking up the receiver from the phone on her desk, she called through to Mulgrew's office and informed him of Connie's arrival. Replacing the receiver, she looked at Connie.

"Mr Mulgrew is ready to see you now. If you'll just follow me, I'll take you to him."

The receptionist stood up, smiled and moved out from behind her desk. Like her colleague she was young and attractive. Her dark brown hair was piled up into a beehive and she was wearing a pretty beige blouse and a navy pencil skirt, which came to just below her knees. Connie walked with her down the corridor to the right past a number of doors and a large, open plan area with desks for a number of men and women carrying out administrative tasks. At the end of the office was a door and the receptionist halted to knock on it. Hearing a growl of acknowledgement from inside, she ushered Connie into the room.

"This is Miss Campbell," said the receptionist, leading Connie towards a large desk behind which Mulgrew was standing.

"Thank you, Jane," said Mulgrew, smiling. "That will be all."

"Yes, Mr Mulgrew."

Jane turned and walked back towards the door. Connie noticed Mulgrew's eyes following her out of the room, but she detected no salaciousness in his look, rather more an appreciation of seeing a pretty young woman. In that, Mulgrew was no different to the majority of men that Connie knew.

Coming out from behind his desk, Mulgrew smiled and offered Connie his hand. The gesture surprised her, but without hesitation, she shook it. His grasp was firm but not too tight. The respect that he was showing towards her, challenged the previous notions that she had developed from hearing the stories about him. If he were indeed nothing more than a bully, then the trappings of success provided by this impressive suite of offices, a host of employees industriously working for his company and his polite, welcoming manner, all provided a veneer of respectability far removed from the portfolio of crumbling properties in Ardwick and elsewhere. Connie focused her mind. She was here to find out just how far Mulgrew would prove to be a reasonable man. Would he have a side to his nature that she could appeal to on behalf of Gillian and Steve?

"Take a seat young lady," said Mulgrew, motioning to the chair in front of his desk. "Would you like a drink?"

"No thank you," replied Connie, sitting down.

"Normally, I wouldn't see anyone about one of my tenants," said Mulgrew. "As you know, I employ people to deal with that kind of thing. But I've heard all about you from Bill Yates and I've got to say that you interest me Miss Campbell, or can I call you Connie?"

Connie had observed Mulgrew carefully whilst he was speaking. He was in his late fifties, but he looked younger. A tall, broad and powerful man, Mulgrew clearly took care of himself. He still had a good head of brown hair, with no signs of balding. He was clean-shaven, which emphasised his strong, firm jaw line and his eyebrows and sideburns were neatly trimmed. He was a man who cared about his appearance. The faint line of a scar under his right eye and across the top of his cheekbone, gave a suggestion of a violent encounter in the past. Yet for Connie, that could only be a matter of conjecture. Seeing him for the first time, his appearance was pleasant and welcoming.

"Connie's fine, Mr Mulgrew."

"Well then, you should call me Josiah."

"Yes, of course," replied Connie.

Her voice was calm and business like. She fully intended to control her emotions. Most of all, Connie didn't want to give the impression to Mulgrew that he could 'soft soap' her. She was here about a serious matter and she wasn't going to allow him to forget it.

"Do you know Connie," said Mulgrew, "I approached Joe Greening about his firm taking on our audit work. Fancy that, we could have met one another before today. Joe wasn't interested though. Of course, he was polite enough to make an excuse, claiming that Greenings were too stretched at the time and he wouldn't be able to give us the attention that we deserved. We both knew that it was nonsense. Joe's old school. Any whiff of impropriety and he'll have no part of it. Do you think I'm crooked Connie?"

The question took her completely by surprise. Connie had expected their conversation to be circumspect, that they would be carefully skirting around the issues. Mulgrew however, was striking openly at the very essence of her fears. She looked at him, determined not to avert her eyes. Yet uncertain of what to say, she made no response.

"I built this company up in the 'Thirties.' Took on housing tenants," continued Mulgrew. "It came about from me being a builder. It was tough. People don't realise now just how hard it was back then. I learned early on that you can't sympathise. You need your rents, or you go under. So yes, you couldn't afford to go soft on people. If the word got around, everyone would miss their rent. After all, who couldn't have used the excuse of hard times to justify not paying. After the war, I got clearance and building contracts. I branched out and now I'm here." Mulgrew paused, raising his arm to indicate the splendid, modern office they were sitting in. "But Connie, when people strike deals with me, I have always insisted that they honour them. You want to talk about Steve and Gillian. I didn't force them to rent the house in Smith Street. They knew the score. If you live in one of my houses, then you have to pay me for it. I don't feel sorry for them, especially when I've got a fire damaged house on my hands. I'm not the man to come to if you want any sympathy."

"But you've got insurance," said Connie. "It can't be the first time that you've had tenants who had a fire?"

"Yes, I've had others. But I don't recall any of them being in arrears though."

"I'm asking you Josiah, if you would be prepared to give them some leeway, please? They have a young child and if you make them pay, they won't be able to afford to rent anywhere else."

"So, why is that down to me? What makes it my responsibility?" replied Mulgrew, clearly unmoved by her plea.

"It doesn't," replied Connie. "But it's the right thing to do and you can afford it."

"More than you!"

Mulgrew laughed and his face softened.

"Bill told me that you'd paid two weeks rent for them, but this situation is beyond your means, isn't it, Connie?"

Connie nodded, acknowledging his point. She couldn't possibly disagree.

"You care too much Connie. You're an idealist. You've made quite a few waves for me lately with your opposition to building the new council estates."

"How do you know that?" asked Connie.

"Oh, I'm very well informed. I know everything that goes on in this city; everything that goes on in your party too. I have to. There are some big contracts out there and I intend to get them."

Connie was shocked, Mulgrew seemed to be alluding to the fact that he had access to inside information and influence over the tendering process.

"You're a clever girl Connie. I've checked you out. You've got business acumen, a good head on your shoulders. I can make very good use of you. In fact, I'll double what Joe Greening's paying you right now."

"No, thank you."

"Don't be too hasty young lady. Do you really think that your party comrades are all as honest and upstanding as you are? Why don't you earn what you're worth, instead of worrying about those who only have themselves to blame for their failures."

"I don't believe that there are that many who would so easily sell out their principles. One or two perhaps. There's always someone. No, I won't accept it," replied Connie, firmly.

Mulgrew smiled. He liked Connie. He respected her, because unlike so many of her contemporaries, she still believed in something. He knew that her values weren't for sale at any price.

"If I wanted to Connie, I could reel off a list of councillors and officials from here and elsewhere, that have been in my pocket whilst I've been expanding my business over the last fifteen years. I won't do that of course and if you ever tried to repeat what I've said to you, you'd never have any evidence to back it up. Corruption you may want to call it, being accommodating is what I prefer to say. I don't need to put pressure on anyone, or threaten them, because they understand the mutual obligations we have when we come to an understanding. What's more, my company always delivers value on the contracts that we get awarded. You see Connie, you can be like 'Old Joe' and live in the vain hope that you can make the world the way you'd like it to be, or you can be like me and embrace the world for what it really is and profit from its imperfections."

"So, what you're saying to me Josiah, is that you can buy almost anyone?"

"Not everyone Connie. I know that I could never get your support and that's why I admire you. You're single-minded, just like me, when it comes to anything you believe in. Because of that, I've allowed you to come here and challenge me in my own office. I wouldn't let anyone else do that."

"So, what about Gillian and Steve?"

"Well normally Connie, I would ask what's in it for me?"

"To be able to do the decent thing."

"But that means nothing to me Connie."

He looked calmly at her. She had nothing to offer him and they both knew it. He sighed and leaned forward in his chair.

"Well, against my better judgement, I'm going to give you what you're asking for. I won't pursue Gillian and Steve for the arrears. No one, including them, will know that I've been soft though. Bill Yates will see them and tell them that you Connie, have paid off their arrears. You won't tell them any different, for if you do, the deal is off. The one thing that I have to protect is my reputation. People need to know that I'm tough and ruthless if necessary."

I won't," said Connie. "But I feel there must be another reason why you're prepared to help them."

"Let's just say Connie, that you're not the only one lobbying on their behalf and in this other instance, I'll be getting something valuable in return."

Mulgrew's comment intrigued Connie, but she knew better than to push him for any clarification.

"I'd like to think Josiah," continued Connie. "That perhaps a little part of you does actually want to do some good."

"I'm not as bad as people say Connie. All those stories about me. Who knows if they're true?" Mulgrew smiled, but it was a sinister smile more akin to a grinning alligator waiting to devour an unsuspecting victim. "But what I do know, is that it doesn't hurt to let these stories develop a life of their own. In that way, no one will ever dare to cross me."

Mulgrew sat quietly for a few seconds.

"I think we're finished now Connie. I hope you fully appreciate how generous I've been."

Connie nodded.

"Yes. I do Josiah and I'm sure that Gillian and Steve will too."

"Do you really think that it's going to make a difference to them Connie? I'm sure you've been told before that you're wasting your time on them."

"I have, but I hope so."

"We need crusaders like you Connie, but I don't expect that you'll be getting very far with your ideas of social justice."

"Well, I'm not going to give up."

"I'd be disappointed if you did. Remember Connie. If ever you do have a change of heart, there's a job right here waiting for you."

The two of them shook hands and said farewell, Mulgrew accompanying her to the door. Back in the lift, Connie tried to make sense of Mulgrew. He seemed something of an enigma. She had no doubt that he had a violent and criminal past, yet his sharp intelligence had kept him out of reach of the law and over recent years he'd become respectable. The knowledge that 'Old Joe' had turned him down as a client, one who would have proved very profitable for the firm, indicated to her that there was real substance to the rumours of corruption that attached themselves to Mulgrew's company. Yet he had treated her with respect; recognised her ability and not her gender. In that sense, he reflected a liberal view that was totally at odds with the hard image he'd earned in the streets of Manchester. Connie suspected that few individuals called into his office, would have received the same generous treatment that she had. Nevertheless, it was hard to shake off the feeling that as pleasant as he had been, Mulgrew had an intimidating aura around him.

As the lift doors opened, Connie immediately saw Tom rushing towards her.

"Oh, thank goodness Connie," he said, clearly relieved. "I was starting to get worried."

"Why?" asked Connie.

"You were up there for ages."

Without thinking, Tom put his arm around her shoulders and gave her a hug. Connie stood back. She noticed the relief on Tom's face, his sharp intakes of breath expressing his genuine and deeply felt concern.

"I was just about to come up Connie. I wanted to find out what was going on."

"Don't be daft," replied Connie. "Mulgrew was very reasonable. Come on, let's get out of here and get back to work."

Outside, walking down Portland Street, their conversation continued.

"You were in there for three quarters of an hour Connie," said Tom.

"Oh," said Connie, surprised.

Glancing at her watch, Connie could see that it was now almost three o'clock.

"It's just Mulgrew's reputation Connie. That was what made me worried."

Connie smiled, but she was pleased that Tom hadn't taken the lift to the twelfth floor and behaved like some kind of mediaeval knight going to the aid of a damsel in distress. It seemed that there was every chance that he would have done, had she remained any longer in Mulgrew's office.

"I've told you Tom, I'm a big girl now and I don't need any man coming in to save me. Unless, of course, I ask them to."

Tom's face went bright red. He was clearly embarrassed.

"Oh no, no Connie. It wasn't like that at all."

Connie smiled reassuringly.

"I know Tom. I'm sorry. You needn't have worried. You're just a big softie, aren't you?"

She shook her head at him gently.

What on earth do you think could have happened to me, when so many other people were around?"

"I just thought that he might threaten you," replied Tom, rather sheepishly. "I thought you might be feeling uncomfortable."

"No, quite the contrary. He's agreed to let Steve and Gillian off, but we mustn't tell them or anyone else. As far as the world is concerned, I'm the one who's paid everything off for them. You don't know anything about this Tom. Do you understand?"

"Yes, Connie. The result is the important thing."

"That's right. I've had enough of Josiah Mulgrew. Let's get on with the rest of the day."

The incident was now closed and the two of them returned to Clayton House to continue with the afternoon's work.

Chapter 32

It seemed to Connie that of all the men she had met in her life, the only one to excite her was Ralph. She knew that they were different. Their social backgrounds, their politics, their aspirations for the world around them. Yet, didn't opposites attract? Didn't she just find herself at the mercy of emotions that she simply couldn't control, or actually want to control? Slowly, her feelings for Ralph were becoming more intense. The more they spent time together, the closer their relationship became. Connie loved his company. His intelligence came to the fore when they were together, he had a genuine sense of humour and she could therefore not fail to be attracted by his good looks.

For Ralph, Connie had gone far beyond the realms of a challenge. A boyish desire to woo and win a beautiful woman. He now appreciated everything about her. He recognised her uniqueness and knew that if he were ever to make a lasting impression upon her, he would have to act with maturity and sincerity. In all, Ralph would have to abandon the profligacy of youth and Connie was the wake-up call that alerted him to the need to do so. To win her love, Ralph believed that he was finally prepared to change.

Joe Greening could see the difference in Ralph's behaviour whenever Connie was present and he'd been keen to send the two of them out to represent him in meetings with clients, such as the one planned at the 'Midland.' Connie enjoyed these occasions. She was a woman empowered, able to make presentations and conduct negotiations with some prominent local businessmen. It pleased her that 'Old Joe' had complete faith in her abilities and although prospective clients attached a greater degree of importance to Ralph, not being at all egotistical, Connie was prepared to accept the fact with good grace. After all, Ralph was the boss's nephew, it was natural for them to be more deferential towards him.

It was during a meeting at the 'Midland,' the week before Easter, that Connie became aware of just how much Ralph thought about her. She'd been making a presentation to a team from a local food processing company and having finished, had left the room. On her return, she had started to open the door and then quickly stopped, as she could hear one of the delegates making a personal comment about her.

"Well, I don't know about her having a head for figures, but she's certainly got an outstanding one of her own!"

There was laughter before another voice responded.

"Yes. I'd punch her numbers any time!"

It was typical of the juvenile comments that Connie had faced throughout her career, but almost immediately she heard Ralph's voice booming out.

"You'd better take those comments back right now, or I'll see you both outside!"

There was silence. Connie was shocked, fearful that the men would come to blows. Yet her fears were soon allayed as meekly, the two voices responded.

"I'm sorry Ralph," said one.

"Yes, we didn't mean anything by it," added the other.

"I'll have you know that Connie is the finest accountant in our company. She's better than all the rest of us put together. You should be grateful that there's a chance that she could be working with you."

The room was silent; the delegates chastened.

"Now," continued Ralph, firmly in control. "We'll hear no more about it."

Slowly, the buzz of conversation returned. Connie was still at the door. She carefully pulled it shut, deciding to walk around the hotel lobby for a few minutes, before returning. She didn't want Ralph to know that she'd overheard him, or create any embarrassment for their guests. After all, she knew that Greenings wanted their business. Then she chuckled to herself, realising that she was becoming quite the pragmatic businesswoman.

The incident hadn't been mentioned by Ralph when the evening had ended and Connie appreciated the fact. Not only did he not want to hurt her feelings, but more importantly, she was pleased that he wasn't using the incident to try and curry favour with her. His support had been genuine and she had been impressed with his confident and assertive approach towards bringing the delegates in line. It meant that when Ralph approached her, just before the Easter break, to ask if she'd like to go out for a drive, Connie agreed.

He'd come into her office just after dinner. She had been with Tom at the time and he'd asked her a couple of questions about an account that they had been working on. Unusually, he had quickly departed, only to reappear ten minutes later, almost as soon as Tom had returned to his office. Entering, he had closed the door behind him. Connie was surprised. He would only have done that as he had something confidential to discuss. Sat in her chair, she lay her hands on the desk and looked up at him.

"Yes Ralph?" she asked, quietly.

Connie," he said. "We've got the Easter weekend coming up and I wondered if you're free to go for a run out in the Dart."

"Oh," replied Connie, surprised.

"Yes, she needs opening up a bit and I thought that you may not be doing too much over the break and we don't want you overworking at home, do we? So, I thought it would make a nice change for you."

"Where would we be going?" asked Connie.

"Well. Wherever you want. Distance is no object."

"We do want to be able to get home though, don't we Ralph? We wouldn't want to stay out overnight."

Connie smiled. Leaning her head on one side, she gave him an enquiring look.

"Oh, I say Connie!" replied Ralph, trying to appear hurt at the thought that his motives were being called into question. "I hope you're not suggesting that I'm trying to be anything other than a gentleman."

Connie laughed.

"Well, are you Ralph?" she asked, cheekily.

"I should say not!"

Ralph was flustered. Connie was teasing him and he was unsure of how to respond. She was making him wait for an answer. He couldn't believe that he was allowing her to do that. He was sure that he wouldn't have done it for anyone other than Connie.

"Blackpool."

"What?" asked Ralph.

"Blackpool," repeated Connie. "I want to go to Blackpool."

"I was thinking of somewhere more tranquil," said Ralph.

"Well. If not Blackpool Ralph, then we can forget it."

"Oh, Blackpool sounds fine to me Connie," said Ralph, quickly.

"Yes, Ralph. A little bit working-class for your liking perhaps, but you'll have to slum it for a day, won't you?"

"Oh, I'm sure that I'm absolutely going to enjoy it, Connie."

"Are you really Ralph?" asked Connie, with a touch of gentle sarcasm in her voice.

"Oh, yes. Yes, I'm certain," replied Ralph, eagerly.

Connie burst out laughing. Ralph looked at her bewildered. What had he said that was so amusing? Seeing his face, Connie was reminded of a lost and confused little boy and in consequence, her laughter intensified and became so infectious that Ralph couldn't help but follow her example.

"You are a terrible tease Connie," said Ralph, when he'd finally stopped laughing.

"Yes, I know I am," replied Connie, mischievously.

Her eyes were shining and her broad smile made Ralph feel as if he was being bathed in a wonderful, warm glow. She was such a pretty girl and so exciting. His heart raced when she looked at him like that. His body tingled as if it had been charged by electricity. It was an experience that no other woman had ever given him. He wanted her desperately, but he knew that he would have to wait and that delay made him desire her all the more.

"So, when will we go?" asked Ralph. "This Saturday, or is Monday better?"

"Easter Monday," replied Connie.

The playful exchange between them was indicative of their burgeoning relationship. It was clear beyond any doubt that Connie and Ralph had developed a real affinity for one another. Just how far those feelings would go, would most likely be determined by their upcoming trip to Blackpool.

Chapter 33

Ralph had arranged to pick up Connie at eight in the morning. He had followed her directions carefully, driving past the ABC, along Stockport Road, down Syndall Street and then second on the right into Howard Avenue. Noticing that the road came to a dead end, he turned the Dart around and parked outside number fifteen. He'd noticed that there were only a couple of cars parked along the road. It didn't surprise him. It was a poor area and owning a car was beyond the means of most of the inhabitants. To Ralph, Howard Avenue was an alien world. Although he was familiar with Manchester's terraced streets, he tended to move through them quickly and the thought of having to live here, was anathema to him. He found it confusing that Connie continued to stay here. He just couldn't think of one reason why she would do so. It seemed to him nothing short of ridiculous. But then, that was Connie, an amazing woman who, without trying, was slowly winning his heart.

Getting out of the Dart, Ralph gave it his usual admiring glance. It was his pride and joy and as he looked back down Howard Avenue, he suddenly became concerned, thinking that if he were to go into Connie's, his vehicle may not be safe. He was thankful that it was a chilly morning and so he'd kept the roof up, giving the impression that the car was more secure and thus less welcoming to prying eyes and fingers.

"Don't worry Ralph. No one's going to damage your baby!"

It was Connie. Concerned for his beloved Dart, Ralph hadn't noticed her opening the front door and stepping out on to the pavement. Shuffling away from the car, Ralph's face went red and a guilty expression flitted quickly across his features.

"Oh, no. No Connie," he replied, hesitantly. "Nothing of the sort. I just thought I'd seen something on one of the wheels."

"Come off it, Ralph," replied Connie, chuckling. "You think that you've come into a nest of Vipers and a den of iniquity, don't you?"

"No. No, I don't," said Ralph, with a notable lack of conviction.

"You 'toffs.' You always stereotype the working classes, don't you? It's all right Ralph, you and the car will be perfectly safe."

Connie smiled. It was a reassuring sign to Ralph that he hadn't upset her. It was the last thing that he'd intended to do. Nevertheless, he knew that she was right. From his background, it was inevitable that he would grow up distrustful of the working classes. He had come to believe all the warnings he'd been given about their rough, crude manners, their loose morals and their hostility to their social betters.

"Anyway Ralph. I'm all ready to go. So, if you start the car, I'll just nip back inside and get my bag."

Having returned, Connie locked her front door and got into the Dart alongside Ralph.

"Hopefully, we're early enough to avoid the traffic," said Ralph. "It should be a nice drive Connie, especially when we get out into the countryside."

Back down and on to Stockport Road, Ralph followed the A6 towards the city centre and then into Salford, through Pendleton, Swinton and Walkden. The traffic was light and the Dart made good progress out into the open country.

"I suspect the traffic will build up as we get nearer to Preston," said Ralph. "But now they've built the new bypass, we'll be able to avoid the town and push straight on to Blackpool."

"It's all right," said Connie. "I'm enjoying the ride. There's no rush."

"Yes, although it's a shame it hasn't warmed up a bit more, so that I can take the hood down."

"Well, at least I won't get blown all over the place," replied Connie.

"That's half the fun of it," said Ralph.

Connie was enjoying herself. It was good to get out for the day and she was finding motoring a pleasing experience and Ralph good company.

"I've been thinking of taking driving lessons myself Ralph."

"You should. Get mobile. It makes it so much easier to get around."

The conversation flowed back and forth and it seemed to Connie as if the time was flying by. It wasn't long before they'd put Chorley behind them and were approaching the Preston Bypass, the first stretch of motorway to be built in the country.

"I've been looking forward to this," said Ralph. "We can open her up a bit now."

With that, he began to depress the accelerator and the Dart's V8 engine roared into life. The car seemed to take off, the scenery rushing by.

"I thought the limit was seventy," shouted Connie, trying to make sure that Ralph could hear her over the increased noise of the engine.

"It is," replied Ralph.

Connie glanced at the speedometer, which was just visible behind the steering wheel. She could see that Ralph was doing 75 mph.

"Sorry Ralph," shouted Connie, "I thought that you were going a lot faster."

"No," replied Ralph. "It only seems that way because we're sat closer to the ground and you hear more noise in a convertible."

Without being asked, Ralph relaxed his foot on the accelerator and the Dart slowed back down to 55 mph. He didn't want to spoil Connie's enjoyment of the journey, sensing that she didn't like going too fast. Connie felt pleased. Ralph had respected her feelings and wasn't trying to impress her by posing as a new Stirling Moss or Jack Brabham. It seemed that when he was alone with her, Ralph acted with maturity and good sense, a far cry from his reputation as a selfish playboy.

Arriving in Blackpool, Ralph followed the signs for the Promenade. The traffic had built up by now. It was the first bank holiday of the year and the resort acted like a magnet to people from all over the country. They were eager to get some fun and entertainment into their lives, having gone through the long, dark and damp winter days. Connie however, didn't mind the queues of cars moving slowly towards the North Pier. Looking in front of her, Connie could see the Blackpool Tower rising impressively into the sky and she knew that they were entering the famous 'Golden Mile.' Connie began to feel excited, just as she had as a little girl when her mam had brought her here on a day trip organised by the 'Rutland'. She remembered it is a magical day and she was eager to see if Blackpool was still as captivating to her as an adult, as it had been when she was a child.

Connie wasn't disappointed. The pavements were thronged with people of all ages, smiling and laughing. There were a host of attractions: arcades full of slot machines; gypsy fortune tellers; snack bars; cafés; fish and chip shops; pubs offering music and dance; bingo; shops selling buckets and spades, Blackpool rock and candy floss; oyster bars; a ghost train; freak shows; fun houses; cinemas and theatres. Everything you could possibly want was here, even Louis Tussauds Waxworks near the Central Pier.

Driving on past the South Pier, Ralph parked the car. They'd arrived at the Pleasure Beach. Turning to Connie, Ralph could see that her face was radiant.

"You're really excited, aren't you?" he asked, smiling.

"No, don't be daft Ralph. I was just taking it all in. Having a good nosy."

"Really?" said Ralph, indicating that he didn't believe her.

"Yes, really," replied Connie, who wanted to conceal her childlike enthusiasm from him.

Ralph had been touched by her reactions on the 'Golden Mile.' She was wide-eyed, almost innocent. Connie had shown a vulnerability that he had never previously seen. At work, she avoided any signs of feminine weakness. Ralph felt an overwhelming desire to put his arm around her and hold her close. Yet he knew it was too soon; he had no wish to give Connie the wrong impression. If something were to develop between the two of them, it had to be because Connie wanted it to. There was a real uncertainty about how the day's events would unfold and for Ralph, that made it all the more thrilling.

Getting out of the car, the pair were hit by a cold blast of air coming from the cold waters off the south shore. They were both prepared however. Connie muffled up in a jumper, slacks, coat and scarf, still appeared gorgeous to Ralph, who was wearing a thick jacket, jumper and scarf himself.

"Whoa!" exclaimed Ralph. "I hope you're nice and warm Connie."

"Yes Ralph, I'm fine."

Heading into the Pleasure Park, Connie had to make a confession.

"I'm afraid that the roller coasters scare me a little bit Ralph."

"Oh?" replied Ralph, unable to hide his disappointment.

"Well, I don't mind waiting for you if you want to go on them."

That thought was furthest from Ralph's mind. If he couldn't go on them with Connie, then he wouldn't bother. After all, they were supposed to be there together and to Ralph, that meant that they should share their experiences. The 'Big Dipper,' the 'Grand National' and the aptly named 'Rollercoaster,' wouldn't be enjoying Ralph's company today.

"I'm all right on any of the other rides Ralph. It's just rollercoasters."

"Never mind," said Ralph. "There are plenty of other rides we can go on."

And there were, but they started at the 'Fun House.' Stood watching and listening to the laughing man located outside it, Ralph felt unnerved.

"There's something sinister about that laugh Connie."

"Don't be daft Ralph. It's just infectious."

"No, it's definitely sinister," insisted Ralph, shaking his head.

"Woooo!" said Connie eerily, suddenly tickling the top of Ralph's arms and shoulders as if she were a scary ghost.

Ralph pulled away from her laughing, having enjoyed the feeling of her fingers on the bare skin at the top of his neck.

"Come on, let's go in then," said Ralph.

Inside, Connie tackled the moving floors, revolving barrels and other obstacles with real gusto. She found it difficult to keep her balance though and was amazed at how Ralph seemed to negotiate it all without any concerns whatsoever.

"Oh, aren't you the clever so-and-so," said Connie, noting how pleased Ralph was with himself.

"Well, there's nothing to it really," replied Ralph, confident that he'd impressed her.

Connie smiled. She was delighted that Ralph had thrown himself into the spirit of the day. As he'd never been to Blackpool before, she hadn't been sure how he would react. The resort's reputation had been built firmly on its appeal to the working classes, therefore it wasn't necessarily attractive to those who came from more privileged backgrounds. Blackpool was a place that was designed to make people forget their troubles, go out and simply have a good time. Ralph certainly seemed to be doing that now.

After the 'Fun House,' it was time to try out some of the rides. The 'Derby Racer,' a large carousel with four rows of horses, was Connie's first choice. It was surprising to Ralph, given that it moved quite quickly. He assumed that as Connie didn't like roller coasters, this ride may also prove testing for her. As Connie was about to mount up on one of the outside horses Ralph, without thinking, gently lay his hand on hers.

"It's better to go on one of the inside horses Connie."

She turned her head towards him and the two of them made eye contact. There were long, lingering looks on both sides, before Connie finally averted her eyes to avoid any embarrassment.

"Why's that Ralph?" she asked, quickly.

"The inside ones go slower, as they travel far less distance. If you sit there first, then you can see how it goes."

Connie smiled and did as he suggested. As the carousel started, she looked across at him. His concern for her was endearing and she thought about how unusual that feeling was. Normally, she would have questioned any man who suggested to her that she shouldn't do something. Yet now she had willingly followed his advice and with that realisation, Connie began to understand that she was starting to fall for him.

The carousel was followed by a trip through 'Alice's Wonderland.' It was a ride that was relatively new to the Pleasure Beach and it took visitors through scenes from Alice's adventures. As a child, Ralph had been unimpressed with the story, but now Connie was sat next to him and they had a 'Cheshire Cat' carriage all to themselves. The fact that there wasn't much room, meant that they were pressed against one another and with the darkness descending, Ralph felt a degree of intimacy developing between them. The sense of familiarity continued as they travelled on the 'Ghost Train' and Connie, laughing nervously, pressed into him as she tried to avoid the dangling arm of a skeleton.

The rides, it seemed, were pushing the pair of them together, whether they wanted it or not. Finally, feeling more confident that she could cope with any of the attractions, Connie assured Ralph that she would be fine if they went on the 'Whip.' It was a 'waltzer' type ride, carriages spinning about as they went around. Pulled back into her seat by the force generated by the revolutions of the carriage, Connie felt a little giddy. She rested her head on Ralph's shoulder and moved her body against him. He looked down into her face and could see that she had become very pale. Freeing his arm, Ralph put it around her and held her tight, occasionally patting her arm as an act of reassurance. As the ride came to a halt, Ralph helped Connie to her feet and out of the carriage.

"Come on let's go and find a seat Connie. Take a breather and you'll be okay."

Connie nodded hesitantly, allowing Ralph to put his arm around her once more. She still felt a little unsteady and appreciated his help in getting her to a nearby bench. Sitting Connie down, Ralph crouched in front of her.

"Take a few deep breaths Connie, you'll soon be as right as rain."

He was smiling at her but Connie could tell that he was still a little concerned, even though she was starting to feel a lot better. She looked into his blue eyes and raised a smile in return.

"Sit down Ralph. Here, beside me," she said quietly, patting the bench for emphasis.

Ralph moved next to her and sat down.

Without warning, Connie suddenly took his hand.

"Thank you, Ralph," she said, softly.

"What for?" asked Ralph, surprised.

"For being lovely and bringing me here."

Ralph blushed and turned away. He didn't know what to say. Connie smiled, she felt in control and prepared to take the next step. Leaning across to Ralph she turned his face towards her and kissed him gently on the lips. She felt Ralph respond, slowly at first and then with intensity and passion. She felt a tingle of excitement and as their lips slowly parted, she could see that he, like her, was taking a deep breath in order to get his emotions under control. Laying her head against his shoulder, Connie felt warm and calm. It seemed so right. She just knew that Ralph was the man she had been waiting for. She enjoyed being with him and today he had proved to be a perfect companion. But more than that, she felt a real attraction to him. He was handsome and she desired him and she knew that he desired her. Yet if he was to be serious about her, then he would have to wait, for Connie had no intention of taking their intimacy to the ultimate level, unless they were married.

Ralph, softly stroking Connie's shoulder, didn't need to be told that Connie was an old-fashioned girl. He'd considered whether that was why he'd been so determined to win her; that, in common parlance, 'we always want what we can't have.' But he knew that it just wasn't the case. Today had proved it. Not once had he tried to take advantage of her, although there were times when he could have. The kiss that Connie had given him had shaken him to his foundations. It was raw and powerful and had true meaning. Her affection hadn't been lightly given and Ralph was determined that he wasn't going to lose her. As difficult as it was going to be, for his desire for Connie knew no bounds, he would play by her rules in order to keep their relationship alive.

Finally, lifting her head from Ralph's shoulder, Connie sat up.

"I'd like to go on the tram and ride along the Promenade."

"Yes, Connie. We can catch it here. We can go and get something to eat and then get the tram back to collect the car."

Standing up, the couple began to walk towards the entrance. Making the first move, Connie put her hand in Ralph's. He turned to her and smiled, the two of them walking together, side by side.

Chapter 34

It was almost ten o'clock when Ralph had dropped Connie off at home. It had been a long day, but eventful and enjoyable and her sense of contentment at the development of her new relationship with Ralph, meant that she had a restful night's sleep. Over the next few days, it became clear to both of them that a strong emotional bond had been created between them by the events at Blackpool. They increasingly sought out each other's company and although it was never said, the two of them were effectively 'going out together,' just as enthusiastically as a teenage couple. It was natural then that Ralph had come to pick her up at Howard Avenue, the Saturday after their visit to Blackpool. Ralph had arrived just after dinner, attracting the attention of a gang of young children who were keen to admire the Dart. Sitting in the front room, Connie had heard Ralph pull up outside and looking out of the net curtains, she was amused to see Ralph stood on the pavement, looking aghast at the kids swarming around his pride and joy. Moving quickly to the door, she opened it and went outside to rescue him.

"Oh, hi Connie," said Ralph, clearly relieved to see her.

Connie smiled. She recognised all the kids. They were the sons and daughters of her neighbours in Howard Avenue.

"It's all right Ralph. They don't get much chance to see a fancy sports car close-up. Take the hood down. Let them have a look inside."

"Oh, yes Mister. Go on," said a grimy looking lad.

Around ten years of age, he was wearing a thick jumper, which was full of holes and about three sizes too big. His jeans were tatty and frayed. He seemed to be the self-appointed leader of the assembled gang.

"He will Jim," said Connie. "But none of you need to be putting your hands all over the car, do you?"

She could see that Ralph, who'd had the Dart waxed and polished ready to pick her up, was struggling hard not to lose his temper.

"No Connie. Come on kids," said Jim, talking to his comrades. "Don't touch the car."

Hearing the voice of authority, the others stepped back and then turned expectantly towards Ralph.

"Go on then Ralph, take the top down," said Connie.

Slowly, Ralph unattached the top and pulled it down. There was a collective sound of amazement as the kids peered over to look into the beautiful interior of the Dart.

"Hey Ralph, how fast can it go?" asked Jim.

"Yeah. I bet its dead fast," said a small boy by his side.

Ralph was taken aback, shocked that this errant youth would have the audacity to address him, an adult, by his first name. He looked bewildered and Connie chuckled.

"Go on Mister," she said, mimicking the voice of a child, "tell us how fast it goes. I bet it's not much faster than a bus."

Ralph didn't initially see the funny side of Connie's remark, but when he looked at her and saw the cheeky smile on her face, his attitude soon changed. Shaking his head and sighing out loud, he turned to Jim.

"Of course, it's much faster than a bus."

"I know," said Jim. "Connie's just being daft. But how fast can it go?"

"Daimler claimed that it could reach 120 mph. I've not gone that fast though."

"Have you ever done a ton in it?"

Ralph hesitated. He looked across at Connie. He had, but was unsure of how she'd react if he told them. He saw her looking straight at him. It was clear that she was eager to hear his answer.

"Well, Ralph?" asked Connie.

"Yes, I have, but only on a very open, straight stretch of road. And of course, children," said Ralph, "I shouldn't have."

The answer pleased Connie. She preferred him to be honest.

"Okay kids," said Connie, "let Ralph get the hood back up. You've all had a good look now."

"Can we watch your car Mister?"

Ralph looked at Jim. The latter's request had confused him.

"Watch my car?" he asked.

"No. He doesn't want you to. Neither do I," said Connie, interrupting.

Jim and the other kids looked disappointed and slowly made their way back down the Avenue.

"What did the lad mean?" asked Ralph.

"He wanted you to give them money in exchange for keeping an eye on your car. To keep it safe."

"What!" exclaimed Ralph. "That's extortion. Who does he think he is? Al Capone!"

Connie burst out laughing. Ralph was outraged. He really had no inkling about what life in Ardwick was like.

"What's so funny?" asked Ralph. "I don't think it's funny. It's unbelievable!"

Silent, Ralph suddenly had a thought.

"Oh God Connie!" he exclaimed, "they're going to scratch the Dart. Do you think I should have paid them?"

Quickly, Ralph's mood had shifted from anger to panic. His face was a picture. Connie was laughing fit to burst. Gradually calming down, she tried to reassure him.

"It's all right Ralph. The car's safe. They'd never touch it, especially as they know that you're visiting me."

"But they said …"

"No Ralph," said Connie interrupting, "they wouldn't. They just implied that your car might get damaged if it's not being watched. It won't and if you had given them money, they would have cleared off anyway, as soon as you went inside."

"Well, the absolute scoundrels. How can you live with these people Connie!"

Once more, Ralph was outraged and Connie burst into fits of laughter.

"Stop it, Ralph!" she said, with difficulty. "Please, stop it! I can't laugh anymore!" begged Connie.

Almost bent double, Connie was finding it difficult to get her words out.

Ralph looked perplexed. Why on earth was she laughing at him? He waited quietly until she had finally gained control of herself and spoke to him again.

"It's okay Ralph. It's just that you've been so sheltered. You know nothing about the real world and real people, do you?"

Ralph looked at her concerned.

"It's not your fault," continued Connie. "You're just different. You don't understand what life is like around here. And don't worry Ralph, I don't mind you being different."

Connie walked towards him and looked up into his eyes.

"You've not kissed me yet. Aren't you pleased to see me?"

"What, kiss you here in the street?" asked Ralph, uncertainly.

"Why not?"

Ralph needed no second invitation. He put his arms around Connie and kissed her fully on her soft, inviting lips, feeling her warmly respond. It was a kiss charged with longing and emotion. Connie could sense Ralph's desire and felt the intensity of the passion within herself too. She stepped away, knowing that the atmosphere between them was becoming too heated. There was a pause, the two of them standing quietly on the pavement as they struggled to get their feelings back under control.

"I'd best check the hood again," said Ralph.

"Yes," replied Connie, grateful for the breathing space that a return to the commonplace had provided. "I need to get my coat. Come inside Ralph and I'll show you around."

Opening the door, Connie led Ralph into the front room. He couldn't fail to be impressed by the choice of furniture and her eye for decoration, yet he felt that it was wasted here. Connie's decision to remain in Howard Avenue had aroused Ralph's curiosity. These two-up two-downs, with their outside toilets and no bathrooms, were part of the past. He was eager to find out why she was still here.

With time to spare, Connie made them both a drink. Sat at the kitchen table, they each had a steaming mug of tea with an open biscuit tin placed between them.

"You know Connie, I respect your work with the Labour Party and your love for Ardwick ..."

"No, you don't Ralph," said Connie, interrupting him. "But it's okay."

"Well," continued Ralph, "I have to ask, for all that work and effort that you and others have put in, what's changed?"

"What do you mean?"

"Well Connie, it's not 1945 anymore, is it? People are aspirational now and with aspiration comes individuality and selfishness. It's all about 'I'm all right Jack.' The idea of community will die. People will move out of these areas once they have money and those that remain will be scattered to the new estates when they knock down these old houses. The chance of building your socialist community, has gone. Capitalism has triumphed."

Then what do you propose that we should do about it?" asked Connie.

"Make the best of it. We can't deny ourselves the fruits of our labour. Why shouldn't we have good things? Why shouldn't you? To me it seems so natural. You need to accept the fact, Connie."

Ralph looked at her fondly and took her hand. His words, though critical, weren't seen by Connie as condescending. She wanted him to continue. After all, if there was to be a lasting relationship between them, she needed to understand his thoughts completely.

"You've got such a wonderful heart," continued Ralph. "Because you're so intent on helping others, you don't believe that you should concentrate on making life better for yourself."

"And you've come to that conclusion because?" asked Connie.

"Because you still live here. Yes, I know that you've bought some lovely, expensive furniture, but you're still determined, despite your success, to try and remain a member of the working-class."

"This is my home, Ralph. This house, this street, Ardwick, made me what I am."

"Do you think for a moment Connie, that your neighbours feel the same as you? No, they don't," continued Ralph, shaking his head. "They'd all love to have what I've got. They wouldn't hesitate to change places with me, if they could. They'd leave here right away and wouldn't give a second though to those left behind."

"No, I can't believe that Ralph. You're wrong. Some people might act like that, but most wouldn't."

"I'm not wrong Connie. The 'brave new world,' the great socialist community, never had a chance. You can't see it for yourself, because you're too emotionally committed to the dream."

Connie stared at Ralph. Her eyes were fixed on his. The hint of a smile crossed her lips.

"Do you know Ralph, you really are a 'con man', aren't you?"

"What?" asked Ralph, concerned.

"You're 'happy-go-lucky' with everyone at work and when you mix with the clients. You play the part of 'good old Ralph' to perfection, don't you? But then, when you're with me, I see a completely different side of you. Your knowledge and intelligence, the depth of your conversation. I think that you're far more of an enigma than I am."

"I know Connie," said Ralph, smiling. He was relieved that he hadn't upset her. "When you're young and the boss's nephew, you learn very quickly that you have to be the life and soul of the party, unless you don't want people talking to you. With the clients, it's the role I'm expected to play. Uncle Joe is the serious one. You should think of the pair of us as a kind of double act."

Connie laughed.

"What, like Morecambe and Wise?"

"No, silly."

"I know Ralph," replied Connie, smiling and gently touching his hand.

It was clear that Ralph still hadn't got the measure of her sense of humour. He was quiet for a moment, thinking that he should explain to Connie why his conversation with her had seemed relatively serious.

"When I'm with you Connie," continued Ralph, "I feel able to be myself. I care about you and I wanted to let you know that I think that by living here and giving so much to everyone else, that you're putting too many demands on yourself."

"I'm not being hard on myself," replied Connie "and I don't feel guilty about the money I earn. Difficult as it is for you to believe, I do actually like it here. I know that I may well have to move out at some stage, but at the moment, I don't have to."

"What happens if you ever decide to settle down with someone Connie?"

The question was innocently asked but when Connie hesitated, Ralph became aware of the significance of what he'd said.

"Well, when that comes about, I suppose I'll have some thinking to do," said Connie eventually.

"Yes, perhaps your husband wouldn't be too keen on living here," replied Ralph.

The conversation had taken an interesting turn. Each of them knew that they were speculating about what could happen between them in the future. Yet neither of them wanted to admit the fact to the other.

"Maybe so Ralph. Who knows?"

Connie stood up and took their mugs and plates over to the sink. She turned to Ralph.

"Come on then Ralph. We'd best be getting off. That is if you still want to take me out."

"Of course, I do," said Ralph, eagerly.

Connie laughed.

"Oh, hang on, let's hope that the Dart's all right," she said, a hint of concern in her voice.

Momentarily, she saw a look of concern on Ralph's face and then he smiled.

"No, Connie. You're not getting me this time!"

"I don't know what you could possibly mean Ralph," replied Connie, pretending to be wounded by his comment.

The two of them laughed. Ralph was finally getting to grips with her unusual sense of humour. The day was going well. They were learning so many things about one another and there was an openness and honesty to their conversation. It was enough to give the pair of them much food for thought. In a relatively short time, they had become very close to one another. If they decided to take things further, then those questions about settling down would become real and immediate.

Chapter 35

The following day, Sunday, Connie had arranged to see Kath. Her friend was going to Southern Cemetery to take some flowers to the grave of her husband and daughter. Kath went regularly, but this was the first time she had asked Connie to accompany her and it was an indication of how close their relationship had become. It would take two buses to get them there, the long journey giving them ample time to catch up on recent events. Boarding the bus to Piccadilly, the two women sat down and Connie told Kath about her outings with Ralph and how she was becoming increasingly attracted to him.

"It sounds like it's becoming serious Connie," remarked Kath.

"Yes, I suppose that it is."

"Serious enough that you might get engaged?"

Direct as ever, Kath got straight to the heart of the matter.

"Well, I think that he might ask me."

"And what would you say?"

"I suppose that I've not really thought about it."

"But what does your heart tell you?"

"I really like him. He's so different when he's with me compared to when he's with others."

"Is that good or bad?"

"It's good, because I know that he tries harder for me. He cares about me. He's affectionate and yes, he's very handsome."

"But?" asked Kath.

"Engaged. Married. I'm not sure that I'm ready for that," replied Connie.

"Is anybody ready for it?" asked Kath. "I'm not sure that anyone can really know what marriage has in store for them."

Connie nodded.

"And how's Tom?" asked Kath.

"He's fine," said Connie.

"About you going out with Ralph?"

"I don't think he's that aware of it. We don't go out of our way to advertise our relationship," replied Connie.

"Oh love, sometimes you have a real innocence about you," said Kath, concerned.

Connie looked at her confused.

"You must have noticed how Tom looks at you," continued Kath. "I've seen it every time he's come with you to the house. He can't take his eyes off you."

"Tom's fine. He's accepted that I don't want to go out with him. I told him so when he asked me. I wouldn't ever dream of leading him on or upsetting him. He's my friend Kath."

"Oh, if it were only that simple Connie."

"But why shouldn't it be?"

"Because it rarely is. The lad's still carrying a torch for you."

"But that's not fair Kath. It's not my fault."

"I know love, but you're going to have to treat him carefully. Especially as you spend a lot of time with him."

"Yes, I suppose so."

Arriving at Piccadilly bus station, the two friends walked the short distance to their next stop. They found that their bus to Southern Cemetery was just about to leave and they quickly clambered on board and sat down.

"Marriage can be wonderful Connie," said Kath, re-opening their conversation.

"Do you think that people change after they get married?" asked Connie.

"I'm not the best one to ask about that Connie. Stan and I were only married for a short time and for much of it he was away fighting."

"I know that you told me that he'd been out in Egypt and at Gallipoli, but didn't he come back to England, to Manchester?"

"Yes love, he did, in early 1917. His regiment were brought back to go and fight in France. They were given some home leave and I was able to spend a few days with him before he returned."

"That must have been awful Kath. Not seeing him for so long, but knowing that he'd be off again in no time at all."

"Yes, but I kept my feelings to myself. I couldn't let Stan know. I didn't want him to worry. But it was so good to touch and hold him again. It was when I got pregnant with Alice."

It was the first time that Kath had directly referred to her daughter. It was a subject she found difficult to talk about and then only to those who'd gained her confidence.

"The thing I remember most when he left London Road Station to return to France, was seeing his uniform and hating it. When he was in the Territorials when I first met him, all I could think about was how handsome he looked in it. How very foolish I was. It was the very thing that would take him away from me."

Connie nodded, signalling her understanding. She was listening intently.

"Every day the women at Hyde Road used to dread getting a letter telling them that their husband or sweetheart had been killed and it seemed to us that the fighting would go on forever. We kept our spirits up as best we could, but whenever anyone got the news, we all felt it."

Kath paused and looked out of the window. Connie could tell that her story was still a painful one.

"Stan got wounded at the end of March in the fighting at Baupame," she continued. "They were overrun by the Germans, but they got him to safety. I didn't know anything for weeks and then got news that he was being brought home. At least I could be thankful for that. He ended up in a temporary hospital at Moseley Road School in Fallowfield. They had special uniforms for them, blue with white shirts and red ties. You could see hundreds of them, all over Manchester, from lots of different hospitals. Stan had been badly gassed and hit by shrapnel. He was so weak and found it difficult to breathe. He could hardly walk, but they got him out into the fresh air. I was able to take Alice to see him, when my bosses didn't object."

"Object? asked Connie, in amazement.

"Oh yes, love. You had shifts to work, a war to win. Men were being lost all over. What did another one matter?"

"But surely?" said Connie.

"Different times love and it was much the same for women in the Second War."

"How did you manage with Alice?"

"My mother looked after her. I moved in with her when I was expecting. I didn't take any time off work until I had her and went straight back afterwards. We needed the money."

Connie shook her head. She couldn't envisage how difficult it must have been.

"Stan never recovered. He knew that he wouldn't. He told me that his love for me would live on through little Alice. I told him not to be silly. I insisted that he'd get better, but we both knew. I really loved him Connie and it hurt so much to lose him. But I had to stay strong. Stan told me that I had to be there for our daughter. And then I lost little Alice too."

Once more Kath paused. Connie held her breath. She wasn't sure what to say. She thought that perhaps she should tell Kath that it was all right to stop; she needn't upset herself anymore. Yet sensing that Kath wanted to tell her, Connie took hold of her hand and pressed it gently.

"Alice was a victim of the Spanish flu," continued Kath. "A terrible, awful disease. It came at the end of the War. We were all terrified of it.

It spread so quickly and it was deadly. My mother had noticed Alice was struggling to breathe, then she started to go blue. She sent for me at work. We went to the MRI. There was nothing that they could do. I like to think that she'd gone to join her dad."

"Oh, Kath," said Connie, a slight tremor in her voice.

"No, it's all right love. Don't get upset," said Kath. "It's just that once in a while I need to tell someone and remind myself of just why I still want to support the call for peace and justice in the world."

Connie nodded, her resolve fortified by the reassuring warmth and softness of Kath's hand.

The bus had now arrived at Southern Cemetery and together with the majority of the passengers, who had also come to visit the graves of their loved ones, Kath and Connie got off. Striding purposefully through the entrance, it was clear that Kath came here regularly. The cemetery was huge and it could be a bewildering place for those who were unfamiliar with it. There were many large memorials to some of Manchester's wealthiest citizens. Connie shook her head. Didn't they realise that all were equal in death?

"Yes Connie," Kath remarked, when seeing her friend's reaction. "They don't seem to realise that all the money in the world won't impress God."

"Have any of these people, or their families, ever read the New Testament?" asked Connie. "I'm sure that it says something about a rich man, a camel and the eye of a needle," she added, mischievously.

Going on a little further, Kath stopped. She turned to Connie and pointed out a series of family graves to the side of the path that they were walking down.

"I passed here so many times before I noticed," she said.

Connie looked at her enquiringly.

"These headstones, the three of them. The first one here and then, past this next one, look at the two that follow."

Kath pointed carefully at the headstones she wanted Connie to look at.

"What do you notice about them Connie?"

"What do you mean Kath?"

"The writing. What's been written on them?"

Connie stared at each of them in turn, reading the names of the people that had been interned in these large family graves. But she had no idea about what Kath was getting at.

"You're like I was," said Kath, finally breaking the silence. "I didn't see it for ages and then, perhaps as more names were added, it suddenly became clear to me."

Once more, Kath paused. It was almost as if she was hoping that her companion would come up with the answer. Connie though, was mystified and waited eagerly for Kath to reveal what it was.

"It's the first name on each headstone. Each of them is a young man, a soldier who lost his life in the Great War. The names that follow are of his grandparents and then his parents. You can see the huge tragedy brought about by the conflict. Parents, most certainly grandparents, don't expect to outlive their sons or grandsons. Yet this is what the Great War brought us. If you go around this cemetery, you'll see so many similar headstones. A complete and utter waste of lives."

"Yes, I see," said Connie.

"You know Connie, after the last war so much rubbish was talked about appeasement, about giving in to the dictators. Every family in Manchester in the 'Thirties' had been robbed of some of their young men because of the fighting in the trenches. Why wouldn't we all support the League of Nations, peace and collective security? In those days there were so many anti-war groups in Manchester. I was a member of the Women's International League for Peace and Freedom. We had an office on Princess Street. In July 1937, there was a Manchester and Salford Peace Week. We had a Women's Day with a big meeting on Platt Fields and Ellen Wilkinson spoke at it. We were desperate that what had happened to young men like Stan, should never happen again. Hitler wanted it to be different though."

"Yes," said Connie. "He did."

"I accepted that we had to fight Nazism, but we weren't wrong to do all in our power to try and build a new, peaceful world."

"No, you weren't Kath, but you won't find much support for that view in the history books."

"That's the problem Connie. No matter how much death and destruction there is, you still get those with an interest in spreading violence and conflict."

It was a sobering thought, but given Kath's experiences, one that she couldn't avoid whenever she came to visit her husband's final resting place.

"Come on Connie," continued Kath. "Let's get these flowers to Stan and Alice."

Walking on, the two of them passed many rows of graves before finally turning right on to a narrow path. They advanced another fifty yards, before Kath halted in front of a large headstone upon which the name Stanley Edward Cooke was etched in black lettering. Underneath him was the name of his daughter, Alice Elizabeth Cooke. Connie could see that Kath had lost her husband on September 5th 1918 and that on

January 7th 1919, their daughter had followed him. Alice had been less than thirteen months old. She wondered how Kath could possibly have coped with the double tragedy. Somehow, she did.

Connie could see that Kath had put her new flowers on the floor ready to place them in the vase, once she had emptied it.

"I'll do that for you Kath. Is there a tap back where I saw the bins?"

"Yes, love. Just turn right when you get back to the main path and there's one a few yards further down. You'll see it."

Connie followed her instructions, emptied out the old flowers into the bin and then washed out the vase and filled it with clean water. Meanwhile, Kath unwrapped her flowers and trimmed the stalks ready to put them in the vase.

"Thanks love," said Kath, as Connie bent down and placed the vase at the front of the headstone.

Carefully, Kath placed her bouquet into the vase. She adjusted the flowers and then stood up and moved a couple of steps back to evaluate her alterations to the arrangement.

"Yes, they're nice," declared Kath, with satisfaction.

"Yes, they are. They look beautiful," said Connie.

The women moved back a little further and admired the flowers. They were silent. Connie, conscious of leaving Kath to her own thoughts, retreated a short distance. She understood that despite the long passage of time, it would never get easier for her companion to accept the loss of both her husband and daughter. She knew that Kath was a devoted Christian, but someone who shunned organised religion. Kath had explained to her that war and injustice had made it so.

"I saw both Anglicans and Catholics preach for fighting against Germany in the Great War. I saw the Vatican pandering to Mussolini, Franco and Hitler and the Church of England support the monarchy and the establishment. Organised religion," Kath had said, "simply exists to control the words of Jesus; in reality, to deny them. For after all, Jesus was a revolutionary. Yet if you can deny his ideas to ordinary people, then Christianity can keep the working classes down, rather than liberate them."

"But don't you ever lose your faith in God?" Connie had asked. "The world is so hard and so little seems to change?"

"Jesus has shown us the way things should be. It's men who continue to deny us the world that God wants."

Kath's powerful words had illustrated her natural intelligence. To the party intellectuals, with their backgrounds of deep academic study, she would have appeared a strange, little old lady whose views, though quaint, were the result of pure emotion and therefore not soundly based.

Connie however, recognised that Kath had lived an authentic, working-class life and it meant that her understanding of the shortcomings of society and the reasons for it, were far more valid than those who hadn't. Kath was in the tradition of James Keir Hardie. He'd been desperate to create a party of and for, the working classes, with members of Parliament from the very class who knew what it was like to be cheated and exploited.

Having finished a final, silent prayer, Kath looked round to see that Connie had remained standing at a respectful distance. She appreciated the empathy shown by her young friend.

"Well Connie, it's time we were heading back."

Connie nodded. The women linked their arms and walked slowly back along the path to the Cemetery's entrance.

"Do you know Connie," said Kath. "If you truly love someone, that love will always be there and in fact, it continues to grow. I love Stan more with every passing day. No one could ever have replaced him. Through truly loving someone, you finally realise the meaning of life. When you do make your choice Connie, be as sure as you can that he really is, that one special person."

"I will," said Connie, quietly.

"Yes love. Just make sure that you do."

Chapter 36

Connie had heard nothing from her mam since she had returned to Frank before Christmas. She was disappointed that Doris hadn't taken her up on the offer to return to Howard Avenue, but deep down she wasn't surprised by her decision. Since Doris had left, Connie had accepted that she was unlikely to become a presence in her life, but confronted by Frank's abusive behaviour, Connie's conscience began to bother her. She knew that her mam wouldn't appreciate any interference in her affairs and feared that if they argued, Doris wouldn't seek her help in the future. Yet the visit to Southern Cemetery with Kath, had made Connie aware of how precious family relationships could be. She therefore decided that, despite the potential difficulties, she would go ahead and visit her mam.

Doris had told Connie that she had moved into a house on Polygon Avenue. Connie decided to go there after work and find her. It wasn't far. Connie walked down Syndall Street, then crossed over Stockport Road and made her way back towards the ABC, past Shakespeare Street, Legh Place and Wilson Street, before turning left into Polygon Avenue. Starting logically, Connie knocked on the front door of the first house at the top of the near side of the Avenue. Receiving no reply, she moved on to the next. Getting halfway down, she had found no one who seemed to know of Doris or Frank, then she finally got a positive response.

A young woman in her early twenties opened the door, a baby in her arms. Connie apologised for disturbing her and then asked if she knew her mam.

"Do you mean Doris, who lives with Frank?" the woman asked.

"Yes," replied Connie.

"They were here. Just across the road at number twenty. But they've gone."

Oh?" asked Connie.

"Yes," the woman replied. "About a month ago. I can't say that anyone was sorry to see them go."

Realising that Connie may take offence, she quickly apologised for her words.

"Oh, I'm sorry. I didn't mean to be rude."

"No, that's okay," replied Connie. "I'm not surprised. I don't suppose it was very peaceful with them around, was it?"

The young woman shook her head.

"You're right there. Every Friday and Saturday it was the same. They'd come home from the 'Shakespeare' arguing and he'd be shouting at her, threatening her in the street. Then, once they'd gone in the house, it would usually 'kick-off.' Their neighbours tried to stop it at first, but gave up. Your mam wouldn't let the police help and after they'd been a few times, they didn't bother coming back."

Connie wasn't surprised. She'd expected as much. It seemed that her mam was still defending Frank, making excuses for him and putting up with his behaviour.

"Do you know if they still go in the 'Shakespeare?'" asked Connie.

"Hang on a minute," said the woman. "I'll just get my hubby."

Leaving Connie, she went back inside. After a couple of minutes, a young man pushed his head around the door. His face wore a look of irritation. He was annoyed that his wife had sent him to see their visitor. Seeing Connie however, the look vanished. He pulled open the door and smiled, obviously impressed by the sight of her. Connie could see that he had been getting ready to go out. His hair had been neatly combed and he was wearing a freshly ironed, white shirt and a blue tie.

"Hello love, I'm Sam. How can I help?"

"I was just asking your wife, if she knew whether Frank and Doris still go in the 'Shakespeare.'"

"Not regularly," replied Sam. "But I've seen them in there a couple of times. Why?"

"Well, I'd like to get a message to Doris. She's my mam. I want her to contact me."

"Oh," replied Sam. "She knows where you are then?"

"Yes, I only live in Howard Avenue, off Syndall Street."

"Oh, right."

He looked confused. Connie realised that he was wondering why she had no idea that her mam had moved, when she lived so close to her.

"I've had to keep away from them with Frank beating my mam," explained Connie. "She's defended him for years and there's been nothing I could do about it. That's why we don't see each other very often," she explained.

"I see. I understand. It must be tough to take," said Sam.

"Yes, it is."

"I'll keep an eye out for them, but it'd be an idea to have a word with the landlord. I go into town at weekends and that's probably when they're most likely to be in."

"Yes. Thanks," said Connie.

"I'll tell you what," continued Sam. "If you come in and wait, I'm going down there myself tonight. I'll walk down with you and we can have a word with the landlord together."

He smiled at her but Connie quickly declined his offer.

"Thanks all the same, but I've bothered you and your wife enough. I'll whip over there now and have a word."

"Oh, okay," replied Sam, not attempting to hide his disappointment at her decision. "You're sure?" he asked again, smiling.

"Yes," replied Connie. "I'd better be getting a move on. I've got a lot to do tonight."

Turning away, Connie walked quickly down the street, eager to put some distance between them. The young husband's behaviour had annoyed her. Not once had he taken his eyes off her, weighing her up from head to toe. She was sure that his offer of accompanying her to the 'Shakespeare,' was with the purpose of asking her to have a drink with him. She shook her head unconsciously at the thought. There he was going out, leaving his young wife at home with their baby, whilst he was chasing after other women. Kath's advice was so true; you had to be certain of choosing the right one. It seemed to Connie that so many young women were at the mercy of the whims of their husbands, as soon as they'd had their first child. Connie felt embarrassed that Sam's wife probably knew that he'd been trying to 'pick her up.' Yet it wasn't Connie's fault that Sam couldn't appreciate how lucky he was. His wife was pretty and they had a beautiful baby, yet all he could think of was his own personal pleasure.

Reaching the End of Polygon Avenue, Connie crossed over Stockport Road to the corner of Shakespeare Row. Here was located the 'Shakespeare Hotel,' a 'Chesters' pub that was popular with local residents. Entering the lounge, Connie went to the bar, spoke to the landlord and asked if he would get her mam to contact her if she came in. Yet he didn't appear too optimistic. It seemed that Frank and Doris hadn't been seen for a couple of weeks, but at least he promised to do the best that he could. A week later however, Connie came home from work and picking up the post from inside the front door, there was a letter from Doris. It was short and to the point. Her mam told her that they had moved to Moston, yet provided no address. She insisted that Frank was 'getting better' and that he 'hardly ever' raised his hand to her now. Connie knew that it wasn't true and had no doubts that Doris had withheld her address to stop her daughter witnessing his abusive behaviour. Finally, Doris reminded Connie of how proud she was of her and insisted that if she ever needed Connie, then she would be in touch.

The letter provided little in the way of reassurance for Connie that her mam would be all right. Yet, there was little more that she could do. When she thought about Frank and her encounter with Sam, it was so easy to believe that if you shared your life with someone, it was almost destined to end in tears. Yet Kath had provided an alternative view. One where romance could blossom into lasting devotion. Connie recognised that her success in her chosen profession, had been achieved alone. She hadn't been forced to consider the needs of any partner, so decisions were uncomplicated and easy to make. Yet it also meant that she had lived a life devoid of real love and affection and as Connie got older, she had an increasing sense that as a woman, she remained incomplete. Now that she was going out with Ralph, she couldn't deny that when she was with him, her spirits lifted; she felt an inner glow of satisfaction. She had never felt such a connection with anyone else before. Connie therefore considered whether her negative thoughts about marriage and relationships were a natural test of her resolve and her commitment to Ralph. Ultimately, life was there to be lived and if she was ever to experience real love, then Connie had to accept that there would always have to be an element of risk. Having become so close to Ralph, Connie determined that with him, she would be prepared to take a chance.

Chapter 37

Almost a month had passed since Ralph had taken Connie to Blackpool. It had been a special day, sealed with a kiss from Connie that had ensured his capitulation to her charms and beauty. The only woman who had ever threatened to tame his wild bachelor instincts, Connie had done it without even trying. Ralph had to admit that he couldn't envisage a life without her and he was now determined that she would become his wife.

Ralph knew that Connie was eager to visit the City Art Gallery, where they were running an exhibition of the works of Ford Madox Brown. A Victorian artist, famous for producing the Manchester Town Hall Murals, Brown was a significant figure in the pre-Raphaelite movement. Although not particularly appreciative of art himself, Ralph saw the exhibition as an ideal opportunity to make Connie a proposal of marriage. When he suggested to her that they go to the exhibition on Saturday afternoon, she was delighted and immediately agreed.

Approaching the City Art Gallery, Connie admired its classical frontage. The deep portico supported by six Ionic columns providing a grand entrance to the building. She mounted the steps and entered inside with a childlike enthusiasm that made Ralph smile. He loved to please her and recognised that this was another way in which she had changed him. No longer selfish, he understood that in a committed relationship, it was often far more satisfying to give than to receive. Yet as they went around the gallery, he found it difficult to muster any enthusiasm for the paintings themselves. To Ralph, it was just a matter of splashing paint on canvas. In truth, he thought that photographs were far preferable to paintings. They represented life as it really was. Artistic interpretation, hidden meanings and messages, meant little to him. In fact, Ralph was convinced that the art world was full of sharp operators, cleverly exploiting the intellectual susceptibilities of their intended audiences. Yet Ralph wouldn't have dreamed of voicing his opinions. Connie was enjoying herself and he had no desire to upset the positive atmosphere between them, especially as he was waiting for the ideal moment to make his proposal.

Connie however, hadn't failed to notice his indifference and when they had seen most of the collection, she looked at Ralph and smiled.

"You don't think much of painting and artists, do you Ralph?"

"They're all right. Some of the paintings have been good."

"Such as?" she asked, looking at him closely, her eyebrow lifting slightly, an unconscious expression of her curiosity.

Ralph was silent, finding it hard to think of any such painting.

"Yes?" asked Connie, expectantly.

Her eyes opened wide in anticipation of an answer that was exceedingly slow in coming. She could see his face strained in concentration and knew that he was struggling desperately to recall the name of a painting that had made any kind of an impression on him.

"Come on then Ralph," said Connie. "It shouldn't be too difficult. Which ones?"

Connie was teasing him, almost revelling in his discomfort. She was trying hard to keep a straight face, desiring to maintain the impression that she was serious about expecting a response. Yet it was impossible for her not to smile, especially when she noticed his bewildered expression and as he stared at her, utterly confused, she suddenly burst out into uncontrollable laughter.

"Shush!" said an old man who, together with his wife, was stood contemplating the picture to the side of Ralph and Connie.

"Oh, I'm sorry," said Connie, her laughter stifled by his firm reprimand.

The man tutted, dismissive of her apology. He slowly moved on, continuing to express his dissatisfaction at Connie's behaviour, until his wife finally and firmly, told him to shut up.

"Oh dear," said Connie to Ralph. "I think I've upset him."

"Yes," said Ralph. "Let's hope he doesn't get us thrown out."

Connie chuckled quietly.

"You'd like that Ralph, wouldn't you?" she asked, smiling.

Ralph tried hard to resist, but Connie's witty response meant that he couldn't help but burst out laughing.

"I was right all along, wasn't I?" asked Connie, with a gleam in her eye. "You're just not an art lover are you, Ralph?"

"I'm sorry Connie," said Ralph, looking down at the floor like a naughty boy. "I have tried."

"Don't be daft," said Connie. "It doesn't matter. I've enjoyed looking at the pictures and I'm grateful that you brought me. I probably wouldn't have bothered coming on my own. I'd have always found something else to do. Come on, let's go and get a drink in the café"

"Connie," said Ralph, quietly.

"Yes."

"Come and sit over here for a minute."

Ralph pointed to a large bench in the middle of the room.

Connie was curious. Ralph's voice sounded soft and urgent, suggesting that he was about to say something important. She followed him without question and sat down beside him.

Turning towards her, Ralph looked directly into her eyes.

"Connie, I knew that you wouldn't appreciate grand gestures, so I wanted to ask you here, where it's quiet and simple. I don't want to waste words, I just want to tell you that I've never felt as happy as when I'm with you and I'm asking you if you'd consider being my wife."

Connie was surprised. She hadn't expected Ralph to raise the question of marriage in the surroundings of the City Art Gallery. She became unsure of whether she had heard him correctly, so her initial response was to ask him for clarification.

"Are you wanting me to think about being your wife, or actually asking me to marry you, here and now?" enquired Connie.

Ralph looked confused. He thought that he'd been clear in what he'd said.

"I'm asking you if you'll marry me, Connie. I want you to be my wife."

Having asked her again, Ralph feared that he was about to be rejected. A sinking feeling moved down through his chest and into the pit of his stomach and at that moment he knew just how desperate he was for Connie to accept him. As the seconds ticked slowly by and he waited for Connie's response, it seemed like forever. Finally, Connie smiled.

"Yes, Ralph. I would love to be your wife."

Unable to contain himself, Ralph threw his arms around her and kissed her on the lips, feeling her respond with warm compassion. Overcome with joy, neither of them remembered where they were, until the affected coughing of a patrolling museum guide brought them back to reality. Separating, they saw an elderly, pleasant faced man smiling at them.

"Steady on you two," he said cheerily. "We're not supposed to encourage that kind of thing in the public galleries you know."

"Oh, we're very sorry," said Ralph. "We got a little carried away."

"I'll say you did, but it's not every day that you make a proposal, is it?" continued the guide, looking at Ralph. "Congratulations to the both of you."

"Thank you," said Connie.

"May I be permitted to say what a lucky young man you are?" added the guide, turning his attention towards Ralph.

"Yes. I certainly am, aren't I?"

Getting to their feet, Ralph and Connie said farewell and headed off to get a drink of tea and discuss their plans for the future. Sat in the gallery's café, Connie looked across the table at Ralph.

"Listen to me carefully Ralph and don't get upset, but I want to wait a few weeks before we announce that we're engaged."

Ralph looked bemused.

"But why Connie?" he asked.

"It's a huge commitment that you're making Ralph and I want you to be absolutely certain that it's what you want."

"Connie. Do you think I would ask you to marry me on a whim? I've given it long and deep consideration. I've never been more certain of anything."

"Well, just do it to please me Ralph," insisted Connie. "I wouldn't forgive myself if I didn't give you the opportunity to reconsider."

"You are a strange one Connie, but yes, I agree."

"Thank you," replied Connie. "If you still feel the same way at the end of the month, we can announce it at the start of June."

Ralph nodded in agreement and Connie smiled.

"Besides Ralph, it will give us time to think about how long the engagement should be and where we'll live."

"Not in Ardwick I hope," said Ralph, quickly. "Oh Lord, save me from the dreaded two-up two-down."

"Okay Ralph, you don't have to take the Michael."

"Yes, Miss!" said Ralph, playfully.

Connie laughed. She just couldn't get angry with Ralph, even when he was casting aspersions, albeit humorously, on her home and neighbourhood.

"Yes Ralph," she said, trying hard to be serious. "There are some important matters that we need to think about."

"Good old Connie," said Ralph. "Practical as ever."

"Someone will have to be Ralph."

"Well, I don't mind it being you," said Ralph, smiling.

"I've no doubt that it will have to be!"

Connie shook her head, but she was happy and delighted that Ralph couldn't hide his pleasure at her acceptance of his proposal. Today had been a wonderful day and Connie hoped that it would prove to be an auspicious start to the rest of their lives together.

Chapter 38

Connie soon broke her own stipulation that she and Ralph should refrain from announcing their engagement. It came when she went out with Paula for dinner at the Lyons Café. Technically, she wasn't confirming that she and Ralph were actually getting engaged, but that they were thinking about it.

Connie had decided on this course of action as she knew that Paula would be the soul of discretion and that as the two of them were so close, she wanted to get an inkling of what she felt about her growing relationship with Ralph. She also believed that Paula could alert her to the possibility of some negative reaction from the staff at work. After all, Connie was well aware of the criticisms of Ralph's behaviour in the past.

Connie's news hadn't come as a surprise. Paula was aware that her friend had been dating Ralph. She'd noticed the looks of affection between them and seen them holding hands, when they thought that no one was looking. It concerned Paula, as she had no wish to see her friend get hurt. On the other hand, she found it hard to believe that Connie, who was so confident and astute, could possibly become another of Ralph's victims. In their last conversation about Ralph, Connie had defended him stoutly and with that knowledge, Paula avoided any suggestions of negativity about their likely engagement. Paula was conscious of the fact that if Ralph did let Connie down, the latter would need her support. Therefore, Paula remained circumspect and after their conversation, Connie was no wiser as to how news of her engagement would be received at Greenings.

There was one area though in which Paula was willing to give Connie advice. It was one familiar to her friend, as she'd already received it from Kath during their visit to Southern Cemetery.

"When you break the news of your engagement Connie, try to let Tom know before the rest of the office."

"Why?" asked Connie.

"So that he's prepared for it. Don't let him be shocked in front of everyone else," replied Paula.

Connie was silent. She felt frustrated. She understood that Paula and Kath didn't want to see Tom upset, but why should that have anything to do with her relationship with Ralph. If she'd acted unfairly towards Tom, she could have understood, but she had always been open and honest with him.

"I don't understand why he would be shocked," replied Connie, eventually.

By her friend's reaction, Paula understood that the subject was a sensitive one. She realised that she would have to proceed as diplomatically as possible.

"I'm afraid Connie, that Tom's still carrying a torch for you. All I'm suggesting, is that it's best for you to be aware of how he feels."

"I still don't see it Paula," insisted Connie. "I've made it so clear to Tom that there can never be any romance between us. He's accepted that. Surely, if he hadn't, we wouldn't work together so well. The pair of us are a great team."

"Yes, you are Connie. But he's so happy around you that you're bound to get on well together. Give him the chance and he'll understand your feelings for Ralph. He's decent and considerate. I'm just suggesting that you give him a little more time to get used to things."

They sat quietly. Connie knew that she couldn't simply dismiss the views of her friend, when Kath had offered her the same advice. She felt tense and then a little guilty, because she had no wish to upset Tom. She admired so much about him and he had been such a good friend to her since she had arrived at 'Greenings.' And she finally recognised that she would have to deal sensitively with him over the matter of her engagement.

"Yes, Paula. I see your point," said Connie, eventually. "I'll talk to him first and I'm sure that he'll understand. In fact, I know he will. You'll see."

It was Connie's signal to Paula that the subject was closed and the two women went on to talk about other concerns. That afternoon however, alone in her office, Connie mulled over their conversation and came to a decision. If by the time of next week's local party meeting, Ralph hadn't indicated his desire to pull out of their engagement, Connie would take the opportunity to inform Tom of their plans. Acutely conscious now of Tom's ongoing affection for her, it was a task that Connie wasn't looking forward to. Yet having accepted her friend's advice, she was convinced that it was the right thing to do.

Chapter 39

The local party meeting had passed off routinely and at its close, Connie had asked Tom if he'd like to go for a coffee at the 'Wimpy Bar' on Hyde Road. Although it was getting a little late, Tom didn't hesitate to accept, eager to spend the extra time with her. Furthermore, he suspected that she may have something she wanted to share with him. He'd come to that conclusion as throughout the evening, Connie had appeared quite distant. She hadn't followed the proceedings very closely and unusually for her, she had made very few contributions to the discussions. It simply wasn't the type of behaviour that Tom normally associated with Connie and if she needed his help in any way, he wouldn't hesitate to give it.

Connie had chosen the 'Wimpy' as it was located next to the ABC and she expected other customers to be present. That would rule out any chance of Tom reacting emotionally to her news, a scenario that she was desperate to avoid. Although she had tried to be dismissive of her friends' concerns about Tom, the closer Connie got to having to tell him, the more nervous she became. When they entered the café, got their drinks and sat down, Connie found that her nervousness had translated into a real sense of negativity. She began to feel irritated that she would almost appear apologetic to Tom, for falling in love with someone else. The choice of the 'Wimpy' also proved to be a poor one. It was brightly lit and appeared cold and sterile; a poor environment to encourage empathy and understanding. Furthermore, there weren't any other customers present. In the silence, Connie stared down at the table, disinclined to start the conversation.

Sat quietly, Tom looked at the set of cruet placed in the middle of the table, next to which was a large, glass sugar dispenser, with its wide hollow tube projecting through a shiny metallic top. With Connie's continued silence, Tom felt certain that something was wrong, but he waited, prepared to give Connie as long as she needed to tell him what it was.

At last, Connie started to speak. Small talk at first, about tonight's meeting and matters at work. Tom responded warmly, but he still had the impression that there was something more important to come. Finally, he could wait no longer.

"Connie, is there anything the matter? Are you all right? You seem worried about something."

Tom's voice expressed real concern.

"Everything's fine," replied Connie.

"Are you sure?" asked Tom, unconvinced.

"Yes, of course, I'm sure."

Tom sensed a hint of irritation in Connie's voice. He was surprised. It just wasn't like her. She was usually so cheerful and positive. On her part, Connie could see by Tom's expression, that her response had failed to provide him with any kind of reassurance.

"Honestly Tom. There's nothing wrong," she continued. "I'm completely fine."

"Oh. That's good Connie," said Tom, relieved.

Connie had finally got through to him, but it now seemed clear that however she gave him the news of her engagement, a sombre mood had descended over their conversation. It was directly at odds with the supposedly joyful news that she was about to impart.

"I've got some news to tell you Tom."

"Oh?"

"Yes, it's about Ralph and I."

Tom held his breath. His heart sank. He dreaded what she was about to say.

"We're about to get engaged," said Connie.

The sentence was short and to the point. There was a sense of irrevocability about it and the words pierced straight through Tom's heart like an arrow. Connie watched as the blood drained from Tom's face and his eyes, that had been fixed intently on hers, dropped away as he looked down to the table. He was quiet. There was no response. Connie had hoped that, even if Tom was upset to know that he'd lost her, he would stoically offer his congratulations and they could quickly move on. But it wasn't to be. All her worst fears seemed to have been realised and she began to regret that she had ever considered meeting him over the matter. She'd been stupid. It was a private concern for Ralph and herself. Her good intentions had led to nothing but unpleasant complications. Yet the silence was unbearable and she knew that she'd have to speak again.

"Well, aren't you going to congratulate me Tom?"

It was a situation that was finely balanced, but one about to spiral out of control. There had been obvious misunderstandings between the pair of them since they had sat down and now it was about to get worse. Connie had intended her statement as a way to bring the matter to a conclusion, but Tom, with his deep concern for Connie, incorrectly assumed that her question was an open invitation to provide an opinion on the proposed union. As such, he found himself uttering words that risked driving a wedge between them.

"Are you sure that you're doing the right thing?"

The question came as a shock to Connie. She looked into his eyes and saw despair and then wondered if it could perhaps be envy.

"What do you mean?" asked Connie.

It was a question posed more as an accusation. She was determined that he would answer and Tom knew immediately that she wasn't happy. He now wished that he hadn't said anything. But it was too late. The words were out now and he knew that the developing conversation would have to play out in its entirety, regardless of the consequences.

"I'm sorry Connie. I thought that you were asking me what I thought."

He paused. It was a final opportunity for either of them to have halted the conversation, but it didn't happen.

"Go on. Go on then. Tell me," Connie insisted. "Let's hear what you've got to say."

She couldn't help it, but she was starting to get angry. Her unusual demeanour was starting to become intimidating to Tom and he felt that he had no option but to answer her.

"I know that you like Ralph," said Tom, "but he's not all that you think he is. He doesn't respect women; he uses them and then discards them. He brags about it. I know that you're strong Connie and I hope he's changed, but I don't want him to let you down."

"No, Tom. You don't know him. He has changed. I'm not a fool, even though you seem to think that I am."

"No. No, I don't," insisted Tom.

"Yes, you do. I know that Ralph was foolish in the past, but he was younger and immature. He's not like that anymore. He's proved it to me."

She waited for a response, but Tom was quiet. It seemed that he had nothing left to say. And his silence now angered her even more. How dare he upset her like this? He had no right. Who did he think he was? It was her life and she would do exactly as she pleased. Connie's emotions were boiling up inside her and before she realised it, the terrible words came out rapidly and cruelly from her mouth.

"I understand Tom," she said, scornfully. "You're jealous. It was because I turned you down. You can't stand it that I found love with someone else."

Tom looked at her blankly. He'd heard her words but it was as if he couldn't accept them. Still angry, Connie wouldn't let the matter drop.

"Well? What have you got to say for yourself? You were quick enough to criticise Ralph."

Tom looked into her blazing green eyes. She was protecting Ralph like a mother sheltering her young. He wished that the floor could swallow him up, or that he could turn back the clock, but he was left with no alternative but to try and respond.

"I didn't mean to upset you Connie and I'm sorry that I have. You are right about one thing. I was desperate to go out with you, but I've accepted that you feel differently. It doesn't stop me caring about you though and I couldn't bear to see you unhappy. I'd be delighted if you found a man who's worthy of you. One who appreciates how special you are. I can't be jealous, because I want what's best for you and I know that it doesn't include me. I don't dislike Ralph. I've known him far longer than you and that's why I don't believe that he can be trusted. I won't lie and say I think he can, because I care about you Connie."

Tom was silent. Connie had listened to him and slowly her anger began to subside. Paula and Kath had been absolutely right, as she'd suspected all along. Tom had fallen in love with her. Yet, it still didn't make it right that he had criticised her judgement and more importantly, Ralph. She was going to find it very hard to forget.

"Well Tom," continued Connie. "You're wrong and you'll see that you are. I wasn't completely certain that I was going to accept Ralph's proposal, but thanks to you, I now know I will."

Almost immediately, Connie wished that she hadn't said it. Of course, it wasn't true. Not only that, but it was a cruel comment and so very much unlike her. She'd lost control and her words had wounded Tom, a man who loved her and was already so vulnerable. Yet too much had been said by Tom for her to offer an apology and so the two of them sat silently at the table.

Finally, Tom stood up.

"It's very late Connie. Would you like me to see you home?"

It was a ridiculous question, but Tom couldn't stop his natural politeness and concern for Connie emerging once more.

Connie looked at him wearily. Although she was still feeling guilty about her previous comment, she was determined to reaffirm her displeasure at Tom's criticism of Ralph.

"Well, what do you think?"

Tom, standing by the table, made one final plea.

"I'm so sorry Connie. Please, can we still be friends?"

Although Tom was clearly upset, he found no sympathy from Connie.

"We'll have to see. Goodbye, Tom."

Her words were cold and final. They left Tom wondering whether she would ever speak to him again. He turned away from the table and trudged slowly towards the door. Opening it, he didn't look back as he stepped out on to the pavement.

Chapter 40

Alone, Tom was devastated. He had lost his beautiful Connie. He'd upset her and it seemed as if she didn't wish to know him anymore. It was late and he had to get home, but he wanted time to think, so decided that he would walk, rather than take the bus. Tonight, his dreams had been shattered. He had dared to think that Connie would come to see him in a different light; recognise that he truly loved and cared for her. He was certain that eventually, Connie would see Ralph as he truly believed he was, a predator who selfishly used women for his own gratification. But he had completely misjudged the situation and now any relationship he had with her, was in tatters.

Yet Tom remained convinced that Ralph would prove a disaster for her. Ever since he'd started working with Ralph, he'd seen him chase after every new, pretty young woman employed at the office. Ralph always finished with them without any sense of remorse and frequently cheated on them with other women. Tom had witnessed it many times when the two of them were out of town on business. It was this that Tom couldn't bear seeing happen to Connie and had led to his warning to her that evening. But now it was clear that she didn't believe him. In fact, she had been more determined than ever to defend Ralph. It seemed so very unfair. Ralph, not he, would have Connie's unconditional love and then would almost inevitably throw it away.

The more he thought about the situation, the more impossible it seemed for him to stay at Greenings. He wanted to be close by in case Connie needed him, but she'd made it clear that she wouldn't heed his advice and he couldn't bear it if she were cold, or even hostile towards him, because of his words that evening. He had to give her time and space. Only in that way would there ever be a chance to rebuild any kind of relationship with her in the future.

Arriving back home, a plan had already become firmly established in Tom's mind. His ongoing work at Joyce and Hitchcock hadn't gone unnoticed. The firm was in the process of expansion and Mike Joyce believed that Tom would prove an ideal candidate to be brought in to head up their accounts and finance department. He could oversee their plans for expansion and restructuring and take a seat on the board. Mike was an excellent judge of character. He recognised that Ralph was the face of Greenings. He'd accompanied Connie on her presentation, but that was due to him being Joe's nephew and heir apparent when Joe retired.

But it was clear to Mike that over the last couple of years, it was Tom who was the creative force of the company. Although quiet and unassuming, he was intelligent, hard-working, organised and efficient, capable of bringing the best out of everyone.

Yet, Tom was being overlooked at Greenings. Mike, a self-made man, was convinced that it was because he let the boss's nephew take all the plaudits for himself. And that wasn't the way at Joyce and Hitchcock. The company had been built on cooperation and trust; workers and management a united team. Mike saw that Tom's personality would fit perfectly into the culture of his company.

As a consequence, at the end of February, Mike had made Tom a very lucrative offer. It was considerably more than he was getting at present, with a recognition of his worth and status. Mike had set no time limit on Tom's acceptance and when Tom politely declined the offer, reiterated that it remained open should be change his mind. That had been unlikely whilst Tom remained close to Connie, but now with their friendship hanging by a thread, Tom felt that it was best for them both if he accepted Mike's offer.

Although he would have no difficulty in making the break with Greenings, Tom knew that he couldn't possibly depart without leaving some form of communication for Connie. He understood that whatever happened, he would always love her and she had to know that should ever the need arise, she could always depend on him to be by her side. So, at three o'clock in the morning, he sat at his desk to compose a short letter to her. Although the hour was late, he'd had no sleep and had walked half way across Manchester, his mind was sharp and his words precise. How could be possibly feel tired when every shred of nervous energy he possessed, had to be utilised to write the most important letter of his life? As he sat there however, it proved to be a far from easy task and scribblings out and torn up drafts plagued his attempts to complete the letter to his satisfaction. He was still writing as the early light of dawn made its appearance outside, but finally, he was satisfied and once more, he read through his neat, final draft.

   'Dear Connie,

   I know that you are angry with me at the moment and I understand why. I'm truly sorry that I've upset you and only wish that I could take back the words I've said. I do really hope that you can find lasting happiness with Ralph and there will be no one more pleased than I, if that is the case.

   For a few weeks now, I've been thinking over an offer I've had from Mike Joyce to join him. It's too good an opportunity to turn

down and so I've decided to accept it. It's all happened so quickly
and I realised that I wouldn't get the chance to tell you personally,
so I've mentioned it in this letter.

I do hope that one day you can once more consider me as your
friend. And I want you to know that if ever, for any reason, you
need my help, I will always be there to give it.

Love,

Tom.'

The letter was very much to the point. Tom feared that she may be so
unhappy at his behaviour, that anything longer would have been
discarded without a second glance. Shorter, Connie would be more
inclined to read it. Tom was desperate for her to accept that he was sorry
and he had said that. And he wasn't being disingenuous; he did wish to
see her happy. If not with him, then with someone else. But Tom knew
that he had been dishonest about his new job. He had only taken it
because he'd upset her and in so doing, had effectively ended their
friendship. Yet his letter focused on the benefits of his new position, so
that there was no chance that Connie would ever feel responsible for his
departure. Most important of all though, Tom saw his letter as a lifebelt
for a drowning man. It was a plea to Connie to let him back into her life
at some point in the future. It was all that was left, but gave him that faint
glimmer of hope that enabled him to carry on.

Chapter 41

Prior to setting off to work, Tom telephoned Joyce and Hitchcock and asked to speak to Mike. Tom wanted to confirm that his offer was still on the table.

"Yes," replied Mike. "Of course. I told you that. Why?"

"Well, I've given it a lot of thought and I'd like to accept it."

Mike was delighted.

"That's great Tom. What was it that made you change your mind?"

Tom paused. He knew that he couldn't tell Mike the whole truth.

"Well, I suppose I realised that if I didn't, I'd be showing no real ambition."

Mike seemed satisfied with his response.

"I see. Yes. A good enough reason I'd say. I think that you're right. You've moved beyond the responsibilities that Greenings have given you. What about your period of notice Tom? How much do you need to give them?"

"I don't need to give one as far as I'm aware."

"Well, I suggest you check that with Joe Greening and don't panic if he wants you to work another couple of weeks. I'm happy to wait."

Oh," said Tom, unable to hide his disappointment.

"Well, I can see that you're eager to start," replied Mike. "I suspect that Joe won't be too unhappy for you to finish today. We're a big client for him now and he'll probably not want to upset us, if he can help it."

"Right," said Tom, suddenly sounding more enthusiastic.

"Ring me later," continued Mike "and you can let me know when you'll be starting."

And that was it. So straightforward. Yet Tom still needed to see 'Old Joe' and arriving at Greenings, he headed straight for Paula's desk. It was just after eight thirty, so Tom knew that Joe wouldn't have any meetings or appointments quite yet. Seeing Tom approaching, Paula greeted him.

"Hi Tom!" she said cheerily, giving him a bright and engaging smile.

Tom, avoiding any exchange of pleasantries, came straight to the point.

"Is Mr Greening in his office yet Paula?" he asked.

Paula was surprised by Tom's somewhat sharp and direct response. He seemed in such a hurry. He wasn't the calm, friendly and polite figure that she was so used to.

"Are you all right Tom? Is there something the matter?" she asked, sympathetically.

Tom hesitated. He'd been so intent on getting in to see Joe Greening that he hadn't realised that he'd been dismissive of Paula's original greeting. Pulling himself together, he responded to her with more consideration.

"Oh, no. No Paula. I'm fine, thank you."

Everything about Tom's demeanour told Paula that he was anything but.

"Oh, I see," she replied. "Well, he's definitely in Tom, so I can go and ask him if he's able to see you."

"Yes, please Paula. Thanks."

Paula got out of her chair and walked over to the door behind her. She knocked confidently and hearing Joe respond, she entered. A short time later she emerged with a smile and confirmed to Tom that Joe would see him.

Gratefully, Tom moved towards the door that she was holding open. Closing it behind him, Paula went back to her desk. Tom's behaviour and his request to see the 'old man' had intrigued her. She was positive that whatever the reason Tom was in Joe's office for, it must be something important.

Entering the room, Tom saw Joe Greening sat behind his desk.

"Come in Tom," said Joe, smiling. "Take a seat."

Tom sat down quickly.

"Thank you for seeing me Mr Greening."

"That's all right, Tom. What can I do for you?"

Suddenly, Tom's resolve seemed to desert him. He hesitated, unable to get out the words he wanted. Joe realised that the young man was about to tell him something that he feared would elicit an unfavourable response. As a result, he tried to appear as reassuring as possible. He smiled and encouraged Tom to begin.

"Come on lad. Spit it out. I won't bite!"

Slowly, Tom began to speak. Uncertain at first, but then in a stronger, steady voice.

"I'm sure you know that I've been very happy here Mr Greening. I'm very grateful that I've benefitted so much from the opportunities that you've given me. I believe though, that it's now time for me to take on a new challenge."

"Oh!" said Joe, surprised.

Tom's news wasn't what he was expecting to hear. Although his employee hadn't yet finished, he was certain that he was about to tell him that he'd found another job. Joe had been caught out. Tom had never seemed too ambitious, seemingly prepared to allow others to accept the prestige and plaudits for his own hard work. Tom was a real diamond and now Joe was beginning to regret that he hadn't done enough to keep him.

Having paused on hearing Joe's interjection into his explanation, Tom sat silent, looking rather awkwardly at his boss.

"Go on then," said Joe, finally.

"Well, Joyce and Hitchcock have offered me a new position with a seat on the board."

"I see."

"Yes. I'm happy to keep working here for another couple of weeks, if leaving will cause any difficulties for the firm Mr Greening. Mike is happy to fit in with whatever you want."

"Hmm," said Joe, musing on the situation.

"I don't suppose that there's anything I could do to change your mind, is there?" asked Joe.

"No, Mr Greening!" replied Tom, alarmed at the suggestion. "I wouldn't go for a move to try and engineer better conditions out of you. That wouldn't be right. I definitely want to take the job at Joyce and Hitchcock."

Joe looked at him. Tom was aghast at the idea that he would try to exploit Greenings. It was another example to his boss of why Tom was such a fine young man. He didn't have a selfish or disloyal bone in his body and it was why Joe simply hadn't seen this one coming. Yet Joe felt uneasy. He was unsure whether Tom was telling him everything about his decision to leave. Nevertheless, there was little he could do about that. Besides, Joyce and Hitchcock were important clients and he had no wish to stand in Tom's way and risk upsetting them. Positively, Tom moving there should strengthen the company's links with Greenings. At least that could be a beneficial outcome from this unfortunate situation.

"Don't worry lad," said Joe. "There's no need to work any period of notice. I'll phone Mike now and tell him that you're going with our blessings. You want to get started there right away. You can clear your desk now and be with them first thing on Monday morning."

Joe stood up and walked around the desk. Tom rose from his chair and shook the hand that was extended towards him.

"Well done lad," said Joe. "Don't forget us. We've built up a good relationship with Joyce and Hitchcock. I'm sure we'll be seeing more of you in the future."

"Yes, I assume so," said Tom.

With that, Tom was guided towards the office door and the two men parted.

Sitting at his desk, Joe couldn't deny his disappointment. Tom had been such an asset to the company and he couldn't help but rue the fact that his nephew lacked a similar amount of talent and drive. Thankfully however, he still had Connie. He wondered if Mike had been planning a move for her too. Maybe he had, but that would have perhaps seemed a little too disrespectful. Like Joe, Mike was a man of honour and principle. It would have been a step too far for him to do that. Joe realised that Ralph was now going to have to take on a more proactive role in the company. Since Connie's arrival, he couldn't deny that his nephew had worked harder and acted with more maturity than previously. Yet in Joe's eyes, he still had some way to go. He would need to arrive there quickly though, as Joe wouldn't hesitate to bring in someone else if he didn't.

Chapter 42

Paula looked up from her typewriter as she heard Tom emerge from Joe Greening's office.

"Did you manage to get it sorted out then?"

It was a probing, speculative question. Tom had given no indication of what his visit was about, but naturally inquisitive, Paula was eager to find out.

"Oh yes," replied Tom. "It's all sorted out."

"Oh good," answered Paula.

Paula waited expectantly, hopeful that he would elaborate further. Instead, he reached into the inside pocket of his jacket and pulled out an envelope. He turned it in his hands, read Connie's name on the front and hesitated for a moment. Clearing his throat nervously with a quiet cough, he looked at Paula.

"I wonder if you could do me a favour?"

"Well, I hope so."

"It's this letter. It's for Connie."

"Oh," said Paula surprised. "Can't you give it to her yourself?"

"Well, I'd rather not."

"Why?"

Tom had hoped that she would simply take the envelope off him without any questions, but he should have known better, particularly as Paula and Connie were such close friends.

"Well, it's to let her know that I'm leaving. I'm going to work for Joyce and Hitchcock and I'm expected to get started right away and I haven't got the time to tell her."

It was a strange reply and Tom's behaviour was bordering on the bizarre. Normally, Paula would have offered him her congratulations, but the man she saw in front of her, exhibited no sense of satisfaction at the new job he'd just been given.

"But Connie will be back this afternoon. Surely you can give it to her then?"

"But I can't," replied Tom. "The 'old man' has just accepted my resignation. I have to clear my desk right away."

Tom looked lost and confused. He was making little sense.

"I'm sure that they won't be kicking you out of the office just yet," said Paula. "You can hang on a bit. You're not starting at Joyce and Hitchcock right now, are you?"

Tom shook his head.

"Connie's going to be really disappointed if you leave without seeing her."

"No," replied Tom. "I don't think that she will."

He looked down at the floor, purposely avoiding her gaze. Paula sensed that he was fighting hard to hold his emotions in check and suddenly, she realised what his behaviour was all about.

"She's told you Tom, hasn't she?"

Tom was silent, but Paula felt that he needed to talk. She couldn't leave him feeling so upset.

"When did you find out?" she asked.

"Find out about what?" replied Tom, unconvincingly.

"It's all right, I already know about Connie's engagement. It's the only reason for you to avoid her. I know how much you think about her Tom."

Breathing deeply, Tom sat in the seat next to Paula's desk. She moved her own chair next to him and slowly, Tom began to speak.

"I found out last night," said Tom, hesitantly. "We went to the 'Wimpy' after the meeting and she told me then. And I just messed everything up Paula."

He looked away from her, finding it hard to recall how stupid he'd been.

"No. I'm sure you can't have Tom."

"Yes, I did. I appeared jealous and selfish; as if I didn't want her to be happy. I wasn't pleased for her and I had no right to react like that."

"No, Tom. I know how much you care about her. You're wrong."

Paula leaned closer towards Tom and gently put her hand on his shoulder.

"You warned her about Ralph, didn't you?"

"Yes," replied Tom, "but I shouldn't have."

"Just between us," said Paula, "I've done the same. We've both known Ralph far longer than Connie has and I'm worried that he's going to let her down. Once the news of their engagement is official, others will feel the same way."

"But I should have known how Connie would react. She was bound to take offence. I questioned her judgement and who's to say that she isn't right? Maybe Ralph has changed. Maybe I was, deep down, being jealous. She's wonderful. If anyone could make Ralph change, then Connie could. I've been such a fool. I've upset her and now I may never get to speak to her again."

Tom was a man in turmoil, full of regrets. He was desperate to make things right with Connie, but despaired of ever having the chance. Paula wished that she could hug him and say that everything would be all right, but it was something that she couldn't guarantee. Yet it was clear to her that Tom needed hope and she tried hard to give it to him.

"I'm concerned Tom. I'd love to think that Ralph can change for Connie's sake. But I don't believe that he will. He's charmed by Connie at the moment, but I'm sure that the old Ralph, with his wandering eye, will return. If that happens, then Connie will need her friends around her and you Tom," Paula hesitated to emphasise the point, "you are her very best friend. Please wait. Don't go until she comes back this afternoon. Talk to her. Try to make things up with her."

Tom sat quietly whilst he considered her words.

"No Paula," he finally replied. "I've already thought long and hard about it and whatever I say, it's only going to make matters worse. If that were to happen, I'd never have another chance to make things right. I have to respect Connie and give her all the time that she needs. Its best this way and I've told her in the letter that if she ever needs me, I'll always be there for her."

Getting to his feet, Tom once again offered Paula the envelope. This time she took it.

"Thanks Paula. Please keep being a good friend to Connie."

"Of course, I will. Look after yourself Tom."

"And you too Paula."

Paula watched as Tom walked slowly away, with little resemblance to a man who had secured a prestigious and lucrative promotion. The fact was that Tom already had his dream job, working alongside Connie. Money and status were of no concern to him. What he'd sought was the love of his beautiful Connie. But now she would forever be in the arms of another man, leaving Tom with a feeling of utter despair.

Chapter 43

It was just after three. Hearing the sound of excited chatter, Paula looked up from her desk. It was Connie and Ralph, returning from a site visit in Oldham. The two of them were smiling and Paula noticed as Ralph took hold of Connie's hand and gently pulled her towards him. Resisting, Connie looked at him disapprovingly, but then her words of rebuke were gently delivered.

"Not here. You'll get us both fired."

"But I'm the boss Connie."

"No, Ralph. Your uncle is."

"It's the same thing."

Connie shook her head and smiled.

"I don't know Ralph. What am I going to do with you?"

"Lots I hope," replied Ralph, grinning.

Noticing Paula, Connie turned towards her and smiled.

"Hi Paula."

"Have you got a minute Connie?"

"Yes, of course."

Connie turned to Ralph.

"I'll be with you in a few minutes. Can you have all the folders ready so that we can go over the information for the final report?"

Ralph nodded and then walked off down the corridor towards his office.

"What is it?" asked Connie.

"I have a letter here for you."

"Oh. Who's it from?"

"Tom. He left it this morning."

Paula noticed Connie's demeanour change almost immediately, signs of irritation on her face. Tom wasn't exaggerating when he said that he'd upset her.

"Huh!" said Connie, dismissively. "What's he left a letter for? How could he possibly think that I'd be bothered to read anything that he wants to write?"

They were rhetorical questions, clearly not requiring a response from Paula.

"Anyway," she continued, "there's no need to look at the letter when I'm going to have to suffer his disapproving looks for however long."

"No, you're not," said Paula, quietly.

"Not what?"

"You're not going to have to put up with any of Tom's disapproving looks."

For a brief moment there was a flicker of concern on Connie's face. It suggested that despite her harsh words, she still cared about him. But quickly, her reply indicated that she still felt wounded by his criticism.

"Why? Because he's now decided that I should marry Ralph after all. That it's the best thing that could happen to me? I'm sure!"

"No, Connie," said Paula, calmly. "Because he's got a new job at Joyce and Hitchcock and he won't be working here anymore."

Paula's words stopped Connie in her tracks. She was stunned. It was the last news that she'd expected to hear. Still holding out Tom's letter, Paula pushed it gently towards Connie's hand.

"Well," asked Paula. "Aren't you going to open it?"

Taking the envelope, Connie took a couple of steps back. Taking out the letter, she carefully unfolded it and began to read. Paula watched as her eyes moved across and down the page. Having finished, she replaced the letter back in its envelope.

Connie was quiet. It would probably have helped her if Tom's letter hadn't been full of remorse, for then she could have dismissed it as unworthy of her attention. But she could feel his emotion; his desperation to be her friend and confidante once more. As such, it made her question her behaviour towards him. It was a fault that she sometimes demonstrated; a dismissiveness towards someone who had hurt her feelings. It was so far removed from her usual, generous nature.

"Yes, you're right Paula," said Connie, eventually. "It seems as if he's got himself a new job. I suppose it's the best thing for him. Such an opportunity wouldn't have come up for him here."

Paula nodded. Whatever else Tom had said in the letter, it was clear that Connie had no desire to share it with her.

"Well, Paula. I'd best get along and go over those figures with Ralph."

"Yes, he's going to be wondering where you've got to."

As Paula watched Connie walk off down the corridor, she saw her fold the envelope and place it in her jacket pocket. Paula knew that Tom had promised Connie that he would always stand by her. The fact that she had kept the letter, gave Paula hope that if she ever needed to, Connie would still be prepared to reach out to Tom for his support.

Chapter 44

Whilst Connie had been speaking to Paula, Ralph had returned to his office. Realising that the folders they needed were in the records department, he phoned through to request them. A few minutes later he was sat behind his desk and into the office walked a pretty young woman with a large number of folders in her hands. Veronica was now eighteen and far more self-assured, having worked at Greenings for several months. Wearing a beige blouse, tightly fitting, black pencil skirt and heels, she looked very elegant.

"Just put them there, on the front of the desk," said Ralph. "Your arms look like they'll drop off if you try holding on to them any longer!"

Ralph smiled and watched as Veronica moved closer to the desk. Suddenly, she stumbled and quickly, without thinking, Ralph was out of his chair to catch her before she fell to the floor.

"Are you all right Veronica?" asked Ralph, concerned. "I thought we'd lost you then."

"Yes, I'm fine Mr Greening."

Veronica straightened her skirt and stood back. She fixed her eyes on Ralph and then lowered her head. She closed her eyelids slowly, opening them again, her elegant, long lashes drawing Ralph's gaze to her deep, blue eyes. Veronica fascinated him. Her youth gave the impression of innocence, a demure young girl, yet when he saw her around the office, he was always struck by her eye-catching figure and good looks. Often, when he'd spoken to her, she had looked at him flirtatiously, a look that threatened to stir his desire. Yet Ralph was determined to suppress such feelings. His days as a philanderer were behind him and he was intent on staying faithful to Connie. She was the woman he had learned to love and he wasn't going to throw it all away.

"I've told you before," said Ralph, kindly. "You don't have to be so formal. Everyone here calls me Ralph. You make me sound as if I'm as old as my uncle."

Ralph's comment was light-hearted but it provided an opportunity for Veronica to compliment her boss.

"Oh no, I didn't mean to do that Mr Greening. Why, all the girls in the office think exactly the opposite."

Veronica smiled, Ralph unconsciously drawn towards her soft lips which, slightly parted, revealed her lovely, white teeth.

"Well, I'll let you get back Veronica. I'm sure that you've got some important jobs to get on with."

"Yes, Mr Greening."

Veronica turned and walked slowly out of the office, Ralph watching the gentle sway of her hips as she disappeared down the corridor. He couldn't deny that it was a pleasing sight, but then shook his head in order to erase the image from his mind.

It wasn't long before Connie arrived. Entering, she closed the door behind her and then walked slowly over to the desk.

"Come here Ralph."

Connie held her arms out towards him. Ralph, looking up, saw her radiant, beautiful face. A shaft of sun light was forcing its way through a gap in the blinds and was playing around the locks of hair that lay delicately on her cheeks. Needing no further persuasion, Ralph leapt out of his chair, quickly advancing the few steps towards her. Taller, Ralph looked down at her, his eyes not failing to notice the opening at the top of her blouse, revealing the beautiful, bare skin on her neck. It was her modesty that so excited him. Her blouse only ever had at most, its two top buttons undone, so keeping the top of her breasts out of sight and leaving him longing for more.

Embracing, the couple shared a long, passionate kiss. For Connie, aroused as she was, it was a show of affection that would need, for the moment, to prove fulfilling enough. She was determined that until she was married, there would be no further steps of intimacy. Yet for Ralph, such ideas were alien. His past experiences had conditioned him into feeling that a passionate kiss was an indication of more to come. Sliding his hand down Connie's back, he gently squeezed her thigh and then started to move his hand around towards the inside of the top of her leg. Suddenly, he felt a sharp tap on his hand and Connie gently pushed him away.

"You know we'll have plenty of time for that later Ralph," she said, quietly and without obvious censure. "I've always told you, I'm an old-fashioned girl and if we do get engaged, it's going to stay that way until my wedding night."

"Yes. I'm sorry Connie."

Silent for a moment, Ralph was suddenly struck by Connie's choice of words.

"What do you mean 'if' we get engaged? I thought that we were going to announce it."

Connie noted Ralph's concern and smiled. It was reassuring to see such an obvious sign of his commitment. It crossed her mind that she had been justified in being angry with Tom, who had so strongly questioned the integrity of the man she loved.

"I'm just giving you the chance to consider your options Ralph. If waiting is too difficult for you, then maybe I'm not the one you're looking for."

Connie's insistence that he behave like a gentleman, excited Ralph. In the past it had been far too easy for him to get what he wanted. Yet the fulfilment he'd gained then, was nothing compared to the thrill of anticipation he felt now, waiting for the moment when Connie would finally surrender to him.

"You are the one Connie," insisted Ralph. "I'll try harder. I promise. But when I look at you, I just can't help it."

Connie smiled.

"Well, you're just going to have to."

She looked so confident and assured; defiant. It was no good. She looked even more beautiful and Ralph wanted her so much. His pulse raced, he literally trembled inside and he had to catch his breath. Did she have any idea of how difficult it was for him? If she did, she wasn't giving anything away. He was so desperate for relief, but there was no chance of that. Somehow, he had to calm himself down, but it was a difficult task when all he could see was Connie, the source of his torment, stood before him.

Connie fully understood Ralph's predicament and it pleased her. She wanted him to desire her, but realised that her continued presence would simply increase the sexual tension that now filled the room. She looked into Ralph's eyes. She could see that they were silently pleading with her to give him more. And he was so handsome and she couldn't help but feel the temptation to do so. But no, she mustn't. It wasn't how it should be and somehow, Connie found the strength to resist. Calmly, giving no sign to Ralph of her own inner turmoil and desire, she walked towards the door.

"I've left some important papers in my desk Ralph. I'll have to go and get them. I'll be back in a bit."

Ralph nodded. He understood that she was giving him the chance to calm down. Leaving the office, Connie closed the door behind her, intent on giving Ralph the privacy to deal with his obvious discomfiture, however he could.

Chapter 45

Later that afternoon, Connie was back with Ralph in his office. By that time, Ralph also knew about Tom's departure and expressed surprise at his decision.

"I can understand why he needs to leave, for there isn't really the chance for him to progress any further here. But I never expected it to happen."

"Why?" asked Connie, who was determined to keep the details of her fallout with Tom from her fiancé.

"Well, I never thought he was particularly ambitious. Good old Tom. Everybody loves him, but he's far too soft. I thought he'd be with us forever."

Irritated and angry with Tom a short time ago, Connie now found herself slightly annoyed by what she judged to be Ralph's condescending tone. After all, everyone at the company knew that there was no one to match Tom for his work rate and ability. Tom may feel uncomfortable taking the credit for his achievements and he was certainly no self-advertiser, but the company had benefited greatly from having him as an employee. Quickly, she sprang to Tom's defence.

"Well, I'm sure that Tom will do very well at Joyce and Hitchcock and I expect that your uncle is going to be very sorry to lose him."

Ralph liked it when she felt strongly about something. Her voice would become animated, her words passionate and she looked even more beautiful. Mischievously, he saw an opportunity to push her further.

"That's just like you Connie," he said, playfully. "You always have to protect the poor 'waifs and strays.'"

"I hardly think that describes Tom," replied Connie, showing signs of irritation that encouraged Ralph to tease her all the more.

"Well, perhaps not exactly," he replied, "but it's like his work for the Labour Party. Why would a man from the business community mix with those socialists? Perhaps he's just looking for a cause to feel good about himself. No, he's too soft Connie. He's unable to support tough decisions for the benefit of us all, just in case we break a few eggs along the way."

Finished, Ralph waited for the inevitable fiery response. He'd baited the hook and knew that Connie was about to take it.

"So, I'm wasting my time trying to help all these 'charity cases', am I?" asked Connie.

"Well, it's different for you Connie. You're a woman. You have a mother's instinct. You naturally want to help others."

Ralph smiled at her. He knew that he had her. Connie had failed to realise that he was playing with her.

"It's different for men," he continued. "Men have to be tough. For example, these welfare programmes. Yes, some people are in real need, but there's too many idle wasters out there. They need discipline and hard work. They need to get themselves sorted out. Self-help; self-reliance. That's what will bring them success and prosperity."

Ralph had just lit the touch paper and settled back to watch as Connie exploded into life.

"Oh, really Ralph! And you've achieved it all through self-help, have you? Your position here today?"

She paused and looked at him intently. She was angry; her eyes shone fiercely. Any other man would have been stopped in his tracks, but not Ralph. He knew that she was referring to his own advantages, particularly the fact that he was the boss's nephew. It didn't bother him. He was too self-confident to allow such considerations to undermine him. Looking at her, taking in her words and seeing her frustration with him, Ralph saw the vivacity that so enchanted him.

"Connie," he said, quietly. "Do you know how utterly beautiful you are when you lose your temper? You're absolutely gorgeous."

It shouldn't have worked on her and she knew it, but it did. Smiling, Ralph continued.

"I'm sorry Connie. I was only teasing. I know that I shouldn't do it. Especially given the way you look now. I just don't know how I'm going to be able to stop myself from taking you in my arms."

Connie let out a deep sigh and shook her head.

"Do you forgive me?" asked Ralph.

He stood looking at her, a cheeky grin on his face. A naughty schoolboy waiting to be punished by his pretty teacher.

"It wasn't funny Ralph. You should know better than that. You've known Tom for a long time and he's always been your friend."

"I know Connie. I'll be pleased to see him again when we go to work at Joyce and Hitchcock. I do hope that he does well there. I'm sure he will, or Mike Joyce wouldn't have offered him the job. It's strange though. Knowing Tom, I would have expected him to stay around and say goodbye to us. We could have gone out for a celebratory drink together."

"Yes, I suppose we could have," replied Connie.

"Did you have any inkling that he was going?" asked Ralph.

"No," replied Connie.

"Oh," said Ralph, sounding surprised. "You seem to be far closer to him than any of us here. I thought that he might have mentioned something to you."

"No. The first I knew about it was when Paula told me earlier today."

Connie had answered Ralph's questions truthfully. She had no intention of ever lying to him. But she had chosen not to tell Ralph about her disagreement with Tom. Connie had resolutely defended her fiancé and saw no reason for Ralph to know, now that Tom had departed. Yet her words in Tom's defence had indicated to Connie that she hadn't completely turned her back on him. He had been wrong to question her relationship with Ralph, but she now believed that they could be friends once more in the future, when the passage of time had healed the wounds of the present.

Moving closer to Connie, Ralph put his arm around her shoulders and pulled her gently towards him. Seeing his familiar, roguish smile, Connie was unable to resist him. The two of them shared a long, lingering kiss before Connie pulled herself away and called them back to their work.

"That's enough Ralph. There's been too much kissing and canoodling for one day. We need to get back to work"

"Yes, dear," replied Ralph, playfully saluting her.

"Ralph!"

"Sorry!" said Ralph, laughing.

The two of them sat down around the desk and continued working on their report.

Chapter 46

The Thursday after Tom's departure, Connie was at the party office in Ardwick. She had a feeling that Tom wouldn't be present, a fact that Harry quickly confirmed.

"I'm afraid, it's going to be a little difficult for a while Connie. Tom's left. He said that his new job will need all his attention. He's talking of moving to Stockport and getting involved with the Party down there."

"Well Harry, I know that he's taken on a lot of new responsibilities. I suppose it will be easier for him to help out closer to his job."

Connie felt sure that Tom had made the decision so that she wouldn't feel uncomfortable being around him. She had no intention of telling this to Harry though.

"Maybe so Connie," replied Harry, "but Tom's hardly gone to the ends of the earth. I don't see why he can't make it back here."

"Never mind," said Connie. "Hopefully, we'll be able to find someone else to help us."

"Yes, I hope so, but his behaviour still seems a little odd," continued Harry, as he picked up a folder and handed it to Connie. "It would be great if you could see the people at these addresses. I've not put any awkward customers in there."

Connie looked through the pages. She was familiar with the individuals and families concerned and nodded appreciatively.

"Shall we arrange to meet back here afterwards?" asked Harry.

"Well, if it's all right with you, I've got a lot on at work tomorrow and I'd also like to drop in on Kath. I've not seen her since last week and I want to check that she's okay."

"Yes, that's fine Connie. You've got very close to Kath, haven't you?"

"Yes, I have. She's lovely and someone I can really talk to."

"I told you she was pretty special, didn't I?"

Connie nodded in agreement.

"Look, don't worry," said Harry, "we can catch up on any new issues next week and if you feel that there's something urgent, you can give me a ring at school."

Watching Connie depart, Harry felt a twinge of disappointment. He'd been looking forward to talking to her later on. His admiration of her had continued to grow. Pretty, but strong and forthright, she had the endearing qualities of kindness and compassion. She cared about the poor and disadvantaged and wanted to do everything in her power to help them. Harry understood that Connie had captivated him and no other woman had done that before.

Focused on his work at school and for the Party, Harry cut an austere figure. Through circumstances however, he had found little time for romance in his life. Before he met Connie, Harry had spent many years caring for his widowed mother. Her ongoing bronchial complaints had ultimately developed into cancer and he'd suffered the pain of losing her, following a long, heroic and drawn-out battle to survive. As her only child, Harry had found it exceptionally difficult to secure the care and attention that she needed, while still continuing with his job in education. It was another compelling reason that drove him on towards the vision of a socialist future, where the weak, the ill and the vulnerable, would be protected by a reforming government that operated within a society driven by compassion.

Harry had already recognised Connie as a kindred spirit. In his imagination, he'd already seen her as the ideal woman to have by his side when he eventually pursued his dream of getting into Parliament. Harry had already told her that he'd appreciate having her help on that journey, but his words had no romantic allusions attached to them. Consequently, Connie couldn't possibly have detected his desire for a more intimate relationship. Nevertheless, he felt convinced that he would be able to offer Connie the love and attention that she deserved. Yet ironically, Harry had no knowledge of Connie's growing relationship with Ralph. Tom and Connie had never discussed Ralph in his presence. As such, Harry's growing affection for Connie wasn't held in check. By the time he did become aware of Connie's love for someone else, it was too late for him to extinguish his desire for the two of them to be together.

Without intending it, Connie had captivated three different men, all of whom adored her. Tom had already fallen victim to his disappointment at losing her. It remained to be seen what the passage of time would bring to her relationships with Harry and Ralph.

Chapter 47

Outside, clutching her folder of appointments, Connie made her way around the streets of Ardwick, visiting those who found it difficult to see Harry at the party office. The people she met were for Connie the saddest of cases. There were the old people who were too frail to leave their homes and the deserted young mothers, left to care for the children and babies so casually discarded by their wayward fathers. There were those too, who had problems with their homes and Connie needed to visit the properties herself, before attempting to coax some remedial action out of their landlords.

Since the Tory Rent Act of 1957, controls on rents had been removed and they had risen rapidly. It was the reasonable operation of 'market forces', the government had claimed and it would encourage private investment in new housing and so solve the housing crisis. But of course, every time houses were let to new tenants, the rent could be raised and the poorest and most vulnerable were in danger of being squeezed beyond their capacity to cope. Furthermore, Connie knew that regardless of rental income increasing, too many landlords were disinclined to pay for essential repairs to their properties. Before the new law, a standard two-up two-down terrace in Ardwick could be rented for twelve shillings a week. Now, there were cases where rents on newly let properties were rising towards two pounds, with rates to be paid on top. Connie believed that a Labour victory at the next general election was crucial. The Party already had plans to introduce a new Rent Act, one that would establish local authority rent officers who would determine and register a fair rent for all properties. Furthermore, Labour intended to protect vulnerable tenants by only allowing them to be evicted, if their landlords had taken out successful proceedings in the County Court.

Yet laws were good intentions, written down on paper and Connie couldn't believe that they would provide the ultimate answer to unscrupulous landlords. Connie was well aware of the intimidation that many would apply to their tenants. She had met Josiah Mulgrew. He was far too clever to be linked to the thugs who could enforce his authority over 'awkward' tenants. Connie also understood that the working classes had an ingrained distrust of the forces of law and order. The police, the courts and the authorities were all looked on as outsiders, not public servants who could be trusted to help them. After all, the very poorest often found themselves pursued by the police and punished by the courts.

They were reluctant to approach them with their problems and individuals such as Mulgrew, knew that to be the case. The real answer lay in an acceleration of the housing programme. The compulsory purchase and renovation of existing housing and the construction of new estates for those currently without homes of their own. Rents would be set reasonably by the local authorities, who would own these properties. Yet progress was painfully slow and Connie had to admit that since the end of the War, her own party had failed to tackle the issue just as much as their Tory opponents.

By eight thirty, Connie had finished her last visit and was soon knocking on Kath's back door. Once inside, Kath threw her arms around her and gave her a peck on the cheek.

"Come in love. It's good to see you. Sit down, I'll put the kettle on."

Sitting at the kitchen table, Connie watched her friend go through the familiar routine of making a brew. As she did, Kath chatted away, talking about trivial, everyday matters such as the weather, or the prices in the shops. Having placed the teapot, resplendent in its colourful, striped cosy, the mugs, milk and sugar on the table, Kath was able to sit down, give Connie her complete attention and the conversation could become more serious.

Taking a sip from her mug, Connie expressed her satisfaction.

"Ah, thanks Kath. I needed that. I always know that I'll get a proper 'cuppa' here."

Kath smiled, please with the compliment.

"Well you know yourself Connie, you've got to leave it long enough to brew. Too many people rush it. They don't warm the pot and they want to drink it too soon. It never tastes right that way."

Connie nodded appreciatively.

"How's that young man of yours then?" asked Kath. "Is he treating you well?"

"Yes, he's fine and of course he is."

"Good, I hope he realises how lucky he is to have such a wonderful girl like you."

Connie looked down.

"Don't be embarrassed love. Where is he going to find someone to compare to you?"

Connie shook her head and smiled. She knew that there was no point in challenging her opinion.

"We're going to get engaged Kath. We'll be telling everyone next week."

"Oh, that's lovely. Have you set a date?"

"No. We've not done it yet."

Kath hadn't met Ralph yet, but knowing Connie, she felt sure that he must be a young man with fine qualities. Almost inevitably however, Kath's mind wandered over to the question of Tom.

"And how's Tom taken the news?" she asked. "I suppose he was disappointed, wasn't he?"

Connie hesitated. She was unsure how she would answer the question. She took a sip of tea, in order to give herself more time to think. But it was no good trying to hide her feelings from Kath. Her friend could tell that the engagement had created difficulties between Connie and Tom.

"He's not taken it too well, has he love?"

"No."

Connie stared down into her mug, unable to make eye contact. She couldn't help feeling guilty, now that her initial anger with Tom had passed. The problem was that although Connie could be quite dismissive when talking about the matter to Paula, Kath recognised that deep down, she still felt affection towards Tom. It may be the affection of a friend, but it had given Connie a sense of responsibility for Tom's welfare.

"Well love," said Kath, "don't you think it's best to talk about it?"

Connie looked up and nodded.

"I just don't understand Kath. Why do I feel like the 'villain of the peace?' I don't see why getting engaged to Ralph means that I have to take Tom's feelings into consideration."

"If you really do believe that you owe him nothing," replied Kath, "then there's no reason for you to feel frustrated. Tom's a sensible lad. He wouldn't do anything silly and certainly nothing to cause you upset. You don't need to worry about him and in time you can be friends again."

Kath reached across the table and put her hand on Connie's. She patted it reassuringly. Connie took a deep breath, the incident with Tom had upset her and with Kath, she could finally admit it. Yet her friend wasn't finished.

"You're a lovely girl Connie, so warm and considerate. It doesn't surprise me that you're concerned about Tom. Is that all though?"

"What do you mean?" asked Connie, surprised.

"Is it, that perhaps you feel a little more about Tom than you're prepared to admit?"

"No, I don't," replied Connie, with certainty. "I can assure you of that. Tom has never been other than just a friend. Ralph excites me, he makes me feel alive. That's what I want in a man."

"Yes, I know," replied Kath. "You're young. I understand, but love is strange. Sometimes you can mistake passion and desire for love. Love often grows slowly over time and you can find it in the most unusual places."

Connie was surprised by Kath's words. She was showing a depth of understanding that made her wonder if she was talking from experience. The thought crossed Connie's mind that perhaps Stan's personality had been similar to Tom's. Nevertheless, Connie didn't feel inclined to broach the matter with her friend.

"I know that every woman takes a gamble on the man she chooses," said Connie. "I know that Ralph has had other women in the past. Yet I feel sure that he's the one for me."

Kath nodded.

"I know that Tom's a lovely guy," continued Connie "and everyone likes him. I keep thinking that he's bound to meet someone else and then he'll forget all about me. He's got a fantastic new job; a big promotion. He'll be too busy to worry about what I'm doing."

"But won't you be seeing him when the two of you are helping Harry?"

"No. Tom's taken a break from the Party to concentrate on his new job."

"And not to save you from any embarrassment Connie?"

Connie was silent. Both she and Kath knew that it was the real reason for his decision.

"Never mind love," said Kath. "Things will turn out all right between you and Tom. You'll see."

Glancing at the clock, Kath saw that it was almost ten.

"Hadn't you best be getting off love? It's getting on a bit."

"Yes Kath, I need to be up early for work tomorrow morning."

"You always are. You work too hard love. I hope that boss of yours appreciates it."

"Yes, I'm sure he does. Joe Greening is decent enough. I can't think of many others who would have given a woman like me the opportunity that he has."

"That's right love. I can't disagree with you there."

Connie smiled. The two women warmly embraced before Connie opened the door, went out into the backyard and set off home to Howard Avenue.

Chapter 48

The following day, just after dinner, Connie and Ralph met up in his office to talk about the announcement of their engagement. Connie was insistent that there would be no grand party to follow. She believed that their commitment to one another was personal and private.

"You know Ralph. All that matters to me is that you love me. It's about us, no one else. I want us to quietly announce our engagement. I don't want any fanfares or parties. My commitment is to you. Trust is the key to any relationship. It can't be bought and paid for. It's the same with the wedding. I would prefer it simple. A civil, not a church service. Although I suspect," she added, "that it may cause some problems with your family."

"Yes, I'm sure it will. I suspect that my mother and uncle will expect something grander. They'll want to show off the family at its best to their friends and associates."

"I understand," replied Connie, "but it's not right. I can't justify the expenditure and for what? It won't affect our happiness, or our capacity to build a successful marriage. Relationships thrive on the character and honesty of man and wife, not on the cost of a wedding dress or the size of the reception."

"Don't you think that you're being a little inflexible?" asked Ralph. "Aren't you reading too much into it? Surely most women want the best and brightest occasion that they can have. It makes the day extra special and it gives them something that they can remember. I agree with you about the engagement Connie, but isn't the wedding different?"

Ralph paused, giving Connie time to consider his words.

"I suppose you've got a point Ralph. I won't change my opinion though. A grand, white wedding is being unnecessarily profligate. I understand that getting married is a family event. Working-class parents also give their daughters the best wedding that they can afford. Yet I still prefer to have a small, intimate reception for close friends and family. I know that we'll have to compromise with your mother and uncle, but I won't allow matters to get out of hand."

Ralph could see that Connie was determined to stand her ground. He suspected that she felt uncomfortable that the 'profligate' spending would be carried out by his wealthy family. He was sure that Connie wanted to maintain her independence and a low-key wedding would enable her to meet half of the costs herself. Ralph wondered if she would ever be comfortable with being well off. He had been born into it; wealth was natural to him. Connie found her success, the money she earned at Greenings, difficult to accept at times. Ralph saw no reason why she should and as he had done in the past, he gently chided her for it. The result was that bizarrely, from a discussion based on love and marriage, Ralph and Connie found themselves entering into a political debate.

"I think Connie, that you're only concerned about expense because you're thinking about your friends and neighbours in Ardwick."

Ralph smiled and looked closely at her. He knew that he would soon have her biting back.

"It's because you think that you can't show that you care for them, if your wedding is so expensive," he continued. "You don't have to live a life of austerity to prove that you genuinely want to help the poor."

"That's not true Ralph," said Connie.

She was determined not to get drawn over the matter, but Ralph knew that eventually, she would be unable to resist.

"You see Connie, I don't see any other socialists who think like you do. Crikey. Harold and his cronies don't go without, do they? Most of your Labour lot aren't slow in putting their noses in the trough, are they?"

Ralph had a satisfied look on his face, he was confident that his comments had hit the mark.

Connie was annoyed but the worst thing for her, was that she believed there was an element of truth in what he'd said. Too many in the Party had lost sight of their principles and Wilson and the National Executive had been eager to expel members of the Socialist Labour League for being too radical. The struggle between left and right in the Party was gaining strength because of it. Disillusion with the leadership's perceived lack of commitment to real social progress, was leading once enthusiastic party members to look to the radicalisation of trade unions, as a means of challenging the power of the establishment.

"Well Ralph," she replied, after a pause. "There's always the danger of vanity rearing its ugly head where politics are concerned. It's the nature of the beast. We all have to be a little egotistical if we want to tell others how they should live their lives. And there is a fine line to tread between being an agent for good, a facilitator of change, or someone who revels in their own importance and confuses the public good with their own advancement. It's all too easy. Lenin was right. He said that no one should hold any position of influence within the Party for more than a couple of years. Any longer and the bureaucratic mindset takes over. Officials become distant from the people they represent and their only concern becomes that of holding onto their privileges and their position. The interests of the common good are lost without trace."

Connie sounded almost melancholic. It wasn't the response that Ralph had hoped to elicit from her. She was taking matters too seriously and he was determined to lighten the mood.

"Oh Lord, Connie! Lenin! You do worry me sometimes. Just what on earth goes on in that head of yours?"

Ralph smiled, an action that initially irritated his intended. Connie frowned.

"Don't be condescending Ralph."

"Now, why would I do that?" asked Ralph.

Once again, he smiled at her and stretched out his hand across the desk to where she was sat and took her left hand in his. Gently, he stroked her fingers and then looked into her eyes.

"Yes, you really are so beautiful when you're angry Connie. It's worth it just to see how gorgeous you are."

Ralph grinned cheekily and Connie, although she was determined to resist his flirtatious advances, couldn't help but smile.

"Don't Ralph. You know I'm being serious."

"I know Connie, but the world would be a very dull and dreary place if we spent our time being serious all day now, wouldn't it?"

Ralph looked impishly at her, waiting for her to respond.

"Well, wouldn't it?" he repeated.

Unable to resist his cheeky smile, Connie shook her head and sighed.

"Honestly Ralph, one of these days I'm going to really sort you out."

"Oh, yes please Connie. There's nothing I'd like better!"

He smiled again. Still holding her hand, he caressed it softly and looked seductively into her eyes.

"Stop it, Ralph! Pack it in!"

"What?"

"You know what!"

Connie disengaged her hand from his.

"I've told you before. You need to make an honest woman of me before any of that Ralph."

"Any of what?" asked Ralph, feigning surprise.

"Trying to get 'fruity.'"

"Fruity!" replied Ralph, a puzzled, almost comical look on his face.

"Yes" said Connie, starting to laugh as his expression turned into one of incredulity. "Fruity!"

"I can assure you, that I wasn't doing anything improper Connie."

"Oh, really?" asked Connie.

"Yes, really," replied Ralph, with all the sincerity that he could muster.

"Okay then Ralph, let's forget it. Anyway, look at the time, we should be getting back to work."

"I don't know," said Ralph. "I thought I was supposed to be the boss. I'm more convinced than ever that Uncle Joe's going to put you in charge once we're married. I bet you'll be a real little slave driver!"

Ralph laughed and smiled, the two of the them parting with a kiss as Connie set off back to her office.

Chapter 49

It was Saturday, May 30th 1964 and four weeks to the day since Connie had accepted Ralph's proposal. They had agreed that they would announce their engagement at work on the following Monday and realised that Connie would need an engagement ring for the occasion. Ralph had arranged to arrive at Howard Avenue at ten o'clock in the morning, pick up Connie and take her in to town to buy one. When Ralph arrived, Connie was ready and waiting for him in the front room. When she heard the Dart pull up outside, she opened the front door and stepped out ready to greet him. It was no time at all before Ralph had got out of the car and was sharing a kiss with his intended.

"That was nice," said Connie, smiling after their lips had finally parted.

Ralph stood back, eagerly taking in every aspect of his fiancé's appearance.

"You look lovely Connie. You make a chap ever so proud to take you out on his arm."

Connie smiled. She was wearing a simple, yellow dress suit. The pretty, short-sleeved top, had four buttons beneath an open style collar. The skirt reached to just below her knees and the tailored design hugged her figure, creating an overwhelming impression of grace and elegance, even though the outfit passed for 'casual wear.'

Shaking his head, Ralph let out a long sigh.

"It shouldn't be allowed Connie."

"What?"

"You, wearing that outfit. It's not fair. How am I supposed to be able to concentrate on anything today?"

"Well Ralph," said Connie mischievously. "You're just going to have to, aren't you?"

She turned and walked back to the front door.

"I'll just get my coat Ralph and then we can make a move."

Ralph watched her walking away, his eyes drawn to her swaying hips and her soft, supple legs and slim ankles, beautifully defined by her stiletto heels. He breathed deeply. She excited him so much. He wished that they were already married and then he could make love to her, but at the moment, she remained tantalisingly out of reach. Ralph hadn't expected that it would affect him like this. He'd believed that the closer they got to their engagement and marriage, the easier he would find it to cope. Yet the reality proved to be so different and whenever she appeared, whatever she wore, regardless of what she was doing, his desire for her was uncontained and he was desperate for relief.

Focused as he was on Connie, Ralph had failed to notice the approach of two young men, attracted by the sight of the Dart. He was taken completely by surprise when one of them suddenly addressed him.

"Is that your car?"

Recovering, Ralph turned round to see a young man with red hair and freckles. He was with his friend, who had black hair and a quiff. They were both wearing overalls and were smiling at the fact that they had made Ralph 'jump.' It was Johnny and Bob.

"Are you okay pal?" asked Johnny. "I think we caught you by surprise, didn't we?"

"Ah," said Bob. "He's daydreaming about Connie, isn't he? She gets everyone like that, doesn't she Johnny?"

He turned to Johnny who stared back silently at him, his usual reticence returning whenever Connie's name was mentioned.

"That's my fiancé, I'll have you know," said Ralph, clearly irritated.

"I know," replied Bob. "I'm sorry. I didn't mean anything by it. Honest."

Ralph nodded, realising that he had been a little premature when reacting so negatively.

"I'm Bob and this is Johnny."

Bob pointed towards his friend.

"I'm Ralph."

Holding out his hand, Johnny and Bob shook it in turn.

"It's a smart car, the Dart," said Bob.

"Yes, it is," replied Ralph, who was now beginning to warm to the young man, especially as he had praised his pride and joy.

"They go pretty fast, don't they?" asked Johnny.

"Yes. They've clocked them at a hundred and twenty."

"That's the same as our 'Interceptor,'" said Bob. "I bet we could beat you in a race," he added.

"Have you two got a Royal Enfield Interceptor?"

Ralph couldn't hide his surprise. The company had only been making the impressive motorbike for a couple of years and they didn't come cheap. Ralph assumed that young men their age couldn't have afforded one, especially when they lived around here.

"We did it up," said Bob. "Go and fetch it Johnny and bring both of the helmets."

"Okay."

Johnny set off down to his house at the far end of the Avenue. Like Ralph, he too loved his chosen mode of transport and was eager to show it off at any opportunity.

"A friend of a friend," continued Bob, "knew this guy who crashed a 1962 Interceptor. He got the insurance and let them take back a bit of the pay out, so that he could keep it for spares when he got a new one. His missus wouldn't let him buy another bike and so he let us have it for a few quid. Johnny's an apprentice mechanic and he's put it right. We needed a new set of front forks and a front wheel, but we managed to get them trade through Johnny's boss. It's as good as new."

Just as he finished speaking, Ralph heard a roar. He looked down the road and saw Johnny astride the Interceptor. Having started it, he quickly rode the short distance back to Connie's house. Pulling back the throttle a few more times, Johnny smiled with satisfaction, before shutting off the engine.

"Sweet," said Johnny.

"As a nut," continued Bob.

Ralph looked at it. It certainly was a beautiful machine. Red, silver and black, there was no sign at all that it had been written off in an accident.

"You've done a good job on it," said Ralph, admiringly. "She's a beauty."

By now the Interceptor had attracted a small audience. A group of kids had gathered round to gape at both it and the Dart. With few of their parents able to buy and run a car, the chance to look at the two magnificent machines made them feel as if all their Christmases had come at once.

"It's called a 750 Interceptor," said Johnny, "but it actually has a 736cc twin cylinder engine."

Ralph nodded. Johnny was speaking his language. Technical specifications that were lost on most people, fascinated him.

"So that's why I've not seen you two about. You've been spending all your time on the bike."

It was Connie. She'd slipped out of the front door and had stood behind them, listening to the conversation.

"Hiya Connie," said Bob.

Johnny nodded. Even though he had a crash helmet on, it was plain to see that he was blushing. Quick to notice, Bob had a suggestion for his friend.

"Why don't you take Connie for a ride on the back? We've got an extra helmet here for her."

Johnny looked at Connie. He studied her face. He wanted to ask her, but fearing that she would turn him down, searched for any signs that she wasn't keen on the idea.

"You'd like to, wouldn't you Connie?" said Bob, trying to encourage her.

Connie could see Johnny's eyes widen and his mouth open slightly in anticipation of an affirmative answer. She hadn't the heart to disappoint him and actually, when she looked at the powerful, gleaming Interceptor, she thought that a ride on the back would be quite thrilling.

"Yes, if Johnny doesn't mind," said Connie, smiling reassuringly at him.

"No. I'd love to," said Johnny, delighted that she'd agreed.

"Well, I'll have to nip in and put some pants on," said Connie. "I won't be able to sit on there with my skirt on."

"Hmm," said Bob. "I suppose not. We didn't think of that, did we?" he continued, turning to Johnny.

"No, we didn't," replied his friend.

Connie went back inside to get changed. Whilst they waited for her, Johnny faced a barrage of requests from the kids, demanding that they also be allowed to ride on the back of the motorbike. Being told firmly that there was no chance, given that they were all too young, Bob and Johnny had to suffer a crescendo of disappointed groans. Ralph meanwhile, was becoming concerned. Much as he admired the Interceptor, he feared the dangers inherent in a young man riding a powerful bike around the streets with Connie on the back. It was a fast machine and he was sure that Johnny would take it through its paces to impress her. Ralph had done it many times in the Dart when he'd been with his other girlfriends. It was his immaturity; an assumption that women would see him as being as slick, powerful and attractive as his car was. Johnny wouldn't be able to resist the opportunity to show off. So, when Connie emerged, wearing a thick jumper and pants, Ralph decided that it was time to intervene.

"I'm not sure that you should be doing this, Connie."

Connie looked at him. It was a sharp and somewhat cold stare.

"Doing what Ralph?"

"Going on the back of the bike."

"Oh? Why not?" she asked.

Ralph realised by the tone of Connie's voice, that she was displeased. He knew that he'd already lost the conversation, but it was clear to him that Connie demanded an answer.

"Well, you're not used to riding on the back of a motorbike. You might end up coming off."

"Don't be so stupid Ralph! Johnny wouldn't let that happen. And do you think I'm some weak and feeble female who needs to be wrapped up in cotton wool? You don't have a clue whether or not I've been on the back of a bike before, do you Ralph?" continued Connie.

"Well, no. I suppose I don't," said Ralph, somewhat sheepishly.

It was a real telling off. Ralph had been put firmly in his place. The kids had averted their eyes, looking down at the floor. Connie's disparaging words all too readily reminding them of a scolding from their mam.

"I'm sorry Connie. I didn't mean…"

"Just get it straight Ralph. No man tells me what to do. If I want to ride on the back of the bike. I will."

Connie's words were followed by a deafening hush.

"Well?" asked Connie, looking expectantly at Bob.

"Yes Connie?" replied Bob, wondering if he was about to feel the full force of her displeasure too.

"Are you going to give me the helmet then?"

Bob smartly did as he was told and helped to adjust the strap after Connie had placed it carefully on her head. Seeing that she was ready, Johnny kickstarted the Interceptor back into life, pulling on the throttle and eliciting some mighty roars from the engine. Connie sat astride the back of the cushioned seat and put her arms around Johnny's waist in front of her. Almost immediately, they were off. Quite slowly at first, as they travelled the short distance to the end of Howard Avenue. Once they'd turned left down Syndall Street however, Ralph, Bob and the kids could hear the engine roaring into life. Bob turned to Ralph, eager to reassure him.

"Don't worry Ralph. Johnny won't be stupid. He thinks the world of Connie."

"We all do Mister," said a small voice to the side.

"Connie's lovely," added a little girl as Ralph looked round.

Ralph tried to smile, but the next ten minutes seemed like an hour. He was worried sick, convinced that his beloved Connie was going to end up in a terrible accident. He hadn't anticipated that she would be away so long and as a quarter of an hour came and went, he expressed his concern to Bob.

"Where can they be? I thought that they'd be back by now."

"Don't worry Ralph. Johnny's gone down Stockport Road. They've probably been held up in traffic. It gets quite busy on a Saturday morning."

"Yes, I Suppose so," replied Ralph, eager to latch on to any reassuring comment, however insubstantial.

"I wouldn't mention anything when she gets back," said Bob. "I thought I was going to cop for it when she wanted the helmet!"

Bob grinned. It was far easier for him to see the funny side of the morning's events.

"Yes," replied Ralph. "I rather put my foot in it, didn't I?"

"That's our Connie for you. She's lovely, would help anyone, but she knows what she wants and she'll always stand up for herself."

"Yes, people round here seem to like her, don't they?"

"We all do," said Bob. "Everyone respects her for what she's done with her job and everything else. What people like especially though, is that she hasn't changed a bit. Anyone else would have been away from here long ago, but not Connie. She's one of us."

As Bob finished speaking, Ralph thought he could hear the sound of the Interceptor. Concentrating, he heard the noise increase. It was definitely a motorbike and he was sure that it was making its way up Syndall Street. Bob too had picked up on it. More familiar with the sound generated by the bike's twin cylinder engine, he smiled.

"That's them," he said, turning to Ralph.

A few seconds later, the Interceptor turned the corner and accelerated past them to the bottom of the Avenue and turning around, roared back towards them, coming to a halt alongside Ralph and Bob, the kids cheering as Johnny turned off the engine.

Getting off the back of the bike, Connie took a couple of steps on to the pavement and unfastened her helmet. Taking it off, she handed it to Bob.

"Well, what do you think Connie?" he asked, eagerly.

"It was good," said Connie. "It picks up speed so quickly. You can really feel the force of it."

Her eyes were gleaming, she had a rosy complexion from riding through the open air. Carefully moving her hand through her hair to remove the impression of the helmet, Connie then threw back her head and shook it, so that her hair fell naturally back into position. Ralph watched her attentively. Her face was glowing; her actions unintentionally seductive. He felt an overwhelming urge to take her in his arms and kiss her but here, on the pavement, surrounded by Bob, Johnny and the motley collection of kids, he fought off his inclination.

"So, Johnny looked after you all right then Connie?" asked Bob.

Connie nodded.

"Yes. He's very good. It would be great to go out with him when the roads are less busy and he could open it up a bit more."

"She kept telling me to go faster," said Johnny, who had left the Interceptor on its stand and was now taking off his helmet beside them.

"Oh, really," said Ralph, a look of disapproval briefly registering on his face, before rapidly disappearing as Connie stared sternly at him.

"So, do you prefer the Interceptor to Ralph's Dart Connie?" asked Bob.

It was the key question. He, Johnny and Ralph eager to hear her verdict, the kids also waiting expectantly for a response.

"Well," said Connie slowly, giving the impression of someone who had deeply weighed up the merits of both contenders. "I've got to say that I like them both."

The kids groaned. She was sitting on the fence. Surely, she could come down on one side or the other? The men weren't happy either. They were desperate for her to show favour towards their own particular vehicle. It seemed like a microcosm of the class struggle. Ralph, not only eager for Connie's support as her fiancé, but as a symbolic reassurance of his superiority over Connie's Ardwick friends, whilst they were desperate to see the defeat of the 'posh toff' from outside.

"But Connie, you must think it's far more exciting on the back of a bike, than sat in a car?" asked Johnny.

Riding with Connie on the Interceptor, her arms around his waist, had been an electrifying sensation for Johnny. He knew that their physical contact had no meaning for Connie, other than her safety, but to him their closeness had been the partial fulfilment of his fantasies about her. Looking closely at him, Connie saw his eyes pleading with her to side with them and she understood implicitly that he was looking for an acknowledgement that their ride together had been as special an experience for her, as it had been for him. And Connie really didn't have the heart to disappoint him.

"Well. I suppose if I was really forced to choose between them, I'd have to go for the Interceptor."

A huge cheer broke out, smiling faces looking towards Ralph, who couldn't help but be amused by their reaction. He suspected that Connie's judgement was driven by her generosity in not wanting to upset Johnny and Bob, especially the former. He'd seen the way that Johnny was around her; it was obvious he was captivated by Connie. No, Ralph thought, he may have lost this particular battle, but he was the one who would be getting the girl and that gave him every reason to appear as a gracious loser.

"Okay lads," said Ralph. "You win, but once the wind, the rain and the snow returns, the Dart will soon be number one with Connie again."

"Yes. Of course, Ralph. Whatever you say," said Bob, laughing dismissively.

"Well lads. I need to get changed," said Connie. "Ralph's taking me out. Thanks for the ride."

"It's okay Connie," said Johnny, who blushed as she smiled at him.

"Johnny will take you out any time. Won't you Johnny?" said Bob, grinning.

Unable to answer, Johnny merely nodded his head. It was so tough falling in love with a beautiful, older woman who ultimately, was out of reach. Yet no one could ever take away from him, the meaning of this special day.

Turning back to the Interceptor, Johnny gave his helmet to Bob, disengaged the stand and wheeled the bike back down to his house, followed by Bob and the kids still clamouring to get a ride.

Chapter 50

Driving into town, Ralph tried to explain to Connie why he'd been so concerned about her riding on the Interceptor.

"I don't think you had any idea of how worried I was. Did you Connie?"

"Aah, aren't you just a big softy, Ralph?"

Connie was poking fun at him and Ralph knew it.

"No, Connie. I was. I'm serious. Anything could have happened to you."

"So?"

Ralph glanced across at her. Bob was right. Once she had an idea in her head, it was hard to shift her. Ralph decided to try a different tack.

"I respect that it's your decision to make, but you might not always get it right."

"Where men are concerned Ralph, I've told you. I won't be treated like the little woman. If I want to do something, then I will."

"Hmm. Just like the jewellers I suppose."

"Yes Ralph, we need to park near Oxford Street to pick up my engagement ring from 'Beaverbrooks.'"

Ralph winced. It was a sore point with him. Able to choose a ring from the most expensive jewellers in Manchester, Connie had been insistent that they would buy it from a cheap, chain store. In fact, Connie had already picked out her ring and paid a deposit on it, so that she could have it correctly sized for her finger. It was a simple design, made of nine carat gold with a single diamond.

"I suppose that you want to pay for it yourself," said Ralph, with a touch of petulance.

"No," replied Connie. "I want you to buy it. You know that I didn't leave the choice of the ring to you, because you would have got something ridiculously expensive. It's what the ring symbolises that matters to me, not its value. You can't put a price on love."

As much as Ralph could appreciate her feelings, he knew that once they were engaged, everyone would want to see Connie's ring. He expected that his mother and her friends would see Connie's decision to wear it as peculiar. They believed that a stunning engagement ring was an opportunity for a woman to impress; a thing of beauty that would bring prestige to its wearer. Ralph was also concerned that he may appear miserly, unprepared to spend lavishly on his intended. But such feelings were irrelevant. By marrying Connie, Ralph had to accept that she would challenge not only his own personal convictions, but the conventions of his friends and family too.

Having parked, Ralph and Connie were quickly inside Beaverbrooks. Connie noticed how Ralph looked around them before they entered the shop. She was quietly amused, knowing that Ralph didn't want to be seen going into the jewellers by anyone who might know him. Once inside though, Connie had to accept that Ralph had behaved impeccably. Polite towards the young woman who served them and expressing his pleasure when Connie tried on the modified ring and the fit was perfect. He even agreed with the assistant when she commented on the beauty of the ring. Ralph could actually acknowledge to himself that the ring's simplicity reflected the purity of Connie's character, but he wanted something grander, something that shouted his love for her from the roof tops. So ultimately, as they left the jewellers, Connie proudly wearing the ring, Ralph couldn't help but feel somewhat disappointed.

Outside, on the pavement, Connie stopped. She took Ralph's hand and looked into his eyes.

"The ring is beautiful Ralph. Thank you for buying it for me," said Connie, smiling. "Aren't you going to give me a kiss now that we're engaged?"

Not needing a second invitation, Ralph put his arms around her and pressed his lips softly against hers. The kiss seemed to go on forever and as they enjoyed the sensual pleasure of the most intimate connection that the pair of them could share before their marriage, any vestiges of disappointment over the purchase of the ring, were soon removed from Ralph's mind.

Eventually parting, Connie smiled mischievously.

"Why, you're a fine kisser Mr Greening."

Her eyes were shining, her lips slightly parted and Ralph reached out for her again, only for Connie to take a step back.

"Steady," said Connie, tenderly, "we'll be making a public spectacle out of ourselves, if we're not careful."

Ralph had forgotten where they were. Public shows of deep affection weren't generally appreciated by shoppers going about their business in Manchester. Furthermore, rebellious teenagers may be expected to defy convention, but not a couple like themselves.

"Now that we've got the ring," said Ralph, changing the subject, "would you like to have another look around the art gallery? We didn't see everything last time, did we?"

"No, that's right Ralph. That would be lovely. It'll give you a chance to calm down a bit too."

Connie rolled her eyes and smiled.

"What do you mean? Calm down a bit!"

"You know Ralph."

Connie grabbed his hand.

"Come on Ralph. Let's get going then."

"Oh, Connie! I don't know!"

He sounded exasperated and she realised that she shouldn't tease him so much. Connie knew how easily Ralph could be aroused when they were together. It pleased her to know how much he wanted her, but she also knew that the pressure would mount on her to give him more. And it wasn't that she didn't want to, but she was adamant that kisses and cuddles wouldn't lead to anything more. After all, if he truly loved her, then he would be prepared to wait. No matter how much Connie thought of Ralph, she simply couldn't afford the risk of giving in to him and then see him walk away from her. It was how the vast majority of her contemporaries felt, determined to remain chaste before marriage and so preserve their reputations. After all, they were members of an unforgiving society, that showed no sympathy for young women who didn't.

Taking the lead, Connie steered Ralph towards the top of Oxford Street. On their left they could see the Midland Hotel, its glitz and glamour far removed from the humble simplicity of Beaverbrooks. In front of them, across St Peter's Square, was the beautiful Central Reference Library. Connie had spent many hours within its walls and was always captivated by the classical beauty of its circular design, its upper floors recessed behind a multitude of Doric columns. Turning right, the couple walked around St Peter's Square to Mosley Street and down towards the City Art Gallery. Such a wonderful collection of buildings, in such a small area, thought Connie. How proud she was to be a Mancunian.

Yet on the far edge of St Peter's Square, at the corner of Dickinson Street, Connie looked at an edifice that stirred very different emotions within her. It was an imposing, yet solid and functional three storey building, brick built with an impressive tourelle on its corner and an attractive frieze running just below the roof. It was 102 Mosley Street and it was the old Clarendon Club premises that had now become the home of the St James Club. As they walked across Dickinson Street and into Mosley Street, Connie looked across at the recessed archway and the steps leading into the building. A gentleman's club, Connie wasn't welcome inside its doors. To her, it was a bastion of male privilege and control, everything she'd had to fight against in her career. She knew that many of Manchester's business elite were members, given the opportunity it provided for them to make contacts and strike deals in its comfortable surroundings. She didn't judge all its members harshly; the club's rules were symptomatic of attitudes towards women in all areas of society. Yet such institutions, across the length and breadth of the country, denied the gender equality that she craved. Had Ralph been a member, she doubted very much whether she could have agreed to their engagement.

Reaching the Art Gallery, Ralph and Connie went inside and walked around the exhibits that they had missed on their previous visit. After a while, Connie suggested that they take a break and have a drink in the café. Without realising, they had been on their feet for quite some time. Sat together, Ralph looked at Connie. She was so beautiful and he moved his hand over the table and started to stroke her fingers. Connie could feel his affection for her and she responded to him with soft caresses of her own. She smiled and looked into his clear, blue eyes.

"Never mind Ralph, we'll soon be married," she said, sympathetically.

"Not so soon, Connie. It will all have to be arranged. It's going to take time."

"That's only if you insist on it, Ralph."

"But we can't just ignore our family and friends."

"Why not? I'm not marrying them, Ralph. I'm marrying you."

Ralph sensed real intent in her words. She was looking straight at him, bold and certain. He knew that she was far stronger than him. When he floundered before obstacles, she simply swept them aside. Small in stature she may be, but he knew of no one more determined.

"Neither of us is a member of a church," continued Connie. "Besides, we have an obligation to the sanctity of marriage, whether the ceremony is civil or religious. A church wedding and all the organisation it entails, just isn't necessary. We don't have to wait around to get married Ralph. We can do it in twenty-eight days at the Register Office."

I wish it were that simple," replied Ralph, unconvinced.

"It can be," insisted Connie. "If you really want it to be."

Ralph didn't answer. He'd not been brought up like Connie. She'd been independent in thought and deed since her early teens. Furthermore, without the talent required to make himself indispensable to his uncle, or to forge a successful business career by himself, Ralph's inheritance of his uncle's company was dependent on him conforming to family expectations.

"You can talk to your family Ralph. Explain that you don't want to wait to get married. I'm sure your uncle would be sympathetic."

"Well, he probably would," replied Ralph, "but it would upset my mother and you've still to meet her. I want you two to get on together."

"I'm sure that we will Ralph and remember, we both decided that I wouldn't see her until after we were engaged."

"I know Connie."

"Well, if the Register Office isn't an option, then you're just going to have to be patient Ralph."

She looked at him. There was something else that she needed to get straight.

"Ralph, I appreciate, as I've already told you, that getting married can involve families too. That's why I've agreed to be flexible. But when we're married, it's just you and me. I won't accept any interference in our lives together. It won't work otherwise."

"I understand Connie," replied Ralph. "I can assure you, that you'll always come first."

"Come on then Ralph," said Connie, smiling. "Finish your drink. I'm going to take you out for tea."

Chapter 51

Back in the car, Ralph asked for directions to where Connie intended to take him.

"Oh, just drive us back to my house Ralph."

"Why? Are you cooking something for us Connie?"

"No, Ralph."

"So where are we going?"

"You'll see."

Arriving at Howard Avenue, Ralph parked the Dart outside Connie's house. The two of them got out on to the pavement. The road was deserted, the kids were all inside having their tea.

"That makes a difference," said Ralph.

"What does?" asked Connie.

"Not having your fan club milling around when you're out here."

"Fan club. What do you mean? asked Connie, confused.

"Your fan club," repeated Ralph, smiling. "They're always here. Different kids, Bob and Johnny, all of them desperate to see you."

"Don't be daft Ralph," said Connie, dismissively.

"No, it's true. You're like some kind of local celebrity."

"Now you're really being daft," said Connie, firmly.

"When you went off with Johnny on the bike, they were all singing your praises. I think they were letting me know that I'd better treat you well or else!"

Connie stared straight ahead, determined to ignore him.

"You're getting embarrassed, aren't you Connie?" asked Ralph, chuckling. "Fancy. It's the first time I've seen you like that," he continued.

"No, I'm not," said Connie, determined to prove him wrong.

"Well, I think it's nice Connie. They all see what I do. A beautiful, kind and considerate woman. I can understand why you've stayed around here for so long."

"Oh, so the working classes aren't all scoundrels then? You're changing your tune, aren't you?" asked Connie, smiling.

"I didn't say that I wanted to live here," said Ralph, "just that I can see why you might want to live close to neighbours who obviously think a lot of you."

"Oh, good Ralph. It's reassuring to know that you're still a 'toff' at heart."

The two of them laughed.

"So, what about my tea then?" asked Ralph. "I'm getting hungry."

"Come on," said Connie. "It's not very far."

Connie and Ralph linked arms and started walking down towards Syndall Street. Once there, they turned left and walked down to Stockport Road.

"Right Ralph," said Connie, as they reached the main road. "We need to get across."

It was just past five o'clock and the road was busy. Carefully, the pair of them waited for a gap in the traffic on their side of the carriageway and advanced towards the middle of the road, waiting for a similar gap on the city bound side, before completing the crossing.

"There you are Ralph," said Connie, pointing a few yards along the pavement.

Ralph followed the direction of her arm and saw that she was indicating a fairly large café. It was double fronted and had large glass windows and three doors. On the bottom of each window were long signs with the words 'Cafe,' 'Vimto' and 'Snacks,' emblazoned on them. Vimto, a cordial made from the juice of grapes, raspberries and blackcurrants, was Manchester's iconic drink, created in the city almost sixty years ago. Yet a sign hanging from the wall above, made it clear that 'Pepsi Cola' was also available, something more cosmopolitan in the heart of Ardwick. On a big white sign above the whole frontage of the café, was the name 'A. Chiappe' written in black, joined-up writing.

"You were good enough to take me to 'The French', so I've brought you to 'Chiappe's' in return. It's the least I could do."

For a moment, Ralph thought it might be Connie's idea of a joke, but he knew better than that. She would never treat her working-class heritage so lightly. It meant far too much for Connie to have done that.

"It's really a 'chippy,'" continued Connie, "and as far as I'm concerned, it's the best one in Manchester. It's lovely and clean and they've got a café area. You'll enjoy it. The food is every bit as good as at 'The French,' but you won't need wheelbarrows full of money to pay for it!"

This was a real departure for Ralph. Whenever he went out for a meal with a lady, it had to be at one of the most prestigious and expensive restaurants. He wanted to show some enthusiasm for Connie's sake, but fish and chips! Unable to stop himself, Ralph couldn't resist the temptation to question her choice of culinary establishment.

"Wouldn't it be just as good to have them in the paper? We can find a bench somewhere to sit down and eat them."

Connie looked at Ralph and saw disappointment etched into his face. He resembled a sullen and dispirited child and Connie couldn't hide her amusement.

"Oh Ralph!" she spluttered, convulsed by fits of laughter. "Stop it!"

"Stop what?" asked Ralph, confused.

His response only had the effect of increasing Connie's hilarity.

"Oh no," pleaded Connie. "Stop it. It hurts!"

Connie was almost bent double, struggling to catch her breath and her fiancé was at a complete loss, unable to understand just what he'd done to amuse her so much. Furthermore, as customers were coming out of 'Chiappe's,' they were stopping to watch Connie's antics on the pavement. Their attention was starting to make Ralph feel uncomfortable.

"Come on Connie. You need to settle down so that we can go in and get something to eat."

His calm and slightly serious tone, helped to soothe Connie's mood and gradually, the laughter subsided and she was able to take in a couple of deep breaths and relax.

"Come on then Ralph," she said finally. "Let's go."

The two of them went towards the open door and then made their way to a seating area that served as a café. They sat down at a table against the far wall and Connie handed Ralph a copy of the menu.

"I'm going to have steak and kidney pudding, mushy peas and chips," said Connie. "It's my favourite. The fish is lovely here Ralph. You'll probably be happiest with that."

"What type of fish is it?" asked Ralph.

"Cod. It's always Cod in Manchester 'chippies.' If you go further afield, some places prefer Haddock."

"Well, go on then," said Ralph. "I'll have fish, chips and peas."

"They're mushy peas Ralph."

"I know. I'm not a complete novice in these matters, Connie."

"So, you've roughed it before, have you Ralph?" asked Connie, a twinkle in her eye.

"You can stop teasing Connie. I'm not falling for it this time."

Ralph looked fondly at her and placed his hand on hers, only to be interrupted as a young waitress came to take their order.

Looking around the café, Ralph was impressed. The Formica table tops were spotless, as were the cruets. The chairs were neat and tidy and the floor, gleaming. The tiled walls reflected the electric lights, making the café bright and welcoming. At the far end there was a large queue of customers waiting at the counter for their orders.

"There are a lot of people here Connie," remarked Ralph.

"Yes, that's because it's such a good 'chippy.'"

"I suppose so."

"You see," continued Connie, "the gourmets who frequent the top restaurants, assume that they're the only places where you can get the best quality food. People who live around here, are just as particular about what they eat. You'd be amazed at how many fish and chip shops change hands regularly. People take them over, but don't produce decent food. As soon as that happens, the customers go elsewhere and the business is sold on again."

"But it's only fish and chips Connie."

"No Ralph. You need decent potatoes and fresh fish. You have to throw away unsold items from dinner, before you open at tea time. Customers hate warmed up food. You need to change the dripping in the fryers frequently and above all, everything has to be spotlessly clean. The working classes are far more aware of that than the rich."

"Oh," said Ralph. "Why's that then?"

"Because working class women do their own cleaning and having a pristine home and kitchen is extremely important. If any 'chippy' or café isn't really clean, they'll notice right away and they won't give them any custom."

"I see," said Ralph.

"How many of your mother's friends do their own cleaning Ralph?" asked Connie.

"Well, none of course. They get domestics in for that sort of thing."

"See?" said Connie.

"So, are you going to be doing all the cleaning when we live together?" asked Ralph.

"Of course. I do it now. I always have."

Ralph shook his head. He didn't understand.

"Why do it, when you don't need to?"

"Because I'd hate the thought of someone else having to clean up my mess."

"Déjà vu," said Ralph.

"What?" asked Connie, confused.

"It's the same conversation as we had that night in 'The French', when you cleared your plates and stacked everything up so nicely."

"It is, isn't it?" said Connie, smiling.

"But you know Connie, you do work very hard for the firm. Not only in the day, but at home too. It doesn't leave you with a lot of time. Don't you think that in the circumstances, it makes it all right to get someone to help you with the cleaning? No one could accuse you of being lazy."

"It doesn't matter," replied Connie. "I wouldn't trust them to do it properly anyway."

"I don't know Connie. You're modern in so many ways and yet so traditional in others. Sometimes you're a real enigma."

"Hopefully, that's why you love me, Ralph. And you 'toffs,' should know better than to stereotype us working-class girls. We're all different. I hope you realise that."

The young waitress returned with their cups of tea, followed by two buttered barm cakes and then their meals. Eating his Cod and chips, Ralph had to admit that it was exceptionally good. His first instinct had been to remove the batter from the outside of the fish, but he thought that such a decision might create a poor impression on Connie. He therefore cut into the battered fish and placed it in his mouth. The Cod was moist and succulent; the batter light and crispy. Together they were a delight and Ralph found that the mushy peas acceptably complemented the flavour too. All in all, Ralph had thoroughly enjoyed his meal.

Drinking their teas, the two lovers looked at one another with quiet affection. It had been a long day and a revealing one for Ralph. The incident with the motorbike, his conversation with Bob, the purchase of the ring and the visit to 'Chiappe's,' had given Ralph a real insight into just how much Connie's values had been shaped by her life in Ardwick. He now knew why she often seemed a woman of contradictions. It was because she effectively lived in two different worlds. Part of Ardwick, but with a career that moved in vastly different circles. Marriage to Ralph would bring those worlds even further into contrast and he hoped that they would overcome the difficulties it might bring. He understood the dilemma that Connie felt because of her material success. It threatened to draw her away from everything that was familiar. He believed that a powerful reason for her remaining in the old two-up, two-down in Howard Avenue, was because it gave her the physical proof that she hadn't sold out her heritage and values. The middle classes, thought Ralph, could never feel like Connie. They never had any feelings of guilt attached to their material success. It was their holy grail and they had been brought up to believe that they should cherish it. It was a concept that Connie would always find difficult to accept.

Chapter 52

On Monday morning, June 1ˢᵗ 1964, Ralph and Connie had announced their engagement to the staff at work. The news was generally well received, although there were those, such as Paula, who weren't convinced that the relationship would end up being either lasting or stable. Yet for the present, they were prepared to keep such feelings to themselves.

Particularly pleased at hearing the news was Joe Greening. He'd been impressed by the change of attitude Ralph had displayed since Connie had joined the firm. She had been a steadying influence on him and his desire to win her affection had made him more mature and willing to accept responsibilities. Marrying Connie would, Joe believed, complete the process. At that point, he would feel more confident of eventually handing the family business over to his nephew. Most importantly, Ralph would have Connie at his side, a woman admired for her professional capabilities in a business dominated by men. She had won over so many new clients by her practical, no-nonsense approach and her kind, warm personality. At a time when most intelligent young women could hope at best, to be the adored personal secretary of the boss, Connie had achieved far more. Through her ability, she was close to earning a place at the 'top table.' She had so firmly established her value to Greenings, that it was unthinkable that she could be replaced.

Joe's only concern, in the days following the announcement, was that the couple should quickly set a date for the wedding. He had no wish for his nephew to fall back into old habits, but was aware that matters were perhaps being delayed due to difficulties with Ralph's mother. As a result, Joe sent Paula to find Ralph, with the instruction that he should come to his office.

"What's it about Paula?" asked Ralph, when she had found him.

"I don't know. Your uncle didn't tell me."

Ralph never liked unplanned meetings with his uncle. It only seemed to happen when the 'old man' was unhappy about some aspect of his performance. Worse still, it reminded him of his vulnerability. Whilst everyone in the firm assumed that he was the heir apparent and his mother had impressed the idea upon him too, Ralph was never quite so certain. He always felt a sense of humiliation when he had to explain himself to his uncle; had to say the right things to avoid giving any offence to him. It hurt Ralph's ego. It was the only situation in his life where he had to defer to another's will and he didn't like it. Meetings often left him with the sense that he was dispensable. Joe was well past retirement age, yet he clung on to the reins of power. Ralph wondered for how much longer he would have to play the role of the dutiful and obedient nephew and having done so, what if Joe reneged on his promise that the company would be his?

Nevertheless, when Ralph arrived in his uncle's office, he showed no signs of dissatisfaction. Smiling, he confidently strode towards the chair in front of Joe's desk and sat down, waiting to be informed of the reason for him being there. As was his wont, Joe was straight to the point.

"I wanted to ask you some more details about your engagement Ralph, if you don't mind that is?"

"No, of course not," replied Ralph, well aware that he could hardly have given any other response. "What would you like to know?"

"Well, you won't be surprised that your mother's been on to me about you not wanting an engagement party. She'd really like you to have one."

"I know," replied Ralph, "but neither Connie or I want one. We don't think it's necessary."

"You, or Connie?" enquired Joe, looking carefully at his nephew.

"Both of us, but actually, mainly Connie. She thinks our commitment to one another is all that's important and she feels that the expense is unnecessary. I'd rather you didn't tell mother though."

Joe nodded.

"Yes, Ralph. We wouldn't want her blaming Connie for depriving her of an extravagant engagement party. It does sound very much like Connie though."

Joe paused.

"And what does your mother feel about Connie?" he asked, eventually.

"Well, they've met a couple of times and they seem to get on well. But it doesn't matter. I've chosen Connie and she's accepted me and that's all I'm concerned about."

Joe nodded his head in agreement. He was pleased with Ralph's response.

"Quite right. I've told your mother what a real diamond Connie is and that she's the perfect wife for you and that leads me on to the wedding."

"Yes?" asked Ralph.

"The date of the wedding," said Joe, "When's it going to be? It all seems a little vague."

"Well, Connie and I have compromised on the wedding. We were wanting to do it quickly at the Register Office, but we know that's going to upset the family. So, I'm afraid we're waiting on finding a suitable venue and when we do, there's going to be a delay in finding an available date."

"I see," said Joe. "It would be best to get married as soon as possible, but then again, if you do that, it's bound to make things difficult with your mother. And it will be Connie who'll be blamed, along with me of course, because your mother will say I could have stopped the pair of you!"

Ralph nodded in agreement.

"This delay worries me, Ralph. I don't want any distractions coming along and ruining things. You're so lucky to have Connie. You'll never get anyone else like her. Appreciate what you've got and don't allow temptations to lead you astray."

"What do you mean?" asked Ralph, barely able to hide his irritation.

"You know full well Ralph. You mustn't be cavalier with Connie's affections, like you've been with others in the past."

As he spoke, Joe leaned forward in his chair, looking for any signs of concern on his nephew's face, but Ralph held his gaze, projecting a real sense of sincerity to his uncle.

"That's history now. I was younger back then. Connie's made me realise the error of my ways. She's the woman I want to marry and spend the rest of my life with. I won't do anything to risk that."

Ralph spoke with emotion and conviction, Yet Joe was still determined that his nephew would know how important it was that he didn't let Connie down.

"I do hope that you're being honest with me Ralph. If you fail Connie, it will be the worst thing that you've ever done. I'm not sure that you recognise just how lucky you are that she's agreed to marry you."

"Of course, I do," said Ralph, firmly.

"She cares about you Ralph," continued Joe. "She's not bothered about you being the boss's nephew, unlike most of the women you've had. She's honest and money could never buy her affections."

"Oh, I know that," replied Ralph.

"If you don't stay faithful to Connie, I know that we'll lose her and I don't want to see that happen. I've already lost Tom and that's left a big hole in the company. One that I'm finding hard to fill."

"Hang on," interrupted Ralph. "Tom's departure wasn't anything to do with me!"

Ralph's displeasure at his uncle's warnings had pushed him into an assertiveness that he had rarely demonstrated against him. Joe hadn't intended their discussion to become so heated, but he simply couldn't dismiss his knowledge of Ralph's previous behaviour. He was insistent on following the conversation through to its logical conclusion.

"Are you sure?" he asked.

"Yes," insisted Ralph.

"I'm not, Ralph. It was clear that Tom idolised Connie. Perhaps your engagement is what pushed him to leave."

"But, how can that be my fault?" said Ralph. "I can't hold back my feelings because I might upset Tom."

"Of course, you can't. I agree. But if you mess Connie about, then Tom needn't have left and it would be your responsibility that I've lost a valued member of the firm."

"Well," said Ralph forcefully, "you haven't anything to worry about on that score. I've told you, my behaviour towards Connie will always be honourable. I've never been more determined about anything in my life. Connie and I will be married."

Ralph was defiant and Joe was left with no choice but to accept the protestations of his good intentions. As he left the office, Ralph felt angry. He thought of Tom and how he'd been able to leave Greenings so quickly. Yet Tom had no stake in the company, he had nothing to lose. Ralph felt trapped. The promise of his inheritance was too much to give up. However much his pride had been damaged by his uncle's exhortation to 'do the right thing,' he would remain compliant. Furthermore, however much Ralph tried to change, few would accept that he had. It seemed as if others wouldn't allow him his sense of redemption. Because of this, a seed of doubt was planted in Ralph's mind. An idea that his critics would be right after all and his new life with Connie was fated never to happen.

Chapter 53

Happy as he was to enter into his engagement with Connie, Ralph increasingly found himself under the intense pressure of his mounting desire for her. It was this that threatened to put the couple's relationship in jeopardy.

Ralph's desperation to make love to Connie had led him to be increasingly amorous, but she had stopped him at every turn. It had disappointed him and to some extent had been surprising, as he could tell by her response when they kissed and embraced, that she was a woman capable of deep passion and emotion. He had felt her body stiffen as he had held her; listened to her quiet sighs and experienced the sensation of her slowly rising bosom. The sweet surrender of her lips and her delicate fingers softly wrapping themselves around his, as they pressed ever tighter together. Then, when they parted, she would fix him with her beautiful green eyes, inviting him to stare into the very depths of her sweet, sensitive soul. She captivated him. The beautiful enchantress who had him completely under her spell, pushing him towards a fever pitch of expectation, which risked driving him into impetuosity.

Yet all Ralph's pleas went unheeded. Connie was adamant and refused to acknowledge his claim that his public commitment to her, through their engagement, released them from the traditional expectation of no intimacy before marriage. If they were to make love, she told him, it must have true meaning. That would only be when they were joined in matrimony and had made their lifelong commitment to one another.

Ralph regarded Connie's attitude as another example of the contradictions that were inherent in her character. She was, in his mind, a product of the newly emerging 'Swinging Sixties.' She embodied the spirit of women's liberation and she vigorously fought against the old order. Yet at heart, Connie was, as she had always told him, an old-fashioned girl. One who believed in the virtues of traditional morality. A just and honest society, she'd told him, couldn't be built on any other foundation.

"You see Ralph, I've thought a lot about this. Freedom and liberty are too easily confused. They are very different things. The Timothy Leary's of this world would have you believe that taking away all societal and moral restraints, will bring freedom to individuals. But he's wrong. That type of freedom leads to exploitation, especially for women. Now liberation is different. It will bring women's equality and practical improvements. Women can be protected from their husbands and treated equally at work. More women can become managers and politicians, even prime ministers. And it has to be a world where women are accepted on their own terms. No, liberation can't be achieved without responsibility. Many 'so-called' new ideas, enslave women. We don't need 'free love', but stable relationships underpinned by love and commitment. Too many men mistake sex for love and women too. Sex can't rise beyond being anything other than just a physical act, if two people aren't committed to one another in every way. Only that commitment can bring the unity of purpose between two people that, when they make love, brings a higher, spiritual meaning to their lives."

When she had finished speaking, Ralph had simply stared at her. He didn't know what to say. He wanted to admit that he didn't have a clue who Timothy Leary was. Yet in the context of what she had said, such honesty was irrelevant. It was quite clear what she meant and a firm and final statement to him that the consummation of their relationship would have to wait. Facing that reality, Ralph was disappointed. He had continued to believe that eventually, Connie's attitude would soften; that the powerful emotions generated by their mutual desire, would overcome Connie's scruples. Ralph could no longer be in any doubt that it wasn't going to happen.

Connie had held out the promise of a point in the future, when they were married, where their intimacy would have a deeper meaning. Ralph would experience a level of enjoyment and sense of fulfilment that he had never reached with anyone else before. Yet Ralph would have to wait and he was finding it increasingly difficult to control the hormones that were coursing through his body. Ralph loved and appreciated Connie. She was beautiful and exciting, but for the moment, unattainable. And the delay in being able to make love to her, made it more difficult for him to ignore the alluring forms of other women who crossed his path. Ralph was a man with powerful desires and prior to meeting Connie, he had been used to having them satisfied. Only time would tell if he would be able to remain loyal to his fiancé and stand by his commitment to her.

Chapter 54

The challenge to Ralph's fidelity wasn't long in coming. It arrived in the shape of someone he saw almost every day.

Veronica was a young woman who had become infatuated with her boss. Her initial conversation with Ralph had made a huge impression on her. He was good-looking, welcoming and charming. Since then, he had always been attentive to her, showing a genuine interest in how she was getting on. Consequently, she had become convinced that a much closer relationship with him was possible, more intimate than that between a member of staff and her employer. When she returned to the typing pool and sang Ralph's praises, Veronica found that the older women were somewhat dismissive of her views. It was generally felt that Ralph was just 'a charmer' and it was suggested to Veronica that she should be mindful of him 'trying it on' with her. It seemed to Veronica that no one had a good word to say about Ralph and she simply couldn't understand why. Out on a dinner break with Alice, the office manager who'd taken the young woman under her wing, Veronica took the opportunity to find out more about her boss.

"Why do the other women say such horrible things about Ralph?"

It was a question that came as no surprise to Alice, aware as she was of Veronica's growing admiration for Ralph.

In the process of stirring her tea, Alice stopped and looked up. She didn't immediately respond, but observed her young colleague closely. A married woman in her late thirties and with two teenage children, Alice had worked in offices since leaving school at fifteen. She'd experienced at first hand the amorous advances of a number of bosses. Many seemed to consider their secretaries and typists as part of the chattels of the company and so liable for their own personal use. It had often proven difficult for her to ward off their attentions, especially as she needed to keep her job. Moving to another required a reference and if you'd failed to please your employer, they could spitefully portray you as a difficult or incompetent worker.

Over the years, Alice had known many young women like Veronica. They were naïve. Keen to believe in the fairy tale romances that saw the pretty young secretary win the heart of the powerful and handsome boss. It helped if they had their own steady boyfriend or fiancé; it could stop them falling for the predatory instincts of these 'glamorous' men. Yet for someone as young and vulnerable as Veronica, her inexperience of life meant that she had few defences to protect her from emotional exploitation. Alice knew of Ralph's reputation and had seen how he had compromised other young women who had worked at the company. Veronica's fascination with him concerned her. Alice had to do the best she could to warn Veronica away from Ralph, but if she was too headstrong to follow her advice, Alice feared the worst.

Taking a deep breath, Alice began to talk slowly and calmly.

"You're right Veronica. Ralph's charming. He's really handsome and when he talks to you, you can feel like you're the sole focus of his attention. Yet, he's the same with any woman he takes a fancy to. It's the way he is. You mustn't think that his attention is any more than that. You're a pretty girl Veronica. Ralph was bound to be nice to you."

"But he spoke to me for ages. Insisted that I called him Ralph and not Mr Greening."

"No doubt he complimented you too. Made light of your age. Treated you like a mature woman."

"Yes, he did."

"And you think that he believes that you're special. Don't you?"

Veronica blushed. Alice had hit the mark, but her young colleague didn't respond in the way that she expected.

"Well, yes I do, because he meant what he said. I know that there's something between us."

"Oh, Veronica!" exclaimed Alice, shaking her head. "Can't you see it's a game to him? He's involved with Connie. If he really cares for someone, it's her. He's not serious about anyone else and if he were to show an interest in you, when he's engaged to her, what kind of a man does that make him?"

There was a pause and Veronica pursed her lips. She was thinking intently about what Alice had told her. Finally, she responded.

"No, Alice. Ralph's sincere and kind. I can't believe that he's the type of man who would lie and use people. Perhaps he did like Connie, but that was before he got to know me and if Connie isn't right for him, he should be able to change his mind."

Alice was shocked by Veronica's words. She was displaying an unpleasant side to her nature. One that indicated that she wasn't quite as innocent as her elder colleague had assumed. Unsympathetic to Connie, Veronica had shown a selfish and egotistical side to her character. Ironically, such qualities made her far more vulnerable, should Ralph return to his predatory ways.

Veronica was young and impressionable, but she was also ambitious and just how far she was prepared to go, became apparent over the next few days. Always well turned out, Alice noticed how Veronica's heels became a little higher, her skirt a little shorter and her blouse a little tighter. Veronica had long legs and a fine figure and she was making sure that Ralph would be impressed.

Yet Alice and Ralph weren't the only ones to notice the changes in Veronica's attire. The other women in the office could see that Veronica was intent on gaining Ralph's attention and now that Connie and Ralph had announced their engagement, there was a real concern that it would only be a matter of time before their boss would betray his intended.

The opportunity came with Connie's absence from the office to carry out a site visit in Rochdale. She'd gone with one of the trainee accountants; the job not important enough to need Ralph's presence too. Ralph was alone in his office when he picked up the phone and requested that Veronica be sent to him with some documents. It was Alice who had taken the call.

"Oh, hi Alice," said Ralph "I need the file on 'Walkers.' Could you send Veronica with it please?"

"Yes, of course Mr Greening."

"And I might need Veronica to help me to table some figures. You don't need her at the moment, do you?"

"No. I'm sure that we'll be able to get on just fine without her."

"Good. That's good," said Ralph. "Well, I'll expect her with the file right away then."

Alice replaced the receiver and sighed. She suspected the worst. Ralph had asked for the most inexperienced member of her team, to help him put together a report for one of their main clients. The only reason it made any sense to her, was because she knew that Connie was out of the office. Alice looked across at Veronica who was busily typing a letter. She was a good worker and much as she had shown little regard for Connie, Alice couldn't help but feel protective towards her. She began to think that perhaps she should have told Ralph that Veronica was needed for other tasks and offered to help him herself. Then she doubted if it would have made a difference to him. And, if not today, how long would it be before he engineered another opportunity to be alone with Veronica? So, with a sense of foreboding, but also a recognition that there was almost an inevitability about what would happen, Alice called over to her young colleague.

"Veronica."

Veronica stopped typing and looked up.

"Yes," she replied.

"Stop what you're doing. You can finish it later. Mr Greening, Ralph, wants you to take a folder to his office and he may need you to stay and help him work on it."

"Me?" asked Veronica, surprised.

"Yes. You. He's just asked for you."

Alice saw a broad smile break out on Veronica's face. Indifferent to the effect her actions may have on the other women in the office, Veronica reached into her handbag at the side of the desk, took out a small hand mirror and looked into it. Satisfied with her appearance, she quickly slipped the mirror back into her handbag and got out of her chair. Taking the 'Walkers' file off Alice, she walked quickly and purposely away.

Chapter 55

Ralph was convinced of his love for Connie. She was the only woman he had ever considered marrying. It was because he understood that only she had opened up his heart and soul. Connie had talked to him about the difference between love and sex; that the latter could have no meaning without the former. To Ralph, desperate to satisfy his libido, her words offered a lifeline. He began to believe that if he did transgress, lapse from his faithfulness to Connie, his actions would have no real significance. She would still be the only woman that he loved. Furthermore, if Connie never knew, it could have no impact on their engagement and most importantly, their life together after they were married. It was with these ideas in mind that Ralph's thoughts began to be preoccupied with Veronica.

For Ralph, Veronica's tender age accentuated her charms. Her long blonde hair and blue eyes, that seemed to light up every time she saw him, complemented her pretty face and splendid figure. He was sure that of all the young typists and secretaries that Greenings had employed, she was undoubtedly the prettiest. Her innocence attracted him. It fed his ego to think that he could be the first man to make love to her. He fantasised about it happening in his office, in the middle of the working day, his colleagues in the rooms all around them. How daring and exciting it would be; forbidden lust, secretly fulfilled. The thought made his pulse quicken and his body tingle in anticipation. As time passed, Ralph became a man possessed, any second thoughts about the possible consequences of his intended actions, relegated to the recesses of his mind. In fact, the thought that he'd be betraying Connie, excited him all the more. He imagined how delicious it would be to guiltily partake of the forbidden pleasures of Veronica's young and compliant body.

Having replaced the receiver after his call to Alice, Ralph took a deep breath. He needed to compose himself but when Veronica knocked on the door, his heart skipped a beat, he felt short of breath and could already feel himself becoming aroused. Filled with desire, Ralph wouldn't hesitate to act on impulse. He'd been desperate to make love to Connie, but she had refused his advances and now he couldn't wait any longer. He was determined that right here, right now, he would make love to Veronica.

Ralph knew, of course, that Veronica had to share his desire, but he was confident that she was ready to accept his advances. He had flattered and charmed her and she had responded. He had seen it in her eyes, the way they softened and gazed longingly at him and lately, her choice of attire indicated that she was eager to gain his attention. Veronica was inexperienced as a lover and consequently, all too vulnerable to his compliments. Ralph was in no doubt that he could seduce her.

Sat behind his desk, Ralph responded to Veronica's knock with a loud and cheerful 'Come in!'

The door opened a little tentatively, Veronica making her way slowly into his office. It was obvious to Ralph that she was nervous and uncertain, a fact that excited him all the more.

"Don't be shy Veronica. Take a seat."

Ralph smiled, gesturing towards the chair at the side of his desk. Slowly, Veronica walked forward, tightly holding the requested file. He watched, fascinated as she gracefully sat down and then crossed her legs. The hem of Veronica's skirt lay well above her knees and Ralph couldn't help but be drawn towards it.

"Oh, your file Mr Greening. Silly me. I almost forgot!"

Veronica smiled. She slowly uncrossed her legs, stood up and leaned over the desk. Intentionally or not, as she stretched forward, Veronica's open blouse revealed a brief glimpse of the top of her breasts. The vision was as unexpected as it was welcome and for a moment, thrilled by what he had seen, Ralph was lost for words, before finally muttering his thanks to her.

Veronica, noticing his reaction, was gaining in confidence. She sat back down and slowly crossed her legs again. Ralph was certain that she had pulled up the hem of her skirt a little higher than she had done before. For a moment, he wondered whether it was in fact Veronica who was taking control, yet the thought soon disappeared from his mind. Ralph couldn't envisage a scenario where this young woman, with her own personal ambitions, could be using him as a stepping stone to realising them. Gathering his wits about him, he finally continued the conversation.

"You must call me Ralph. I've told you before. We don't need to stand on ceremony. Not the two of us. Now do we?"

He smiled at her and she smiled back. Picking up the file, he walked around the desk and placed it close to the edge facing Veronica. Moving to the side of the office, he took hold of another chair and drew it close to hers.

"There, that's more comfortable. You need to get ready Veronica. We can make some notes as we go through the figures."

Veronica opened her pad and readied her pen. Whilst Ralph looked at the file, she inadvertently moved the top of the pen towards her lips.

Parting them slightly, she rested the pen between them before slowly removing it when she noticed that Ralph was watching her. Tossing back her head, her long, blonde hair danced across her shoulders and as she glanced at Ralph once more, she could see that his eyes were still fixed upon her. Instinctively, Veronica sensed that he wanted her. She had captivated him and here, alone in his office, with nothing to distract them, she was convinced that she had a chance to win his heart.

When Veronica had fantasised about being in Ralph's arms, she wasn't certain about how it would happen. She did know however, that he was a man of the world, whilst she embodied the inexperience of youth. It wasn't enough for her to be daring and flirtatious. Ralph would have to see her as a real woman, despite her tender years, if she were to successfully compete with Connie for his affections. And it was then that Veronica realised what a dangerous game she was playing, but it was one that she had to win, if she wanted to stake her claim to Ralph. Veronica therefore decided that if the opportunity came, she would throw caution to the wind. Events would have to take their course. Veronica assumed that if Ralph wanted, and she allowed him, to take possession of her body in every intimate detail, that it would signifying his commitment to her. It was a fatal misjudgement and one that she would come to regret.

Waiting to record Ralph's thoughts, Veronica noticed that his mind seemed elsewhere. His eyes had barely scanned the pages of the file. He seemed hesitant, yet Veronica sensed that something was about to happen. Suddenly, Ralph took her hand. Holding it gently, he raised it to his lips and kissed each of her fingers, softly in turn. He then slowly caressed her palm and putting his arm gently around her shoulders, he eased her slowly towards him. Feeling no signs of resistance, he kissed her gently on the lips. Initially, he felt no response, but it was unsurprising to him. Her inexperience meant that she was in need of guidance. He knew that for Veronica this really would be the first time. Kissing her softly once more, he stroked her hand and felt her fingers begin to tighten around his. Pulling his lips slowly away from hers, he kissed her on the cheek.

"Veronica," he whispered. "I'm sorry, but you're so beautiful. I just had to kiss you. I couldn't help it."

Ralph kissed her again on the lips and this time he felt her respond. He knew there had been a chance that she could have resisted him, but that time was gone. Now, aroused and excited, Ralph encouraged Veronica to her feet. Stepping away from the chairs, the two embraced. Sharing a lingering kiss, Ralph sensed the depth of passion that he'd released in Veronica. Placing his arms around the small of her back, he pulled her towards him, eager to let her know of his desire for her. He moved his hands over the back of her skirt, caressing her hips and thighs as he thrust himself against her. He knew that it could happen now, but making love to Veronica had excited him even more than he'd imagined. He was desperate to take his time, for the pair of them to make love without any kind of restraint.

Slowly, Ralph disengaged himself from Veronica.

"Not here," he whispered softly. "I know a place. Somewhere special, where we can really be alone."

He kissed her gently on the forehead and then looked directly into her eyes. The two of them were still breathing deeply, aroused by their passionate encounter.

Come on," said Ralph, at last. "We'd best sit down."

Smiling at Veronica, Ralph took her hand and led her back to her chair. He noticed her radiant face, flushed with the excitement of their long and amorous embrace. He then watched as she smoothed her skirt and blouse and as she sat down, he looked at the top of her beautiful breasts and imagined the pair of them lying naked together and being able to explore every inch of one another's bodies.

"I suppose we'd better get back to these accounts," said Ralph, picking up the file.

"Yes Ralph," replied Veronica. "I'll need something to take back to type up for you, won't I?"

Having completed the task, Veronica left the office. She was now on a mission and the game was still in its infancy. She must have her night of passion with Ralph and make him realise that she was everything he would ever need. Aware that office gossip could undermine her plans and perhaps lead Ralph to reconsider his feelings towards her, Veronica took care to return to her desk unflustered, carefully carrying both the file and her notebook.

With Veronica's departure, Ralph could hardly contain his excitement. Since going out with Connie he'd experienced a period of enforced celibacy and now through Veronica, that was about to change. Yet Ralph was determined that his relationship with Connie would remain unaffected and he had already formulated a plan to secure that objective. He intended to persuade Veronica to become his mistress. She was young and willing to please him and he had the money to buy her the gifts that he assumed would keep her silent. He was also certain that given her beauty, she would prove attractive to his friends and associates, one of whom would eventually take her off his hands.

It was Connie that Ralph believed he loved. She was the one that he would marry. Connie's support would be crucial in helping him run Greenings and without her, he doubted that his uncle would be willing to stand aside. And although Connie was denying him the pleasures he desired until they were married, it didn't lessen his feelings for her. Veronica's conquest would be easy and as such, he valued her far less. Connie had an indefinable quality that had beguiled him from the first moment he'd seen her. For Ralph, Veronica would never be more than a distraction and one that he believed he could manage as he pleased.

Ralph would find out however, that he had met his match. Veronica's expectations went far beyond what he was prepared to accept. He'd underestimated her strength of purpose, unaware that she had set her sights on becoming nothing less than his wife. Although he didn't yet know it, from the moment Ralph placed his hand upon Veronica's, his relationship with Connie was effectively over.

Chapter 56

The following day, Alison and Paula took their dinner break together. Sat in Lyons Café with a cup of tea and sandwiches, there was only one topic of conversation.

"He had Veronica alone in his office yesterday afternoon. Came up with some excuse about having to work on the figures from the 'Walkers' file. Just why did he need her there? It's just not right," said Alice.

"Huh. I'm sure that all Ralph was interested in was Veronica," replied Paula, dismissively.

"Yes, there's no doubt about it. Just lately she's been giving him every encouragement. I'm sure she believes that she's got a chance with him."

"Well, more fool her. The only person who matters to Ralph, is himself. We all know that," said Paula.

"She asked me why we're all so negative about him," remarked Alice. "I warned her that she should keep away from him, but she seems intent on not listening."

"I know Alice, but all of us could get our heads turned at her age. I know I didn't always listen to good advice. When you're young, you think that you know best."

"No Paula," said Alice, shaking her head. "Veronica's different. I saw it in her face. We were sat right here, just like we are now. There's a lot more to her than meets the eye. She's ambitious. When we first started, we dreamt that we could marry the boss, have a life of luxury, everything we wanted. Then we realised that the boss was already married, or that they only wanted their wicked way with us, or perhaps they were nothing to look at and unpleasant anyway. We knew then that it was far better to live in the real world; just do the job and go home. Veronica though, will do anything to get her claws into Ralph. She honestly believes that she can manipulate him; that she'll end up living out in Cheshire, the wife of a successful businessman. She's really determined."

"Well, she's going to be disappointed," said Paula.

"The thing is," continued Alice. "I wouldn't care. Veronica deserves everything that's coming to her, but it's Connie that I'm worried about."

Paula nodded, but was quiet.

"I don't know if I can be the bearer of bad tidings," said Alice, "but I hate to see Ralph carrying on behind her back and getting away with it."

"Yes," replied Paula. "I see your point."

"You're her closest friend in the office Paula. Isn't there some way we could warn Connie and tell her to keep an eye on him?"

Alice looked at Paula, awaiting a response. Paula could see that she was concerned. Like everyone at work, Alice felt real affection towards Connie and was unhappy at the thought that Ralph and Veronica were betraying her trust.

"I don't think there's anything I can say," replied Paula, choosing her words carefully. "Before Connie started going out with Ralph, I did warn her about him. I told her about some of the tricks he'd pulled and the women he'd used. She wouldn't listen to me. She believed that he's changed and wanted to give him a chance. And you know her yourself Alice, she likes to see the best in everyone. Whatever I say to her, I know how she's going to react. She won't see anything wrong in Veronica working with Ralph. Connie's not the jealous type. She'll just ignore me. Worse still, she may fall out with me and I'll lose a friend. No, we'll just have to wait and see what happens. We need to be there to support her if something goes wrong."

"Surely, we can do something?" asked Alice.

"No. We can't. She won't listen to us and perhaps, we just might be wrong."

"Oh yes, I'm sure you believe that Paula!"

"Well," Paula paused. "You know I don't. But it doesn't stop me hoping for the best."

"A man like Ralph. How can he fool someone as clever as Connie? It's ludicrous," remarked Alice, shaking her head in amazement.

"Because we women are stupid," replied Paula. "We've got feelings. We need to love someone and don't the Ralphs of this world know it. He's such a charmer. He's at it all the time. He knows that women find him attractive and once he picks someone out, he makes them feel so special, that they'll never question how genuine he is. It was like that with Sandra and even with Connie. Veronica will find out that he'll do exactly the same to her too."

"And after everything comes crashing down, you can bet that Ralph's going to be fine," continued Alice. "He'll still be running the company with his uncle, making the big money. Untouchable."

"Well, hasn't that always been the way?" asked Paula. "The rich and the privileged. They always do whatever they want and get away with it. I just wish for once that somehow, somewhere, one of them didn't."

Alice nodded in agreement.

"Come on," continued Paula. "It's time we were getting back, or they'll be after us next!"

Rising from the table, the two women returned to work.

Chapter 57

A fortnight had passed. Connie was busy at work. She was alone in her office. Ralph was with clients in Salford but he was at the forefront of Connie's mind. Last night they had been discussing the arrangements for their wedding. Connie had been surprised. Ralph had suggested that they set it for the following summer. That was twelve months from now and at odds with Ralph's previous desire to get married as soon as possible. Furthermore, he now seemed to be far more sympathetic towards his mother's wish to have a grand reception, when he'd previously agreed with Connie's desire to refrain from excessive expenditure. Connie had challenged his change of attitude.

"I can wait until next year Ralph, but since we got engaged, you've been in such a hurry to get married. Why the sudden change?"

She looked at him closely, curious to hear his answer.

"Well, we've got a whole life ahead of us Connie and I want everything to be right. I realised that if we rush things, we might regret not having good memories of the day to look back on. I want you to get on well with all the family too. I don't want them to think you're being distant and unfriendly. I want them all to see how wonderful you are and accept you as my wife and part of the family."

"But that didn't seem to bother you too much before Ralph. So why now? Are you sure that you're telling me everything?"

Connie suspected that Ralph was holding back, especially as he seemed a little uneasy at her insistent line of questioning.

"Yes Connie. There's no other reason."

Ralph was attempting to reassure her, but Connie wasn't convinced. She felt certain that something else was bothering him. For the past few days, she hadn't needed to fight off his amorous advances. It had relieved her of the pressure of his expectations, but when he was eager and aroused, she found it a reassuring expression of his desire for her.

"You've hardly kissed me tonight, Ralph. Are you getting fed up of me? We don't have to get married if you're having second thoughts. I've no problem with us breaking off the engagement, if that's what you want."

"Oh no! No Connie! Of course, I want to get married. I'm trying hard to respect your feelings You know how I get when we kiss. I can't control myself and it's not fair for me to put you under pressure. I only want to please you, Connie."

Ralph was shocked by her words. His liaisons with Veronica may have provided satisfaction, but they had also affected his behaviour towards Connie. He had been careless. Connie would always challenge situations that confused her. Ironically, although Ralph credited Connie with making him more caring and reliable, he knew that if he was going to keep her, he would have to fall back on his old traits of cunning and deceit. Once he'd started down the path of deception, Ralph found it all too easy to continue. Very soon he would create a whole tissue of lies, in an attempt to hide the truth of his relationship with Veronica.

With sheer duplicity, Ralph responded to Connie's concerns by suggesting that she was the one who seemed to be having second thoughts about the wedding.

"The way you're so against us having a proper wedding ceremony Connie, might suggest to some that you're the one who's uncertain about getting married, or at least that you don't want anyone to know that you are."

"That's nonsense Ralph and you know it."

"But it's not me that you need to convince Connie. Our friends and family will think that it's very strange if we don't have the celebrations that they expect. You said yourself, that all parents make sacrifices for their daughter's wedding."

Ralph was proving to be sharp, clever and manipulative. He was playing on Connie's emotions, eager to avoid her concern about his lack of physical affection towards her. By so doing, he hoped to remove any suspicions that he might be finding satisfaction elsewhere.

"You already know my feelings, Ralph. There are far better things to spend money on and it's no guarantee of a happy marriage."

"Yes, I know Connie, but I thought that once we actually got down to setting the day, you might have a change of heart."

"But why would I? Why would that alter anything?"

"Because then getting married becomes a reality. And then perhaps you'd realise what a special day it is. For you, me and everyone else."

"Ralph. You know that the expense of a huge wedding is wrong on so many levels. There's…"

"Oh, here we go again," interrupted Ralph, unwilling to let her finish. "You're bleeding heart concerned that you're actually spending money that could be used to help the poor and downtrodden."

"Well, yes. That's some of it, but not all."

"Why is it so wrong for you to be appreciated for a change?" asked Ralph. "I don't interfere with your Labour work, it's not my business, but I think it goes too far when you let your politics take away any enjoyment of your own life. Like I've said, your wonderful Harold doesn't deny himself, does he?"

"Well, perhaps he should. He's cosied up to the bosses a little too much."

"Well maybe you have too Connie. You're a member of management now, aren't you? And what about me? I'm one of the bosses. Are you going to try to deny what I do, once we're married?"

"Don't be silly Ralph. It's you that I love. Your position means nothing to me; never has and never will."

Ralph smiled and moved to embrace her. Connie responded warmly and the two were soon sharing a long and passionate kiss. Separating at last, Ralph took Connie's hand and looked into her eyes.

"I'm sorry Connie. Please forgive me. Organising this wedding is just too much about keeping other people happy. I've let it get on top of me. We're not waiting for these fancy venues to become available. We'll find somewhere smaller and there's an end to it. We can be married in the autumn. All I'm bothered about is you."

"I know Ralph. Don't worry. I could tell that something wasn't right. I'm just pleased that you've told me, because our marriage can never amount to very much if we're not open with one another." Connie paused, as if to emphasise the point, before continuing. "I think we've just had our first little tiff!"

"And you've ended up the winner," replied Ralph, with a smile.

"Well, yes. It's a woman's prerogative to always be right," added Connie, before the two of them burst out laughing.

Ralph felt relieved. He'd safely navigated his way through a difficult situation. He knew that from now on he would have to make sure that his ardour for Connie appeared undiminished. The fear that he would lose Connie had produced a sobering effect on Ralph. He now regretted his seduction of Veronica. He would disentangle himself from her. The wedding would be brought forward and he and Connie could move on with their lives.

Sat in her office, Connie also felt relieved. She and Ralph had ironed out their difficulties and their relationship seemed as strong as ever. Feeling positive, Connie set about her work with her usual purpose. As dinner time approached and she prepared to go for a break, Connie was interrupted by a knock on her open door. Looking up, she could see that it was Veronica. Initially, Connie assumed that it must be a routine matter of company business, but as she waited for Veronica to speak, Connie could see that the young typist looked rather nervous. Thinking nothing of it, Connie gave her a broad smile.

"Hi Veronica."

There was no response. It was obvious that Veronica was feeling uncomfortable, almost apprehensive. It seemed very mysterious, even more so as Veronica started to sniffle. She was clearly upset and on the verge of tears.

Getting out of her chair, Connie moved quickly towards her.

"Why, whatever's the matter? Come on, sit down," she said, soothingly.

Connie shut the office door to afford the pair of them some privacy and then put her arm around Veronica and moved her over to a chair at the side of the office. Taking the seat next to her, Connie sat down and waited for her tears to subside. Only then would she be able to get to the bottom of the reasons for Veronica's state of distress.

Chapter 58

Eventually, Veronica settled and her tears stopped. She took a series of deep breaths, composing herself the best that she could. Connie could see that she was now ready to talk. She patted Veronica's hand gently, encouraging her to release the burden that was such a weight upon her shoulders. She did wonder however, why Veronica had chosen to approach her. After all, there were other women, such as Alice, who she knew far better. But perhaps it was an issue that could only be sorted out by management. As Veronica began to talk, it soon became clear that she had chosen Connie for a specific reason. Not one due to any matter related to work, but because the source of her upset was Ralph.

"Believe me Connie. I never meant it to happen, I'm so sorry."

Veronica's voice started to break and falter. She bent her head forward and wiped away the tears that once again, were welling up in her eyes. Gently, Connie encouraged Veronica to continue, patting her softly on her knee.

"Go on Veronica," she said, quietly. "Tell me what's happened."

Slowly, Veronica lifted her head and looked despairingly at Connie. Around her eyes, the skin was streaked with black mascara, washed out by her tears. She was silent. Unable to speak.

"Come on Veronica. You've been brave enough to come in here. You need to tell me what's bothering you. We can't have you upset like this, can we?"

At Connie's words, Veronica began to sob once more. It seemed as if she had been broken into little pieces. Yet her refusal to talk, had alerted Connie to the possibility that what she was about to reveal, would have an impact on her too.

Slowly and quietly, Veronica finally began to speak.

"I've come to ask you to let him go Connie."

Veronica paused. Connie didn't respond. She wasn't sure what Veronica was talking about. It made little sense.

"Please, Connie. Please, let him go," continued Veronica.

"Who? Let who go Veronica?"

There was another pause. It was as if Veronica couldn't utter the name, or simply assumed that Connie would know who she was referring to. Finally, the name emerged.

"Ralph."

Connie was confused. Did she mean her own Ralph? Just what was Veronica saying?

"I'm sorry Veronica," said Connie, as gently as possible, "I'm still not sure what you mean."

Having managed to reveal Ralph's name, Veronica became more assured.

"Me and Ralph. We're in love. It just happened and I'm sorry Connie, but I want you to let him go."

Connie was shocked. It was the last thing that she'd expected to hear. But she was determined to remain calm. She had to be in possession of all the facts. Veronica was young and impressionable. She had seen for herself how much Veronica had enjoyed the attention that Ralph had given to her. But that was Ralph's nature and what he saw as being friendly, could be misconstrued by a young woman as something more significant. It could well be that she had developed an infatuation with her handsome, unmarried boss and was misinterpreting the interactions between them. Connie wouldn't jump to any conclusions. She accepted that other women found Ralph attractive, but she wasn't jealous and despite his chequered past, she had no reason to believe that he'd been unfaithful to her. Nevertheless, Veronica had alleged that she and Ralph were in love and so she would listen to what she had to say. Veronica must surely be putting forward evidence to support her claim and if it included nothing of substance, Connie would steadfastly support her fiancé.

Calmly, Connie addressed her young colleague.

"Why do you say that you and Ralph are in love? What's happened for that to be the case?"

"Because he's told me that he loves me."

"When?"

"Many times. At work. When we've been together. When you weren't there, Connie."

"You're saying that he's done everything in secret?"

"Yes. He told me that you mustn't know. That he didn't want to upset you."

"But Veronica, if you say he's told you in secret, how can I know if you're telling the truth? Does anyone else know?"

"No, because he calls me into his office."

Veronica's answers were vague and still confusing. As yet, they contained no hard evidence to prove Ralph's guilt, although it was logical that if he wanted to cheat on Connie, he would cloud his actions in secrecy.

"I'm sorry Veronica," said Connie. "I only have your word. I need more than that."

"But we made love. He took me to the Grosvenor Hotel. Someone there will remember us. They're bound to. He bought me this necklace."

Veronica pointed to a thin, but exquisite gold necklace around her neck. It was adorned with a small, ornate pendant. Certainly, it looked expensive, but Veronica was a pretty girl and Connie was sure that she had plenty of admirers. Any of them, eager to win her favour, could have purchase the expensive gift.

Connie continued to look closely at Veronica, but her countenance didn't change and there were no signs that she was lying. Nevertheless, Connie was still unsure, unconvinced that Ralph had acted as Veronica had claimed. She had no wish to prejudge him. After all, he could just be the innocent victim of a young woman's romantic fantasies.

Connie's calm and considered approach towards Veronica's claims was beginning to trouble her competitor, who was now showing signs of desperation in her desire to convince Connie that she was telling the truth.

"I am being honest Connie. Truly I am," pleaded Veronica. "He loves me; he wants me. Ralph told me that the only reason we're not together is because he's engaged to you. He won't see you hurt and can't think of any way to finish with you without doing that. And that's why I'm here. I love him and you're all that stands in the way of us being together. Please, let him go. Let him be happy."

Once again, Veronica started to cry. As she looked at her, Connie realised that the situation was becoming too difficult. Veronica's revelations had shocked her to the core, but she had somehow managed to maintain her composure. Her instinct had been to show sympathy to Veronica yet, if what she'd said was true, her betrayal made her no better than Ralph. And if it was the case that she had lied about her fiancé, could Connie ever excuse Veronica for trying to end their engagement?

"Come on Veronica," said Connie, eventually. "Don't cry. I'll talk to Ralph. We'll get to the bottom of this. I promise."

Slowly, Veronica calmed down and dried her tears.

"You might want to wipe your eyes and get cleaned up," suggested Connie. "I won't talk to anyone else about this, unless you want me to."

Connie's calm words had, for the moment, poured oil on troubled waters. The crisis had been averted. The problem of determining the veracity of Veronica's allegations still remained. Connie was determined to find out what, if anything, had happened. Unless she did, Connie knew that her marriage to Ralph wouldn't be going ahead.

Chapter 59

Alone once more, Connie had to think carefully about how she would handle Veronica's allegations. It was important that she acted quickly for everyone's sake. If Veronica's claims were true, then she would probably need help and support. If they proved false, the fact needed to be established quickly. Any unnecessary lapse of time would mean a greater chance of others finding out and given Ralph's past history of casual relationships with other young women at the firm, people would be quick to condemn him. If Ralph was innocent, that would be unfair. Connie realised how difficult the situation was for her too. She had always had complete faith in Ralph. Now, her feelings couldn't be allowed to prejudice her attitude towards Veronica's allegations. Ultimately, if she discovered that Veronica had told the truth, Connie would be devastated.

Before approaching Ralph, Connie decided that she would carry out her own investigations. She would try and find out if there were any indications that Ralph may have been unfaithful, or at least had acted inappropriately towards Veronica. There was one person who Connie believed could help her. Someone who always seemed to have an insight into the relationships between most members of staff. It was Paula. She was centrally located at her desk in the company's reception, close to Joe Greening's office and a point of contact between management and staff. Effectively, Paula had a foot in both camps and importantly, she was liked because she was discreet. Consequently, she saw and heard things that would normally remain hidden from others. Connie also knew that Paula was friends with Alice, who may have given her some information about Veronica's character and behaviour. The only problem for Connie however, was that in the past she had been dismissive of Paula's warnings about Ralph and it meant that in approaching her now, Paula may view her actions as hypocritical and selfish.

Leaving her office, Connie went to see Paula at her desk.

"Hi, Paula," said Connie, appearing relaxed. "Have you got anything planned at dinner?"

"No," said Paula, smiling.

"Do you fancy going with me? I don't seem to have talked to you for ages."

"Yes, okay," replied Paula. "I'll be able to go at half twelve. I just need to finish off a couple of letters."

"Right. I'll see you then," said Connie.

To avoid the possibility of other staff from Greenings being in the Lyons Café and overhearing their conversation, Connie persuaded Paula that they should go to the Alasia Snack Bar on Newton Street for a change. Her friend agreed, accepting the suggestion without any suspicion that Connie had an ulterior motive for her request. Having arrived, they sat down and talked generalities, but it was clear to Paula that Connie wasn't fully focused on their conversation and that she had something else on her mind. Paula was wary of asking about Ralph, given that their last conversation about him had proved awkward. However, to Paula's surprise, Connie herself soon brought the subject of her fiancé into the discussion.

"Paula," said Connie, her voice suddenly sounding serious, "I need to ask you about something involving Ralph. But it has to remain confidential between us."

Paula felt uneasy. What was it that Connie was about to ask? More importantly, would her response compromise the relationship between them? Rather uncertainly, she responded.

"Well, perhaps I'm not the best person to ask Connie."

"No, you are. Don't worry Paula, I won't mind whatever your answer is."

"But I don't know what the question is. I might not be able to answer it and if I do, how do I know that it won't upset you. I don't want to fall out with you Connie."

"I know that, Paula. I realised it when we spoke about him before. You only wanted to make sure that I knew about Ralph's past. You wanted to protect me. I'm sorry that I was a bit short with you, but I do love Ralph and have always wanted to trust him and believe that he's changed."

Connie paused.

"But?" asked Paula, encouraging her friend to continue.

"Well, I'm not sure that any of what she says has any truth in it, but Veronica saw me this morning and claims that she and Ralph are in love and that she's been seeing him behind my back."

Again, Connie paused.

"And?"

"Before I tell Ralph, because I'll have to, I wanted to know if you'd picked up on anything?"

Paula hesitated. She felt uncomfortable. She was worried that she would upset Connie by telling her about her conversation with Alice.

"Well," she said, eventually. "I'm not in any position to know anything really Connie."

It was a noncommittal answer, given as convincingly as possible. But Connie noticed how her friend averted her eyes and how she quickly picked up her cup of tea to take a sip, in order to avoid adding anything to her answer. It seemed like a planned diversion; that Paula was being disingenuous.

"You know everything Paula. Everything that goes on at Greenings. What about Alice? Has she mentioned anything?"

Connie received no reply, yet her friend's silence only convinced her that she did have information to impart. Insistent, Connie pressed Paula for a response.

"Paula. It's important. Not just for Ralph and I, but for Greenings too. Even if it's not true, we both know it's going to cause a problem and the sooner I can get to grips with it, the less disruption it will cause to everyone. I need to know what there is to go on. Please Paula, just let me know about anything that may have happened between the two of them."

As she considered the situation, Paula began to think that if she didn't tell Connie what she knew, then she was probably letting her friend down. Paula couldn't give Connie any definite proof that Ralph had betrayed her, but she would at least be alerted to the likelihood of it. Never mind the firm, if Ralph had cheated on her, it would be far more devastating for Connie. Taking a deep breath, Paula began to speak.

"Okay Connie, but what I'm going to say doesn't prove anything. I've no wish to cause any trouble, but Veronica has definitely got her eye on Ralph. When he's in the main office, Ralph speaks to Veronica quite a lot, but he's always done that with the younger women."

"It might be that she's fantasising then?" asked Connie, encouraged by her comments.

Paula looked at her. She could clearly see that Connie wanted to think the best of Ralph, but she hadn't finished yet; hadn't related the full details of what Alice had told her.

"Well, there's a little more Connie."

"Oh?"

Her friend was clearly disappointed. It didn't make it any easier for Paula, but she knew that she had to continue. She was determined to be as factual and honest as she could. What Connie then made of the information, would be up to her.

"A couple of weeks ago, when you were out, Ralph was working in his office. He needed the 'Walkers' file and specifically asked for Veronica to bring it to him. The pair of them were together for most of the afternoon."

"And why did he say that he needed her?" asked Connie.

"To help him analyse the figures," replied Paula, repeating what Alice had told her.

Connie was quiet. Paula could see that she was puzzled by her answer.

"But she's just a typist, not an accounts clerk" said Connie, quietly to herself. "Why wouldn't he ask for an accounts clerk? It doesn't make sense."

Paula understood that Connie's words were an expression of her own, personal thoughts, rather than questions she expected her friend to answer. Connie was quietly reflecting on Ralph's request and she was having difficulty discerning any logical reason behind it.

"Connie," said Paula, beginning to feel uncomfortable with her friend's continued silence.

There was no response.

"Connie," repeated Paula, a little louder.

Still lost in thought, Connie again failed to react. Paula lay her hand on her friend's shoulder.

"Come on, Connie."

"Oh. Sorry," her friend replied.

"Time's getting on. We need to get back to work."

"Yes. Yes of course, Paula."

Connie was hesitant, her mind was still processing what she'd been told.

Paula rose from her chair.

"Come on then Connie. Let's go."

Following her lead, Connie got to her feet. She looked at Paula. Her friend was concerned. Worried that she'd been upset by what she'd heard and perhaps unhappy with her for being the bearer of bad news. Not wanting to give that impression, Connie had the presence of mind to reassure her of their continued friendship.

"Thanks Paula," said Connie, managing to smile. "I appreciate what you've told me. I know that it wasn't easy. But I needed to find out and you were the only one that I could trust to tell me. I'm going to talk to Ralph and tell him what I know. I'll see what he says."

Paula nodded.

"Perhaps there's a simple explanation," she said, trying to offer Connie the hopeful possibility that Ralph's actions had been entirely honourable.

"Hmm," replied Connie. "What do I think?"

Connie had posed the question, for at that precise moment in time, she had to admit that it certainly didn't look promising. She needed answers from Ralph and she would get them. He would be honest with her because if he wasn't, she would break off their engagement. The truth would have to come out, regardless of the possibility that it would prove humiliating for her.

Chapter 60

Connie had already arranged to go out with Ralph the following evening. When he arrived at Howard Avenue at seven to pick her up, Connie opened the front door almost as soon as he'd knocked on it. Expecting to get straight off for a pleasant night of relaxation, Ralph was to be disappointed.

"Come in Ralph."

"Why? Aren't you ready?"

"No. We need to talk."

Her voice was quiet and insistent. He noticed that she hadn't smiled at him. Ralph briefly entertained the thought that he should ask her for a kiss, but he sensed that any attempt to lighten the mood, would be unappreciated.

"Go through to the kitchen Ralph. We can sit at the table."

Ralph walked through the door, past the stairwell and into the kitchen. He sat at the table, Connie taking the seat opposite him.

"When we became engaged," said Connie, "you made a commitment to me and I to you. I want to believe in you Ralph and I want to keep loving you, but there's something we have to sort out first."

Connie paused. Ralph could see that she was deadly serious. He'd never known her like this. Her voice seemed devoid of feeling; her words cold and sterile. Whatever she was about to say, he knew it would be something of real consequence.

"What's the matter Connie?" asked Ralph.

He felt uncomfortable. He couldn't understand her strange demeanour. What could possibly have happened to threaten their relationship?

"Veronica came to see me yesterday, Ralph. She claimed that the two of you are in love and that you've already spent the night together."

Connie showed no signs of emotion. Her words were short, precise and factual.

At the mention of Veronica's name, Ralph understood why Connie was being so cold and distant. He was shocked that she knew about his liaison and the fact that the information came from Veronica herself, made it all the more surprising. Ralph had been arrogant; certain that he could control Veronica and ensure her silence. But he had failed to understand that Veronica saw their hastily arranged encounters, as the start of a real relationship. She was playing for greater stakes than simply being 'the other woman'. Over the past few weeks Ralph had become so obsessed about gratifying his sexual needs, that he didn't have the capacity to show any empathy towards the young woman that he'd taken advantage of.

As Connie paused, Ralph's mind was working overtime, thinking about how he could redeem the situation. He was desperate to hold on to Connie. He was fearful that if he admitted his guilt and pleaded for her to forgive his human frailties, that she would refuse him and he would lose her. He therefore decided that the only course of action open to him, was to lie.

Outwardly, Ralph appeared calm. His face betrayed no signs of emotion. If Connie believed that her revelation would shock him into some kind of immediate confession, or angry dismissal of Veronica's claim, she was wrong. Ralph had often been devious and manipulative in the past. He had tried to change, but his liaison with Veronica was now forcing him to return to his old ways. Connie was giving him the opportunity to explain himself and he knew how sharp and intelligent she was. Whatever he said had to be plausible. A mere rebuttal of Veronica's claims wouldn't be enough.

"Well?" asked Connie, having given Ralph time to respond. "Is she telling the truth?"

The posing of the question told Ralph that all was not lost. Connie was going to give him a chance. She wasn't simply going to believe what Veronica had said. She must still have some doubts and so Ralph was determined to exploit them. Appearing assured, he spoke confidently, his voice never faltering.

"I suppose I shouldn't be surprised by this," said Ralph, with a sigh. "What a silly girl."

He looked at Connie, but saw no reaction.

"I should really know better Connie, but I honestly thought that she was a nice girl. I thought that I could help her to settle in; give her a chance to show what she could do."

Ralph paused, keen to see the effect that his words were having on his intended. But still, Connie's face was expressionless.

Ralph shook his head, as if he were chastising himself before continuing. He sighed once again, giving the impression of a man who'd been badly wronged. A man who shouldn't be having to defend himself against something that had never happened.

"We worked together on the 'Walkers' account in my office. I cleared it with Alice beforehand. She was fine about it. Surely, she would have warned me if there was likely to be a problem with Veronica. Yes, Veronica spent time with me and helped by giving me quicker access to all the figures. She saved me the time of continually having to stop and go through them. I thought it would be good experience for her and now she's claiming this!"

Ralph paused. He looked at Connie, imploring her to accept his fidelity. Once more he shook his head in disbelief. Yet Connie was unmoved. What he had told her clearly wasn't enough.

"I can't pretend to know how these young women's minds work Connie," continued Ralph. "It seems that she's taken my friendliness for familiarity. I suppose that I should feel sorry for her, but I don't. To think that she's been prepared to try and cause trouble between us."

Ralph was hoping to see some sign of agreement from Connie, but there was nothing. He realised that his explanation was going to have to go further than he intended. His task was going to be more difficult than he could ever imagine. He was speaking to Connie and if anyone could resist his charms of persuasion, it was her. He knew that he couldn't simply ignore Veronica's claim of their night together at the 'Grosvenor.'

"To finish compiling our recommendations for 'Walkers,' I agreed to meet with Giles Parker at the Grosvenor Hotel. I thought that Veronica should come along too. It would give her some experience outside the office and she could make notes on anything that Giles was concerned about."

It was an audacious move by Ralph. Giles Parker was his friend. They played golf together and just like Ralph, Giles had an eye for the ladies. Ralph knew that he would verify his story. But so too did Connie and it wasn't enough for her. His explanation didn't seem plausible.

"But Ralph, why would you do that? It's not usual. Not with a client like 'Walkers.' Such meetings normally take place at the 'Midland.'"

"Not always Connie. They're an important account. One we can't afford to lose. Giles had some serious concerns, so we had to arrange to meet at short notice. It's better in the 'Grosvenor' in such situations. A nicer atmosphere, informal and so perfect to smooth any ruffled feathers."

Ralph smiled reassuringly.

"So, you're telling me that if I check at the office, there's going to be a record of the meeting and a list of the expenses?" asked Connie.

"There will be Connie, when I get around to it. I'm afraid that I've been a bit lax there. I paid it out of my own pocket, just like I did on the night that McVitie's didn't turn up to meet us at the 'Midland.' When you're the boss's nephew, you're not so keen to get it financed beforehand."

Ralph was confident that he'd covered every angle, but Connie still appeared to be unconvinced of his innocence.

"I'm sorry Connie, but I don't know what else I can say. I've fallen victim to my own stupidity. For whatever reason, Veronica has become obsessed with me. She's imagined I'm in love with her and has used the fact that we went to see Giles at the 'Grosvenor,' to fantasise about us taking a room together."

Ralph was feeling increasingly secure, certain that he was safe. Yet nothing he had said so far, had convinced Connie. His story was too neat and tidy and it made no sense. Yes, Veronica could be misguided, or even vindictive. Connie realised the attraction Ralph provided for so many women and perhaps her claims were made in order to force him into rejecting Connie and accepting her. Yet it somehow didn't feel right. Connie had hoped that she would have secured a satisfactory answer by now. She was frustrated and the continued uncertainty was undermining the trust that she had shown in Ralph. There was no alternative. She had to keep pushing her fiancé for answers.

"What you say is very plausible Ralph and I know that Giles will support you. Yet, I had Veronica in my office. If she's misguided and vindictive, then she's a very convincing actress. She was adamant that you spent the night together at the 'Grosvenor.' We're going to be married Ralph, I have to know the truth. Are you're telling me that no room was booked at the 'Grosvenor' and that nothing has happened between you and Veronica?"

"Yes," said Ralph.

Connie stared into his eyes. Ralph looked straight back. His face betrayed no emotion, he appeared sincere. His confidence was underpinned by the fact that he'd booked the room under an assumed name and Ralph was sure that none of the staff knew him there.

"This all seems so unfair," continued Ralph.

There was an edge to his voice suggesting that he now believed it was time for him to go on the offensive.

"What more can I do to prove my innocence? Surely you believe me? One thing I'm going to do though, is give Veronica her marching orders. I'll do it first thing in the morning!"

"No Ralph. You mustn't."

"I certainly will. Causing all this trouble. She's got no place at Greenings!"

Calm and assured throughout their conversation, Ralph was now in a rage. Waiting for him to calm down, Connie spoke quietly and softly.

"No, Ralph. I mean it. If you take any action against Veronica, then we're finished."

Ralph was shocked.

"What, after all she's done to destroy our relationship, you're going to stand by her?"

"Yes, for now Ralph. I promised her that I'd look into what she's said. I asked her to give me some time. We need to think carefully before we do anything. After all, you need to prove your innocence to everyone. Sacking her out of hand won't help matters, will it?"

"Well, she'd better make sure that she stays out of my way!"

Connie nodded.

"I'm sure that she will Ralph."

Getting up from her chair, Connie beckoned Ralph towards the front room.

"Come on Ralph. I think you'd best go. We both need some time alone to consider things."

"I don't need to consider anything," said Ralph. "I love you Connie and only you."

"I'd still like you to go Ralph," insisted Connie. "I certainly don't feel like going out anywhere."

Connie walked into the front room and Ralph followed. Opening the front door, Connie stepped aside and watched Ralph walk through her small front 'garden' and out on to the pavement. There were no further words between the two of them and before Ralph had got into his car, Connie had already closed the front door. It had proved a frustrating night for her. She was no further forward in her quest for the truth.

Chapter 61

Connie had already considered what she would do if her discussion with Ralph didn't provide her with satisfactory answers. Connie knew the name of a firm of private detectives and the next day she telephoned them to set up an appointment at four-thirty that afternoon.

Phillips & Co, Private Investigators, were located in Marsden Square off Market Street. It was a short walk from Clayton House but Connie gave herself half an hour to get there. She wanted plenty of fresh air and the chance to consider whether she really should take a step, from which there could be no turning back. As a result, she walked slowly down towards 'Pauldens' at the top of Market Street, taking time to look in the windows of the numerous and varied shops she passed: 'Thorntons;' 'Timothy Whites;' 'Dunn & Co;' 'Harrops' and 'Bentons.' Reaching the Rylands building, Connie was at 'Pauldens,' a department store she preferred to 'Lewis's,' but one she had no desire to go in and look around today, even if she had the time. Moving on, she could see 'Henry's' in front of her. Beyond that was the entrance to the 'Cinephone' cinema, a venue that had shocked polite members of Manchester society, when they had started to show continental 'blue movies' to local filmgoers. Before she reached there however, Connie turned by the side of 'Henry's' and into the cobbled entrance to Marsden Square. As she walked on, Connie could see tall buildings on either side of her. There was evidence of a mixture of different businesses, so typical of Manchester's centre and which made the city more interesting. Yet with the whole area targeted for redevelopment and investors speculatively buying up properties, it would only be a matter of time before things changed.

Looking at her watch, Connie had only five minutes until her appointment, so she quickly made her way over to the entrance to Phillips and Co. The building was rather dilapidated and in order to reach the offices of the private investigators, Connie had to climb up three flights of relatively narrow and rickety stairs.

Phillips & Co specialised in matrimonial cases for Manchester's wealthy elite. If a partner was suspected of cheating and it was true, they could invariably prove it. It seemed the logical place to come. Yet Connie had hesitated. If she took this course of action in order to check up on Ralph, it suggested that there wasn't any real trust between them. And if that was the case, then it was tantamount to an admission that she shouldn't be marrying him. Yet she knew that Ralph could only be vindicated by a thorough investigation of Veronica's allegations, that proved she had lied. If Connie took no action, she knew that Veronica would inevitably go public with her claims. So, despite all her misgivings, Connie had to accept that engaging Phillips & Co was the only logical step she could take.

Connie therefore found herself sat in front of a large and cluttered desk, piles of paperwork spread across its top and hanging over the sides. Across from her was a balding, bespectacled, middle-aged man, in a rather shabby grey suit.

"Hello, I'm Jim Phillips, it's Mrs Campbell I believe."

"No," replied Connie. "Miss Campbell."

"Oh, I'm sorry. Sue, my secretary, must have taken the details down wrong."

"She probably assumed that it was my husband I wanted you to investigate but actually, he's my fiancé."

"Ah, I see," replied Phillips. "We do get a lot of work for engaged clients. You're by no means unique Miss Campbell."

The revelation gave Connie some reassurance, but she still found it difficult to tell Phillips precisely what her concerns were.

"I'm not comfortable about coming to see you Mr Phillips," began Connie, somewhat hesitantly, "but I do need to know if my fiancé is being truthful."

Phillips looked sympathetically at the pretty, young woman in front of him. He knew how difficult it had been for her to come to see him. She was experiencing a sense of guilt, like so many of his clients, for failing to have trust in their partners. His role was to reassure her that what she was asking him to do, was reasonable.

"Don't worry Miss Campbell. We're the soul of discretion. Your fiancé needn't ever know that we've investigated him, if that's what you want."

Connie nodded.

"I do have to warn you though," he continued, more seriously, "that we can uncover aspects of someone's behaviour, that those closest to them can find disturbing. If we believe that's the case, we always give our clients the option of being spared the full details."

"Oh?" asked Connie.

"Yes. For example, if a client wants us to take photographs as evidence of infidelity, we don't have to show the pictures to them. They can simply be kept on file by us, or lodged with the client's solicitor."

Explaining the methods his company would employ to check into Ralph's past and current behaviour, Phillips then went through what his charges would be and asked Connie if she was happy to go ahead and engage his services. Connie gave her assent and on Phillips prompting, related the details of Veronica's allegations and the responses that Ralph had made to them.

All the time that she was speaking, Phillips listened attentively, stroking his chin, nodding his head to show his understanding and letting out an occasional 'hmm' to expresses interest in a particular detail or circumstance. Occasionally, he would pick up his pen and write down a note, obviously considering what she had said to be particularly important. When she had finished, he stretched back on his chair, took a deep breath and took off his glasses and cleaned them with a small cloth, before putting them back on. Leaning forward, he spoke quietly to Connie.

"I think this case is a very straightforward one, Miss Campbell."

"Please, call me Connie. I seem to have told you so much about myself, it seems strange to continue to be so formal."

"Well Connie, it certainly shouldn't take too much time or effort to get you an answer. I'm assuming that you're only concerned about finding out whether anything has happened between Ralph and Veronica. You don't want us to have him followed. Is that right?"

"Yes," replied Connie.

"Fine. What I'll do is send someone down to the 'Grosvenor.' I'm sure it won't surprise you to know that we have a lot of contacts in all the hotels in town. If clandestine meetings go on, it's usually there that they happen. What I'll need though, is a photograph of Ralph. "

"I've got one with me," said Connie, who had anticipated his request. Reaching into her handbag, she took the photo out and handed it to him.

"Thanks. That will speed things up a bit. I'm sure you've already realised that if they did get a room, it was probably under an assumed name. Yet we can show the photo to the receptionists and the cleaning staff and find out if Ralph was with a young woman in one of the rooms. Obviously, we can't prove what went on in there, but I think we can safely assume that there's only one reason for them sharing a hotel room. Don't you agree?"

Connie slowly nodded her head.

"But won't the hotel staff keep quiet about it? Won't the management expect them to turn a blind eye to any goings-on?"

"Well yes, but we also pay staff for their information and as we're discreet and their boss will never find out about it, they'll tell us what we want to know. They're also aware that if they don't provide reliable information, we won't approach them again."

"Oh."

"There's no reason for staff to be dishonest and if we had any doubts Connie, we wouldn't give you the information."

"Okay," said Connie, reassured.

"So, you still want us to go ahead?" asked Phillips.

"Yes," said Connie, with a sigh. "I don't see any other way."

"Fine. We'll get on to it right away. Don't worry, it won't cost you a great deal Connie. It's just a few hours to get to the hotel, talk to our contacts and make the payments to them."

Phillips stood up, came out from behind the desk and walked towards the door. Connie got out of the chair and followed him. He opened it and they were outside in the small reception area, where Sue, Phillips elderly secretary, was sat typing a letter at her desk. Noticing them, Sue stopped typing and smiled sympathetically at Connie.

"Well, goodbye Connie," said Phillips, shaking her hand. "It's Tuesday today, can you make it on Friday morning, say at nine thirty?"

"Yes. That shouldn't be a problem," replied Connie.

Descending the rickety stairs, Connie was soon back outside in Marsden Square. The bright July sunshine felt warm and she instinctively looked up into the blue, cloudless sky and took in a long, deep breath. She still felt uncomfortable about what she'd done and wished that there had been some other way. Yet Ralph had left her with no alternative. On Friday she would know for definite the truth of Veronica's claims and that would determine whether her engagement to Ralph would have any chance of survival.

Chapter 62

It was Friday morning. Jim Phillips looked up at the clock on the wall opposite his desk. It was almost half past nine and it wouldn't be long before Connie would be arriving to be told the facts about her fiancé. Phillips found it the most soul-destroying part of his work. There were so many men and women who were prepared to betray the trust of their loving and devoted partners. And when he considered Connie, he could understand it even less. She had sat in his office, an extremely beautiful and intelligent young woman, who was desperate for her fiancé to be innocent of all accusations. Phillips couldn't help but feel angry. Infidelity was cheating; there was no better word to use. 'Cheats' casually broke the rules of honesty and commitment. They were prepared to do anything to get what they wanted, deceiving the people closest to them and giving no thought to the devastating consequences of their actions. Nevertheless, if such people didn't exist, Phillips recognised that he would have a far less lucrative business. But it still made him despair. The self-destructive nature of human beings was a mystery hard to fathom. But it was now time for Phillips to put his feelings to one side and remain professional. If he betrayed no emotion and dealt plainly in facts, he found that his clients, however unpalatable the information may be, could cope far better.

As the hands of the clock reached half past, there was a knock on the office door.

"Come in!" said Phillips, loudly.

The door opened. Standing there was Sue, with Connie slightly behind her.

"Miss Campbell's here for her appointment Mr Phillips."

"Ah, yes."

Phillips rose from behind his desk. He walked the short distance towards Connie. Offering her his hand, Connie shook it firmly. Phillips motioned towards the chair at the front of his desk and returned to his own seat behind it. He watched as Connie sat down. She really was a pretty young woman. Dressed for work, she was wearing a plain black jacket and skirt and white blouse open at the neck, a thin gold necklace resting against her smooth, white skin. The simplicity of her attire highlighted her long, light brown hair, piercing green eyes and attractive figure. He couldn't help but wonder at the stupidity of her fiancé. Connie was the woman of any man's dreams and yet Ralph had been prepared to risk losing her. The news that Phillips was about to give to Connie, meant that she would never trust Ralph again. As such, their relationship was doomed.

"Right, Miss Campbell."

"Please. Call me Connie."

Phillips nodded. He knew that was her preference, but he'd felt that the seriousness of the situation meant that he should appear as official as possible.

"Well Connie, we've carried out our investigations and I'm afraid that I have bad news."

Phillips paused. He wanted to give Connie the chance to prepare herself. Studying her face, he could see that she betrayed no signs of emotion.

"Our contacts at the 'Grosvenor,'" he continued, "verified the fact that your fiancé booked a room and that he then spent the night with a young woman. The description of her matches the one that you gave us of Veronica. As Ralph has admitted to you that they were together at the hotel, it seems clear that the two of them are involved in an intimate relationship."

Phillips paused, giving Connie time to digest the information. Eventually, she nodded in acknowledgement.

"I see," said Connie.

"As you're not married to Ralph," Phillips continued, "there's no reason to pursue the investigation any further. You don't need to prove anything to the courts for example."

"No, of course not," agreed Connie.

The two of them shared a moment of silence before Phillips tried to draw out something positive from the investigation.

"It's not a pleasant job we do by any means Connie, but at least it provides necessary answers. It gives you the opportunity to make decisions about your future, with everything out in the open. You don't have to use the information, but at least you don't have to suffer the uncertainty of not knowing whether your doubts about your fiancé are true or not."

"Yes," replied Connie. "I really didn't want to approach you. I wanted to give Ralph the benefit of the doubt. Yet I knew that I had to act on what Veronica had told me. There were just too many unanswered questions. Too many details that didn't seem right and I knew that our relationship couldn't survive in an atmosphere that lacked trust."

"Well, if people were honest towards one another, those questions wouldn't exist. And then there would be no reason to use the services of someone like me."

Connie nodded in agreement and sighed.

"Yes, that's right. It's the problem with people, isn't it? The constant need to find someone with honesty and integrity."

Phillips observed Connie closely. She seemed to be handling his revelations calmly. She had a dignity that ensured that she wouldn't allow herself to become visibly upset. However, Phillips knew that regardless of the fact that she had, on arrival, been fully prepared to hear the worst, deep down the confirmation of Ralph's betrayal, was bound to hurt her.

Slowly, Connie raised herself from her chair.

"Well, thank you Jim for all your help. If you give me the bill, I'll write you out a cheque."

"It's okay," said Phillips, "we don't expect the money right away."

"No. I want it cleared. Put everything behind me."

"Right," said Phillips. "You'll need to take the evidence with you though."

Phillips picked up a large brown envelope. Inside, it contained the details that had been collected from his investigation.

"Yes. Thank you. I suspect though, that once he knows I've had investigations carried out, he'll come clean."

"Well, perhaps," said Phillips, who knew many instances where partners, even when confronted with photographic evidence, would continue to maintain their innocence.

"You've been very kind and reasonable Jim, but please don't take it the wrong way when I say that I hope I never have to use your services again."

"I understand," said Phillips.

Given Connie's composure, he felt able to offer a smile of encouragement.

"It isn't the only kind of work we do, though admittedly, the most lucrative."

Leading Connie towards the door of his office, he opened it and showed Connie into the reception where Sue was sat working at her desk.

"Miss Campbell would like to settle the bill. Can you see to it Sue?"

"Yes, of course."

"Well, goodbye Connie. I hope everything works out for you."

"Oh yes, I'm sure it will," replied Connie.

Connie gave all the signs of being a very resilient young woman. Phillips was pleased. It suggested that she would be able to rebuild her life. Too often those who had been betrayed suffered huge emotional damage. Connie, Phillips believed, had no intention of being a victim and in the long run, he knew that Ralph would suffer far more, unable to forget that he had lost her through the stupidity of his unfaithfulness.

Chapter 63

In the days following their conversation about Veronica, Ralph had noticed how reserved Connie had been towards him. He sensed that she hadn't believed his protestations of innocence and she'd made it clear that she wouldn't discuss the matter again, until she'd had time to consider her options. She also continued to insist that he take no action against Veronica. The latter's continued presence at work was a constant reminder of his foolishness. Finally, following her meeting with Phillips, Connie had told Ralph that she would meet him that evening at seven, in the bar at the Brunswick Hotel in Piccadilly.

The 'Brunswick' was in reality, just a pub. It was somewhere that Ralph wouldn't normally have chosen to go, but Connie insisted that it was a neutral venue, where it would be better for them to discuss matters. They hadn't been there for a night out and as the pub was usually quite busy, Connie hoped that the presence of other people would ensure that their conversation remained civil. The choice of venue sent out a clear message to Ralph. He understood that Connie was trying to distance herself from the intimate places of their past. He was convinced that she no longer saw him as her fiancé and lover, but as her adversary. His wit and charm would prove ineffective weapons in trying to regain her trust.

Connie was already waiting for him when he arrived at seven. She was sat at a table by the window, gazing out at the busy crowds of people outside. It was Friday night and young Mancunians were already out and about, hoping to enjoy their evening after a hard week at work. Connie wished that she could be as carefree as them too, but tonight that was impossible. Unlike the happy couples she watched walking hand in hand past the window, she knew that her evening was destined to come to a premature end and would result in the breaking off of her engagement. Her decision to do so was painful, but it was one that she knew she had to take.

As Ralph walked over to join her, his heart sank. Looking out of the window, Connie was softly brushing her fingers across her cheek, teasing back a loose lock of hair that had fallen out of place. As usual, she looked immaculate and he noticed her cute little nose, which he loved to kiss and her soft, inviting lips. He wondered just why he had been so careless. And at that moment he could feel nothing but anger towards Veronica. He had, by now, convinced himself that she was to blame. He had simply flirted with her but she had exploited his weakness, aroused his desire and set out to destroy his relationship with his beautiful fiancé. Ralph's transgressions with Veronica had led him to regress to a point before Connie's resurrection of his character. Like he had in the past, he now refused to accept any responsibility for a situation for which he only had himself to blame.

Holding his emotions in check, Ralph told himself that all was not yet lost. Perhaps, after all, his relationship with Connie could be saved. As such, he appeared calm and confident as he reached the table.

"Hi Connie. Seven o'clock. Just as we arranged."

He smiled and sat down opposite her at the table.

"It's busy tonight," he continued. "I thought I was going to be delayed."

"Yes, it is," replied Connie.

She looked at him intently, but further words weren't forthcoming. Connie's response was decidedly frosty, but Ralph chose to ignore it and continued to make small talk in an attempt to make the atmosphere as pleasant as possible.

"Well, it is Friday night. The end of the week. Everybody's out in town for a good time."

Ralph smiled, hoping for a response, but Connie was unmoved. She was determined that he would face the music. There would be no turning back; his charm now ineffective against her. Slowly and calmly, she spoke.

"I've had time to think Ralph and I'm giving you a final chance to tell me the truth. Did you and Veronica spend the night together?"

A small part of Connie still wanted Ralph to admit his infidelity to her. To be honest enough to face up to his indiscretions and show genuine remorse for what he had done. Surely there must be some goodness in him. She couldn't have been so wrong in her assessment of his character. Yet his response made it clear that she was.

"I don't understand you Connie, or what all the fuss is about. Veronica is manipulative and scheming. She's fooled you because of her age. She may be young, but it makes no difference. She's purposely lied about me. Can't you see that? I love you Connie. Why would I risk losing you? I'd be stupid."

Ralph's words were an attempt to appear as sincere as possible. Connie inwardly shuddered. In the silence she stared at him, his eyes focused on hers, willing her to believe him. And she realised that he had become a monster. He was like a man she had never met, displaying an evil side to his nature that had hitherto been so well disguised that, without the evidence she possessed to the contrary, was insidious enough to convince anyone of his spotless character and good intentions.

"I gave you the chance Ralph and you didn't take it."

"What do you mean?"

"You know what I mean."

"No. I don't."

Connie looked at him closely. He was adamant that he was innocent. She had no choice but to reveal her evidence.

"I went to a private detective Ralph. You did spend the night with Veronica. In the Grosvenor Hotel, after the meeting you claim to have taken place with Giles Parker. For all I know, it's not the only time. But that doesn't matter. For me, once is enough."

"I don't believe you Connie. You wouldn't do that. You wouldn't go to a private detective."

Ralph seemed convinced that she wouldn't. Connie therefore reached down to the side of her. Besides her handbag she had a documents folder. She picked it up, laid it on the table and unzipped it. Ralph watched as she took out a large, brown envelope.

"This is a copy of the report from the investigators. I've got another one, so you can have it if you want Ralph."

She rested her arms on the table and opened the palms of her hands towards him. She gestured to him to take the envelope. She felt calm. She wasn't sad or angry, if anything she felt a sense of relief. Relieved that she was rid of him; that he would be out of her life. His defences had been lowered. She saw the shock on his face; the realisation that he'd been found out when he'd been so confident that he wouldn't. In a faltering voice, Ralph tried to justify himself, to even criticise Connie.

"I've done nothing wrong. Don't you see? It's Veronica. You've let her destroy us, Connie. How can you allow her to do that?"

Picking up the envelope, Connie put it back into the folder and zipped it back up. She reached down to pick up her handbag and stood up.

"I assume that you don't want the envelope, Ralph. I'll take it with me. I wouldn't like it to fall into the wrong hands."

Stepping away from the table, Connie started to walk towards the exit.

"Wait! Wait Connie!"

Ralph shouted after her in a despairing voice, couples at the surrounding tables looking up from their conversations. Connie had no intention of continuing the discussion and having met Ralph in such a public place, there was no chance that he could force her to do so. Once outside, she breathed deeply. She felt liberated and understood the good fortune that she had encountered in escaping from her engagement. Their relationship had been a poisonous one, but she hadn't known it. Now, the veil of secrecy had been lifted and she was free to see clearly again.

Crossing Portland Street, Connie made her way to the bus stop, eager to get home. Ready to embark on a new phase of her life, Connie realised that she couldn't continue working at Greenings. Having lost her fiancé, Connie knew that quickly, she would have to find another job.

Chapter 64

The idea had come to her as she sat on the bus on the short journey home. Over the last few days, Connie had thought about the letter that Tom had sent to her when he'd left to work at Joyce and Hitchcock. Now that Tom's concerns about Ralph had been vindicated, Connie understood that he hadn't acted out of jealousy, but through a genuine concern for her happiness and well-being.

Back in Howard Avenue, Connie soon had Tom's envelope in her hands. She reached inside it, took out the letter and read the reassuring words. Tom had promised his support if she ever needed it and this was the moment when she did. Connie felt vulnerable. For all her success at Greenings, most other employers wouldn't see beyond her femininity. Whilst some would be prejudiced against her gender others, although recognising her ability, would still see her appointment to a senior position, as a visible and unacceptable challenge to the notion of male supremacy. Importantly too, although Joe Greening had been very good to her, Connie couldn't be sure how he would react to the news of her broken engagement and it was here that Tom's help could prove crucial to her future prospects. Connie had worked closely with Mike Joyce and as a highly respected local businessmen, a reference from him could overcome the hesitancy of potential employers, should Connie's reference from Greenings prove to be less than enthusiastic. Now employed by Mike, Tom would be able to approach him on Connie's behalf.

Nevertheless, it proved to be a troubling weekend for Connie. Her initial relief at being free of Ralph, was soon replaced by worry and doubt. She was a woman in a man's world and had to accept that consequently, she faced an uncertain future. Being quite frugal, she had accumulated a reasonable amount of savings and she still had the remainder of her father's legacy. Yet she knew that it wasn't enough to survive a period of sustained unemployment. The thought entered her head that perhaps she would have to forget any lofty ambitions and even accept a job as an accounts clerk. Yet if that was the price for ending her association with Ralph, then so be it. She hoped however, that it wouldn't come to that.

At eight o'clock on Monday morning, Connie dialled the number for the office at Joyce and Hitchcock. Employed at an engineering company, Tom started work at an earlier hour than most of his fellow accountants.

It was fortuitous for Connie, as it meant that she could make contact with him before starting work. Quickly, Connie had reached the switchboard and was soon being put through to Tom.

"Hi Connie! It's good to hear from you."

The enthusiasm of Tom's voice allayed any concerns that his attitude may have changed towards her. His words in the letter were true. He would be there, if she needed him; he would never withdraw his friendship.

"Hello Tom," began Connie, quietly. "I'm sorry to bother you and so early but …"

"Bother me? You'd never bother me Connie," said Tom interrupting, eager to stress that his concern for her was as great as it had ever been.

Connie paused, momentarily concerned that he may be getting the wrong signals. Perhaps her call had reignited his romantic feelings. Quickly however, she dismissed the notion and continued with the call.

"I'd rather not go into details yet Tom, but I've decided to leave Greenings."

"Oh," said Tom, clearly surprised.

"Yes, but I'm a little concerned. I know that Joe Greening didn't want to lose you, but Mike knew that you were good at your job, so you didn't need a reference. I'm concerned that Greenings might not be positive in their support of any job applications I make."

"And you think that Mike may be able to help you, Connie?"

"Yes. We were both involved in the work Greenings did for him. Mike knows me well and I wonder if you could ask him if he'd be prepared to act as a referee for me, should I need him to."

Connie paused whilst Tom digested what she'd said. Her words were interesting to him because Joyce and Hitchcock's continued expansion, meant that they were looking to recruit a new chief accountant. Tom was increasingly involved in other projects and would be vacating the position. The timing of Connie's phone call could therefore prove beneficial for both parties. Certainly, Tom knew of no better candidate than Connie for the job. Nevertheless, the decision to offer the post to her would need Mike's approval. Concerned not to raise Connie's expectations and also conscious that she may prefer not to work with him again, he decided not to mention the opportunity, until he was certain that the job would be offered to her.

"Mike won't be here until around nine. I'll see him as soon as he gets in. If you're able to ring back at ten, I'll be in the office to let you know. I'm sure he'll be willing to lend his support. He thinks a lot of you Connie."

Tom's words were reassuring and just what Connie needed to hear, but after she put the phone down, she knew that it was going to be a nervous wait. Furthermore, she was worried about going into work. She may have to see Ralph again and that would be difficult. She had acted with real dignity in the 'Brunswick' but with the passage of time, she was feeling increasingly angry. He had made a fool of her. She had supported him against the warnings of her friends and the members of staff at Greenings, who were aware of Ralph's past and never believed that he would change. By going out with Ralph and announcing their engagement, she now appeared to be lacking in judgement. Supposedly mature and intelligent, she had fallen prey to his charms, just like any number of infatuated teenagers who'd worked in the office. Moreover, she would have to face Joe Greening and explain why she wanted to leave. Although she preferred not to talk about the breaking off of her engagement, she suspected that she would have to.

Knowing that this would probably be her last day at Clayton House, Connie had no qualms about turning up late. She stayed at home until ten and then, feeling nervous, she made her return phone call to Joyce and Hitchcock. Almost immediately, the switchboard operator answered and she was put through to Tom.

"Hi Connie. Thanks for ringing back."

Tom paused, before continuing.

"I've got some news for you Connie. Good news, I hope."

Once more he paused. Connie noticed that he seemed rather nervous.

"Yes, go on," prompted Connie.

"Well, it would depend on how you feel of course, and you may not want to, but there's a job going here that would suit you down to the ground."

"What type of job?" asked Connie, assuming that if Tom felt she may not want it, it was unlikely to carry as much responsibility as her current post. As such, her voice didn't display much enthusiasm for what he'd said.

"It's a chartered accountant we want Connie. We've been expanding and with new responsibilities, I don't have the time to head up the accounts and planning section any more. Mike's dead keen to offer you the job. He says that you know the firm inside out and will be perfect. He'll increase the salary you're on at present. You can come in and see him this afternoon, if that's okay? Of course, only if you're interested in the job."

Connie was stunned. The offer was completely unexpected and now she was the one who was silent.

"Connie? Connie, are you still there?"

Tom was worried. For a few moments he thought the worst. That Connie had put the phone down and was rejecting the offer out of hand. Perhaps she'd thought that by taking the job, it would make her beholden to him. That wasn't the case, but he remembered how critical she had been of him on that fateful night when they had fallen out and he now hoped that Connie would accept that he was acting out of good intentions.

Gathering her thoughts, Connie was finally able to give Tom the response he craved.

"Yes. Yes, Tom. I'm still here."

"Oh good. I thought you'd been cut off," said Tom, trying to conceal his fears.

"No," said Connie. "Why didn't you mention the job earlier?"

"Well obviously I had to talk to Mike first. I was pretty confident that he'd want to offer you the job, but I didn't want to let you know until I knew for definite."

It was an honest and logical answer, but Connie still wasn't satisfied.

"Why did you think that I might not want the job, Tom? From what you've said, it's better than the one I've got now."

She heard Tom take a deep breath.

"Well, after what happened, I thought you might not want to work with me again."

Connie sensed the pain in his voice and for the first time she really understood just how much their falling out had affected him. Connie suddenly felt very humble and appreciative of the fact that, regardless of how she had treated him, Tom was so genuine in caring for her.

"No, Tom. I was wrong. I'm sorry. I'm so grateful for your offer."

"It's not my offer Connie. It's Mike's. He's the boss. I can't take any credit."

"Yes, I know Mike has the final say, but he's not going to employ anyone without knowing that you're happy with it, is he now?"

Tom was quiet. Connie knew that he would never seek personal plaudits; never want others to praise him.

"I'd love to take the job Tom. Even if it means I've got to work with you again!"

Connie started laughing and at that point Tom knew that the dark days of the past were over. The two of them could once again be friends.

"Can you get in this afternoon Connie?"

"Yes. I'll have to go and see Joe Greening first to give him my resignation. It makes it so much easier for me, now that I have a job to go to. Will three o'clock be okay?"

"Yes, fine. I'll be waiting for you at reception when you get here."

"Okay Tom. Bye."

"Bye Connie," replied Tom, softly.

Putting down the phone, Tom sat back in his chair. The thought that he would shortly be seeing Connie again, when he'd believed that she was lost to him forever, had left him in a state of mild shock. Today, his life had changed for the better. Once more he would be near the woman he loved and admired. And if she never did see him as more than just a friend, then so be it. There was one thing that Tom was sure of. As far as love and romance were concerned, for him it was Connie or no one. He would never accept second best.

Chapter 65

Having ended her phone call to Tom, Connie then called work. It was Paula that answered.

"Hi Paula, it's me, Connie."

"Connie! Where have you been?" replied Paula, clearly relieved to hear her friend's voice. "Are you all right? We were starting to get worried."

"Oh," said Connie, surprised. "You haven't heard anything then?"

"No," replied Paula, sounding confused. "Should I have?"

"Oh, it's nothing," replied Connie. "It doesn't matter. I'll tell you later."

Paula was curious to know more, but she knew better than to try and get her friend to elaborate any further. She would have to be patient.

"Is there something you want me to do Connie?" asked Paula, changing the subject.

"Yes. Can you get me in to see Joe Greening before dinner please? It's important."

"He'll see you at any time Connie. You can just slip in to his office."

"I know Paula, but it needs to be a little more formal than that. I might need to talk to him for longer than usual."

"Okay. Just hang on while I check his diary."

Connie's request provided Paula with a sense of déjà vu. It reminded her of the day that Tom had left.

"Can you get here for eleven thirty? I can get you half an hour. Will that be long enough?"

"Yes. Thanks Paula. I'm on my way in now."

Connie hung up the phone and set off to catch the bus. She arrived at Greenings with a few minutes to spare and headed straight to Paula's desk. She didn't go to her own office. Anything that she wished to pick up, she would do so later.

"Can you come with me for a chat after I've finished my meeting, Paula? You haven't anything else planned, have you?"

"No. I'm due a break then, so I'll get someone to cover."

"Thanks. I appreciate it," said Connie, a faint trace of a smile flickering across her face.

Paula now knew, beyond any doubt, that something serious had happened. Her friend needed her support and she was determined to give it.

"Come on Connie," she said, encouragingly, "I'll 'buzz' the 'old man'. It's eleven thirty."

Connie took a deep breath as Paula informed 'Old Joe' that she had arrived to see him. Putting down the phone, Paula told her to knock and go in. Advancing towards the door, Connie tried to remain calm. Knocking, she heard a pleasant 'come in.' Turning the handle and walking into the room, she saw Joe looking up at her from behind his desk. He was smiling broadly, clearly unaware of the issues that she and Ralph had been going through.

"Hello my dear. What can I do for you? You're keeping that tearaway nephew of mine in line I hope," said Joe, pleasantly.

Connie sat down. She felt uncomfortable. Joe Greening had been so good to her and he'd been delighted when he'd been told that she was going to marry Ralph. Connie knew that Joe felt that she was a good influence on his nephew and so the news that she was about to give him, would be unwelcome. But then, none of this was her fault. It was Ralph who had proved unfaithful. Moreover, he didn't seem inclined to inform his uncle of the problems he'd created for the firm, by his liaison with Veronica. Connie knew that she mustn't forget that if she were to deal confidently with her boss.

"I can't thank you enough for the opportunities you've given me Mr Greening, but I've come to tell you that I've decided that I want to leave the firm. I'll work my notice if you want me to, but I'd rather go now if that's possible. I'm not involved in any critical work at the moment. There are others who can take on my responsibilities, until you can get someone to replace me. As you know, there are plenty of good people out there."

Connie's opening statement was word perfect. It was exactly how she'd been rehearsing it over the weekend. She now paused, considering that it was up to Joe whether he wanted to pursue an explanation for her decision. Looking at him, Connie could see that he was shocked. He had no idea, prior to seeing her, that the matter she wanted to talk to him about, was her resignation.

Slowly, Joe began to gather his thoughts. He looked closely at Connie. For a moment he considered whether her words had been uttered in jest. She didn't really mean what she'd said and would soon smile and tell him what she was really concerned about. But this was Connie. She would never behave like that and as the seconds ticked by, her face remained deadly serious. There could be no doubt that she meant what she'd said. And Joe just couldn't understand it. Why now? Surely, she was happy at work. She was highly valued, was engaged to his nephew and she must know that in the future she would have an even greater role in the running of the company. Surely, he could get her to reconsider. Whatever it was, they could sort it out.

"You've shocked me, Connie. I didn't expect this. Is there something wrong? Something that I can do for you?"

He was stunned, all traces of the pleasant countenance that had greeted her as she'd entered the room, removed by the words she had said. And, for the first time, Connie recognised his frailty; the weakness of an old man confronted by events that he feared he could no longer control. In contemplation of how this meeting would play out, she had assumed that he would be angry with her. He would be full of recriminations, believing that she had betrayed his trust and support. Yet it simply wasn't the case and now she had no desire to upset him any further, by revealing the details about her break-up with Ralph.

"No, thank you Mr Greening, but my mind is made up. I believe it's time for me to take on a new challenge."

"But why? Why now? I thought that you were happy here."

"I have been and you've been very kind to me."

"So, please Connie. I think I deserve a better explanation. Don't you?"

Joe looked intently into Connie's eyes, imploring her to clarify her decision. Connie recognised his vulnerability and it moved her. It was becoming difficult. Joe Greening was a man who ran his business with confidence and authority. It wasn't like him to ask for the goodwill of any of his employees. His request made her realise just how much her news had upset him. Reluctantly, she understood that he would have to be told everything. Perhaps it was for the best that he learned that the engagement was off and that it was the reason why she had decided to leave.

"I need to go because it's impossible for me to work here now," she said, quietly. "Ralph and I have called off our engagement. It wouldn't be good for the company if I stayed. I'm afraid that I won't be able to work closely with him again."

At the mention of his nephew's name, Connie saw Joe's face change. Shock and disbelief were now replaced by anger. Connie noticed his eyes staring at her. His mouth had closed, he'd gritted his teeth and his jaw was set firm. He breathed heavily.

"What's he done? What's that 'good for nothing' nephew of mine been up to this time?"

Connie was silent.

"You don't have to protect him for my benefit. Come on girl, let it out."

Joe was animated. Not for one moment did he believe that the breakdown of their relationship, could be down to anyone but Ralph.

"It doesn't matter," said Connie. "The fact is that our engagement's off and as I've said, it just isn't possible for me to work with him anymore."

Connie hoped her explanation would be enough, but it wasn't. Joe was convinced that there could be only one reason why their engagement had ended; Ralph had been unfaithful. He was determined to find out the truth.

"He's been chasing after other women, hasn't he? He's done it before and now, he's done it again!"

Joe stared at Connie, waiting for a reply. She looked down, averting her eyes, an action which told him that he was right.

"I see. You won't deny it."

Connie remained quiet. She was still looking at the floor.

"One thing I know about you Connie, is that you won't lie to me. And you won't let anyone take the blame for something that they haven't done. If Ralph was so 'sweet and innocent,' you'd tell me."

Connie knew it was no good, she may as well confirm what Joe suspected. She raised her head, looked at Joe and nodded.

"Yes," she said. "He has."

"Who?" demanded Joe.

"No. I'm not telling you that."

Why?"

"Because it's not fair."

"Fair!"

"Yes. Ralph can be very persuasive. Why should someone else have to suffer too?"

"Well, Ralph will probably tell me."

"He shouldn't and you shouldn't make him," replied Connie, firmly.

Joe shook his head at her. He was amazed at Connie's reaction, unable to understand why she would be so generous and forgiving to the woman who'd helped to destroy her engagement.

"Fine," said Joe, "that's up to you. As far as Ralph is concerned, you can stay and I'll sack him! You're worth far more to this company than he is."

"No. You mustn't do that and I need to leave. I've too many bad memories here now."

"But why shouldn't I sack him? He needs to be taught a lesson. All his life he's been indulged and he's had it far too easy."

"No. It's not just Ralph's fault. He can't help himself. I should have known that. I was naïve to believe that he'd become more responsible. That he was ready to settle down and share his life with someone. I was wrong. He's still far too immature. He needs more time."

She paused, allowing Joe to consider her words before continuing.

"I was hoping that you'll allow me to leave today without working out my notice."

"Yes. Of course, Connie. I just wish that you'd reconsider. Surely you can? I'll put you in charge. Ralph will have to do whatever you tell him."

"No. It's very kind of you, but I need to go."

"Yes, I understand," said Joe, finally resigned to losing her.

"If you need a reference from me Connie, just ask. I'll keep my eyes and ears open in case anything suitable comes up for you."

"Thank you," said Connie.

She thought it best not to tell him about the offer from Mike Joyce. After all, she knew how disappointed he'd been to lose Tom and now she was following him to Joyce and Hitchcock. Connie felt that Joe had suffered enough setbacks for one day.

As Connie departed, 'Old Joe' watched her with sadness and regret. She was a lovely young woman. Able, pretty, hard-working, kind and considerate. His nephew was such a fool. Privileged and spoiled, he'd had it too good. Joe thought of his own youth and the terrible times he'd experienced in the trenches. It had taught him how precious life was and how important it was to grasp all that was beautiful, good and noble and never let it go. It was the reason he'd worshipped his beautiful Elizabeth. Joe had wanted to believe that Connie would have a similar effect on Ralph. But his nephew was a lost cause. Unfortunately, without children of his own, Joe knew that once again, he would have to suffer his nephew's stupidity. Whether he liked it or not, Ralph would inevitably take the reins of the company from him in the future. Whether he would be as successful as he himself had been, Joe seriously doubted.

Chapter 66

Leaving Joe's office, Connie saw Paula ready to go out. Alice was sat in her chair, covering for her so that the two women could go out for dinner together. Alice smiled at Connie, a reassuring smile that filled her with sadness. She knew that she had made some good friends at Greenings and now she would be leaving them behind.

"Thanks Alice, I've got some news for Paula," said Connie. "I'm sure she'll tell you about it later."

Alice nodded, Paula had already told her that Connie had turned up late and seemed agitated. Alice was sure that it would have something to do with Ralph. As her conversations with Paula had revealed, Alice was already convinced that something was going on between Ralph and Veronica. Her assumption had to be that Connie had found out.

Turning to Paula, Connie asked if she would go with her to her office. She wished to collect some personal items: a framed photo of her mam and dad taken before he'd left to fight in France in 1940 and a couple of ink pens that she'd used through her short, but successful working life. They had brought her luck in her chosen profession and she hoped that they would do the same at Joyce and Hitchcock.

"Stay with me please Paula, if Ralph comes into the office."

"He's not here Connie. He left shortly after nine. He's gone to a meeting at 'Walkers.'"

"To see Giles Parker, I assume."

"Yes, that's right Connie."

Connie shook her head. She couldn't believe it. Ralph was still trying to cover his tracks. He was no doubt ready to deny everything that he felt his uncle would be told. If not by Connie, then by Veronica. Paula's news was like instant therapy for Connie, another reminder of just how foolish she had been to put her trust in such a man.

"Are you okay?" asked Paula.

"Yes. I'm fine," replied Connie.

Paula wasn't fully convinced, but she knew that all would be revealed once they were away from the restraints created by being at work. After all, walls have ears and Connie clearly wanted to control what people knew about the situation.

Leaving the office, the two of them walked down Newton Street. It was busy with lots of people moving along the pavement. They headed towards the Alasia Snack Bar and going in, sat down and ordered two teas and a couple of cheese barms. Connie realised just how hungry she was. She hadn't eaten since early yesterday, so worried had she been to resolve her situation at Greenings. She tucked eagerly in to her barm cake, relieved that the future now seemed a little brighter. Most importantly, she was encouraged by the fact that however badly Ralph may have treated her, others, such as Tom, Mike Joyce, Joe Greening and now Paula, had shown her real kindness.

Paula sat quietly at the table. She knew that Connie would speak in good time. She watched her friend become more relaxed, the longer that she was away from the office. Having finished eating, Connie sat back. She allowed herself a smile. Slowly, she began to tell Paula about how she had initially confronted Ralph. That he'd been circumspect in his response and that in consequence, she felt that she had no alternative but to hire a private detective. From the way she spoke, Paula could tell that Connie wasn't comfortable with her actions.

"Well Connie. What else could you have done?" asked Paula. "You gave him every chance to be honest. You never really believed him though, did you?"

"No, I didn't Paula. And I suppose that when I knew that I didn't trust him, it should have been obvious that the engagement couldn't last. So perhaps I needn't have gone ahead with having him investigated."

"No, Connie. You did the right thing. If you hadn't, you would have come to believe that you'd been unfair to him and that he really had been innocent. Now you know for definite that he wasn't, so there's no need to feel any sympathy towards him."

"Well, yes. I can see that, Paula. And slowly, I've come to accept how self-centred and selfish he really is. But then again, I should have seen it. A part of me believes that it's just the way he is and that he can't help it. I'm sure Veronica could accept it. Being married to him, a ring on her finger, the status that comes with it. She'd probably be happy to turn a blind eye to whatever he gets up to when he's not at home. I'm sure that there's a lot of other women out there who would feel the same way too."

"Well, there's no chance Veronica will get anywhere near him again Connie. It's Ralph's way. He's had what he wanted. What else has she got to offer him?"

"That's a bit harsh," said Connie.

"No, it isn't," insisted Paula. "You're silly Connie. You feel sorry for her. She knew exactly what she was doing. All the girls warned her about Ralph and she ignored us. She didn't give it a second thought when she betrayed you. Did she?"

"Well, no she didn't," replied Connie. "But I was fooled by him too Paula. You forget that. He's done it to so many women. She's a victim just like everyone else."

"But she wanted him knowing that he was engaged," replied Paula. "When he had his other flings, he was single and fancy free. She betrayed you, Connie. You were good to her and she came to you in order to get you out of the picture. Surely you can see that, can't you?"

Connie was quiet. Paula knew that she wasn't going to say anything negative about Veronica.

"I don't know Connie, sometimes you're far too generous for your own good."

"Veronica did me a favour. I don't approve of what's happened, but I blame Ralph, not her. By telling me, Veronica made sure that I avoided making a complete fool of myself by marrying him."

Paula could see the logic of Connie's words, but still felt that she was being far too forgiving. Yet, it was Connie's way. Furthermore, Paula realised that Connie's emotional ties to Ralph were ended. She wouldn't invest any feelings of anger or remorse into him anymore. The relationship was dead; she was determined to move on.

"What did you see 'Old Joe' about Connie? continued Paula. "I'm assuming that you don't mind me asking."

Connie recounted how she'd resigned her job, but had been forced to tell Joe that the engagement was over because Ralph had cheated on her.

"What will you do now?" asked Paula, concerned.

"It's fine. I have a new job to start at Joyce and Hitchcock. I'm going later this afternoon. It's actually a better position than here, except I'll mainly be working in the office there."

"And Tom?"

"He's been great. I rang him this morning to ask for his help and I've ended up with the offer of a job. I can't believe how lucky I've been."

"I told you he cared about you. Didn't I?"

"Yes. He cares about me as a friend Paula. I know that I'll never have to feel any other pressure being placed upon me. And it was Mike Joyce who had the final say in making me the offer. I don't doubt that they've employed me because they believe in my ability to do the job."

Paula nodded in agreement. Nevertheless, she knew that Tom was still in love with Connie. Paula believed that he was the ideal antidote to Ralph, yet Connie still wouldn't be able to see it. Tom may be kind, generous and dependable, yet highly unlikely to gain the place in her heart that she held in his.

Chapter 67

Connie soon settled into her new job at Joyce and Hitchcock. Working with Mike and Tom, she was with familiar faces, who respected her talents. Greenings quickly became a distant memory and thoughts of Ralph faded from her mind. Furthermore, Connie continued to assist Harry in his Ardwick ward with the two of them developing an ever-closer working relationship. It received a further impetus when, on September 15th 1964, Conservative Prime Minister, Alec Douglas-Home, saw the Queen at Buckingham Palace and asked for a dissolution of Parliament. It meant that there would be a general election a month later. The news wasn't unexpected. The economy seemed to be struggling, the Tories had suffered from the Profumo scandal and had recently lost leader Harold Macmillan, who'd resigned the premiership due to ill health. Harry had been delighted with Douglas-Home's decision.

"He thinks he needs to establish his own status and authority," he told Connie. "He's nothing but an inept 'toff' and he's going to have to struggle to prove that he isn't. He'll never do it."

As the election campaign unfolded, it seemed to Connie that Harry's view was proving correct. Douglas-Home, conscious that Harold Wilson was seen as a man of the people, took the decision to tour the country on a soapbox, appealing directly to the voters. It proved a disaster as he was a poor speaker, undynamic and unable to deal with the constant heckling that plagued his appearances. Wilson, by contrast, was confident and assured the electorate that "if the past belongs to the Tories, the future belongs to us, all of us."

On the first Saturday of the campaign, Harry had arranged to pick up Connie from Howard Avenue at one o'clock. They were going to attend a rally. When he turned up outside in his trusty Austin A40, Bob and Johnny were walking down towards Syndall Street. The pair were wearing their sky blue and white City scarves and they looked curiously at Harry as he walked into Connie's small front garden and knocked on the door. Quickly, it had opened and Connie had greeted him. The pair of them had then walked back out on to the pavement, where Bob and Johnny were waiting for them.

"Hi Connie!" they said, cheerily.

Connie looked at them and smiled.

"Are you off to Maine Road lads?"

"Yes," replied Bob. "We're playing Derby."

"You're not doing too well at the moment though, are you?"

"We will, we will" said Bob, confidently.

"But you're still in Division Two," said Connie, clearly in a playful mood.

"So?" asked Bob.

"Well, United aren't, are they?"

"It'll change. Don't you fret," said Johnny, rather tetchily.

"She's having you on Johnny," said Bob. "Aren't you Connie?"

"Yes, I'm sorry Johnny," said Connie, smiling and turning towards her young admirer. "I shouldn't tease you when I know how much you love your team."

Johnny blushed, embarrassed by Connie's sympathetic words.

"I'm sorry too Connie," he replied. "I hope you don't think that I was annoyed with you. I wasn't. Honest."

Johnny was imploring her to forgive him, but when Connie made eye contact, he looked immediately at the floor.

"Well," continued Connie, eager to save Johnny from further discomfort, "what do you reckon today then lads?"

"We should be all right," said Bob.

"Yes," added Johnny. "We've got 'Tank' and Jimmy Murray's in good form. They'll get us some goals today."

"Who's 'Tank?'" asked Harry, intrigued by the name.

Bob and Johnny turned towards him in amazement. Until then, Harry hadn't existed for them, so focused were they on Connie. Now he'd brought himself to their attention and his question had almost offended them. Bob shook his head and Johnny let out a deep sigh. It was clear that they found his lack of football knowledge unacceptable and as if to emphasise the fact, Bob turned to Connie.

"You know who 'Tank' is, don't you Connie?"

"Yes. Derek Kevan. England centre forward, but that was when he was at West Brom, not now."

"Still bangs the goals in though Connie," said Johnny. "He got thirty-six last season; thirty of them in the league."

"Yes, I know Johnny, but it's only the second division," replied Connie. "Denis Law got thirty in Division One for United last season and forty-six overall. That was against far better opposition. 'Tank' was great at West Brom, but he's older now."

Connie smiled. Johnny was now enjoying their banter, relishing every moment of being with her. She was more than any man could hope for. Connie was beautiful, kind and she loved motor bikes and football. Where was he ever going to find someone like her?

"Why don't you come with us Connie?" asked Bob. "You can bring your friend here," he continued, nodding his head somewhat dismissively in Harry's direction.

"Well, it's kind of you to ask Bob, but you know I'm a 'Red' and Harry and I have got a rally to go to."

"You're not a 'Red' Connie. You're just having us on," replied Bob.

"Am I not?" asked Connie, with a twinkle in her eye.

Bob shook his head and then switched his attention to the green Austin A40 parked to the side of them.

"So, this is your car then?" asked Bob, looking at Harry.

"Yes."

"Humph," said Johnny.

"You can say that again," said Bob, grinning.

"You'd be better off walking Connie," said Johnny. "You'd get there faster than going in that!"

Connie couldn't help but laugh. It was the second time that Harry had disappointed Connie's young friends. He knew nothing about football and in addition, he had what they considered to be, a terrible car.

"It's not like Ralph's Dart, is it Connie? Now that was a machine," said Bob.

"Yes. Beautiful," added Johnny.

Connie didn't answer. Suddenly things didn't seem quite so funny.

"Where's Ralph then?" asked Bob. "We've not seen him around."

Johnny pulled on his arm. From Connie's continued silence, he'd sensed that the subject of Ralph was a sore one. Feeling protective, Johnny was eager to avoid upsetting her.

"Come on Bob," he said, changing the subject. "We need to be getting off if we want a pint before kick-off."

Johnny winked at his friend, who followed his glance towards Connie. When Johnny then nodded his head towards Syndall Street, Bob understood.

"Yes, Johnny. You're right. We'd best make a move. Bye then Connie."

"Bye lads."

With that, they were off. Connie was relieved that she hadn't needed to go into any details about Ralph. The lads had clearly understood that she was no longer with him and she'd appreciated the fact that they hadn't pressed her on the subject.

"I don't think I impressed your young friends too much, did I Connie?" asked Harry, laughing as they got into the car.

"No, I don't think you did," said Connie, smiling.

Harry's reaction to the lads' obvious disappointment with him, pleased her. It was his capacity to laugh at himself; his self-effacing character and good nature. He didn't have a hint of an inflated ego.

"I was impressed with your football knowledge Connie," said Harry, as they drove to the rally.

"Why? Because I'm a woman?"

"No, silly. You've never mentioned football before, so I thought that you weren't interested in it."

"When I was a teenager," said Connie, "I often went to Old Trafford to see United. Work and study seemed to put an end to all that. But I always keep up with what both teams are doing in the 'Evening News.'"

"Oh," said Harry. "I suppose I should take a greater interest myself. Virtually all the men I represent are football fans, I suppose that it isn't very impressive when I don't know anything about it."

"No," don't do that, said Connie, firmly. "People like you because you're considerate and you care. If you pretend that you're a football fan, they'll find you out straight away. Trying to deceive them won't make you any friends. Just be genuine. Be yourself."

Harry was silent, thinking about what she'd said.

"Yes, you're right Connie," he said, eventually. "I can see that you've given me some good advice there."

"People around here will accept you whatever your background, as long as they can see that your heart's in the right place," continued Connie. "Like Martin Luther King, they judge people on the content of their character."

The conversation emphasised to Harry just how much he was coming to depend on Connie's insight and support. She was a clear voice of reason; a sounding board off which he could bounce ideas. She had not only become extremely valuable to him in his political work, but the ending of her engagement had reignited his romantic aspirations towards her.

As the general election campaign neared its end, Harry's confidence in a Labour victory, began to look misplaced. As polling day approached, the Tories seemed to have rallied and actually took a narrow lead in the opinion polls. Harry and Connie didn't doubt that Ardwick's residents would return Leslie Lever, just as they had in 1959. As polling day approached, they decided to help out in one of the Manchester constituencies that had a sitting Tory MP: Blackley; Moss Side; Withington and Wythenshawe. Of these, Moss Side and Withington had a strong tradition of support for the Conservatives, so it seemed difficult to obtain a swing to Labour large enough to take either seat. Of the others, Labour's best chance of victory lay in Wythenshawe. They had lost by just over a thousand votes at the last election. With the building of more council houses in the area and a popular candidate in Alf Morris, the constituency seemed ready to fall into Labour's hands. Therefore, it was in Wythenshawe that the two of them concentrated their efforts in the final days of campaigning, distributing leaflets and knocking on doors to extol the virtues of the Party. Present at the declaration of the Ardwick result, which saw Leslie Lever returned with a thumping majority, Connie and Harry were also delighted to hear that Alf Morris had won in Wythenshawe, with a swing of over ten per cent. However, the British public hadn't delivered to Labour the ringing endorsement for which they'd hoped. Overall, they only had a slender four seats majority in the Commons. It meant that they wouldn't be able to introduce the major reforms that they wanted. After all their campaigning, Connie and Harry knew that inevitably, if Labour were determined to bring about a further transformation of society, it wouldn't be long before they would be forced to call a second general election.

Chapter 68

Christmas and New Year had come and gone. Connie had effectively rebuilt her life after the disappointment of Ralph's betrayal and her departure from Greenings. Work couldn't be going any better. Every morning, at five past seven, she would catch the bus outside the ABC and make the journey down Stockport Road, through Longsight and into Levenshulme. At the city boundary, just before reaching McVitie's, she would get off the bus and cross over the road opposite the 'Speedy Service Motor Depot' and walk up to the junction of Crossley Road. Turning right, she would then walk past a number of pleasant, 1930s semi-detached houses. All were well maintained and had significant front gardens which sloped down towards the road as it dropped to go underneath the railway bridge. Connie loved walking past the bushes and wide variety of shrubs that they contained. It brought to her a sense of the countryside, providing a stark contrast to the bricks, paving slabs and cobbles that were the essential fabric of Ardwick. Under the bridge, she was soon approaching the site of 'Fairey Engineering' and she now knew that she was in Stockport. Crossing the road, Connie made her way on to the small industrial estate which housed, for the time being, the premises of Joyce and Hitchcock.

The company was growing rapidly and this had meant that Connie's responsibilities were evolving too. She was an integral part of the senior management team and together with Tom, had played a crucial role in the financial planning of the company's expansion. It was clear that they had outgrown their current premises and the search was on to secure a new and viable location for the next stage of the firm's development. With the benefit of hindsight, Connie could recognise that her new job had provided her with opportunities she wouldn't have had back at Clayton House. Moreover, in Mike she had a boss who valued her. As a company, Joyce and Hitchcock believed in meritocracy. Unlike at Greenings, family or special interests had no place in the running of the company.

Connie was working exceptionally hard. This was nothing unusual and it had certainly helped her to forget about Ralph. She'd also quickly rebuilt her relationship with Tom. It had been helped by the fact that he felt differently now. He accepted that his role was to be a shoulder to cry on, should she ever need it. His desire to be her lover and her husband still remained and he still couldn't find solace in any other woman, but there was no inner conviction, as he'd had in the past, that one day Connie would be his. Connie had accepted a couple of invitations from Tom to go and watch performances of The Wayves, but other than that, the two of them had spent no time together outside of work. With Harry though, things were different.

Connie had continued working with Harry on Thursday evenings. Her commitment to the Party had increased during the general election campaign, to a point where she spent a great deal of time with the local councillor. She couldn't help noticing that his behaviour towards her had slowly changed. Always kind and considerate, there was now a tenderness in his voice when he spoke to her, he smiled far more in her presence and it was clear that he now regarded her as more than just a colleague.

Connie couldn't deny to herself that she found Harry attractive, both physically and intellectually. He'd made a huge impression on her when she had first heard him speak and his work for Ardwick's residents had gained her admiration and respect. So comfortable in his presence, Connie's feelings quickly began to grow and soon she began to consider that perhaps this was the relationship that she wanted after all. With Harry she would be committing herself to someone who shared her aspirations. He wanted to fight for equality and justice and was prepared to give up so much to help others. Connie still wanted someone to share her life with. Just because her relationship with Ralph had ended so unfortunately, it hadn't destroyed her faith in finding a man who could complete her life.

It wasn't too long before Harry decided that he would ask Connie to become his wife. Just before Easter, the two were sat together in the party office, having carried out a series of meetings with local residents. They had dealt with several testing issues and Harry, as usual, was grateful for Connie's capacity to put a reassuring arm around the shoulder of those on the verge of despair. The two of them were now enjoying a quiet cup of tea and in order to please Connie, Harry had brought along some chocolate digestives; McVitie's and not 'Cadburys,' as they were the ones she always insisted upon. Sensing that Connie was fairly relaxed, Harry saw the moment as opportune.

"Connie, I'd like to ask you something," he said, quietly.

"Yes."

"I hope you know just how much I think of your work here Connie. The way that you advise and support me. I've come to rely on you so much and I've tried to let you know how grateful I am."

Harry paused, waiting to see how she would respond.

"Yes, Harry. You've always been appreciative, but you've no need to be. I do it because I want to."

"Yes, I know you do Connie. Yet I think we make a great team together and, if I may be so bold, I've become very fond of you."

Harry paused, giving his words time to sink in before he continued.

"You're a very beautiful, kind and intelligent woman; the only one I've ever felt I could give my heart too. With you by my side, I feel that anything is achievable. I'll get a chance to run for Westminster soon and I would love you to help me, not just as a party colleague, but as my wife. I can't help it Connie, but I've fallen in love with you."

It wasn't the most romantic approach that Harry could have made but Connie knew that his words were genuine, that they came straight from the heart. They weren't words that were intended simply to impress; shadows without substance which would bring no guarantees for the future. No, Harry had given her the vision of a partnership together. One of equals where they would fight for a better world. And Connie found Harry handsome too, an important consideration given that she was a warm blooded and sensual woman. When she observed Harry, she was sure that under his quiet and measured exterior, a passion and fire raged which wouldn't disappoint her in their moments of complete intimacy. Connie therefore had no hesitation in speaking the words that Harry longed to hear.

"Yes Harry. I'd love to be your wife."

She leaned forward and kissed him softly on the cheek. It was the first intimate moment that they had shared. Turning his head towards her, Harry kissed Connie fully on the lips. Almost spontaneously the two of them stood up and embraced, Connie feeling Harry's strong arms pulling her towards him. Their kiss was long and lingering. Connie could sense the desire that he felt for her. Yet, ever the gentleman, Harry disengaged himself and took a step back, before placing his hand on hers and looking straight into her eyes.

"Thank you, Connie. You can't imagine how happy you've made me."

"And you, me," replied Connie, softly. "Come on, let's sit back down," she continued. "We need to agree on how we organise everything."

Connie's practical approach sat well with Harry. He was eager to let her take control.

"I'm happy to go along with whatever you decide Connie. You're the only person who matters in this."

It was therefore decided that they would be married at the start of the summer school holidays, at the end of July. The ceremony would be at the Register Office at All Saints and they would have a small reception for their closest friends on the following Saturday evening. Like Connie,

Harry wasn't a believer in expensive and extravagant ceremonies. In any case, having lost his mother, Harry had no other close family members to consider. Their marriage was one which would be based on love and mutual respect and both of them believed that their civil ceremony would not only prove frugal, but would also, precisely and without any fuss, outline their marital obligations to one another.

Chapter 69

It wasn't long before the happy couple had set a suitable date at the Register Office. They were both eager for the arrangements for their wedding to be well in hand. Thinking back, Connie recognised that what she found so appealing about Harry, was the fact that he had come the closest, of any man she had known, to earning her complete respect. With Harry, she was never on her guard; she trusted him implicitly. She believed that he was a force for good and that she could help him to fulfil a worthwhile political career. Connie considered that her engagement to Ralph had involved only the fulfilment of her own feelings and emotions, whereas her proposed marriage to Harry had the purpose of helping to serve the needs of others too. Contemplating the situation, Connie believed that her decision to accept Harry's proposal, was an indication of her increasing personal maturity. Her emotions hadn't been neglected however. The embraces and kisses that the pair of them had shared after their engagement, were passionate and intense. Important though, was the fact that Harry never pressed Connie to go any further, respecting the convention of no intimacy before marriage. Connie felt relaxed, never under pressure in the way that she had been with Ralph. As a consequence, the period leading up to their marriage was free of any kind of tension.

The news of their engagement was well received by their friends and colleagues. Kath in particular, had known Harry for a long time and respected him. She could see no concerns for her beloved Connie. Tom too, was genuinely pleased. He had no doubts that Harry would prove to be a loyal and devoted husband for Connie and having accepted that his own romantic notions about her were over, he took the news with exceptionally good grace.

The path of love however, rarely proceeds as smoothly as any happy couple would like. In the case of Connie and Harry however, the challenge to their future happiness came from an unexpected source.

It started in early June, when Connie was approached by a couple of party members who, as tradesmen, were working on the building of new council houses in the city. They were concerned. Corners had been cut, given that the materials being used were of poor quality. The contractor was trying to maximise their profits to the detriment of the project's future residents. The men told Connie that they had seen no evidence of any official oversight of the building programme, so leaving the contractor to do as he pleased. Having promised to respect the two men's anonymity, Connie prepared to look into their claims.

The contractor was Josiah Mulgrew and Connie had little doubt that what she had been told was true. However, she recognised that she had every reason to be prejudiced against him and therefore decided that it would be better for Harry to investigate their allegations. This also made more sense, given that he had been a recent member of the planning committee. Harry had political stature and an access to the machinery of local power, that she didn't. Consequently, when Connie saw Harry a couple of days later, she told him of the tradesmen's concerns. She asked him to take over the case, expecting that he would agree. Yet his response came as a surprise. Harry had no interest in doing so.

"I'm afraid Connie that you've been approached by a couple of disgruntled men who clearly have it in for Mulgrew. It happens all the time. They haven't received the overtime or bonuses that they think they're entitled to, so they accuse the company of contractual misdemeanours in an attempt to get even. I had to consider so many of these allegations when I was on the planning committee. None of them ever amounted to anything."

"That may be so," replied Connie, "but don't we have a responsibility to look into every such complaint, in case it's true?"

"Well, in a sense we do," replied Harry, "but these men aren't prepared to allow their names to go on the record. Surely, if they're telling the truth, they'd be willing to do that."

Connie felt exasperated. She couldn't believe that Harry was so dismissive of the men's allegations. She became animated, her voice urgent and demanding.

"They're working as sub-contractors for Josiah Mulgrew. You know what he's like. I've dealt with him and he intimidates everyone around him. If the men came forward, the least he'd do is to make sure that no other contractor in Manchester, would ever take them on again. The other possibility of what may happen, doesn't bear thinking about!"

Harry was left in no doubt about how passionately Connie felt about the matter. Yet he remained calm, his features betraying no emotion.

"I can't just accept hearsay about Mulgrew," he replied, quietly. "There are too many ridiculous exaggerations about him. I don't agree that your informants can't come out into the open."

"Many of the stories about him are true Harry," insisted Connie, struggling to remain calm. "I've met some of his victims and when I went to his office, Mulgrew made it quite clear that he could be ruthless when he had to be."

"But Connie, the record shows that he's a good citizen. There's never been any criminal charges or legal proceedings taken out against him."

"That's funny," said Connie, shaking her head. "That's exactly what he said."

She paused, giving her words time to register with her fiancé.

"You didn't want me to help Gillian and Steve, did you Harry?" she continued. "You were adamant then that Mulgrew was a reasonable man. Just like you are now."

For a moment, Connie considered the possibility that Harry wasn't being open with her about Mulgrew, but once entertained, the idea was quickly dismissed. Harry stared at her impassively. His mind was made up. He wouldn't be getting involved.

"Well, I'm not letting this go Harry. I'm going to follow it up and I'll start by going to see Mulgrew to find out what he has to say about it. After that, if I'm not satisfied, I'll approach the members of the planning committee myself. If you want to help me, you can do so at any time. I'm so disappointed with you Harry. I can't believe that you're not supporting me on this."

"I know," said Harry. "I'm sorry, but I can't risk my reputation by pushing a cause that ultimately proves misguided. My judgement will be called in to question and it would mean that when another issue comes up, my opinion would carry far less weight. It's the nature of politics Connie. The art of what's possible and what isn't. As much as I know that you're upset, I have to trust my own judgement. I have to think of the situation in the future. We've disagreed on matters in the past. Again, we just have to agree to differ. I'd never not listen to your views Connie, you know how much I respect you, but I'm convinced that I'm right. And I still believe that I was when I advised you not to get too emotionally involved with Gillian and Steve."

Connie listened carefully whilst Harry was speaking. His words reassured her to some extent and she could accept the logic behind his reasoning. That didn't, of course, alter her conviction that he was wrong. Nevertheless, she accepted his idea that they would agree to see the matter differently.

"All right Harry. I understand what you're saying, but I haven't changed my mind. I'm going to see Mulgrew and get to the bottom of this. If I think the allegations are true, then I'll take matters further."

"I wouldn't expect you to do anything less," said Harry, finally allowing himself a slight smile.

Although disappointed that Harry's support hadn't been forthcoming, Connie went ahead and contacted Mulgrew's office. She had to wait several days before receiving a response, but was finally told that he would see her on June 11th at five o'clock.

Chapter 70

June 11th was a Friday. The end of the working week when most people would be winding down towards the weekend. For Connie however, the situation was different. She had a meeting with Josiah Mulgrew to attend, at his offices on Portland Street. This time she wouldn't have Tom's support to sustain her and Harry had made it clear that he wouldn't get involved in the matter. At her previous meeting with Mulgrew, she had sensed that he respected her for having the confidence to confront him, yet behind his polite exterior, there was a hint of menace; something sinister, ruthless and terrible. Connie knew that by reputation Mulgrew wasn't a man to cross and she was about to approach him with allegations that he wouldn't appreciate. She was well aware of the huge rewards on offer from the public contracts for the existing and proposed housing estate schemes. Mulgrew had already won one and was clearly in the running to take others. Connie was well aware that he wouldn't appreciate any investigation into his affairs at this time.

Connie had been a little surprised that he had agreed to see her. What she didn't realise, was that Mulgrew was convinced that she posed no threat to his flourishing business empire. Her request for a meeting had intrigued him and he thought it possible that he may find out enough from his conversation with her, to identify where the voices of discontent had originated.

Closeted with Mulgrew in his office, Connie had been made to feel welcome by her host. He had warmly greeted her, smiling as he shook her hand and invited her to sit down. Once again, her appearance had been pleasing to him. Connie was wearing a pretty, light blue and white check, summer skirt suit, with a white blouse and blue heels. She looked delightful and he remembered the offer that he had made to her the last time she was there; that he would double her salary if she were to join his company. He couldn't imagine any potential clients or associates failing to be charmed, not only by her beauty, but her confidence and intelligence too. She was a woman of substance and one who was doing rather well for herself, having become a key member of the board of Joyce and Hitchcock since their last meeting, an appointment Mulgrew quickly congratulated her on.

Connie was surprised by his knowledge of her departure from Greenings.

"Oh yes, I make it my business to keep track of talented people Connie and you certainly fit into that category, don't you?"

Immune to any suggestions of flattery, Connie was non-committal in her reply.

"Well, I try to do my best Mr Mulgrew."

"Ah! Nonsense Connie. You shouldn't be embarrassed about your abilities. You're a very successful young woman."

He paused, noting that Connie felt uncomfortable at hearing the praise that he was giving her.

"I don't say that in order to flatter you, Connie. We both know it's the truth and by the way, please call me Josiah. I'm well aware that your visit isn't a social call, but I'd rather avoid being so formal."

"All right Josiah. Just as you wish,"

"Well, what are these concerns you have over my work for the Corporation then Connie? I'm not aware from my site managers that there are any problems."

Mulgrew was calm and confident. He was convinced that he held all the cards and that nothing that Connie could put in front of him, would threaten his hand. He sat back in his chair, relaxed as his visitor went through the accusations about the unacceptable cost-cutting that his company was carrying out.

"But Connie," said Mulgrew, after she had finished. "Where's the evidence for this? I don't see any complaints about the quality of the work carried out so far from the Corporation. They'd be on to us like a shot if we were failing to meet the necessary regulations or specifications."

"No," replied Connie, firmly. "I don't believe that they necessarily would. I came here hoping that you were going to take me seriously."

She paused, giving Mulgrew time to consider her words. His response came quickly.

"And do what?" he asked. "Do the right thing? Just like you said to me the last time we met. As far as I'm concerned and the Corporation too, everything is above board."

"But I have evidence to the contrary."

"And where did you get that evidence?" asked Mulgrew.

"You know that I can't tell you that."

"Oh, come on Connie! Are you still intent on making me out to be some kind of hoodlum?"

Connie had to admit that he was convincing. What a clever opponent she was facing. Mulgrew was right about one thing, he wasn't just a hoodlum. Tough, uncompromising, brutal even, he was still highly intelligent; a smooth operator who was able to cover every angle. It was the reason why the law had never been able to touch him. For all her passion and knowledge, Connie knew that she had met her match. Nevertheless, she wasn't about to give in.

"I think I should warn you Josiah that I won't let the matter drop. I intend to go to the planning committee and put my concerns before them."

"Be my guest Connie," said Mulgrew. "I've no intention of changing anything in terms of our materials or working practices. I don't cut corners."

Mulgrew leaned back once more in his chair. Their conversation had reached an impasse. He had enjoyed his little tussle with Connie, but it was now time to move on.

"Well, if that's all Connie, I think we've just about covered everything now. I appreciate your bringing the information to my attention. As you can see though, there's no reason for you to be concerned. My company always delivers to the highest possible standards."

"No reason for concern?" asked Connie.

"Yes. Everything is being carried out just as it should be," said Mulgrew, a serene expression on his face.

"Well," replied Connie, firmly. "We'll just see what the planning committee have to say about it."

"They'll say the same as me. I'm absolutely positive."

Mulgrew paused and looked closely at Connie before continuing.

"Connie, I like you. I admire your nerve. To come to my office not once, but twice and criticise me in the way that you have." Mulgrew paused, shaking his head and smiling appreciatively at her before continuing. "I can't think of anyone else who would dare to do that. But think of yourself Connie. Your own reputation. It won't look good to put forward an allegation that you can't prove and for what?"

Mulgrew's words were familiar, similar to those that had been used by Harry.

"I'm going to do it," insisted Connie, "because whatever you say, it is the right thing to do."

"Do you really believe that you're going to get anywhere Connie? That enough members of the planning committee will be prepared to listen to you?"

Mulgrew was starting to sound frustrated. Connie was an intelligent woman and he couldn't understand her persistence. He'd tried to deflect her criticisms as pleasantly as he could, hoping that she would recognise the impossibility of securing any action on her complaint. Because he liked her, Mulgrew wanted Connie to start acting for her own benefit. She needed to know the truth of the situation. She would get absolutely nowhere and make a complete fool of herself in the process. Mulgrew was showing a generous side to his nature that he rarely exhibited. It was a mark of the impression that Connie had made upon him. It was clear however, that her attitude wasn't likely to change.

"I have to believe that I'll be listened to," she said. "I can't accept, that in my own city, corruption could exist in the way that you're suggesting."

"What corruption?" asked Mulgrew. "I've not said anything to lead you to that conclusion."

"Yet you're so adamant that no one on the planning committee will listen to me, even before I've approached them. How on earth could you know that?"

Mulgrew sensed the satisfaction in her answer. She was convinced that she had caught him out. He looked intently at her. His head was still, his jawline strong, a powerful man with an aura of invincibility, used to subjecting others to his control. Yet when Connie looked into his surprisingly soft, brown eyes, she saw a hint of tenderness, which soon disappeared as he revealed how his influence had crept into every corner of political life.

"Here in my office Connie, I can talk honestly to you. Whatever I say is just between the two of us. The fact is that money greases the wheels of business. My contracts are safe, regardless of anything you believe you can do to change that. Leave things alone Connie. Just accept that it's the way things are."

Connie was silent. Mulgrew could see that she was thinking. He knew that she still wasn't satisfied.

"When I saw you before," said Connie, quietly, "you told me that I wouldn't believe the names of the people you've got in your pocket. Try me."

Mulgrew sighed and shook his head.

"As if I would Connie. That's between me and them."

"But you'd be telling me off the record Josiah. I couldn't use the information, could I? As you've said yourself, I'd still have no real evidence."

"It's a dangerous path you're treading Connie," replied Mulgrew. "It's better that you don't know. Just take my word for it."

"Why would it be so dangerous?" asked Connie.

"Because it would. I don't want you to get hurt."

"So, I'd be in physical danger, would I?" asked Connie. "I won't give in to threats."

Mulgrew shook his head. He was clearly disappointed at hearing her words.

"Do you honestly believe Connie, that there's any chance of you ever being in danger from me? Nothing could be further from the truth. It's what you might find out that can hurt and upset you and it's why I don't want to tell you."

Such as?" insisted Connie.

"You need to let it go," advised Mulgrew.

"No." Connie was insistent. Her stubborn streak had come to the fore and she wanted answers. "I have a right to know what it is that you're not telling me."

Mulgrew recognised her single-mindedness. Her insistent questioning and inability to accept anything other than the truth, had brought him to the verge of a critical decision. He knew that he would have to satisfy her curiosity, but by doing so it would bring her world crashing down around her. It would however, almost guarantee that she wouldn't bother him further about his contracts.

"I could give you a name. One name," he said, slowly and carefully. "I'm telling you for the last time though, leave it alone."

"Why?" asked Connie. "Why should I?"

"Because what I tell you will destroy all that youthful enthusiasm you have. You believe that all your party colleagues share your vision of a bright new world. That they always stand up for their beliefs. You don't know just how wrong you are. Be careful what you wish for. Sometimes, as they say, ignorance is bliss."

Once again there was silence. Connie was convinced by Mulgrew's claim that he had information that would shock her. Yet she had come too far now. It was impossible for her to turn back.

"Tell me the name," insisted Connie.

"I'm not sure that I should," replied Mulgrew. "I admire you, Connie. A pretty young woman with fire in her belly and a kind heart too. I don't want to upset you."

"Tell me. You have to. If it's someone close to me, I deserve to know."

"All right," said Mulgrew, "but it would have been better if you'd never come here. Nothing good will come out of this for you Connie and once I've told you, there's no going back."

He paused, giving her a final chance to pull back from the brink.

"I have to know," insisted Connie, "whatever the consequences."

"Harry Thomas," said Mulgrew, quietly. "There's your name."

Shocked by his revelation, Connie immediately sprang to the defence of her fiancé.

"I don't believe you. You're lying. Harry would never take money from you. You know that we're engaged. You're just being vindictive."

"Of course, I know that Harry's your intended. Why do you think I didn't want to tell you?" replied Mulgrew. "I made it clear that I'd no wish to upset you."

"No," insisted Connie, but her voice faltered, unable to continue. Her head was in a spin, she was recalling Harry's reluctance to accept any criticism of Mulgrew.

"You came here to threaten my business Connie and now perhaps you'll back off. Harry is just one of many. It's not just in your party, the others have people too. Labour, Liberal or Conservative, they're all the same to me. They all have their price and Harry had his. How do you think he could afford that nursing home for his mother? It cost far more than he could ever earn teaching."

Connie shook her head in disbelief. She was still in denial.

"It's not true," she repeated. "I don't believe you."

Yet the evidence seemed so strong and try as she might, she couldn't stop her lip beginning to quiver and her eyes moisten. As Mulgrew had predicted, his words had proved devastating, shaking her to the very depths of her soul.

Mulgrew took no satisfaction from the sight of Connie so clearly in distress. He was well aware that he'd effectively destroyed her dreams of a happy marriage. He had crushed so many others before her. But this time he felt differently. When he had first met Connie, she made a great impression on him. His pleasant thoughts towards her had come to inhabit a soft corner of his cold, hard heart. He thought that if he'd met someone like her when he was younger, before embarking on the construction of his criminal empire, then perhaps he would have stayed on a righteous path. Today however, the reality was that pure, kind and beautiful as she was, Connie was yet another casualty of the unforgiving world of Josiah Mulgrew.

Without a word and desperate to leave his office before Mulgrew could see the inevitable tears trickling down her cheeks, Connie got up and walked towards the door. As she turned the handle, Mulgrew called out to her.

"Forgive him Connie. Show him some compassion. Wouldn't you have done the same if it had been your mother?"

Without replying, Connie pulled open the door and was gone.

Chapter 71

Connie knew that she had a difficult weekend ahead of her. Since leaving Mulgrew's office she'd been going over the details of their conversation, in particular his revelations about Harry. Although she tried, Connie couldn't find any convincing reason why Mulgrew would have lied to her. She needed to see Harry as soon as possible and confront him with Mulgrew's allegations. Early on Saturday she telephoned him and they agreed to meet at Howard Avenue the following morning at eleven. Harry had asked her if there was a particular reason why she wanted to see him, given that they hadn't planned to meet again until Tuesday. Her response was guarded, Connie telling him that it was an important matter and that it couldn't wait.

When Harry arrived, Connie was already waiting for him at the front door. It was a warm, June morning and Connie was wearing a lightweight jacket covering a yellow shift dress and she seemed particularly attractive to Harry as she walked over to his Austin A40. Getting out of the car, Harry went to kiss her, but was surprised when his fiancé turned her cheek towards him, not meeting his lips with her own, as she usually did. Nevertheless, Harry had no idea of what lay in store for him and when Connie suggested that they take a walk down to Ardwick Green, he readily agreed. The park was only a short distance and on the way the couple made small talk, Connie making no mention of her visit to Mulgrew. Once they'd arrived, Connie suggested that they sit on a bench. She chose one in relative isolation. As yet, there weren't many adults around and any children present were too busy playing to pay much attention to them.

"It's quiet here Harry," said Connie, once they were settled. "We need to talk."

Her words were serious and measured and the first definite indication to Harry that something was wrong.

"Oh?" asked Harry, surprised and sounding not a little concerned.

"Yes. I had an appointment with Josiah Mulgrew on Friday."

"I see," said Harry, feeling relieved. He'd begun to think that she was having second thoughts about their marriage and now that didn't seem to be the case.

"You'd have been better staying away from him Connie. It's not a good idea to repeat allegations to someone as influential as Mulgrew. The last thing you want to do is get mixed up with him."

"But you do Harry."

There was a long, silent pause, as Connie stared into his eyes, searching for any signs of nervousness or unease.

"Well, Harry? she asked.

"I've had to Connie," replied Harry, who had now collected his thoughts. "Mulgrew is an important contractor and I was a member of the planning committee. I've met him many times. I may not like the man, but I had a responsibility to work with him."

"That's not what I meant Harry and I think you know that."

"I'm sorry Connie, but I'm not sure what you mean."

Harry was desperate, hoping that Connie wouldn't continue to press him for answers. Yet he knew her too well. He'd seen her in action so many times, intent on pursuing a case, a cause or an argument, to the very end. It had been her stubborn belief, her unwillingness to give into a hostile room and be prepared to court unpopularity, rather than give up her ideals, which had so attracted him when he had first seen her. Yet those same qualities were now threatening to destroy their relationship.

"I thought that it was obvious Harry. I was asking you about the work you've done for Mulgrew. The support that you've given to one another."

Connie had no intention of letting the matter drop and it now seemed clear to Harry that she had found out about his arrangement with Mulgrew. He looked at the colourful flower beds around them. Attractive yellows and reds that provided the delicate, pleasant scents that floated on the gentle breeze. It gave an impression that they were sat in the middle of the countryside, an illusion only broken by the dull hum of traffic in the distance.

"I don't know what he's told you Connie but…"

"Please don't lie to me Harry," said Connie, interrupting him.

"I've no intention of lying to you. I just want you to understand."

Connie could sense the pain in his voice. She knew that Mulgrew had told her the truth.

"Why Harry? Why did you?"

Harry was silent. Aware that their relationship was over, he was now unable to reply. Connie shared his sadness but she needed to understand why he'd sold himself to Mulgrew. Gently, she prompted him.

"Was it for your mother Harry? Mulgrew said that it was."

Harry nodded, but remained silent.

"Please Harry," continued Connie, "I have to know. If you care at all about me, you owe me an explanation."

Harry took a deep breath. Looking at Connie, he sighed.

"Yes Connie, it was."

Harry paused. Connie could see that he was thinking, considering whether he should tell her anything more. Finally, he continued.

"It's easy for you Connie. Once, it was for me. I had principles. I always believed that I would stand by them. They were the bedrock of my very existence. And then I had to stand by as my mother, the woman who had sacrificed so much for me, had to suffer. I knew that if we'd been rich, everything could have been so much easier. And I became angry. Why should she endure so much agony when, if only I had the money, I could get her the help she needed? That was Mulgrew's opportunity. He wanted help in securing contracts and he'd done his research on all the members of the planning committee and with me, he saw his chance. Mulgrew knows how to manipulate; how to bribe and corrupt and he found my weakness. He knew about my mother's condition and after he'd made a presentation to the committee, he asked to see me for a chat. I shouldn't have gone, but then I had no way of knowing what he was going to propose and when he did, it made sense. I did consider that what I was doing was wrong, but I was too weak and Mulgrew so persuasive. I convinced myself that I wasn't the only one on the take and after all, Mulgrew's company was perfectly capable of delivering the houses we needed. He was no worse than any of the other contractors. And I thought of how much I'd given to the community and how I'd never taken anything for myself. I'd helped so many people over so many years and just once I could take something, not for myself, but for my mother. So, I took what was on offer and supported Mulgrew's bids for contracts. It didn't stop me continuing my work for others. I was able to convince myself that it was a small compromise that hadn't really harmed anyone, but the reality is, that like so many others, I was in Mulgrew's pocket."

Harry paused. He took in a succession of deep breaths before continuing.

"You asked me to be honest with you Connie and I will be. I can't tell you that I'm sorry for what I've done. Given my mother's condition, I would do the same again. Despite helping Mulgrew, I've still given everything to the cause. No one can ever say that I haven't supported anyone in Ardwick who's come to me with a genuine problem."

Connie understood Harry's love for his mother and how he'd been desperate to get her the best care possible. She knew that there wasn't a better councillor in Manchester when it came to dealing with residents' problems. Yet she still couldn't agree with what he'd done.

"I know that you wanted to help your mother Harry, but what about all the other families you represent? They're also poor and unable to afford the benefits available to the wealthy few. You took advantage of their trust. They chose you to represent them. They believed in you but then you went to Mulgrew and betrayed them. You took from him what they and their families could never have, in order to benefit not only your mother, but yourself. His help in paying for a nursing home, made your life easier too Harry."

Connie paused, taking her time before delivering her judgement.

"I can't accept what you've done Harry, regardless of any reasons you give. If I do, then it means I'm complicit too. I can't ignore it and carry on as if nothing's happened."

"But I'm finished with Mulgrew now," said Harry. "I'll never be in his pocket again. Don't I deserve any compassion, Connie? What if it had been your mother?"

Harry was imploring her to forgive him, but Connie had already given a great deal of thought to this particular question. Even if she were to show him understanding, it still wasn't the crucial issue that concerned her.

"It's far more than that Harry. You kept this secret from me. It was part of your life that I knew nothing about. After Ralph, I vowed that any man I was going to marry, had to be completely open with me. I would have to be able to see into their very heart and soul, like they can see into mine. You've denied me that right Harry and I can't share my life with anyone who won't allow me to do that."

It was as Harry had expected. Connie wasn't going to forgive him and he had no alternative but to accept it. He'd been secretive, prepared to conceal his agreement with Mulgrew, believing that she would never find out. Connie was right; their relationship had been built on a lie. Harry now realised that it had been unfair to have asked her to marry him.

"What will you do now Connie?" asked Harry, quietly.

Connie stared into the face of a broken man. She had been hurt by his betrayal, but she wasn't vindictive. She had no wish to hurt Harry, although his arrangement with Mulgrew was clearly illegal. Besides, how could she prove charges of corruption against Mulgrew? He was far too clever. Allegations against him were dismissed as hearsay; there was never any firm evidence against him. Certainly, Harry wasn't going to testify against him and she also wondered just how widespread his web of deceit and corruption extended. Did it also include the police, the courts and the political establishment? Mulgrew had warned her that if she launched a crusade against him, she would appear foolish. Connie had to accept that there was little that she could do.

"I'm such a fool Harry. A fool for believing in truth and justice; for thinking that we can build a bright, new world together. I don't know who I can trust anymore. Are you and others in the Party any different to the

Tories? I don't think so. Members talk about helping the poor and the disadvantaged but in reality, how many of them truly care? That's why men like Mulgrew can buy the loyalty of you and others so easily."

Connie paused as Harry looked at her alarmed.

"Oh no, don't worry Harry," she continued. "You needn't concern yourself. You won't see me at any more meetings. I won't be there as a reminder of your indiscretions."

Harry, although stung by her fiery castigation of his behaviour, felt relieved. Connie would take her discovery no further. Nevertheless, he still felt the need to try and rebuild some bridges with her.

"Surely Connie, I know that I've behaved badly, but why do you need to give up? The Party needs people like you."

"Oh, just go Harry," replied Connie, wearily. "Just leave me please. Can't you see that I've had enough?"

Connie turned away from him, an action that underlined her words. Slowly, Harry got up from the bench and walked towards the park gates. Reaching them he turned around to look at Connie. She was still sat on the bench, staring straight ahead of her and showing no interest in his progress. He had lost her, the beautiful and vivacious woman who he'd dreamed would be by his side, helping him to win support, publicity and popularity, in his burgeoning political career. Things would be different for him now. Whatever political ambitions he may achieve in the future, he knew that without Connie, his life would always feel incomplete.

Connie continued to sit in the park for quite some time after his departure. It had been a happy place where she had played with her friends when she was young and as an adult, she often came here when she needed a peaceful place to think. She looked at the flowers and watched the birds landing and flying off, many of them dangling little insects from their beaks. And there, in the background, was the eternal hum, the drone of faraway vehicles that was the sound of the city. It was Manchester, her Manchester and for all the lies and the corruption, she would never fall out with the city and its people.

Walking home, the reality of what had happened began to prove too strong for Connie to deny that it had crushed her hopes and dreams. Her future suddenly seemed so bleak. Entering through the back door of fifteen, Howard Avenue, she sat down at the kitchen table and burst into uncontrollable sobbing. A young woman with no one to console her, whose heart had been cruelly broken for the second time in less than a year.

Chapter 72

Tom had been shocked by the news of the ending of Connie's engagement. She hadn't told anyone of the reasons for it and Tom was sensitive enough not to question her over the matter. In fact, Tom understood that beneath her tough exterior, Connie's heart was aching. As such, he made a conscious decision that the best way for Connie to overcome her pain, was for him not to acknowledge it. Connie wanted to put the past behind her and that would be impossible if those around her seemed unwilling to do so.

By leaving Greenings, Connie had been able to cut her ties with Ralph. Now, in order to sever her relationship with Harry, Connie knew that she had to withdraw from the Labour Party. The decision hadn't been too difficult to take, yet it didn't mean that she would cease to be political. Yet the political world for Connie was now one of fighting for social causes; local issues outside of any party. Mulgrew had opened Connie's eyes to the latent corruption at the heart of all political organisations. Connie knew that it didn't take much to activate it, given the egotistical ambitions of so many who entered the political game, vying for advancement and seeking any advantage to reach the pinnacle of their chosen vocation. Politicians were particularly susceptible to the delusion that only they had the vision needed to guide and protect the community. As a consequence, any methods, fair or foul, needed to secure their place in the political jungle, could be justified.

To Connie, it all seemed so ironic. Before the general election, Wilson had called on the British people to cast out the privileged 'old boys club' under the aristocratic Douglas-Home. Yet when it had happened and Labour were returned to power, what had changed? The new men, whether in government or local councils, wanted to set up their own 'clubs.' Once they had their feet under the tables of power and could enjoy all the privileges that ensued, they would never be prepared to give them up. Thinking back, Connie should have realised what was going on when, following their election victory, Labour's National Executive Committee had expelled members of the Socialist League from the Party. Although she didn't agree with the League's views, Connie now understood the significance of the expulsions. Those effectively purged, were the group most likely to bring principled opposition to the career politicians. It was the latter who wanted to control the Party in order to protect their privileges. By removing their opponents, they had effectively erased the moral conscience that could make them re-evaluate their own selfish ambitions.

Now, Connie was insistent that she would seek out 'truths.' Causes that deserved her attention and for which she would give her talents and energy to support. She therefore became involved in joining and establishing action groups. With them she would fight for the rights of the disadvantaged. It was a world that was rapidly changing in the furnace of Wilson's 'white heat of science and technology'. Yet it wasn't in the way that Labour's leader had predicted. Living in Ardwick, the planners ready to rip apart the heart and soul of the community, Connie saw first-hand that the utopian vision of high living standards, economic security and emotional well-being, would fail to materialise. As other parts of the city were being demolished, it was clear that the most vulnerable and needy, the elderly and unskilled, had become disorientated through the destruction of their familiar homes and streets. It had meant the inevitable loss of the friends and families they had lived with for so long. This was where Connie's help was needed and if people were willing for her to assist them through the terrible process of change, then she would do so.

And sometimes Tom would be beside her, sharing in her causes and offering his support. He still loved her deeply, cherishing every moment that he shared with her. Yet their relationship could only underline his vulnerability. The breaking off of Connie's engagement with Harry had briefly reignited Tom's belief that perhaps one day she could learn to love him. Yet, as the weeks became months, Tom had finally to contemplate the probability that Connie would never be his. But neither did it seem, would she be anyone else's. Connie was convinced that she would never find love again and so her life remained devoid of any romantic diversions.

Professionally, if not personally, both Tom and Connie continued to prosper. They were now an indispensable part of Joyce and Hitchcock which had bucked the trend of failing British engineering companies and was going from strength to strength. The firm was continuing to expand and had relocated part of its business to a new purpose-built industrial unit in Trafford Park. Connie had joined Tom on the board of directors, Mike insisting that she did. When she had expressed reservations about taking the position, Mike had been upset.

"I don't want you to join the board as a token woman; as a sop to feminism. I want you there because you're the only one around here who talks real bloody sense! Let's be honest, its usually women, not men, that do!"

Connie had laughed and gratefully accepted his offer, but had been shocked at his choice of language. None of the men at work ever swore in her presence. The extra responsibility had certainly helped her to keep busy. Connie never had a moment to catch her breath and so contemplate the real emotional void that lay at the centre of her life. With her work, her causes and the support of those around her, Connie was able to gradually overcome the pain suffered by the failure of her relationships with Harry and Ralph.

Chapter 73

With her continued success at work, Connie had become quite a wealthy woman. She could have moved away from Howard Avenue long ago. She was now in a position where she could have bought a house in a leafy part of a South Manchester suburb, or even out in the Cheshire countryside. Instead, she chose to remain in Howard Avenue, even though her home seemed to be existing on borrowed time. Yet Connie wouldn't entirely let go of the belief, shared by many in the community, that at the last minute, a reprieve would arrive. The Corporation would rethink their strategy and instead of building new estates, would modernise the old terraces instead. The much cheaper costs of such a policy certainly made sense. The retention of the social fabric of well-established communities, also made sense. Deep down however, Connie understood that the juggernaut of 'progressive planning,' now supported on all sides of the political spectrum, couldn't be turned back. Architects, politicians and business leaders, had invested too much into their ideas of modernity and everything old must now make way for the new.

New housing was viewed by many as the panacea that would transform all aspects of social injustice. It fitted neatly into Wilson's 'scientific revolution.' Old Britain, including its communities of terraced houses, must be razed to the ground before the new utopia could be established. There were those leaders in Manchester, like Wythenshawe's Alf Morris, who sincerely believed it, fighting continually at Westminster for extra funds for slum clearance and new building. And of course, with profits to be made from the huge construction projects that had to be undertaken, business just couldn't wait to climb on board. So, the numerous little streets with the intimacy they generated between families who had known one another for decades, were gradually replaced by concrete blocks that utilised 'the new techniques of industrial building.' And the soulless environment that the planners had created, provided nothing which its transplanted residents could recognise as familiar, removed as they were from the people and places that had anchored their lives.

Staying in Howard Avenue was also important to Connie as she wanted to be close to Kath. Connie had never had a real opportunity to establish a close relationship with her mam and since she had met Kath, the latter had gradually become the maternal figure that her real mother could never be. Kath had become a source of support and advice and she always offered her thoughts to Connie in a measured and non-judgemental way.

Connie however, was becoming increasingly concerned about Kath's health. It was the front door step that had told her that all wasn't well. Connie had noticed that it wasn't looking pristine. She hadn't mentioned it before Kath had broached the subject herself. Connie learned that Kath had been let down by a young girl who'd been receiving sixpence to brownstone it for her. The revelation came as a surprise, as Kath had always insisted that 'if you want something doing well, do it yourself.' Discreet conversations with Kath's neighbours, informed Connie that Kath was leaving the house far less than usual and often relying on their children to fetch her shopping. Yet to all and sundry, when asked if she was feeling fine, Kath would invariably tell them that she 'felt on top of the world' and that she was 'as fit as a fiddle.' But neither Connie or Kath's neighbours believed that it was true. A proud woman, Kath couldn't bring herself to admit that she was no longer capable of getting about in the way that she once had. All Connie's suggestions that she should visit the doctor, had fallen on deaf ears.

"When your time is up, I'm afraid that's it," had been her response, when Connie had tried to point her in that direction. "When the good Lord decides, then it's not our place to question. Besides, I've been too long in this world without my Stan. I'm more than ready to be with him again."

Kath had seen the alarmed expression that had appeared on Connie's face as a result of her words and had been quick in attempting to reassure her.

"Don't worry love, I'm not going right now. I've got you to think about, haven't I?"

With that, the conversation had quickly changed direction, but Connie was becoming seriously concerned. The past year had taught her that in life, heartache and disappointment were regular, albeit unwelcome visitors. Much as it pained her to recognise it, Connie began to understand that Kath wouldn't be there to support her for ever.

Chapter 74

It was the beginning of December, nine thirty on a Saturday morning and Connie was taking the short walk from her house on Howard Avenue to see Kath. It was a journey she made every weekend, keen as she was to spend time with her. Given her extra responsibilities at work, Connie found it difficult to do more than pop in briefly to see Kath during the week.

Connie walked quickly, a bounce in her step reflecting her eagerness to see her friend. Turning right at the end of Howard Avenue, she strode into Syndall Street, up past the 'Richmond' and crossed over to Apsley Grove. Then she moved on quickly past Thorp Street and Lillian Square towards the premises of 'W. Masterson Ltd,' which marked the entrance to Pleasant View. Cutting through the alley at the back of the corner house, Connie accessed Kath's tiny backyard, where she saw her friend waiting at the kitchen door.

"I thought you'd be here for the usual time," said Kath, with a smile on her face.

Her appearance was reassuring. For all the concerns that Connie had about her, she seemed in fine fettle. Kath's hair, as usual, was neatly up in place and she was wearing a well pressed, black dress and a tidy, white shawl around her shoulders.

"Come in love, I've got the kettle on ready for a brew and Charlie's fetched me some chocolate digestives from McVitie's."

Charlie was Kath's neighbour. He worked at the biscuit factory down in Stockport and as an employee, was able to get the cheap, misshapen and broken biscuits rejected by quality control. It was a fact that made Charlie very popular with the families on Pleasant View. He always made sure that he got Kath a box, especially when he learned that she only bought them to give to Connie with her cup of tea. Many of the neighbours, including Charlie, had been grateful for Connie's help. Like many of the men she'd assisted, Charlie had fallen under her spell. He was impressed by her kindness, admired her beauty and, although it was unusual for a working man to admit, he recognised that she was a woman who should be listened to.

At the mention of the biscuits, Connie expressed concern.

"Oh. I really shouldn't be eating any more chocolate."

"And why not?" asked Kath. "You've never worried about it before. It won't do you any harm. Look at you. What a pretty thing you are. And anyway, you're far too active to lose that beautiful figure of yours."

Connie, embarrassed by her comments, started to blush. Close as she was to Kath, she still felt uncomfortable when receiving compliments from her.

"Why Connie, you are a silly girl," said Kath, noticing her discomfiture. "Of course, you're pretty. If you weren't, then I wouldn't be getting my regular supply of chocolate digestives, would I?"

She winked mischievously at Connie and the two of them burst out laughing. Connie wasn't daft, of course she knew that Charlie liked her.

Sitting at the kitchen table, Connie watched Kath as she poured a small amount of water from the kettle that been boiling on the gas cooker, into a metal teapot placed on a tray by the sink. Picking up the teapot Kath ran the hot water around the inside, 'warming the pot,' before pouring it away down the sink. Satisfied, she opened up her tea caddy and took three large spoons of tea out of it and dropped them into the teapot. She then turned the gas back up on the kettle and when it whistled, picked it up and poured the boiling water into the teapot. Taking a spoon, Kath carefully stirred the contents, ensuring that the tea leaves would infuse the water with flavour before replacing the lid and covering the teapot with a multicoloured, striped cosy. Connie never tired of watching this elaborate process. It said so much about Kath. Her attention to detail; an insistence that everything should be done correctly. It reflected her pride in what she did and her desire to do the best that she could for others.

Taking a couple of small plates, mugs and the sugar bowl out of the cupboard at the far side of the chimney breast, Kath placed them on the tray, alongside the teapot and brought it to the centre of the table. She then walked over and opened the door leading to the top of the cellar steps where, in the cool environment created by the unheated cellar, she kept her perishable items. Returning with a bottle of milk and a box of chocolate digestives, Kath placed them on the table. Opening the box, she pushed it a little closer to Connie, who took out a biscuit and put it on her plate.

"Oh, go on," said Kath. "You know that you want more than one!"

She looked at Connie insistently, then smiled as her young friend placed a couple more biscuits on her plate.

Connie sighed and shook her head.

"You know me better than I know myself."

"I should hope so," replied Kath. "It wouldn't be much if I'd been around all this time and couldn't understand people by now. Would it?"

"I suppose not Kath, but not everyone has that quality. Look at me. I never saw it coming with Ralph or Harry, did I?"

Well, you're nowhere near as old as me love."

"Yes, but I've seen enough of the world to know what an unforgiving place it can be and just how selfish and inconsiderate so many people are."

Kath was concerned for her young friend's state of mind. She understood just how much Connie had been hurt by Harry and Ralph. Connie had given them her heart and they had betrayed her. Although she had put a brave face on it, her world had come crashing down, not once, but twice. Kath was well aware that Connie had thrown herself into her work and tried hard to gain solace from the help that she gave to others, in an effort to try and put her misfortunes behind her. But Connie's spirit, her soul, had been ripped asunder and Kath worried that it may never be repaired.

"You mustn't think like that love. Nothing good can come of it. Don't lose faith. Don't stop living. There is someone out there for you. I know there is," said Kath, encouragingly.

"But that's not what I meant Kath."

"Are you sure love? asked Kath, quietly fixing her eyes firmly on Connie.

Connie felt uncomfortable. She looked down, but then felt Kath's hand on hers.

"Look at me Connie. You have to live. You have to be prepared to let love into your life. It's the greatest thing that there is. You have to try again. You're such a lovely person, you deserve it."

"No, Kath. You don't always get what you deserve and I'm not sure that I've done enough to earn the right to happiness anyway. Why? I can't be arrogant and claim that."

"Now you're being silly Connie," said Kath, firmly reproaching her friend. She paused and gave her a maternal look of displeasure.

"Don't ever be so hard on yourself, young lady," she continued. "There isn't a person on this road who doesn't think that you're a little angel."

Connie shifted uncomfortably on her chair.

"I don't care if I'm embarrassing you. It's true. And besides, I'm old and that means I'm allowed to say whatever I want."

She smiled reassuringly at Connie, who realised that Kath was only being so insistent because she cared. Connie softly squeezed Kath's hand and gently smiled back.

"You're right Kath. I was thinking about men and how they've let me down. But honestly, I couldn't put myself at the whims and vagaries of any man ever again. If I only rely on myself, then I'll never have a reason to be let down or disappointed."

"But there's someone out there for everyone Connie. I truly believe that. Just because you haven't found that person yet, it doesn't mean that you won't and when you do, you'll experience true fulfilment. Love secures that. Without finding love, you'll never know what it means to be truly alive. I found it with Stan and although I was only allowed to be with him a short time, he gave a meaning to my life that has remained with me through all these years that we've been apart. And what love does for me, is that it sustains me with the hope that I will be reunited with him once again and we can be together completely for the rest of time. Only love can do that Connie and you have to pick yourself up and get out there and find it, just like Stan and I did."

Connie was overwhelmed by the power of her words. She couldn't help it as the tears slowly began to run down her cheeks. Connie knew that what Kath had spoken of was a kind of holy grail. It was what Connie had believed she had found for herself with Ralph and Harry. But she had failed and cruel torment filled her mind in those moments when she couldn't suppress such feelings through her work. Connie desperately wanted to believe that what Kath had said was true, but she was convinced that for her, it never would be. Furthermore, Connie was consumed by fear, terrified to take a chance on love, should circumstances provide her with feelings for someone else.

"Come on love. It's all right. You can let it out," said Kath reassuringly, as Connie tried to hold back the tears.

"No, I'm fine," replied Connie, with difficulty.

Connie's breathing was uneven, as she fought hard to keep her emotions in check. Gradually, with the two of them sat in silence, she regained her self-control. Kath had never intended for Connie to react so emotionally, but there was still another matter that she needed to broach with her and she hoped that it wouldn't upset Connie any further. Kath knew that sooner or later it had to be raised if, given her recent bouts of poor health, she was going to have peace of mind for the future.

"Connie love, there's something I've been meaning to talk to you about and I think now is as good a time as any."

"No, don't worry," said Kath, seeing the look of anxiety on Connie's face. "Everything's fine. I've had time to do some thinking and you know how we are when we get old, we have to consider what we'd like to happen when our time comes."

Kath's words weren't at all reassuring. Connie was seized with panic. She reached out to hold Kath's hand, fearing that she was about to reveal some terrible secret that concerned her impending demise. Connie found herself staring into Kath's eyes, desperate for reassurance. Kath mustn't leave her now. Not when she needed her so badly.

Noting her distress, Kath was touched. She loved Connie. She had become like a daughter to her. If ever Kath needed reassurance that in what she was about to say, she was doing the right thing, it was encapsulated in this tender moment between them.

"No, love. I'm sure I'll be here for some time yet. It's just that I've made preparations for when I'm not and I wanted to ask you if you'll be the one to take care of my wishes."

"Of course," said Connie.

She was relieved that, for the moment, there was no impending crisis in terms of Kath's health. Nevertheless, she was still uncomfortable with the fact that Kath was talking about her death. Younger and not having had to come to terms with the loss of someone close, her father having died before she could have any real knowledge of him, Connie had no desire to face up to the reality of human mortality. Inexperienced in such matters, she couldn't fully understand how, as people got older, preparing for their death was a normal process. For the working classes especially, it was something that couldn't be left to chance. Provision had to be made to ensure a proper Christian burial and one that had to be paid for. Kath was old enough to have seen the ignominy of those who'd been given a pauper's funeral. It was a terrible way to leave this world, with little in the way of dignity. Life had been tough; the working classes had been consistently downtrodden. Death and a hope of eternal salvation, where there were no distinctions between rich and poor in God's heaven, should be properly prepared for.

"Come with me," said Kath, "we need to go up to the back bedroom."

Kath got up from her chair and moved over to the door at the bottom of the stairs. She opened it and climbed up to the small landing, gripping the hand rail tightly and pausing at the top to regain her breath. Connie, who'd been following slowly behind her, could see further evidence of how Kath's health had deteriorated. Climbing the stairs hadn't been a problem to her not so long ago, but now it clearly was. Connie thought of asking Kath to consider moving her bedroom down to the front room, as many elderly people did. She realised however, that Kath would proudly dismiss such notions, unprepared to admit to her physical limitations, regardless of the fact that deep down she accepted that they were real.

Going into the back bedroom, Kath told Connie to sit on the end of the bed while she went to the chest of drawers opposite. Opening the top drawer, she pulled out an old 'Huntley and Palmer' biscuit tin. They were the vessel of choice for the older generation. Airtight, they were safe receptacles for any important papers, bank books, letters or certificates that the family held. Closing the drawer, Kath sat down beside Connie on the bed, the biscuit tin resting on her lap. Removing the top, she placed it next to her. Inside the tin, Connie could see a collection of papers and several old envelopes containing letters that had been sent to Kath over the years and which clearly had sentimental meaning to her. Kath rummaged under these various documents and pulled out a book which she then lay beside her, returning to the tin to locate and remove a long, thin envelope. Putting the tin down on the bed, she opened the envelope. Inside was a document and as Kath unfolded it, Connie was able to read the words 'Last Will and Testament,' at the top of the page. Connie was surprised to see such a document, private and personal as it was. She felt slightly disconcerted, unsure as to why Kath was so insistent that she should see it. It wasn't long however, before the answer was forthcoming.

"I need to show you this Connie, as I've named you as the executor and beneficiary of my will."

Kath paused in order to give Connie the chance to take in the information and if she wished, lodge an objection to it. Connie was quiet however, shocked by Kath's revelation. It seemed more formal and final than the request previously made by Kath, about taking care of her wishes.

"As you know," continued Kath, "I've no relatives, but I've come to think of you as part of my family. I would feel very content to know that when I'm gone, you're there to see that I get a proper send off."

Connie took her hand and squeezed it softly.

"You're not going anywhere yet," said Connie, firmly.

"I would hope not," replied Kath. "But when you get older yourself Connie, you'll realise that you want everything settled. It gives you peace of mind."

Kath could see Connie looking at her reproachfully, but she simply smiled.

"Don't worry love. It's such a reassurance to know that you're here for me. The will's legal, drawn up by a solicitor and properly witnessed. It has to be Connie, so that I can make it clear that you're to get any property and money that I have. There isn't very much of course, but I've always been thrifty and I've managed to build up a little nest egg in the bank."

Kath paused in order to put down the will and pick up the bank book. Connie could see that it was from the 'Manchester and Salford Trustee Savings Bank.' Opening it, Kath flicked through its pages, coming to

the most recent entry. It showed that the account amounted to a total of
£282 2s 8d.

"You can see Connie, that I've managed to put away quite a bit."

Connie nodded. She was impressed with Kath's achievement.

"It's surprising how a couple of 'bob' a week mounts up over the
years. You don't need to spend too much on my funeral Connie. You
should have well over £200 for yourself.

"But I don't need anything Kath."

Kath could see that Connie was starting to get upset.

"I know you don't Connie. But that's not the point. If I can't leave
you anything, then I'm being denied the satisfaction that something
good will come from my savings and hard work. You're not taking
anything from me Connie, you're giving me a sense of contentment.
Something that I may never have had, if I hadn't met you."

Kath put her arm around Connie's shoulders and pulled her close.
Connie finally understood that it was right to accept her wishes without
any misgivings. It meant respecting Kath's right to choose.

"I've left instructions in the will on the arrangements I want for my
funeral. I want you to use the Co-op and I want burying together with
Stan and Alice in Southern Cemetery. You'll find all the details in
there."

Kath pointed towards the will at the side of her and nodded,
emphasising to Connie the importance of the information it contained.

"Okay Kath," said Connie, quietly.

Satisfied that she had Connie's support, Kath folded the will back
up, put it in its envelope and placed it in the tin. She then stood up and
put the tin back in the top drawer in the chest opposite.

"The tin will stay in this drawer, so you'll know where to find it
Connie. There's another couple of tins on top of the wardrobe as well
love. There are some special items and letters in there from Stan. I've
never shown them to anyone, but I'd be pleased to think that you'll read
them after I've gone."

Connie nodded.

"Come on then," said Kath, "we'd best get back downstairs. We'll
need to think about what we're going to have for dinner."

It was a rather commonplace remark on which to end what had been
a deep and emotional conversation, but Connie appreciated it. There
was now an opportunity to return to normality; to settle down, relax and
talk about everyday matters. Later however, when she had returned
home, Connie knew that today's events had marked an important point
in her relationship with Kath. Kath wasn't just preparing herself for her
departure from this world, but was also trying to ensure that Connie

would be ready too. Yet Connie knew that she never would be. It would leave a huge void in her life, if Kath was no longer there. Not wanting to face such a bleak prospect, Connie hoped that Kath's health would improve. She desperately wanted to believe that Kath would always be in the background, to make sure that everything was all right. But as the days passed, Connie realised that she was deluding herself and hard as it was to accept, the most important thing she could do was to remain strong for her friend and fully appreciate the time that they still had together.

Chapter 75

As they had done previously, Connie and Kath spent Christmas Day together at Pleasant View. They were certainly 'family' now. Their concern for one another, their love of each other's company, had brought them so close together. The age difference between them had, from the moment they'd met, meant nothing. Kath, although advanced in years, was ever youthful in her attitude to life. She had no emotional investment, as did many of her contemporaries, in the concept of the 'good old days.' The latter was an idea that became ever stronger as many young people seemed to be challenging the social conventions and traditions, that the older generation had grown up with. Many of the latter were irritated by the new freedoms that young people seemed to be enjoying, without accepting the responsibilities that they themselves had been told were so important. Yet Kath didn't agree. She saw hope in the rebelliousness of youth; a guarantee that present and future generations wouldn't fall prey to patriotic and political exploitation.

Kath loved having Connie around her and constantly related her achievements to her friends and neighbours, just like any proud mother would do. This Christmas however, she had struggled to cope but Connie had arrived early at six thirty, claiming that she would feel guilty if she didn't help with the preparations for the meal. Although Kath had reproached her, Connie knew that she was relieved and certainly, unlike last year, Connie's assistance had been needed, as Kath seemed in danger of being overwhelmed. The day had been special. There was an unspoken feeling on both sides, that this could be the last Christmas Day they would share together. Yet neither woman was prepared to allow the mood to become melancholic, rather they wished to enjoy and celebrate the time they did have. The day had made it abundantly clear however, that Connie now had to accept that Kath would increasingly need her support.

And this was when the long-standing network of friends and neighbours came into its own. Connie's concerns were shared by the community around Pleasant View. Young and old, many had known Kath all their lives, which meant that there was always someone to check on her throughout the day. To help tidy up or run errands to the shops and pick up her pension from the post office. Tom too, was a regular visitor, having found out from Connie about Kath's poor health. He'd always appreciated her wealth of knowledge and experience and eagerly listened to the accounts of her exploits in her youth. Connie had wanted to move in with Kath, but she would have none of it, telling her off in the manner of a strict, elderly schoolmarm.

"Don't be silly young lady. You're only around the corner and you've got to concentrate on that job of yours. I expect great things of you and running around after me isn't going to get in the way of it!"

Connie had shaken her head, but knew that it was no good arguing. Besides, she was always at Kath's at six thirty in the morning, before catching the bus to work and would then spend time with her in the evening and over the weekend. It had soon got to the stage however, when Kath had to admit that she could no longer manage the stairs. Connie found out when finding her asleep on the settee in the kitchen, when she'd arrived earlier one morning than Kath had anticipated. She was adamant however, that she wouldn't have her bed brought downstairs, but would continue to use the settee. Connie understood that Kath could never admit to her physical weakness. She had no wish to be treated as an invalid. The pride and self-reliance that she'd shown throughout her challenging life, was not about to be discarded now. It also meant that Kath consistently refused Connie's requests for her to see the doctor.

"Why?" said Kath. "I'm old. I'm like a well-used machine that has started to wear out. I'm like everybody my age."

"Yes," replied Connie, "but perhaps the doctor could help. They might have medicines to make you feel a little better."

Kath had laughed.

"I don't think that the 'quack' will be able to give me some miracle tonic. No, I've just got to get on with it love."

It was a testing time for Connie. A period in which the awful truth of Kath's deteriorating condition, hung over everything she did. Yet she realised that it was Kath, not herself, whose time in this world was drawing to its close and as much as it hurt and upset her, she knew that she had to be strong for her friend.

In reality however, the strength came from Kath. She understood implicitly how much Connie needed her. She was determined to change Connie's perspective on what was about to happen and to reassure her that what lay in store would be a beginning and not an end.

"I've always had faith Connie. I've always believed that eventually, I would be reunited with Stan. That time has come now and it's not something that's sad. I'm looking forward to being with him again. Faith sustains us Connie and you mustn't feel upset."

"I know," replied Connie.

"Do you?" asked Kath. "Do you really understand what this life is all about?"

Connie was confused. She was unsure what her friend was getting at.

"You've done so well for yourself Connie. I feel so proud when I tell everyone about what you've achieved at work and how kind and generous you are, giving up your time to help others. But that's not what's truly important. You need to find love, true love Connie. Without that, you'll never find any real fulfilment in life."

Connie nodded. She couldn't find the words to respond. Her relationships with men had been disastrous, but she had no wish to relay any negative sentiments at this poignant moment.

Kath understood what she was thinking.

"I told you Connie. We must have faith. A belief that life will turn in our favour; that our hopes and dreams will be recognised. You've had it tough, that I can't deny. You've been let down, but there is someone out there for you and you will fall in love and together, your lives will be complete. It's the purpose of life. The union of a man and a woman. It will take you to levels of joy and happiness, such as you can't possibly imagine."

She paused and once again Connie nodded silently in acknowledgement of her words.

"I know it's difficult for you Connie, but give yourself time and don't close your heart. You'll do that for me, won't you love?"

Connie took her hand and looked straight into her eyes.

"I will try. I promise."

Kath sensed the honesty of her words and smiled.

"Yes, I think you will."

It was the last deep and serious conversation that the two women were to have. It seemed as if, having made her plea to Connie and given her advice, Kath was satisfied that she'd completed her final, necessary task, before it was time to join Stan. From that point on, Kath's condition deteriorated rapidly. Now she was in no position to refuse a visit from the doctor and unable to deny his support for Connie's purchase of a bed settee for the front room. Connie finally moved into Pleasant View. Aware that time was short, Tom had arranged for Connie to have an extended holiday. Her entitlement had mounted up as Connie hadn't taken a single day off since starting at Joyce and Hitchcock. Now, she would be solely focused on Kath.

Her final hours came on Saturday, February 6th. Connie and Tom were sat with her in the front room as she lay on the bed settee. She'd been sleeping on and off throughout the morning and into the afternoon, listening to the conversation between her friends in her waking moments and smiling warmly at them. At around three o'clock she had taken Connie's hand and spoken weakly to her.

"Remember what I said Connie. Have faith."

Connie looked at Kath warmly and stroked her hand. She smiled and nodded in acknowledgement of her words.

"I know Kath."

Focusing one more time on Connie, Kath repeated her words.

"Have faith."

Then, her eyes closed and Connie felt Kath's soft hand relax in hers.

Connie sensed instantly that her friend had slipped away. She stared at Kath, her face serene and still. She looked at her chest but could see no signs of it rising or falling.

"Tom. You need to go next door to fetch Mrs Baker. I think Kath has gone."

"Are you sure you're okay to be here alone Connie."

"Yes. Go on Tom."

Tom moved quickly through to the kitchen, out into the backyard and went round to Mrs Baker's back door. In her sixties, Mary Baker had far more experience of bereavement. She knew how to check for signs of life, had washed and laid out the bodies of her neighbours and elderly relatives. Like so many women of her generation, she provided the practical skills necessary to guide those emotionally traumatised, through the process of loss.

Returning with Tom, Mary quickly but carefully, examined Kath. Satisfied, she turned to Connie.

"Yes love. Kath's gone."

Her words, although quietly spoken, brought a resounding confirmation of Connie's fears. A recognition that she had lost her closest friend and confidante. Suddenly, Connie burst into violent and uncontrollable sobbing. Tom, in expectation of such a reaction, had already put his arm around her and now he pulled her close, gently rubbing her shoulder.

"It's all right love. Have a good cry," said Mary, reassuringly. "She was a good 'un. There's not many like her anymore."

"That's true," said Tom, in agreement.

Waiting until Connie's tears had begun to subside, Mary then told Tom what they would need to do next.

"Take Connie into the kitchen Tom. I'll go for the doctor. They'll need to confirm that Kath's passed away for the death certificate. I'll contact the Co-op too, so they can take Kath to the chapel of rest. I won't be long and then I'll come back with my friend Gladys, so we can wash and layout Kath after the doctor's finished."

"Thank you. You've been very kind," replied Tom.

"It's only what Kath has done for so many others. We all try to be there for one another, love."

Mary slipped out of the front door and Tom helped Connie into the kitchen, settling her down on a chair at the table.

"I'll get the kettle on Connie. A drink of tea will do you good."

Connie didn't reply. Staring around the kitchen, it suddenly seemed so empty without Kath's larger-than-life personality to fill it with warmth and humour. She looked as Tom busied himself at the cooker. She'd really appreciated his support over the last few weeks. His help had been given willingly and it was clear to her that Kath had made a huge impression on him too.

It wasn't long before Mary and Gladys returned. When the doctor arrived, Tom explained how Connie was effectively Kath's next of kin, so that he would provide her with the paperwork that she would need to arrange the Funeral. Shortly after, the undertaker arrived and Kath was soon on her way to the chapel of rest. Deeply upset, Connie had been unable to play any kind of role in the afternoon's proceedings. It was clear that after the stress and pressure of caring for Kath, the latter's passing had suddenly left her feeling tired and listless. Mary suggested to Connie that it was best for her to let Tom take her home. She would need a good night's sleep so that she could prepare herself for arranging the funeral and dealing with Kath's personal effects.

Physically and emotionally drained, Connie complied with the suggestion and Tom took her back to Howard Avenue. Going straight to bed, she fell into a long and deep sleep as soon as her head hit the pillow.

Chapter 76

Connie had slept until nine o'clock the following morning. Coming downstairs and entering the kitchen, she was surprised to see Tom sat drinking a cup of tea at the table.

"Morning Connie. Are you feeling a little better?"

"Yes, a little. I don't feel so tired now."

"Good."

Tom smiled, reassured that she seemed to be coping much better than when they had left Kath's yesterday.

"When did you get here?" asked Connie.

"Yesterday. With you," said Tom, looking confused.

"Oh," said Connie. "You didn't go home then?"

"No. I fell asleep on the settee. I thought you might need me again. It was all right to stay, wasn't it?"

Connie could sense his anxiety that he may have upset her. She smiled at him weakly.

"Of course, it was Tom. I appreciate your help. You've been a good friend to me and to Kath too."

"I hope so," replied Tom, quietly. "Would you like me to make you some toast or cereals?"

Connie looked at him with a marked lack of enthusiasm.

"I know that you probably don't feel hungry Connie," continued Tom, "but you didn't eat anything at all yesterday. You need to keep your strength up. There are lots of things you'll have to do in order to carry out Kath's wishes."

Tom's comment had the desired effect and soon he and Connie were sat eating toast and marmalade at the kitchen table.

"I need to go over to Kath's and collect her papers, Tom. Would you like to come with me?"

"Yes, of course I would."

"I'm sure I'll be fine, but I might find it a little difficult without Kath being there."

Tom nodded.

"Can you go into the front room please Tom, whilst I have a wash and get changed?"

"Of course."

Tom had washed his hands and face earlier but was now conscious of the fact that he would have preferred to have a change of clothes himself, having slept in them on Connie's settee. Making his way into the front room, Tom didn't have to wait too long before Connie came in to fetch him. Wearing a beige blouse under a white jumper, with blue slacks, she had dressed plainly. Nevertheless, Tom thought that she looked absolutely beautiful.

Entering through Kath's back door, Connie walked into the kitchen, followed by Tom. She immediately felt the welcoming atmosphere that Kath had always laid on for her. It was reassuring. She felt as if Kath's spirit still inhabited Pleasant View. Connie's eyes were drawn towards the 'Bretby' vase on the mantelpiece. The token of love given by Stan to his wife. She went over and picked it up, looking once again at the red, white, green and brown lines of colour merging together under the glaze. Immediately, she remembered Kath's final words to her. "Have faith."

That she'd focused on the vase before anything else, surprised Connie. It was as if Kath was directing her and reinforcing the message about finding love. Connie took a deep breath and put down the ornament. The tears had begun to well up in her eyes, but she coughed and somehow held them back. Kath wouldn't want her to be sad, she knew that. But it was so difficult not to be.

"Are you all right Connie?" asked Tom, concerned that she had continued to remain silent since they'd entered the house.

Connie had her back towards him, so he couldn't see her face. Fortunately, it allowed her to compose herself and gather her thoughts.

"Yes. Yes Tom, I'm fine."

She turned quickly away from the fireplace and walked towards the bottom of the stairs, determined to stay calm.

"We need to go upstairs, Tom."

Tom followed her out of the kitchen and up the stairs and into the back bedroom.

"If you take the stool from over there," said Connie, pointing to the corner of the room, "you'll be able to see on top of the wardrobe. There are a couple of biscuit tins up there, Tom. Can you bring them down please?"

"Yes, of course," replied Tom who, following her instructions, brought down the tins and placed them on the bed next to where Connie was sitting.

"They contain Kath's letters from her husband Stan," explained Connie. "I'll take them home with me to read later. I don't think I could cope at the moment. I'll get too upset."

"Yes. You're probably right Connie. It's a hard task that you've got before you. Yet don't forget that Kath chose you specially to do it for her. It's upsetting, but it's also an honour."

"Yes, I know," said Connie, who proceeded to open the top drawer of the cabinet containing the 'Huntley and Palmer' biscuit tin.

"I have Kath's will in here Tom. She's got everything planned to perfection. She gave me my orders to take it down to the probate office, so that I'd be able to organise the funeral and collect her savings."

Tom smiled and then chuckled softly, shaking his head in the process.

"Kath certainly knew what she wanted Connie. She never did anything by halves."

"No, she didn't," replied Connie, smiling in return.

"Do you want me to come to the probate office with you Connie. We could go tomorrow morning if you like."

"But what about work Tom. Don't you have to be there?" asked Connie.

"No, I can take a couple of days off to help you," replied Tom. "It's not easy arranging a funeral if you've never done it before. It's not something that people of our age have much experience of, is it?"

"No, it isn't thankfully," replied Connie. "It's good of you to offer Tom," she continued. "I've really appreciated your help."

It was agreed. Connie and Tom locked up at Pleasant View and took the three biscuit tins back to Howard Avenue. Tom stayed until teatime then, confident that Connie would be able to cope without him, went home ready to return next morning to help with the arrangements for Kath's funeral.

Chapter 77

With Tom's help, Connie had carried out Kath's wishes. She had arranged the funeral through the Co-op and now that she possessed the rights to Kath's burial plot in Southern Cemetery, had ensured that once again Kath was united with her beloved Stan and daughter Alice. This time for eternity. With Tom and a number of Kath's oldest friends, Connie had ridden in the funeral car from Pleasant View, accompanying the hearse on its journey to the cemetery. On arrival, Connie was overwhelmed by the attendance at the chapel, so many friends and neighbours having gathered to pay their respects to a remarkable woman. Back at Pleasant View, Kath's house was full to bursting. It was a time of sadness but also one of celebration, as Connie was regaled with stories from Kath's past. Older friends recounted tales of her indomitable spirit, her struggles for the union and her enthusiasm to create a better world in the dark days of the 'Thirties.' There was a succession of neighbours who recounted the times that they had turned to Kath for advice and how she had never refused to help them. And there was the comment that made Connie cry, when Mary Baker talked of the similarities she saw between Kath and Connie herself.

"You're so like her Connie. Kath helped everyone. Always gave of herself. She loved you so much because she saw exactly the same in you. A genuine love for people and a willingness to give your time to anyone who needs it."

It was a difficult day but Tom and Kath's neighbours had helped her through it. There were still of course, a few practical tasks that had, of necessity, to be completed. The formal closing of Kath's savings account and its transfer to Connie was relatively straightforward, as was the return of Kath's pension book. Connie had Kath's 'Bretby' vase and rings with her in Howard Avenue. They would always be a physical reminder of her and if she ever did marry, Connie was determined to wear Kath's wedding ring as her own. There were still other items however, especially the furniture. Connie therefore asked Kath's neighbours to take any pieces they would find useful. A few days after the funeral, Connie believed that she had done everything that Kath would expect of her and so called the landlord and told him that she would hand over the keys and pay the final week's rent. It was the last time she would ever set foot inside Pleasant View.

Connie still had a few days before she had to return to work and over the weekend, she finally felt able to go through the biscuit tins of memories that Kath had asked her to look at after she was gone. Connie realised that she must have had a purpose in doing that, but it didn't become clear until after she had carried out her wishes. Opening the tins, she found some additional photos of Stan in his army uniform and of Alice and Kath's mother. There were also official letters informing Kath that Stan had been wounded, including one from his officer. Stan's medals were also present in one of the tins, but most important and personal to Kath, were the letters that he had written to her from Egypt, Gallipoli and France. Many had been censored; words revealing Stan's location, blacked out. Nevertheless, Stan's outpourings of affection, his obvious intent to write about nothing that could upset his beloved, shone through the pages. It was then that Kath's purpose became apparent. She wanted Connie to know the depth of feeling and fulfilment that came from finding real love. She wanted Connie to never give up on the search for the man who would provide that for her. She'd known that her message would become far more compelling, if Connie understood that it was the last one that she would ever give to her.

Yet, to a great degree, Connie was still grieving and Kath's final message still remained in the realms of her subconscious. When she returned to work, she was almost mechanical in her application to the tasks in front of her. It was as if her daily routine shielded her from the emotional vulnerability exposed by the loss of her friend. Connie functioned effectively, but no thoughts about how she might secure her future personal happiness, entered her head. Kath would have told Connie that she was still 'playing safe.' Terrified of taking a chance on any other man, she was effectively in a state of emotional paralysis.

To those around her however, Connie seemed as confident and assured as ever. Her return to work was seamless. Tom and Mike were amazed by how quickly she was on top of the new business initiatives that had emerged in her absence. To Tom, it seemed as if she no longer had need of his support and had fully recovered from the trauma of losing Kath. It therefore made it easier for him to take a decision that he had been weighing up for some considerable time. As Joyce and Hitchcock continued to expand, Tom had been coming into contact with some large and powerful new clients in the south. His reputation as a young, dynamic business executive was growing and it hadn't been long before informal contacts had been made and offers had been presented to him, providing an opportunity to seriously advance his career. It was something that had never interested him whilst ever there was a chance that Connie may learn to love him. But for a long time now he'd accepted that the chance was gone and although he was a proud Mancunian, who loved the city, its draw wasn't great enough to stop him moving away from the region to pastures new. When he saw how focused Connie seemed to be on her job and how content she appeared, he felt that if ever there was a time to move on, it was now. His beloved Connie seemed to have no further need of him.

Tom had therefore taken the fateful decision at the end of March. He'd received another approach and had been asked by the company to informal discussions in London. Honourable as ever, he'd informed Mike that he was going to listen to what they had to say and was assured by the latter, that it wouldn't impact on his position if he decided that he wanted to stay. Mike still believed that the company hadn't finished with its own plans of expansion. The conversations in London had gone well however and a firm offer was put on the table. It was one that Tom would find very difficult to turn down. He was given a week to come to a decision.

Returning to Joyce and Hitchcock, Tom had informed Mike of the offer and was told to take his time. Mike made it clear that he would like Tom to stay, but would understand if he decided to move on. The two men were the only ones who knew about the situation, until a couple of days later when Mike inadvertently made Connie aware of the fact that Tom may be leaving. It had happened when he casually asked her if she'd feel comfortable taking on aspects of Tom's role within the company.

"Why?" asked Connie. "Is Tom taking on some new responsibilities?"

"No. It's just in case he decides to take that job in London."

"What?" asked Connie, clearly surprised.

By her reaction, Mike realised that Connie was unaware of Tom's offer.

"Oh," said Mike, rather hesitantly. "I assumed that Tom had already told you. It seems that he hasn't."

"No," said Connie, shaking her head in disbelief. "Why would he want to leave?"

"I suppose," replied Mike, "because he sees it as a different opportunity. A new challenge. But shouldn't you ask him yourself Connie?"

Connie didn't answer. She was finding it difficult to process the information that he'd given her.

"Has he told you if he's likely to take the job?" she asked, eventually.

"No, not yet," replied Mike. "They've told him to take a few days to think about it."

Mike was surprised by Connie's reaction. Usually she was so calm, but now she was clearly ill at ease. He could only conclude that she was upset at the thought of Tom leaving.

"Are you all right Connie?" asked Mike, becoming a little concerned.

"Yes. Yes of course," replied Connie, rather unconvincingly.

Mike nodded.

"Well, Mike. If that's everything, I'd best get back to my office."

"Yes, thanks Connie."

Mike watched her as she left the room. She was unwilling to discuss Tom any further with him. Yet it was clear that the news had come as an unexpected shock and the indications were that she would be upset if Tom left and Mike expected that he would.

Back in her office, Connie immersed herself in work. She knew that she needed time to digest Mike's news and try to understand why she had reacted so emotionally. Her mind had always shown an independent capacity to mull over problems and provide solutions. She was confident that when she returned home and could quietly reconsider her feelings, that she would have the understanding she sought.

Sat in the front room, with the radio on quietly in the background, she went over her conversation with Mike. She recognised that his words hadn't just shocked her, but they had induced a feeling of panic. Yet why was that? Was it because she'd relied so heavily on Tom's support with Kath's passing? Did she feel that she may need him again, especially as without Kath, there was no one else to turn to? Or was it more than that? Something else?

It seemed a lifetime ago when she had turned down Tom's request to go out with her and how afterwards she'd told Paula that she would never think of Tom as anything other than a friend. And, except for their disagreement over Ralph, the two of them had been just that, the closest of friends. Tom had stood by her. He'd never lied to or betrayed her and shown no hint of disappointment when she'd agreed to marry Harry. Tom had remained steadfast and predictable. Connie could see that throughout the time she'd known him, Tom had never changed. Yet what was different and had altered her perception of Tom, was that she had changed through the experiences she had gone through with Ralph and Harry. For the first time, Connie realised that the qualities Tom possessed, that had once seemed so unexciting, were now the very ones that would provide her with security, contentment and yes, love. Kath had told her that she would find that special person, as long as she never gave up. The discovery however, had come so unexpectedly. It had been triggered by the possibility that Tom would be leaving. It had brought Connie to her senses. Had made her realise that the source of her future happiness, had lain so close to her all this time. And now she realised it was a race against the clock. Connie must see Tom quickly and let him know that she didn't want him to leave, before he took the irrevocable decision to go to London and so be lost to her for ever.

Chapter 78

Next morning Connie took an earlier bus than usual to work. She knew that Tom was always there before her, so today she arrived at seven thirty and went straight to his office. He wasn't there but Connie stayed to talk to Olive, who was finishing off dusting his desk and cabinets.

"You're early this morning, aren't you love?" said Olive, smiling at Connie.

"Yes Olive. I was hoping to catch Tom, in case he was going off site."

"He's always so busy love, isn't he?" asked Olive.

"Yes, he is."

"I keep telling him that he needs to slow down a bit," replied Olive. "But he never seems to listen. I'm surprised he's not here now. He often turns up before I've finished."

As if on cue, Tom appeared, surprised to see Connie in his office.

"Hello Connie. Is everything all right?"

"Yes, fine Tom."

"Good."

Tom smiled, waiting for Connie to give him an indication of why she was there. Yet Connie was silent and Olive, recognising that she wanted to speak privately to Tom, excused herself.

"Well, I can't be hanging around here chatting. I haven't got around to doing Mike's office yet."

Tom thanked Olive for her work and once she'd left the room, Connie closed the door.

"Sit down Tom, I'd like to talk to you."

Tom smiled. It was his office, but it was just like Connie to take charge. He sat down, curious to find out what was on her mind.

"Mike assumed that you'd told me about your job offer in London, so he mentioned it yesterday. I hope you're not disappointed that I know," said Connie.

"Of course not," replied Tom. "Why should I be?"

"Well, I was surprised that you didn't tell me, Tom. I thought that there might be a reason."

"No, Connie. Of course not," replied Tom.

Connie could see that Tom was concerned that his actions may have upset her. Quickly, she tried to assure him that it hadn't.

"It's all right that you didn't Tom."

"I'm sorry Connie," replied Tom. "I didn't think that you'd be that interested in knowing and you've had a lot to deal with lately, so I felt it wasn't that important."

"Oh," said Connie, quietly.

Tom detected a sense of disappointment in her answer, but he couldn't understand why. Silent, he waited for her to continue.

"I'd like to talk to you about your offer Tom," continued Connie, "but not here. Can we walk down to Cringle Park at dinner? The weather's going to be fine. We can sit in the fresh air. It's better for us to discuss it there. That is, if you've no objections."

Connie's request was puzzling. Tom had genuinely felt that Connie wouldn't have any interest in his job offer and certainly wouldn't want to make any input into his decision, but now she was making it clear that she did. He welcomed the opportunity to hear her advice, yet not for a moment did he consider that she may have another reason for wanting to speak to him.

"Yes, of course. I'd love to hear what you think about the job Connie and it'll be nice to get out of the office and sit in the park. I'll enjoy that."

Having agreed to go, Tom spent the rest of the morning finding it hard to concentrate on his work. He was unable to stop his mind wandering on to the consideration that this may be the last time he would ever share a personal and for him, intimate moment with Connie. Eventually though, it was quarter to one and the two of them walked the short distance down Crossley Road and across into Cringle Fields Park, where they took a seat on the bench in the shelter. It was a pleasant spring day. A little 'nippy,' but in their outdoor coats, the two of them felt comfortable enough to sit and talk. Connie asked him about the offer. She noted that he didn't speak with any particular enthusiasm for the job, a fact that suggested to her that he was still undecided as to whether he would take it. Nevertheless, she couldn't deny that it was an excellent opportunity. The salary and bonuses were well in excess of his earnings at Joyce and Hitchcock and she had no doubt that Tom would be a success and inevitably take his career even further.

"Are you really sure that you want the job?" asked Connie.

"Well," answered Tom, thoughtfully. "It makes a lot of sense to take it."

"But you're happy here Tom. Effectively, you're second only to Mike. He's a decent boss Tom. You work well with him and he's still ambitious. You never know how far the company can go."

Tom was surprised. For a moment he wondered if Mike had put her up to this, but the thought was soon forgotten. Mike would never pull such a stunt and even if he tried to, Connie would certainly not have agreed to it. But Tom still couldn't understand why Connie was trying so hard to persuade him to stay.

"If I did leave Connie, you'd become Mike's number two. He thinks the world of you. I'm sure that you would be now, other than for the fact that I moved here before you did."

It was a typically modest response from Tom, but Connie was having none of it.

"No," said Connie, firmly. "Don't be so silly! We need you here. You're really important to the company and we won't be able to replace you!"

There was clear displeasure evident in her answer, but Tom took it as a positive indication that Connie wanted him to stay. And that forced him into a brave decision. He would take one final chance to try and win Connie's hand. From deep inside emerged a confidence that he'd never previously shown, when talking intimately to the woman who he'd never stopped loving. Turning to Connie, he looked directly into her eyes.

"You say 'we.' That the company needs me. What about you?"

Connie looked down. She didn't reply.

"What about you, Connie?" insisted Tom.

Connie's head was in a spin. Everything seemed to be going too fast. She had hoped that her talk with Tom would secure the result of persuading him that he would be far happier to stay. Beyond that their relationship could be nurtured carefully over time. But, as she was about to find out, Tom wasn't going to allow her that luxury.

"I need to know Connie. I need to know that you want me to stay. That you don't want me to leave for London. I need to know that you will be that special person for me, my friend and lover who I've dreamed of being with forever."

Tom placed his hand gently under her chin and raised her face, so that once more she was looking straight into his eyes.

"You're the only reason I would stay Connie, but if you don't want me, completely, it's best that I go."

Tom was transformed. He was so certain about what he wanted. He was reaffirming his love for Connie, but making it clear that it really was now or never. If she had learned to love him, she must tell him now. If not, it was finally time to go their separate ways.

And suddenly without warning, without Connie wishing it to happen, her eyes started to fill with tears, which then began to trickle down her face. She was overwhelmed with emotion and felt Tom pull her gently towards him, rest her head on his chest and softly stroke her hair. She felt comforted and at peace, knowing beyond any doubt that she didn't want Tom to leave, because she loved him. Finally, able to hold back the tears, she gently released herself from Tom's embrace and looked him straight in the eyes.

"Yes, Tom. I do want you to stay and it is because I want to share my life with you. I want us to be together."

It was now Tom's turn to be overwhelmed. The strength he'd found to make his appeal, now eroded by the emotions triggered by Connie's acceptance of him. The pair of them made a strange sight, clinging silently to one another on a park bench on a bright, crisp, spring afternoon in Cringle Fields. Hardly the most exotic of locations, but the moment could be no more romantic, wherever it had been experienced.

Gradually, the two of them separated and it seemed fitting to Tom that it was Connie who took the lead in the inevitable conversation about what would happen next. After all, she had always been the one in control and he had always been happy to follow her direction.

"I'd like to avoid a long engagement, Tom. We both know how we feel. I think we should arrange to get married quickly."

"Yes. Yes Connie. I agree. I've no wish to wait!"

Connie laughed, seeing the enthusiasm writ large across Tom's face.

"Don't worry Tom, I'm not going to change my mind!"

Tom smiled.

"The register office," continued Connie. "I'm assuming that you don't want a religious ceremony, although if you do…"

"No," interrupted Tom. "A civil ceremony is fine. Getting married is just between the two of us. I'm not bothered about a reception. If you don't want one Connie, I'm happy. Neither of us have any close family anyway, so there seems little point in having one."

"But we can take a short honeymoon Tom. I'd like that."

"Yes, so would I Connie. It'd be lovely."

"And as I own a house and you only rent, then for the time being, we'll be living in Howard Avenue. And without all the 'mod cons' that you've got used to!"

"I wouldn't want to be anywhere else!" replied Tom, laughing.

"Well," said Connie, smiling. "That must be the quickest that a wedding's ever been arranged."

"Yes. It didn't take very long," replied Tom.

"Come on then, we'd best be making our way back to work," continued Connie. "They'll be wondering where we've got to."

The pair stood up and Connie reached down and took hold of Tom's hand. It was the first time that the pair had walked hand in hand, just as lovers do and symbolic of the fact that their lives would now be linked forever.

Chapter 79

Having made their decision, Tom and Connie acted quickly. They went to the register office in All Saints the very next day and paid the fee to give notice of their intention to marry. They set a date twenty-eight days hence, for Friday, April 29th at ten o'clock. Tom gave notice to his landlord, ready to move in with Connie, once they were man and wife. That would of course be after they returned home from their honeymoon. The two of them had wanted nothing elaborate; just the time to be together and away from the familiar distractions of everyday life and work. The couple therefore decided that they would head to North Wales and Rhyl, where there were plenty of guest houses that could accommodate them.

Following their unusual engagement, Tom and Connie had waited twenty-four hours before informing Mike of their intentions. Their decision delighted him, although he found it slightly surprising. He'd witnessed how Connie had been upset by the news that Tom may leave, but hadn't contemplated that the matter would end in matrimony and moreover, in such a speedy fashion. For the business, the news was excellent. Tom would be remaining; unnecessary upheaval avoided. Mike was surprised that they only wanted a long weekend away. It did seem however, to reflect the very practical approach that they were taking towards their marriage. Besides, there would be plenty of time in the summer to have an extended holiday and less need for haste in arranging it.

Mike felt honoured that the couple had asked him to be one of their witnesses, whilst Paula would be the other. The two of them had thus been present to see Tom and Connie become man and wife, Tom placing Kath's ring on his wife's finger to symbolise their union. Photographs had been taken and the four of them had returned to Howard Avenue for refreshments. Yet there was little time to celebrate, as Mike needed to drive the newlyweds to Piccadilly station to catch the train to Rhyl. It was still relatively early in the afternoon and the events of the day so far, had seemed like a whirlwind of activity. The couple were relieved to finally be able to settle into their seats, breathe a huge sigh of relief and relax as the train pulled slowly out of the station. For a short time, the newlyweds sat in silence. They were both experiencing the contentment that came from the fact that they were man and wife. Finally, as the train moved on through Salford, it was Tom who spoke first.

"You don't regret not making your marriage more of a celebration, do you Connie?"

"No, of course not Tom."

Connie smiled at him and held his hand.

"A commitment to each other is all that matters Tom and I know that I've done the right thing in marrying you. How could a fancy reception alter that? No. It can't," continued Connie, shaking her head. "We've made our commitments to one another formally, before the law and if you like, before God too. There can be nothing more important than that."

"Yes. I agree Connie," said Tom. "I suppose that I just wanted the reassurance of hearing you say it again."

She leaned forward towards him and squeezed his hand. The feeling of intimate, physical contact was still new to him. Holding Connie in his arms and kissing her, was something which he'd dreamed about for so long and it had now become a reality. Tom was finding it hard to keep his feelings in check. And now the realisation that they were on the verge of being united completely, meant that when he looked at her, she appeared even more gorgeous than usual. His wife was wearing a fetching pink suit that delicately accentuated her figure and complemented the soft, glowing skin on her face and neck. He couldn't help it, but sat opposite her, he felt full of desire and when Connie caught his eye, she sensed his discomfort, briefly looked down and smiled. She had him completely under her spell and she knew it.

"Think of those cold mountain streams in Snowdonia Tom. I think you need to jump into one of them. Don't you?"

She smiled. She was teasing him, enjoying the sight of his face turning scarlet in embarrassment. She leaned forward and spoke quietly.

"It's a good job we're sat here alone. Never mind Tom. You're just going to have to wait, aren't you?"

She looked at him and smiled again, a mischievous look that hinted at the promise of the night of passion that lay ahead of them.

Breathing deeply, a look of anguish on his face, Tom turned his head towards the window. Concentrating on the onrushing, changing scenery, he tried to repress his amorous thoughts about Connie.

Realising his embarrassment, Connie sat quietly before changing the subject on to more practical and mundane matters.

"I suppose you want to take me to Conwy Castle, don't you?"

"Yes," replied Tom, relieved to have recovered his composure and able to engage once more in conversation. "It's very impressive Connie and you'll get some lovely views from the battlements, including one of Thomas Telford's suspension bridge."

"Oh no. It's not going to be a history lesson, is it?" asked Connie, pretending to be horrified.

"No, of course not silly," replied Tom. "I was just saying…"

Tom paused. He could see the sparkle in Connie's eye and the slight tremble of her lip as she fought back the growing urge to burst out laughing.

"Oh no. You're doing it again Connie."

"Doing what Tom?" asked Connie, raising her eyebrows and attempting to appear as serious as possible.

"You're taking the Michael."

"No, I'm not," replied Connie. "As if I'd do that to you, Tom."

Suddenly, the two of them burst out laughing. Tom shook his head.

"You shouldn't always take me so seriously Tom."

"I know Connie, but you said it so convincingly."

As the journey progressed, the train soon reached Chester and then they were in Wales. Shotton, Flint, then Prestatyn and the train arrived in Rhyl. Turning out of the station, they walked the short distance to West Parade, opposite the beach and found bed and breakfast accommodation at the 'Norfolk Guest House.' Signing the register, Tom hesitated, before remembering that they were now Mr and Mrs Clarke of Howard Avenue, Ardwick, Manchester. It was such a simple task to perform, but one charged with meaning. It was an affirmation, if he still needed it, that his life and Connie's were now entwined. Having settled in their room, the couple then went out for a walk along the seafront. Like all others who lived inland, Tom and Connie found the squawks of the seagulls, the sound of the sea advancing and retreating on the sand and the unmistakable smell of salt water in the air, reassuring. The two of them hadn't been able to resist the temptation to walk on the sand. Hand in hand they were like a couple of giddy children who laughed, joked and frolicked as they dodged the incoming waves. It was the different atmosphere and environment that seemed to heighten their appreciation of their special day and the uniqueness of the coming night that would see their union's consummation.

First however, they found a café. They had to have fish and chips. There was simply no question. They were Mancunians at the seaside. They could do no other on their first night's stay. And then the couple discovered a little pub, set back in the town. It was quite strange, as although it was pleasant and friendly, the conversations between the regulars were carried out in Welsh. Momentarily, it seemed as if they were in a foreign country, a feeling that provided yet another novel experience on this very special day.

Back in their room just after nine, Tom was sat on the side of the bed. He was nervous, different to how he'd felt earlier in the day, when he'd excitedly looked at Connie and had been almost overwhelmed by his feelings of desire for her. Now that they were alone in their room, private and able to do as they pleased, he felt a sense of inadequacy. He realised that he was afraid; uncertain of what he should do. He was inexperienced as a lover. He recognised too, that although Connie had been involved in serious relationships, she'd never gone through the experience of full intimacy with either of the men she had loved. Connie was old-fashioned; the 'Sixties' weren't 'swinging' for her. Yet every man who beheld Connie, couldn't help but be captivated by the essence of her sensuality. It emanated from her whether she intended it to or not. On the train she had found no embarrassment at seeing Tom's ardour for her and her smiles and knowing looks suggested that tonight, he would be relying on her completely. Whatever was going to happen, Connie would be the instigator.

Then suddenly, she was in front of him, removing her jacket and swaying her hips, moving rhythmically as she had done when she had been dancing with Abel. He thrust out his hand attempting to touch the top of her leg, but she had already moved out of reach.

"Wait," she whispered, seductively.

Taking her jacket, Connie folded it carefully. Moving provocatively, she saw Tom's eyes fixed on her, unable to tear themselves away. Slowly, Connie started to unbutton her blouse, then pulling it from her skirt she took it off and laid it neatly with her jacket on the chair behind her.

She looked magnificent. Tom was stunned, his breathing short, he felt he was about to explode. He wanted her so badly and started to get off the bed, only for Connie to move towards him and push him back down.

"No. Ah, ah!" she said, tutting and waving her finger at him in admonishment. "Not now. Not yet."

He looked up at her, his eyes pleading for mercy. The mercy of not having to wait any longer. He didn't think he could. It hurt. He was so desperate. But she was insistent and he sat there as she removed her skirt and as it fell to the floor and she stepped gracefully out of it, he could wait no more. Dropping off the bed, he pulled her to him and pressed his face into the inside of her thighs. He felt her hand slowly, but gently, pulling him away. Looking up, he could see her radiant smile. She stepped back and raised her hands, indicating to him that he should stand up.

Wearing just her stockings and brilliant white underwear, Connie began to undress him. In control, she soon had him standing naked before her. Stepping back, Connie looked him up and down.

"What a fine figure of a man you are, Tom Clarke."

Once more she smiled reassuringly and Tom suddenly felt calm, ready for what was still to come. She could clearly see his rising desire for her, but he felt no embarrassment. He'd told her so long ago that she was the only one for him and what was happening now, had proved it. He felt so comfortable with her, so natural, he loved her so completely and it just felt right. He knew that there wasn't any other woman on this earth who could make him feel like this. He was so fortunate that he had found her and so very grateful that she was one who was taking him through his first experience of making love.

Tom watched as Connie stepped towards the top of the bed and pulled back the covers.

"Go on Tom, get in," said Connie, her words kind, but insistent.

Tom moved between the sheets and slid over to the opposite side of the bed. He watched, almost spellbound, as Connie went back over to the chair, sat down, slowly crossed her legs and carefully, yet seductively, unfastened her stockings, taking off each one in turn and laying it gently over the back of the chair. Then, having removed the rest of her underwear, Tom finally saw her magnificent body in all its glory, before she slipped under the covers and the two of them lay entwined in one another's arms, sharing a succession of long, deep and passionate kisses. As they explored the most intimate parts of each other's bodies, all Tom's fears and inhibitions were forgotten. Carried along on a wave of emotion, two became one, their love and desire for one another ending in an explosion of satisfaction, as they shared the most intensely joyous moment of their lives.

Chapter 80

After a night of uninhibited lovemaking, the newlyweds woke up later than usual to a world transformed. Tom and Connie understood that they had navigated a rite of passage together that meant that their union, their love for one another, was sacrosanct. They now believed that each was part of a whole, that together, they complemented one another. For Tom, the realisation was far easier to comprehend. He had always loved Connie, had never envisaged being with anyone else and so the totality of his union with her, arose naturally out of his expectations. For Connie however, she had already trodden part of this path before, through her relationships with Harry and Ralph. Their failure had undermined her belief in a union of happiness with any prospective partner. As Kath had recognised so incisively, Connie needed to exercise a leap of faith, to continue to believe in the salvation of love. She hadn't consciously made that decision however. Her marriage had come about reactively to the news of Tom's impending move to London. Connie knew intuitively that Tom was important to her, that she couldn't bear the thought of him not being around her, but it was only through their night of passion together, that she finally understood how much she needed Tom to fulfil her life.

Getting washed and dressed, the happy couple went for their breakfast, the knowing smile of Wendy, the landlady, greeting them as they entered the small dining room and sat down at one of the tables. In her late fifties, Wendy had moved with her husband to Rhyl from Liverpool. They'd bought the 'Norfolk' as a profitable business twenty years ago, but over time had seen the decline in the numbers of long stay visitors, replaced by day trippers and those on short stopovers. The business, like others in Rhyl, was becoming marginalised, but Wendy never let it affect her genuine warmth and humour. Over the years, she had seen many couples pass through the 'Norfolk' on their honeymoons. There were rather less these days though. The emerging prosperity for many, meant that it was now possible for couples to visit continental destinations. Tom and Connie struck Wendy as being able to make that choice too, but they were traditionalists who wanted to follow the customary practices of their parents' generation.

"I hope that the room was comfortable for you and the bed nice and soft," said Wendy, a faint flicker of a smile on her lips.

Connie noticed Tom drop his head. He was clearly embarrassed, a fact which couldn't help but amuse his wife.

"Yes, it was fine. Thank you," said Connie, smiling.

The two women exchanged knowing glances as Tom, still silent, seemed to have taken an unnatural interest in examining the cutlery on the table in front of him.

"Have you got anything planned for today? asked Wendy.

"Yes, Tom is going to drag me to Conwy Castle, aren't you Tom?"

Forced to respond, Tom reluctantly lifted his head. Wendy could see that he still felt embarrassed.

"Yes," he replied.

The women looked at Tom expectantly, waiting for him to elaborate on his comment. But that was it. No other words were forthcoming.

"The town's compact, but you've got Britain's smallest house and the suspension bridge to see too," said Wendy. "You can nip over to Llandudno if you have the time."

"Yes," replied Connie. "We might do that."

"I'd take the bus if I were you," suggested Wendy.

"Thanks, we will," replied Connie.

Organised and ready for the day ahead, Tom and Connie made their way to the bus station and boarded the bus to Conwy. The journey proved pleasant. To the right of them they were bounded by the sea and on the left they could see the looming, brooding heights of Snowdonia. It was almost noon when they arrived at their destination and they made their way straight to the castle. Connie was amused by Tom's obvious excitement and indulged his boyish enthusiasm for wanting to climb every tower and walk along every wall possible, regardless of the fact that it seemed to her a rather repetitive process. But she kept quiet, entertained by Tom's excited chatter and determination to keep referencing the little guidebook that they had bought on the way in, to inform her about the castle's special features. Connie had to admit though, that from the heights of the walls, Telford's bridge looked truly impressive and the little boats in the marina were a pleasant and pretty sight.

When their tour of the castle was over, it was clear that today at least, there wouldn't be time to pop over to Llandudno. They therefore found a quiet café, had something to eat and walked around the small town. Camera in hand, Tom was determined to capture as many images of Connie as he could. Yet it had caused him to receive his first 'telling off', Connie concerned that he would use up all of his films before they had a picture of the two of them together. Reprimanded outside Britain's smallest house, he handed his camera to a passer-by, who kindly took a photo of the happy couple. With time running out, the shops closing their doors, Connie and Tom headed back to the café near the bus stop for a hot drink of Horlicks, whilst they waited for their transport to arrive.

Sat quietly at a corner table, they were the only customers. It meant that they could talk intimately to one another without fear of interruption. Tom gazed in awe at his beautiful Connie. She was so wonderful and he felt blessed that she had agreed to be his wife. He was quiet and content.

"What are you thinking about?" asked Connie.

"About what a gorgeous wife I have and how wonderful these last two days have been."

Smiling, Tom moved his hand across the table and laid it softly on Connie's. He was completely in love and determined to demonstrate his feelings for her as often as he could. Stroking her hand, Tom recalled their night of passion. It had been in his mind all day that when they returned to their room, they would have the chance to make love once more. The thought was so exciting, that at times he had to fight back the desire that rose within him when he visualised her beautiful, naked body. He had seen her now and was desperate to lie with her again. He knew that however many times they made love, he would never be satisfied, he would always want more.

Connie smiled and shook her head.

"That's not all. Is it Tom?"

Tom looked confused.

"What do you mean?"

"It's a giveaway Tom."

"What is?"

"Your bottom lip is."

Tom was still confused. He stared in bewilderment at her.

"It's gone all red. So, I do know Tom," continued Connie, looking sternly at him.

Tom involuntarily took a deep breath. It began to dawn on him that she knew exactly what he'd been thinking.

"You're thinking about rude things aren't you, Tom? You're getting all hot and bothered and that's why your bottom lip's gone bright red."

Connie smiled and watched as his face went 'beetroot.' Laughing quietly, she held his hand tightly.

"It's all right Tom. I'd be disappointed if I thought that I didn't get you all excited."

Tom bowed his head. He was still embarrassed and avoiding eye contact. Connie was 'tickled' by his reaction. He'd done everything she could have expected from him to satisfy her last night, yet he was still so reserved when it came to talking to her about such things.

"Never mind Tom. You're just going to have to wait until later on. You can be sure it will be worth it," she added, mischievously.

"Oh, Connie!" said Tom, sighing.

Tom closed his eyes and took several deep breaths, a sign of his growing frustration that Connie was so close, yet it was impossible to reach out to her to satisfy his desire. He could never have imagined that he could feel like this. He sensed that she was taking pleasure from his temporary distress and whether she intended it or not, her words and actions were driving him to distraction.

"Yes Tom?" asked Connie

"You're teasing me, Connie. It's not fair."

I know I am Tom, but then you like it, don't you?"

Connie flirtatiously raised her eyebrows, her beautiful green eyes sparkling as she smiled at him. Her question finally brought a smile from Tom. He felt more relaxed and he knew that she was right. She excited him so much that it almost hurt, but it was the pain of desire and he knew of the pleasure to come when he was finally fulfilled.

"Yes. I do enjoy it, Connie. You're so beautiful," he said, quietly, "and so sexy."

Connie was surprised by his turn of phrase. But his compliments had pleased her.

"You're getting very bold all of a sudden Tom Clarke. I'm going to have to keep my eye on you."

Once more, Tom blushed. He couldn't help it. She had made him feel like a naughty boy who she was telling off and he had to admit that it was a pleasant sensation. Yet he didn't want her to think that his desire was purely physical, because he understood that it was far more than that. Looking into her eyes, he gazed intently at Connie. He wore an expression that she had seen before and one that told her that he was about to discard all his inhibitions and talk to her straight from the heart.

"You're so gorgeous Connie, so pretty and when we made love, I felt an intense and emotional connection with you. It transcended the physical; it was undoubtedly in the realms of the spiritual. If I wasn't totally in love with you Connie, I could never have reached such heights and experienced those feelings."

Connie was silent. Tom's words had allowed her to see into the very depths of his soul. There could be no question that he was utterly devoted to her. There was an honesty about him that she'd experienced with no one else, an unerring sense of putting forward his thoughts carefully and with precision. Connie knew that she would always be safe with him. He would never betray her and he would do everything that lay within his power to make her happy. And now it was her turn to become emotional.

As her eyes began to moisten, Connie turned her face to the side and delicately wiped away a tear.

"Connie, what's the matter? Are you all right? asked Tom.

Taking a deep breath, Connie looked back at him.

"Yes, of course I am."

"But you're upset.”

Connie shook her head. As good as Tom was at articulating and understanding his own emotions, he had much to learn about interpreting hers.

"Don't worry Tom. I was touched by your words."

Tom waited expectantly for Connie to continue, but she was silent. He wanted to hear more.

"Why Connie?"

"Because I was," she replied, smiling.

"But why?"

"I'm not telling you anything more Tom. It’s a woman's prerogative not to have to."

Connie squeezed his hand and smiled.

"Come on, Tom. We need to get moving. The bus is going to arrive in a few minutes."

Standing up, the two of them took their empty mugs to the counter, thanked the staff and went out to catch the bus back to Rhyl.

Chapter 81

After arriving back at the 'Norfolk', the rest of the couple's short honeymoon seemed to pass all too quickly. Waking up early on Monday morning, Tom and Connie were soon washed and dressed, determined to take a final stroll on the beach before breakfast. Walking along the sand, holding hands, they listened to the soothing sound of the tiny waves lapping against the shore.

"Do you realise Connie," said Tom, "that we've not built a sandcastle."

Connie shook her head and smiled.

"Well, you've left it a bit late to think about that."

"No. Not at all. I can do it now," insisted Tom.

Moving away from the water, Tom dropped to his knees to pick up a small piece of driftwood and then proceeded to employ it as a makeshift spade. Digging a small circular trench, he threw the excavated sand into the centre. He then quickly began to form a perimeter wall, inside which he made a tower. Connie was fascinated by the enthusiasm he displayed towards the task.

"I'm going to call it 'Castle Connie,'" said Tom, looking up and eager to gain her approbation.

"I'm honoured, I'm sure," replied Connie, laughing.

Having completed his task, Tom was as good as his word, using his piece of driftwood to write the words 'Castle Connie' around the central tower. Standing back, he looked satisfied with his creation.

"If I'd had more time and a bucket and spade, I reckon that I could have made a better job of it. Never mind it still looks all right, doesn't it?"

"Yes Tom. It does," replied Connie. "Come on, we'd better be getting back or we'll miss breakfast."

As they reached the edge of the sand, the pair turned to take a last look at 'Castle Connie.' They watched in amazement as two dogs ran straight through it and then went racing off down the beach, pursued by their owner. Looking at one another, they burst out laughing.

"It seems they didn't appreciate your handiwork very much Tom," said Connie.

"But they've destroyed 'Castle Connie.' How could they?" asked Tom, smiling.

It was a humorous incident and kept the pair of them in good spirits until they arrived back at the 'Norfolk.' Their train was leaving at ten, so they didn't have much time to get their breakfast, pack their case, say farewell to Wendy and walk to the station. Boarding the train, they sat down, heard the sound of the station master's whistle and felt the train pull slowly away from the platform. Tom felt a twinge of regret that they were leaving. Rhyl would now always be a very special place for him, yet he couldn't help but be excited at the thought of arriving back at Howard Avenue and moving into Connie's house as her husband.

Connie was also eager to get settled into their new life together. She hadn't wanted their honeymoon to be too long, feeling that it was important for them to settle as quickly as possible into the realities of married life. After all, however long they'd known each other, they had never spent as much time with one another as they would now. Living together would be a novel experience for both of them. It would require them to adapt to new situations, to accommodate, understand and appreciate each other's feelings and expectations. Yet with Tom, she was confident that she had a partner who would prove sympathetic towards her needs.

Reaching Piccadilly station at noon, the couple took a taxi. The road seemed unusually busy for the time of day and they made slow progress down London Road and into Downing Street. Looking at the passing scenery, Connie could see just how much had changed since she had travelled on the bus, almost two and a half years ago, to her interview at Greenings when she had first met Tom. The ongoing demolition of terraced houses for the building of the new 'Mancunian Way' and the slum clearance programme, was having a detrimental effect on the businesses and properties that remained. An area that had once been so vibrant, was beginning to look tired and distressed.

Connie knew that it wouldn't be long before they demolished the rest of Chorlton-on-Medlock and then they would be in Ardwick too. The battle to preserve the old communities was all but lost. No matter how many public meetings were held, the wishes of residents to keep their neighbourhoods, were being ignored. And the economic experts who proved that refurbishment was four times cheaper than clearance and rebuilding, were simply dismissed. In new overspill estates like Darn Hill and Langley, the problems of providing facilities, amenities and transport hadn't been addressed; their new residents abandoned. Yet those in charge weren't to be shifted. They desired a new city that erased all vestiges of the old. Convinced that they were visionaries, they arrogantly believed that they knew what was best for everyone else.

As Connie arrived back at Howard Avenue, she knew that they wouldn't be living there for too much longer. Yet now, watching her new husband grappling with their suitcase, she smiled. It was just as Kath had promised her. She had found love and with it, everything had fallen into place. She had discovered the real meaning of her life. And that meaning was Tom, a man who would do anything for her and who loved her completely. Connie knew that wherever they found themselves living in the future, as long as they had each other, there was nothing in this world that together, they couldn't overcome.